Praise for *The Calling*

"Nothing — and everything — is sacred in this powerfully scripted and ambitious novel. From geopolitics to pandemic suffering, religious calamity to personal piety, *The Calling* wrestles with issues that forever unite and divide humanity. With equal parts dignity and censure, Hankins captures the tragedies of Southern Sudan — a realm of deep concern to AIUSA — and uses story as a call to action and advocacy. The effect is a restored conviction that one life, one person, really can make a difference."
Lynn Fredriksson, advocacy director for Africa, Amnesty International, USA

"In this riveting and cinematic novel, Elizabeth Hankins explores the various forces people interpret as divine guidance, including motivations that remain half-hidden even to some who talk the loudest about heeding God's will. She also introduces a courageous heroine who survives abuse to learn the true meaning of love and justice. *The Calling* casts dramatic light on immense human suffering that has unfolded in war-torn Sudan, the largest nation in Africa, largely out of the media spotlight. It is a well-written and fast-paced account of love, loss and resilience. It's enlightening, entertaining and hard to put down."
Mark Bixler, author, The Lost Boys of Sudan: An American Story of the Refugee Experience

"Elizabeth Hankins combines a natural storyteller's instincts with strong dialogue skills — and she enlists her writing ability in service of a storyline that is not only intriguing — it is truly important. I think *The Calling* is a novel that deserves to be published and widely read. It will enrich all who read it."
Brian McLaren, activist and author, A New Kind of Christian

"Elizabeth Hankins' novel, *The Calling*, tells the story of a courageous young woman, the two men who most impact her life, and her growing awareness of the role she has to play in rewriting the history of an entire country. It's a story that portrays the reality of good and evil — from church offices in Boston to oil fields in Southern Sudan, and it traces the disintegration of the moral compass in one man and in the whole world's lack of response to the suffering and death of over two million people that continued unabated for more than two decades. Finally, Hankins poignantly captures the dignity, courage, and faith of the Southern Sudanese in a loving tribute to a people who should never be forgotten."

Faith J. H. McDonnell, director, Religious Liberty Programs and Church Alliance for a New Sudan, Institute on Religion and Democracy

"*The Calling* will indeed call the reader to reflect on and respond to a world in need of hope and justice — yet with reverence and respect. Hankins' narrative is a voice for the voiceless that entertains, delights, saddens and provokes, hopefully to action for the forgotten. This book will awaken something in all of us."

Joel Vestal, founder and president, ServLife International

"*The Calling* will inform you about important developments in Sudan and this volatile region in Africa. Most importantly, this novel will captivate your heart, You'll be inspired to take action and make a difference. Elizabeth Hankins has done an outstanding job and I highly recommend this book."

Dr. Jerry Wiles, president, Living Water International

"Elizabeth Hankins' novel will take you on an unforgettable ride. Pages fly by as you travel up, down and across mind-jarring landscapes where abuse and redemption meet, where religious hypocrisy confronts the power of authentic faith — and where staggering injustice is finally met by two people who embrace the call and courage to help change it all. Powerfully insightful into human nature and the high costs of social injustice, this book will leave you a different person."

John Burke, author, No Perfect People Allowed, senior pastor, Gateway Community Church, Austin, TX

"*The Calling* is gripping, a compelling story with the captivating flair of great fiction set against a real-life backdrop that's so unfathomable, it, too, seems fictional. Yet in the age-old redux of art reflecting life, this book highlights decades-long tragedy and subsequent need in war-torn Sudan. Powerful and moving, *The Calling* is the type of book you never forget having read."

Peter Swann, executive director, Aid Sudan

"*The Calling* is a must-read, combining fascinating characters, tight plot and a redemptive message woven with real-life geopolitical events. Kudos to Hankins for donating all proceeds of *The Calling* to relief and development efforts in the Sudan. Read the book for the story, open your heart to the plight of the Sudan while supporting its recovery. You can't lose!

Scott Harris, missions pastor, Brentwood Baptist Church, Franklin, TN

"It's been said the best fiction depicts truth more accurately than any other form of writing. Case in point is *The Calling*, a story that leaves behind perspective on truths of our time, deep truths that simultaneously engage the mind and burn the heart long after the book is closed. Writing with a clear and compelling style, Hankins weaves a fascinating tale set in multiple locations while keeping a divergent cast of characters universally bound by the pains, dreams and longings that make us human. As she does, she explores the ways so many claim the name of God as they serve the desire for power and privilege. *The Calling* is a shrewd narrative that ultimately invites each of us to test the authenticity of our own motives, our own self-justifications, our own hearts."

Dr. Steve Wende, senior pastor, First United Methodist Church of Houston

The Calling

Elizabeth Hankins

The Key Publishing House Inc.

First Edition 2008
The Key Publishing House Inc.
Toronto, Canada
Website: www.thekeypublish.com
E-mail: info@thekeypublish.com

ISBN 978-0-9782526-4-9 paperback

Cover design and typeset: Olga Lagounova
Cover design is inspired by a new stained glass window by Bovard Studio Inc., replicating design aspects of ancient icons.

Maps are used with permission of the UN Cartographic Section. Africa, Map No. 4045 Rev. 4 January 2004. Sudan, Map No. 3707 Rev. 10 April 2007.
Published in association with Ambassador Literary Agency, Nashville, TN
From CANNERY ROW by John Steinbeck, copyright 1945. Renewed © 1973 by Elaine Steinbeck, John Steinbeck IV and Thom Steinbeck. Used by permission of Viking Penguin, a division of Penguin Group (USA) Inc.

Scripture quotations taken from the New American Standard Bible®, Copyright © 1960, 1962, 1963, 1968, 1971, 1972, 1973,1975, 1977, 1995 by The Lockman Foundation

Scripture taken from the HOLY BIBLE, NEW INTERNATIONAL VERSION®, Copyright © 1973, 1978, 1984 by International Bible Society. Used by permission of Zondervan. All rights reserved.

Library and Archives Canada Cataloguing in Publication
Hankins, Elizabeth,
The Calling / Elizabeth Hankins.
ISBN 978-0-9782526-4-9I.
Title. PS3608.A557C35 2007   813'.6   C2007-905927-9

Printed and bound by BookMasters in USA. This book is printed on paper suitable for recycling and made from fully sustained forest sources.

Though this is a work of fiction with all characters and many places/incidents being a product of the author's imagination, some of the events in this story are based on the more than two decade-long plight of southern Sudan.

The Key Publishing promotes mutual understanding, respect, and peaceful coexistence among the people of the world. We represent unique and unconventional voices whose objective is to bring peace, harmony, and happiness to our human society.

The Key Publishing House Inc.

*Dedicated to the more than two million southern Sudanese
who died in Africa's longest-running civil war.
You are not forgotten.*

PART I

Crucible

"I have greatly wronged thee," murmured Hester.

"We have wronged each other," answered he. "Therefore, I seek no vengeance, plot no evils against thee. Between thee and me, the scale hangs fairly balanced. But, Hester, the man lives who has wronged us both! Who is he?"

"Ask me not!" replied Hester Prynne, looking firmly into his face. "That thou shalt never know." *The Scarlet Letter*, Nathaniel Hawthorne

"Who shall say . . . how often ambition wears the guise of vocation, perhaps in all good faith?" *Les Miserables*, Victor Hugo

Chapter 1

"Oh, God, no . . ." The woman whispered in a voice leaden as the still winter night. "This has gone too far . . ."

"Easy," the man's command was brusque, "we'll frighten her."

The woman shivered as she and the man moved slowly in the darkness. Every few seconds, planked wooden boards beneath their feet alternately groaned and squeaked.

"Poor little soul, look at her," the woman gestured toward gauzy moonlight that framed two children huddled just feet away on a creaking porch swing. "She's a corpse with a heartbeat."

"Shhh . . . Emily," the man insisted, watching the delicate creature grope for the hand of the raven-haired boy beside her. "She'll hear you."

Teeth clicking together non-stop, the pixie child sucked in a shaky breath and leaned forward. In one motion, she pushed her free hand against the slats of the swing and tried to pull herself up. She steadied the attempt by keeping a tight grip on the boy's hand.

The effort was too much. As a look of agony cut across her pale face, the girl's legs buckled beneath her and she fell back into the swing. The chains rattled wildly, almost muting the yelp that escaped her lips.

Stunned, the child winced then blinked hard.

For what seemed like minutes that was all she did. Winced and blinked. Then with renewed resolve, she set her jaw, bit her lower lip. She reached again for the boy's hand, dug her fingers deep into it and inched gingerly to her full height.

"So what are we supposed to do now?"

"Listen," the man's cheeks burned as he faced the woman, "if this is what I think it is, that little girl's life just graduated from misery to hell." His eyes flashed as they flit back to the silent children breathing out air that smoked and swirled like angry wraiths. "And I'll be damned if we sit around and watch any more."

With that, the man pushed past his wife to join the children in a shaft of light that made the world shades of silver.

This was especially true of the child's dress, a shimmering little garment clumsily pinned where a long tear had ripped it from neck to waist.

Her elfin face, too, was cast in shadows, swollen with purple bruises that appeared charcoal in the moonlight.

Close up now, the man noticed glittering wet on the child's cheek, tears escaping from beneath her webbed lashes.

Then from the corner of his own eye, he saw something else.

Another glistening rivulet, this one thick and crimson-black. It snaked from beneath the little girl's dress, down her thigh, onto the gray wooden porch.

Behind him, the woman stifled a scream as the child turned, then collapsed into the waiting arms of the man.

~

Meranda Kaine's own scream cleaved the silence, wrenching her from deep sleep. Damp with sweat though the temperature in her apartment had turned biting cold, she sat up and made herself inhale several shaky breaths. The frigid air burned her throat so badly it made her eyes start watering. She wished the physical discomfort was enough to force back the flood of images that were coming now, ones that typically came first in this dream order.

The stained glass teddy bear and the faceless priest, where had they been? These icons were always precursors to what came next . . .

Mera shook her head, dazed. This time the sequence had skipped. Re-sorted altogether so as to have landed her squarely into the forgotten sphere of two tiny friends, one standing sentry over the tormented other.

And the conversation—another first. A dialogue she barely remembered and one Mark and Emily Frasier never knew she'd overheard.

Glancing at her watch, then out of her apartment window where the setting sun had transformed the Charles River into a gleaming tangerine serpent, Mera chewed a fingernail.

Maybe it was this meeting with Jack Frasier.

Or maybe it was Robert Malcolm Drexel's harrowing question imposed on the way out of philosophy class this afternoon.

"What holds greater weight," the perpetually wheezing professor had scraped out in a baritone corrupted by decades of chain-smoking Camels, "the past with its tethers or the future with its uncertainties?"

The timing of his query had stabbed her mind. Then made everything go blank for a second.

It was just a question to provoke thought, she'd told herself so as to get moving again. One of his pedagogical meanderings leveled at graduating grad students. Nothing more.

She repeated this disclaimer aloud now, a tinny-sounding mantra meant to get her through a quick clean-up and change of clothes before meeting Jack at 6:00 P.M.

But ten minutes later as she grabbed her backpack and headed out the door, she could swear the little children who belonged to her decade-old dream, to a long-ago night thick with stars and frost and shearing pain were staring back at her like they wanted to know how she would answer Drexel's question.

Chapter 2

She couldn't decide what was more beautifully symmetrical, the tiny velvet box or the glittering princess cut that lay tucked inside it. Numbly, she traced a finger over the smooth blackness, across the shimmering hard of the stone. Then she snapped the case shut.

"Jack . . . Jack . . . this is . . ."

"It's what?" Jack stared at her, taking in the hesitance, the tremulous pauses charged with . . . *with what?*

"It's beautiful. Perfect."

"But what? C'mon Mera, I hear the 'but something' in there."

Of course he did. Two decades, four years and a few months had given him more than sufficient practice. A lifetime of practice, that at the moment, she wished he didn't have.

"Look, I've turned this over in my head a million times," she continued, biting her bottom lip so she could get the words out without faltering, "answered it probably a hundred different ways . . . and . . ."

"And . . . what?"

"I don't know. It was just never quite yes."

Jack studied her face, half-incredulous, half-searching.

"Why, Meranda? You love me. I love you. This is what's supposed to come next . . ."

"I *do* love you, you're right. I've always loved you."

"Then, what is it?" The sun was paling over Boston University's campus, final soft bands of pink and gray as they sat outside the Marsh Chapel beneath Martin Luther King Jr.'s *Free at Last* memorial. "Is marrying me some kind of compromise?"

"Jack, tell me you don't believe that . . ."

His wide brown eyes narrowed as he leaned in so close she could feel his breath warm the air between them. "Then tell me what I'm supposed to believe."

"For starters, not that."

"Then what?"

"You're perfect," she whispered, wishing that there was something, anything, that would keep the planed art of his features from withering, the pain out of his voice. "The best friend anyone could ask for. And that doesn't include how handsome and smart and funny you are . . ."

"But not enough of those things for you to want to marry me, right?"

She turned the little box over and over in her fingers feeling the unbearable weight of something so light. If she had been just about anyone else, this whole scenario would have played out in opposite. Everyone liked Jack Frasier, women in particular.

"That's not it. Not even close. Honestly, I can't explain it." Mera groped for the right words, but they weren't coming easily. "All I know is I love you . . . I just can't marry you."

Jack breathed in sharply like everything in his six foot-four frame was throbbing.

"I can wait, Mera. If it's time you need, I'll wait until you're ready."

"No, it's not about time or you or anything else. We're almost done here, and then you're off to seminary next year. I'm twenty-four, you're twenty-five. By now, we should know if we're right for each other."

"*I do* know. I'm as sure about marrying you as I am about being a priest."

Jack obviously wasn't getting it, probably because it had never crossed his mind that Mera wouldn't marry him. Now, though, just two months before she finished her master's in journalism and he wrapped up his in philosophy before packing off to Cambridge's Episcopal Divinity School, this news had to be nothing less than stupefying. And crushing.

"I think maybe the priest thing's part of it." Keeping her voice at a whisper kept it from cracking. "Before you know it, you'll be off doing whatever it is that a priest's supposed to do. And while I love that for you, it scares me."

"Why?"

"The truth?"

"Meranda . . ."

"I'd never fit the mold of a priest's wife." She looked away and tucked her arms tight under her gray sweatshirt. Her teeth wouldn't quit chattering, a result, no doubt, of the night air blowing off the Charles River and her raw nerves. She'd known this conversation was inevitable, known it for months now. But the combination of its reality, Drexel's vexing question and the bothersome dream children was shaking her to the core. "And truthfully, I'm not sure I'd even want to."

Honesty was the best policy, she knew, though contemplating the high price of losing him made her shrivel inside.

"Mold? It's 1988, not the Dark Ages. Where's this coming from?" Jack pressed her, more like he was giving a lecture than asking a question. "And when have I ever wanted you to be something you're not?"

"You haven't. At least not until now. But you're not thinking that my job's bound to mean travel and long hours and . . . sacrifices."

"I can do sacrifice."

"That's not the point and you know it. I want a column in five years, you'll have a parish in five years and you can bet none of this will come without a cost."

"I get that," he said. "That's not exactly breaking news."

"Right. But it's not what's best for you, it's not what you need. In five years, you'll need someone to be there with *you*, work alongside of *you*. You deserve that, and no matter how much I care for you, I know I'm not made to be a priest's wife. I'm just not."

Like she might waver if more time passed, she pushed to her feet and thrust out her hand holding the box.

He ignored it.

Instead, he stood, too, and brushed off his jeans before busying himself with pushing papers into a book. "You know, Dr. Lennox had this idea we debated in Hermaneutics the other day. It had to do with how the word 'calling' gets tossed around, even trivialized, in religious circles . . ."

"Calling?" she echoed, thinking that at least Lennox stuck to ideas. Maybe Malcolm Robert Drexel should take notes.

"You know, you hear it all the time. People saying they've answered some kind of calling."

"Sure. Lots of times, lot of folks. Preachers. Missionaries. Doctors . . . whoever." She wasn't following the digression.

Jack nodded.

"Well, Dr. Lennox was going on his usual premise of words mean things. Or that they should. And what he was saying is that this supposed 'calling' a person is talking about rarely gets measured."

"In what way?"

"He said most times we stop at hearing someone say they're answering God's call. It's like we get lazy and just decide that because someone says he's been 'called,' it's some magical guarantee that he'll spend his life taking the high road. Like it's all about . . ."

"The spiritual version of happily ever after." She finished the sentence with a wry smile.

"Exactly. And that's where Lennox says we do our damage. He said more often than not, we don't bother to test it, weigh it out."

"Jack, you're losing me . . ." Nothing unusual, she mused to herself. Jack had wanted to be a priest from the time they could draw pictures of God in the church nursery. So these seemingly random discourses, even rants, about theological matters were normal. And they usually had a point if she waited long enough or just asked him to spell out what he meant.

"Well, his point was that the real measure of how a person answers God's call is what he does with his life." Jack paused for a second as if reabsorbing the idea. "And that means no one gets the whole truth about a life until there's a biography to look at."

"As in from birth date to death date?"

"More or less."

"Sounds a little rigid if you ask me."

"Maybe. But his whole theory rests on this idea that the answer to a divine call is more about a lifetime of saying 'yes' to God. It has more to do with finding what it is you're made to do and then doing it than it does about running around telling everyone you're His emissary."

Mera turned to face him.

"So what you're essentially saying is you lose whatever spiritual bragging rights you might be holding onto. You don't get to point to a religious commissioning ceremony or hide behind a 'I'm doing this for God' façade." As the words escaped her mouth, she felt their meaning register and stick. "And instead, I guess you mostly let your life tell what it is that you believe."

"Exactly. And it's not that you *never* talk about what it is you believe He's made you to do . . ."

"No, I get that. It's just that you're busier fleshing it out than convincing people that it's your job to live it out."

"Right again."

She smiled. "That's so cool."

"Yeah," Jack agreed. "A lot of gravity to it."

She thought some more before answering.

"Help me out, though. I'm still missing how it relates to you and me."

Jack rested his hands on her shoulders.

"Meranda, I know what you've been through. And I know everything you've worked for is going to make you an unbelievable journalist." He brushed his hand gently over her cheek, stopping to tilt her chin up until her glass-green eyes met his gaze. "It's so obviously what you've been made to do . . . to be. Do you think for a minute I'd get in the way of that?"

She closed her eyes.

"No," she said slowly. Jack Frasier was hurting right now and if anyone didn't deserve pain it was him. "That hasn't even crossed my mind. I know you want what's best for me. And I want the same for you."

"But don't you see? I can't think of anything better for me than you."

"I wish that was true . . ."

"It is," he interrupted, squeezing her shoulders as if the act of holding on tighter might keep her from letting go. "I swear it is . . ."

She looked away, less out of avoidance than the knowledge that studying his angst would leave her emptier than ever.

"Please, Jack, don't. This is killing me . . ."

"You?" he rasped. "Killing *you?*"

For a split second, she let her mind chase the idea of what it would take to be the kind of wife her best friend needed. It didn't work.

"This is crazy," Jack's bewildered stare begged for more than the explanation he was getting. "Crazy. We've been through everything together."

He started to say something else when a pack of students drifted by, two boys, four girls, laughing and chattering and smoking cigarettes. Their breath split the purple twilight with silvery threads that stretched on forever before vanishing like spirits. Behind them, their voices were lilting echoes until all fell quiet and dark again.

Inhaling all the air her lungs could hold, Mera felt the vivid hard of the ground beneath her, the softness of the box between her fingers. She heard the *swish-thump* of her heart beating between her ears, the unrelenting voice in her head that made her deliver the final blow.

"You're right, Jack. I can't think of a single thing I've faced without you. Ever." Her concession was calm but she was forcing herself to say the words. "And it's not that I don't love you because I do. Maybe someday, somehow, you'll know just how much."

As if on cue, they started walking, along Commonwealth Avenue, past the Mugar Library and the University's nearly empty student union. The moon's clear beams fell over his profile, and for an instant, Mera remembered his dark hair and furrowed brow in the light of another moon, years ago. She stopped and faced him and he moved his hands to the back of her neck, playing with her hair.

"Say yes . . ."

"Please don't . . ." She pressed the little box into his unwilling hand.

He started to answer but she leaned close to kiss him, first on the cheek, then lightly on his mouth. She didn't expect a salty wet to trickle onto her lips and surprised, she looked up.

Tears were streaming from Jack's closed eyes — and she'd never seen him cry.

Chapter 3

He should have been used to the pungent smell of Kahlier's tobacco by now, but even after six years, the thick haze still choked him. The odor was always the same, some toxic mystery that snaked into the air from the bishop's cherrywood bowl and stretched into fading blue ribbons that left behind an invisible stench. Whatever it was, though, the old man liked it, would take long drags from his pipe stem, then hold his breath for what seemed like an eternity before breathing out the rancid curls.

"We had a deal, son." Icy words scraped from the bishop's throat. Then hung in the smoky air. "So I'm not making good on my end 'til you take this thing by force."

The old man tended to like combative terms when getting his points across. Especially points about the imperative nature of completing a doctoral dissertation.

"I'm trying, Dr. Kahlier, honestly," Jack stammered. "I was halfway through researching . . ."

"Yeah, you told me. Your deal about McClendon's take on ethics in systematic theology. The same one that sixty thousand other morons already had a fork stuck in."

"Which I know puts me behind, especially if I'm taking Shanklin's parish next month." It was a half-reminder, half-plea for confirmation.

Thomas Kahlier straightened behind his mahogany desk. He exuded power and he knew it, even if he was bald, flabby and practically antediluvian. For the past twenty years, he'd been bishop of Boston's Episcopal diocese, and when he talked, people listened. Especially young clerics in line for rectories of their own.

"Deal's off, boy. I said halfway through with the paper and you'd get that parish. But you're sitting here telling me you don't even have a topic."

"Nottingham's perfect for me, you've said it yourself." Jack struggled to control the terror in his voice. "They're growing, and we both know how starved they are for fresh ideas, new blood . . ."

"I did and you were." The bishop was unaffected. "But you know the rules. None of my boys gets a place 'til they've done their time in the theological trenches."

"I'm trying, though. You know how . . ."

Kahlier raised his hand. A silencing gesture.

"The paper's your hall pass, boy. Your way of showing me you're a producer. Which then means we both look good." The old man sucked hard on his stem, reclining back in the nail-studded leather chair. He clunked his right hand against his desk, the huge bishop's ring on his third finger a reminder of who was who in the room.

Maybe it was the smoky bands, snuffing out any real air that made the walls of Kahlier's study suddenly close in. In any case, Jack was scared now. He thought the bishop was in his corner, that he'd understand despite this latest impediment. After all, Thomas Kahlier had seen to him particularly all these years.

"Sir," Jack decided to hit it from another angle, "for more than six years, I've done everything but stand on my head blindfolded when it's come to following orders. And you know I'm no wave maker or slacker." Jack leaned in until his elbows rested on the bishop's desk. "I've just hit a roadblock and I need a little help. Or at least a little more time."

Just two days ago, he'd learned his dissertation topic was old news — researched and re-researched so many times he just couldn't rationalize trying to breathe life into it again. So he was back at the starting gate, which meant one thing with the bishop: no parish.

"I want you to look into Taize." Kahlier breathed his familiar blue rings into the air.

"Taize?"

"Taize. Sounds a lot like crazy, just with a t."

"What is it, sir, what's Taize?"

"Besides being some village in eastern France, it's a growing ecumenical movement. Supposedly kicked off as a reconciliation shindig after World War II. From what I've read, it started with a few monks taking vows. But it's gotten bigger, broader, or so they say."

"And it qualifies as a dissertation because . . ."

"It works on a couple levels. The faithful come, then go away convinced we can all live together, happily ever after. And anyone else looking for religious drama pretty much gets their wish and calls it meeting God."

"I see." He didn't at all, but saying so could be dangerous.

"Probably nothing more than some feel-good mountaintop frenzy. But it's a topic, and you need one."

"Right," Jack agreed, pushing back his chair and standing to leave. "Absolutely right. And Taize sounds great. First thing tomorrow, I'll pass it by Doc Vernon for approval."

"Sit down, son, I'm not done yet. I'll make the call to EDS, get Vernon to clear it myself. Meanwhile, let's cut a few corners. I want you to get in touch with a man in Chicago. Name's Langford, Seth Langford. He runs some kind of homeless shelter, north of downtown, I think. But you don't drop my name when you talk with him."

Jack nodded, pulling the white collar at his throat like it was choking him.

"In fact, start by calling the *Tribune*. See if someone there can come up with a series they ran about the shelter a few years back. It'll be good background."

"Sounds interesting, sir, but I'm still missing the nexus between Taize and this shelter."

Kahlier cleared his throat, a growling sound thick with phlegm.

"Langford apparently spent time at Taize, really believes in the place. Supposedly got his inspiration there for what he's doing now. Which would make him a decent source of first hand information if you can hook up with him." The bishop arched his eyebrows, something he did when a matter was settled once and for all. Then he reached into his pocket for a match and re-lit the pipe, a tiny flame followed by three long pulls that gave way to a cloud of opaque smoke.

They sat in the silence for a few minutes, Jack in an attempt to be discretionary, Kahlier because he'd long learned that strategic silence on his part gave him the upper hand.

"Well," Jack finally said, "this sounds like a plan. I'll get moving on it tomorrow." He wished he could ask the bishop about Nottingham again, but Kahlier had his limits.

"Remember, Frasier, no name dropping. We can't have folks thinking I'm holding your hand." Kahlier chewed his pipe stem, an idea brightening his pasty countenance.

"Didn't you once say you have a friend at the *Tribune*?"

"Yes sir, Meranda Kaine. She landed a job there a year or two ago."

"Doing what?"

"She's one of their columnists."

"Call her. See if she'll drum up some of this info for you. If she knows of Langford, she might even help out with an introduction of sorts."

Jack eyed Kahlier. Though he was still barking orders and sounding presumptuous, the bishop looked less ominous.

"It's been years since we talked. But I guess there's no reason I couldn't give her a call." The thought of talking to Mera again made his heart skip a beat.

"If you can get this paper squared away, you and Nottingham may make a fine impression on each other." Kahlier's thin lips curled into a half-smile, his eyes narrowing just enough to remind the young priest that everything with the bishop came with a cost. "*If . . .*"

"I hear you, sir." Jack breathed easier, almost sure he was back in Kahlier's good graces, a place he intended to stay.

Chapter 4

"I'm looking for the catch in it, but so far nothing's turning up." Mera was filling Jack in long-distance, still somewhat thrown by the curve of his call a few days ago. They hadn't talked in years, since going separate ways after graduating from Boston. "Really, Jack, this whole thing's almost too good to be true."

"What, the Taize gig, or Langford's shelter?"

"Actually when you get into it, it's hard to tell one from the other. It's like they're part of the same equation." She'd been more than happy to dig for the details Jack was looking for. What she hadn't expected, though, was to be wowed by what Langford was doing.

"So, what did you find out?"

"Plenty. You should be getting the fax about now. I sent you everything we have from the archives on both Seth Langford and Wings Like Eagles."

"What's Langford like?"

"Something of a paradox from what I can tell. To quote one of the articles, 'a curious combination of velvet and steel.' But hey, you decide. And let me know what else I can help with."

Jack paused like he was thinking through the offer.

"After I look through your stuff, I'm gonna give him a call, try to set up a meeting down there."

"My guess is you'll like the guy. Unless this is all hype, which seems pretty unlikely, you'll be amazed at what he's done for the homeless here." Mera fingered the array of articles spread over her desk, all covering either Seth Langford or his brainchild, Wings Like Eagles. "In fact, all this research has given me an idea for my column. I'm thinking about doing another series on him.

27

Something different from the others we've done here."

"Well even if the guy's another Gandhi, I'm planning to keep the hero worship to a minimum," Jack said blandly. "All I'm after is getting this paper squared away."

For a distraction, Mera looked out of her office window. Impossibly blue sky filled with billowy cotton clouds. Fifteen stories down, ant-sized people winding and twisting and looking dead serious about getting someplace in record time.

Jack couldn't have changed that much.

She said it to herself again though she knew the past few days of trading calls and playing catch-up and acting, in general, like old friends had been something of a farce. Jack *was* different now. When he wasn't about being supremely pleased with himself, he had the shifty edge of an operative on assignment. And the attitude to go with it.

"When did you say you were coming down?" she said more lightly than she felt.

"Soon as I get through these articles and sound smart enough to call this guy for an appointment."

"Hey, how about this?" She had an idea. "Once I get the final green light here for another series, I was planning to call Langford. So how about if I just set something up for both of us, different dates, of course. Since we've covered his place so often, it'll make it easier for you."

"That'll work. Just let me know when Langford can swing the meeting." Kahlier's suggestion was falling into place. Mera was already planning the footwork and Jack hadn't even had to ask. "And I don't mind going together if you don't. It'd be good to catch another angle watching you work your deal."

"Fine by me," Mera agreed. "Let me nail down a date. And Jack . . .?"

"Yeah?"

"It's really good hearing from you again."

"Yeah. You, too. Good talking to you, I mean." She knew he

probably meant it, but the words sounded stiff, and she tried again not to read too much into his spurious tone.

The rain pelting her windshield was cold and steady, but not icy like it was going to be later, compliments of an unseasonal Arctic blast. She'd been in Chicago nearly two years now, but this kind of weather still made the curving highways and sudden bends a high stakes obstacle course she liked to avoid.

Jack was due in at O'Hare just after seven, so she'd left the *Tribune* Tower at five sharp, early for her. With thickening traffic and the glacial forecast, the short distance from downtown to the airport could easily turn into an hour-long commute.

Watching the wipers skim sleet beads from her windshield, Mera realized she was tapping her fingers against the steering wheel. She told herself to quit, to relax, before veering west on Interstate 90, where the entire landscape immediately morphed into a barely moving sea of freezing metal. Without a doubt now, the eighteen miles to Terminal 3 would be a crawl.

She glanced down at her fingers again. They were drumming ninety to nothing against the steering wheel.

Why? Why be so nervous? It was just Jack, her oldest and dearest friend. Jack, the only good memory from part one of her life . . .

There was absolutely nothing to be anxious about.

Chapter 5

O'Hare was a tangled maze. Between the slick roads and weekend traffic, there were lines everywhere — at exit ramps, baggage check-in — and passenger pick-up was the worst. It had taken more than thirty minutes to dock in the valet parking lane, another fifteen to get a claim ticket. Now, Mera tried making up for lost time by half-walking, half-trotting, through the terminal where she knew Jack would be waiting.

Minutes later, she found United Airlines' gate 22 still empty, the plane just taxiing in off the runway. She wasn't late after all.

Glad for the few seconds to spare, she slipped into a nearby restroom, barely sidestepping a collision with a tired-looking young mother pushing a stroller harnessing wailing triplets. Catching her footing and then stooping to retrieve a pacifier one of the babies had dropped, she offered the woman a smile before stopping at a sink to splash cold water over her face.

Then she did a double take. Mirrors didn't lie. And what with the long week, frenzied ride and stark florescent lights, there was no question that she was a candidate for some serious intervention.

Racing against time, she fished through her purse for a tube of rose lipstick. Next came a hint of color over her cheeks and a brush through her shoulder length hair. Another look at her reflection and she was satisfied enough to head out.

Back at the gate, Flight 243 was disembarking and Mera recognized Jack immediately. A folded navy garment bag slung over his shoulders, he towered a full head above most of the other passengers and he wore a black shirt bordered by a cleric's collar. She couldn't help smiling as he got closer.

Maybe almost seven years had passed, but Jack had hardly changed at all. His dark hair was still smooth and wavy, his build lean and muscular. The slightly aquiline nose that tipped up at the end, the clean jaw line and pensive brown eyes — they were all the same as she remembered. She'd forgotten how handsome he was.

"Meranda!" He grinned as he spotted her coming toward him.

"Jack Frasier, it's *so* good to see you." He leaned down to hug her and she kissed his cheek. "How was your flight?"

"Bumpy and long, and I'm starving. Where can I take you for something to eat?"

"Well, it's icy and the streets are packed, but Scoozi's dishes up the best Italian in Chicago."

"Scoozi's it is. Let's get my other bag and get out of here." He draped his arm lightly around her shoulder.

Mera felt something inside her unwind just a little. Jack was fine. Or at least he seemed to be. Right now the only thing that was distinctly different about him was his cleric's attire. And that only added something special, maybe even a bit mysterious, to him.

꙳

"This place is so cool." Jack rapped his knuckles on the table, tapped his feet on the varnished cement floor at Scoozi's, taking in the funky blend of Italian art-deco.

"I thought you'd like it," she smiled over the candle flickering between them. "It's sort of retro Tuscan . . . with a Chicago flair to it. And you'll love the food."

"What I love is that we had no wait," he said triumphantly, referring to the absence of a crowd when they'd arrived at the Gallery District's virtually unmarked warehouse. "I'm hungry enough to polish off everything on this menu."

"It's no wonder, considering we got here just a few strokes before midnight."

Jack rolled his eyes in mock exasperation. "It's ten-thirty, you goob."

"Which means if you hadn't taken your sweet time unpacking and hanging on the phone in that hotel room of yours, you wouldn't have missed the local color of a Friday night in Chicago . . ."

Mera was chatting easily, like old times, but it was all Jack could do to act natural. Staring across at her, he couldn't get over how perfect she was. The years had changed her some, etched her features with an even deeper beauty than he remembered. But there was something else now, too. Maybe a clarity, a keenness that seemed to have more to do with goodness than it did the passage of time.

"So, what's up for tomorrow?" Afraid she might read his thoughts, Jack forced himself to break with them. "We're not meeting with Langford until late, right?"

"At four. He said it was the best he could do. But I thought I'd pick you up early and we'd do the Boul Mich tour. That way, you could check out all the history down Michigan Avenue."

He smiled at her, unwrapped his napkin and smoothed it into his lap. Then he picked up a menu before a quizzical look passed over his face.

"Hey, what I want to know is how you got here. You did it, you know."

"Did what?"

"Made your five year goal."

She blushed a little.

"I guess I have Harry to thank."

Jack's eyebrows arched then slanted back down. "Harry?"

"After school, I got assigned to the Boston city beat, which at the *Globe*, can translate into almost anything. I mean I covered tax hikes, clean air legislation. You name it, if it had to do with city affairs, especially dull ones, I got it."

A waiter dressed in black pants and a crisp white shirt politely waited for her to finish talking before he took their order. Then he left.

"So then what?" Jack seemed interested. "How did you get from dull to Miss Human Rights of America?"

"Funny." She rolled her eyes at him.

"Well?"

"Well, just after Christmas a few years ago, one of the senior writers got stuck in New York. LaGuardia was covered in drifts and since all planes were grounded, the editor handed off his story to me."

"Another boring one?"

The waiter was back, bearing a glass of white burgundy for Jack, Diet Coke with lime for her. Taking a sip, she shook her head.

"No. This was one I'd been waiting for, the kind of story I'd been craving to write. Lance Abbott, the senior stuck in New York, was scheduled to cover Boston's streets through the eyes of the city's homeless. So when the editor gave me the go, I was down on the streets in less than an hour." Mera paused, remembering. "It had snowed all day; the world was blinding white, the winds like knives. And before the night was over, we got another six inches. But in a back alley, under this little lean-to made out of an old refrigerator box tied and hitched to a light post, I met Harry."

"So Harry was a homeless guy." Jack took a sip of his wine.

"Yeah. It was so cold that night, the few vagrants I saw were either burning whatever trash they could find in metal bins or were wrapped in trash bags and hunkered under newspaper. But around three in the morning, this Neanderthal-looking man in baggy clothes stopped to huddle in the lean-to where I was."

Jack recoiled. "Creepy, man. That had to be really weird."

Mera shook her head and squeezed the lime into her Diet Coke.

"No. I would've thought that, too, before I went out there. But it wasn't. It was just two cold people sort of desperately the same for the moment."

"That's an interesting way to put it."

"You know, I can still see him, Harry that is. Like it was yesterday, I can picture him through the slowing snowflakes, how the air steamed with his breath . . . how the ice clung in his shaggy beard."

Jack looked uncomfortable. "So what did this guy have to do with you getting here? Don't tell me some long lost uncle of his founded the *Tribune* and he used his connections to get you a job."

"Bad joke, Jack," Mera shot him a mildly disapproving look. "I wrote the story through Harry's eyes. After we'd stood in that pitiful little shelter for ten minutes or so, Harry started talking, sometimes mumbling, sometimes ranting. In any case, it boiled down to once upon a time Harry had a real life. A real family and a friend who swindled what little money he had. The rest, I guess, had to do with his debt stacking up and one thing leading to so many others that there he was. Alone and cold and stuck somewhere between living and dying."

Jack looked only slightly sympathetic and that seemed more out of obligation than genuine concern for Harry.

"So what did you name the story?"

"*A Dirty Golden Halo – The Boston Homeless After Dark.*"

Jack crossed his arms. Leaned back in his chair.

"You care to say why?"

"Why what?"

"*Why Dirty Golden Halo?*"

Through the icy beard that covered Harry's face, Mera could see he hadn't been old, though it was hard to tell if he'd been thirty or forty. The streets had leathered his skin, too, and his hair was so matted, it stood in tufts framing his head. *A dirty golden halo.*

"It was the way his hair stood in a circle . . . in this halo around his head . . ." she answered hoarsely, like the memory had made her breath catch in her throat and stick.

"So you wrote the story you always wanted to write. And here you are."

"Something like that, I guess. But it wasn't like I clamored to get here."

That was an understatement. Within two weeks of writing the story, the *Globe* had been inundated with calls. Everyone from citizens to newspapers around the country hailed the way she'd put a human face on poverty.

But that was how she'd gotten to Chicago, to the *Tribune*. After being nominated for a Pulitzer Prize, something she felt she didn't deserve since the Harrys of Boston still faced the blight of homelessness, Sally Noble had called her. Offered her a job on the City and Region staff, a position that let her cover Chicago's human interests just about any way she liked.

"So do you like it here?" With his right index finger, Jack traced the top of his cleric's collar.

She tucked a wisp of hair behind her ear and smiled at him. "I love it."

"You know, the only thing I remember about downtown Chicago, Chicago in general, is the Navy Pier. And I bet it's changed since I was a kid."

"You'll see it again tomorrow. It's on our way to Wings Like Eagles."

"By the way, how was Langford?" Jack switched subjects. "Father Kahlier said he's something of a rogue, the ragamuffin type."

"Hard to say, considering we talked for all of two minutes," Mera shrugged. "But he seemed nice enough." The waiter was back, this time to set down huge plates of pasta and foccacia bread with herbed olive oil. Out of habit, Mera bowed her head. Jack always said grace.

"God's neat, let's eat," he quipped, merrily irreverent as he dug into his mound of steaming spaghetti. He hadn't lowered his gaze, let alone his head.

"Wow, that was special." Mera's eyes were wide in her face.

"Tell me you didn't learn that hallowed benediction in seminary."

"Nope, it's all mine. One I use when I'm starving and don't need to impress anyone."

A full minute of silence passed with Jack eating bites of meatball and winding spaghetti around his fork and Mera cutting her pasta into tiny pieces like she needed some kind of distraction.

"Well . . . tell me about this Thomas Kahlier," she finally broke the quiet. "You mentioned on the phone what a great mentor he's been to you."

"What a journey the old guy's made." Jack loved bragging on the bishop. "Graduated from EDS himself and got elected bishop over Boston about twenty years ago."

"So how did you meet him?"

"Second semester at EDS, I ran into him. He was doing some kind of lecture and we got talking afterwards. A chance sort of thing, I thought at first. But pretty much since, he's been like a second father to me." Jack shook his head. "Lucky for me."

"What's he like?"

"Incredible, the man is amazing." Jack swirled his wine glass before he downed another sip. "Sometimes I can't believe he's invested so much in me."

"So, is he married?"

"Yeah, I mean he was. Wife died about ten years ago and he supposedly took it hard, never remarried. He has a grown kid somewhere, a son. But he's pretty private about him, except to say the guy's an essential waste."

"*That's* harsh."

"Yeah, I think the kid's an addict or something from the way he talks. But I've never asked."

"No, I didn't mean it was too bad for Dr. Kahlier," Mera clarified. "I was thinking with him being a bishop, he wouldn't be so quick to write off his own son."

Jack's face tensed into tight angles and he let his fork fall onto his plate.

"You don't know what you're talking about, Meranda," he said after several seconds. "You can't make judgements about someone you've never met. How do you know he hasn't done everything he can to help his kid?"

Jack's cheeks were flushed and taking in his cold stare, the sharp tone, Mera's face grew pale.

"Jack . . . Jack . . . I think you misunderstood me," she began weakly. "I'm not attacking your friend. Really."

The shocked hurt on Mera's face told him he'd overreacted. Again. Lately, he'd been so prone to flying off the handle, especially when it came to defending the bishop. But he owed it to the old man, he always told himself. Besides his own parents, no one had invested more in helping shape his life. Not to mention, Kahlier's connections opened doors few men could access. And this was a benefit that appealed more to him with every passing day.

Jack took a deep breath. Recomposed himself.

"I'm sorry, Mera," he offered contritely. "I get a little jumpy about Father Kahlier now and then. You know, Mom and Dad are hard on him . . ."

"They know him?"

"Only sort of. They've met him on a couple occasions, but they don't really get him."

"So he's hard to understand?"

"No, not at all. Really. It's just my folks think he's something of a religious politician." He wiped his mouth with the corner of his napkin. "But, they don't know him like I do. If you only had any idea how good he's been to me . . ."

If rigor mortis could possibly set into oxygen, the air between them was case in point. Jack needed to persuade her that the bishop wasn't Quasimodo's Frollo; for some reason, this was important to him. And he could tell by the look on Mera's face that she needed to be convinced that he wasn't some callous stranger, but the same Jack Frasier she'd known her whole life.

"It sounds like he really cares for you, Jack," she finally said, though he could tell that she'd forced herself to sound reassuring.

"It's taken me more than seven years to get here, Mera, much longer than I'd planned. And whether or not I get Nottingham depends on writing and defending this dissertation." Jack nodded at the waiter refilling their water glasses. "More than anything, I want that parish. It's a great opportunity." He took a bite of bread. "And a perfect stepping stone."

"Stepping stone? What do you mean?"

Jack chewed thoughtfully then swallowed. "Just that. It's a good leg up on what I'm aiming for . . ."

"But, I thought you always wanted to put down roots, stick with a parish," Mera interrupted. "Kind of like Father Duncan."

Without trying, Jack saw Ezra Duncan's dark blue twinkling eyes. He pictured the multi-colored ballet of whiskers at the priest's chin, an appendage that went on forever before it connected somewhere in a brush of beard to his angular face. With his tireless love of people and a gap-toothed grin that appeared only on occasion, Father Duncan had served as his inspiration, his ideal, since he and Mera had been children.

"I used to think I wanted that, too. But moving around would show some diversity in my career, some creativity . . ."

"Career?" she cut in. "You've always referred to being a priest as a calling, something you're made to do."

"And I still think that's right." He looked at her, unflinching. "But there's nothing that says I shouldn't plan to be elected a bishop someday."

Picking up her glass of water, she watched the little squares of ice float then clink against the sides. For a long time, she sat staring, as if in studying the motion of solids suspended in liquid she might somehow comprehend the mystery of what had happened to Jack these last seven years.

"I see." She looked down and exhaled the words so softly that he had to lean in to hear her. "Do you think that's what God wants for you?"

"I don't think God's will is necessarily that cut and dried, Mera. I think it works like this: if my ministry helps others find peace with Him, why shouldn't I shoot for bigger parishes? It ups my chances of hitting that mark."

"Maybe you've got a point . . ."

"You don't sound convinced," he interrupted.

"It's not that I'm convinced or not convinced." She sighed. "Big parishes can be good, great. Being a bishop is a noble thing, too. It's just that . . . that . . ."

"That what?"

She hesitated. "It's just the way you seem to be going about it all. Like religious progress is all in a day's work, something to scratch off a list. Like what's sacred is just . . . well, sort of common." She sighed again. "I don't know. I just don't remember you thinking like this."

Jack winced like the words had stung. "That's not the way it is, I promise. Maybe I'm just not explaining myself right."

She looked up and met his gaze. "I'm just wondering, Jack. Did moving up the church hierarchy help Father Kahlier point people to God?"

Jack stared at her. It was just a question, he knew. No malice intended.

Thomas Kahlier might be something of a despot at times. He knew that. But that was only because he was good at what he did and he knew what he was doing. Without question, the old man ran the Boston diocese like a well-oiled machine. Beyond all this, though, he'd certainly pointed seekers to the divine, to the Christ to whom he was espoused.

Didn't all men of God do that?

"Of course it has." He advised his haunted conscience it was at least a half-truth so the words wouldn't taste so bitter in his mouth. "His whole life is all about pointing people to God."

Suddenly, Jack felt his stomach sour. If Kahlier was such a pious man, why did he always feel this need to cover for him?

Chapter 6

Despite the tension of the night before, the day brought a contrasting easiness, a relaxing familiarity that made the time fly. When Mera picked Jack up just after sunrise, his rapacious ambitions were nowhere in sight, like they'd given him time off. Instead, the old Jack had resurfaced, easygoing, and for all intents and purposes, fun to be with.

The morning dawned bright and clear with just a hint of fresh fallen snow. After grabbing coffee at a downtown Starbuck's, Mera played Boul Mich tour guide and they lost track of the hours until their stomachs signaled a time-out that landed them at a little sidewalk café off of Congress overlooking Grant Park.

The sun beating warm, the air crisp and cold, they sat at a wrought iron table munching thick Reubens and talking like they hadn't since college. She told him how crazy the Boston city beat at the *Globe* had been and he explained that studies and research and travels had kept him at EDS much longer than he'd planned. Lingering over more coffee, she confided that her work kept her so busy that she had no time for a personal life. And he told her getting married was at the top of his agenda now. When he mentioned Thomas Kahlier recommended marriage as a stepping stone to undertaking a parish, she bristled, wondering what else the bishop intended to coach once Jack married. Nonetheless, she reserved comment and Jack drifted to another subject, still amiable and light-hearted.

Before they knew it, the sun was low in the steel-gray sky and they had less than half an hour to scramble from the café to Seth Langford's center north of the river. But with scant traffic, they wound past the Navy Pier in just minutes into a universe of side streets that belonged to another world.

"You gotta be kidding. This is a confounded ghost town back here," Jack said, taking in the sudden shantytown punctuated with cracked sidewalks decorated in colored glass confetti. Broken bottles were everywhere. "All that's missing is the tumbleweed."

With every passing block, the streets stretched further away from the city's pulsing life. Buildings went from vacant to vandalized, most sporting peeling paint and either smashed out or boarded up windows. Graffiti and gang lingo marked just about everything. The few businesses that were operational, a couple of X-rated video shops, intermittent pawn stores and bail bond stops, a dingy hovel marked 'Ike's Diner,' had thick iron bars over windows, signs in them forbidding solicitors.

"I think we're here." Mera finally stopped in front of a gray warehouse, recently refurbished. Over the red double entrance doors loomed a fierce eagle painted on the bricks facing the words, "Wings Like Eagles." Off to the side, a bony leather-skinned woman with yellow hair sucked a cigarette and paced in front of an old man who had slumped against the building. Half-napping, the vagrant opened one eye, buried himself deeper into his ratty trench coat and muttered something unintelligible as Mera and Jack reached for the door.

"If this is what Langford's Taize jaunt did to him," Jack whispered as they walked in, "you can bet this is as close as I'm getting to the place, Burgundy Hills or not."

Mera smiled at his expression. "From what I know, starting this shelter wasn't on Langford's top ten list of career choices. But something big happened in France and here he is."

Jack shrugged. "Note to self: keep away from big French moments."

Before Mera could answer, they were inside, where the floors were lacquered concrete and the depth of the place turned out nearly triple the outside's width gauging by the hallway that disappeared into a curving horizon. It was plain but immaculate, judiciously dotted with sparse furnishings.

The reception area was wide-open, probably fifty feet across, with a large walnut kiosk set to the left against a low glass wall. Behind it, an older, bespectacled woman smiled and handed messages to the endless staff skirting by. In between doling out little pink slips, she tended the ever-buzzing switchboard. Beside her was a slender young man with mousy brown hair garbed in a gray t-shirt and faded Army fatigues. He was intent on his clipboard as he talked into a cell phone, but he looked up to signal something of a greeting.

"May I help you?" The guy finished up his call. Set down the clipboard.

"Yes. Mr. Langford's expecting us for four o'clock. I'm Meranda Kaine with the *Tribune*." She extended her hand which the young man gripped with a polite smile.

"And I'm Mike, Seth's assistant, for all practical purposes. Just have a seat right here," he winked then pointed to a long row of plank benches across from the kiosk, "and I'll page Seth."

Prepared to wait what she figured would be awhile, Mera sat down beside Jack. Since she'd been with the *Tribune*, she had learned it was almost protocol to have journalists wait some undisclosed period before an interview. But within seconds, quick footsteps broke her thoughts.

"Ms. Kaine, Mr. Frasier, I'm Seth Langford. Welcome to Wings Like Eagles." The voice was deep and kind, the handshake solid. But the setting sun's glare through the window completely eclipsed Seth in a blind spot.

"Thank you for seeing us, Mr . . ."

"Seth," he interrupted, "just Seth. And why don't we head somewhere a little less extreme so we can talk?"

Before she could catch a glimpse of him, Seth had turned and started down the endless hall. Sauntering lightly, he navigated them past closed doors and several barrack-looking areas. Then a large cafeteria and some classrooms. Along the way, he greeted what had to be the residents—mostly women and children, but some men, too. Occasionally someone looked a little blank or bleary-eyed, and one man seemed particularly twitchy. But he was the exception.

"How 'bout in here?" Seth pushed open the door to a large conference room, spartanly arranged with a single walnut table and matching chairs that ran the near fifteen-foot length of it. The only visible sign of what might be construed as excess was the yellow topaz paint on adobe-textured walls.

Then Seth turned to face them and Mera breathed in sharply.

Striking. Staggeringly so. The most striking person she'd ever seen.

He was tall, a few inches over six feet with the tight build of a college football player. Dark blonde and wavy, his hair fell to his shoulders, and his sculpted nose and cheekbones would have rendered him perfect before a deep scar over his top lip broke the precision of his features.

But the magic was his eyes. Deep-set but wide, they blazed like two cerulean flames. In his left ear, he wore a small Celtic cross, and his jaw line sported a shadowy stubble.

She forced herself to peel her eyes from his face and sank down beside Jack at the table.

"So you're here to talk about Taize . . . for a doctoral project or something, right?" Seth sat down across from them. He leaned in toward Jack, offering his full attention.

"That's the idea, at least. I hear you're a pretty loyal vet of the place."

"I forget, Mera mentioned how you stumbled onto my name . . ."

"A professor at EDS in Boston."

"I thought Father Kahl . . ." Mera began.

"No," Jack silenced her, noticing the frown that brushed across Langford's face. "Dr. Vernon at Episcopal Divinity mentioned he knew you. Said you were tops as far as first-hand resources go."

"I've known Vernon for years."

Jack looked like he wanted to ask a question, but was opting to refrain. "Well, what I'm here to learn is what got you to Taize, what the place is like and what it had to do with you coming back here to do this."

As if he was suddenly agitated, Langford pulled his fingers through his hair. Then he stood abruptly like he was looking for a distraction. A decanter sitting in the table's center fit the bill, and he leaned over to pour coffee into a styrofoam cup.

"Anyone else want some?"

Mera and Jack shook their heads no, and Langford walked to a window overlooking a decrepit building with glass panes smashed out like missing teeth. He gulped the liquid, his back to them and took a deep breath before he turned around.

"How should I say this? Okay . . . have you ever set out for what you think is a clear path . . . and then some crazy wild card knocks you off course?"

It wasn't so much a question as it was his thinking out loud. Remembering.

"Late seventies, I came to Chicago to go to Loyola, majored in international studies. I planned to go on to law school, figuring I'd end up in war crimes. But during the summer of eighty-two, I headed out to Loyola's campus in Rome for a few semesters. Figured a European hiatus would be a change of pace."

Seth polished off the last of the coffee, crushed the styrofoam cup between his fingers, and tossed it in the trash. Then he sat down again.

"The Rome Center was like home base for me. Whenever I could, I'd be out scouting Italy, seeing stuff I'd only read about in history books and travel guides. Then a buddy, actually my old college roommate, suggested I make my way up to Taize."

"Any particular reason?" Jack was interested.

"No and yeah. I had a lot of personal stuff going on. And my friend, David Brantley, thought a trip there over semester break might help clear my head."

"Did it?"

"Not hardly." Seth shook his head, a smirk-grin turning up one side of his mouth. "Flipped me upside down, inside out. And that's putting it mildly."

"Wait . . . isn't Taize a society of Cluniac monks who got together after the Second World War . . .?" Jack said, like he was having a hard time equating idyllic monastic living to Langford's radical life change.

"That's probably oversimplifying it, though it's not all that complicated," Seth answered easily. "Taize's an ecumenical community near Burgundy, France founded by a Swiss Reformed pastor. Initially, Roger Schultz settled in the village during the early forties. Set up the place to harbor Jews fleeing the Nazis. But after the war, he kept it going — for the orphans, for folks who didn't have anywhere to go. At first, Schultz's plan was to encourage reconciliation and healing from wartime suffering. But since then, it's mushroomed. People come from all across the globe to see his principles put to life."

"Were you able to meet Schultz while you were there?"

"Sure did. He goes by Brother Roger, and he makes a point of trying to connect with anyone who shows up looking for him. Don't ask me how he does it. The summer I went, there must've been thousands clamoring for his attention. Like me, most of 'em were kids, looking to make sense out of life. Hoping to find something bigger than ourselves."

"So did you find what you wanted?" Like a switch inside him had been flipped, Jack's voice was suddenly cool.

"No, Jack, and it was a good thing I didn't," Seth countered smoothly. "I was chasing some mystical encounter that would vanquish my demons. And God knows I had my share of them. But what I got in Taize was better than that."

"How so?"

"For starters, I got a clear view of the Christ. The real One."

"As opposed to one of the bogus messiahs?"

"That's not what I mean," Seth was unmoved by Jack's acerbity. "I grew up around religion, in church. And I could spit out God-jargon smooth enough to convince a priest I was the next St. Francis of Assisi." He chewed his thumbnail thoughtfully. "But inside I was dead … and so was God as far as I was concerned."

A knock sounded on the door. Mike from behind the kiosk excused himself then handed Seth a piece of paper.

"Fax this, then call Jerry Powell." Seth returned the page to Mike after giving it a brief scan and offering his signature. "Tell him we can house fifty more after six tonight."

Mike nodded then was gone again.

"Sorry, we've got an Alberta Clipper headin' our way and most of the shelters this side of town are at capacity. Snow's supposed to pound the city all night."

"You were saying you found God at Taize." Jack sounded patronizing but interested.

"The community at Taize blew me away. The brothers were all different races, different cultures. But they fit together like a jigsaw. Like you said, Jack, they're monks. The crux of Taize, though, is practicing faith where pain and poverty are the worst, whether it's in Africa or the underbelly of Chicago."

"Is that where you got the idea for Wings Like Eagles?"

"Not yet. At first, I wasn't sure whether the whole thing was an emotional high. I mean you had crowds gathering for these reflection services, music that I swear had to come from another world. And the languages," he stood again to pour more coffee into a new cup, but a slight tremor in his right hand made the effort appear epic, "the incredible collision of different languages all in one place made it surreal. Like watching a movie . . . and I guess I needed time to think."

Seth wiped up the coffee spill he'd made then swirled his cup before he drank.

"So I went back to the Rome campus and chewed on the whole thing for another semester. But by the time I went back,

I knew what I was going to do. I had it all weighed out. What I'd gain, what I'd leave behind."

"Gain? What do you mean, gain?"

Seth turned to face Jack straight on.

"You know, before Taize it never once occurred to me that sacrifice is a gain, a privilege if it helps change a life. But that's exactly what it is."

Jack sat back in his chair like Seth's words had stunned him. A full ten seconds of silence passed.

"So, you came back here and started this shelter?" he finally said.

"In a nutshell, yeah."

"Why here and not in some third world country? You had the background in international studies."

"Good question," Seth smiled. "You know where Lower Whacker Drive is? Or the general vicinity of the Tramp Trail?"

"No. I haven't heard of either." Jack stretched his long legs, tugging at his cleric's collar. He'd been taking notes, but Seth's question took him off guard. He put down his pen.

"Remember the stretch of river on the Bob Newhart Show reruns?"

"Vaguely."

"Did you see the Magnificent Mile yet?"

"Earlier this morning."

"Well, just beneath downtown, past the northeast corner of the Loop, lies a very different Chicago. Above, you got Bob smiling near the river, tourists snapping photos of the Mag Mile. But go down about ten yards and there's Lower Whacker. A third world of underground side streets and loading docks and homeless people who get kicked around like stray dogs."

"I had no idea," Mera blurted out. Here almost two years, she'd covered the best, and what she thought was the worst, of Chicago. But Lower Whacker had eluded her.

Sure, she'd seen peddlers singing for change in the subways. And sometimes the snowy Michigan Avenue Bridge was lined with shivering drifters pleading for hand-outs. But the thought that just a two-minute descent would reveal a colony of displaced people was inconceivable.

"I'm not surprised," Seth answered softly, his gaze meeting hers. "Lower Whacker's a well-kept secret, especially since its ceiling is many an upscale shopkeeper's floor."

"So, how does your work help these people?" Jack was impatient.

"Jack, what we do here isn't so much a quick fix as it is a work-in-progress. I'm lucky. I operate from investment proceeds of a large trust besides getting your basic 501c backings and exemptions. So we can afford to be more creative, more intentional here."

"One donor subsidizes your shelter?"

"I didn't say that. We have the usual grants and city aid most of these places get. But Wings Like Eagles has . . . well, an anonymous benefactor who donates a generous sum of money every year."

"What happens if that quits?"

"To be honest, I don't worry much about what ifs." Though his tone belied any irritation, Seth's features had tensed. "The folks who show up here have enough bona fide heartache and baggage to keep me busy for the next century. I figure if this shelter is God's idea, He'll handle the finances."

This answer seemed to have perturbed Jack, and for several seconds, he gave into a sulky silence.

Seth glanced at his watch, then out the window. The sky was charcoal and wind gusts had debris swirling in endless circles.

"Jack, Mera, I really wish I had more time, but another five minutes is all I can go. Tonight's gonna be one of our busiest yet. The City Mission Center closed a few weeks ago and we'll be getting those folks, plus another fifty I told my buddy across town we'd take."

"Real quick," Jack picked up his pen again, "how does Wings Like Eagles echo your Taize experience?"

"That's a good one. I think the teachings of Taize helped me see that poor and hurt is what someone might be, but it's not who they are, who they're created to be. Our staff here comes alongside this city's endangered people. Helps promote their rights, meet their needs."

"Sounds like a long-shot mission statement," Jack said artlessly. "How do you put feet to it?"

"Good catch, Jack." Seth didn't flinch. "It *is* all part of our vision statement. And the how to is pretty simple: broad services that help develop and equip the displaced person. Sure, we do the basic stuff—offer food, places to sleep. But real change happens when you give someone the tools to make it part of them instead of a chance happening."

"And what tools are those?"

"Counseling. Medical help. Life skills and trade classes. Accountability teams. The Midway Center . . ." Seth rattled off the opportunities like he was used to doing it.

"What's Midway?"

"Most folks never figure out what a wicked catch twenty-two homelessness is. Try getting a job when you have no address to show an employer. Then, try renting a place without a job. It's the old gotcha, both ways." Seth's eyes flashed, like the unfairness still ate at him despite long years of doing this work. "See if you can get an interview clutching a dirty backpack with everything you own in it. Then, say you somehow do land a job. Try opening a bank account to cash your paycheck without showing a residence."

He took a deep breath, a swig of coffee, then continued. "While we're equipping our at-risk folks, they can stay at our Midway Center, the warehouse at the end of this hall. They do chores, help run the place while they take classes and get the skills and confidence they need. In a nutshell, we're their address until they get a job, get on their feet. We call it Midway because the person is at the halfway mark of being repatriated into society."

"Repatriate—that's an interesting way to put it." Despite himself, Jack was listening intently again.

"Yeah. It's pretty bizarre how the places where we've lived can suddenly become foreign turf. Places we don't belong anymore. We try, here, to help our people get what they need to connect and belong again. Some of 'em are so torn up, you think they're past hope. But . . ."

He was interrupted again, this time by his beeping pager as the door opened. A woman with curly auburn hair and a generous mouth slipped in and deposited a foot-high stack of folders on the table. Like that was his cue, Seth pushed his chair back and extended his hand.

"Hope this helps with your research, Jack. Again, sorry we have to cut this so short. But give me a call if you get home and see we've left something out." Jack gripped his hand and he and Mera rose to follow Seth Langford from the room.

"Mera, sorry we didn't get to your questions." Seth stopped suddenly, turning to look at her. "Let's talk next week since you're here. Maybe we can hook up for lunch one day. That's how Sally and I have always done it." Before being promoted to editor, Sally Noble had reported on Wings Like Eagles several times.

"Great." She reached to shake his outstretched hand, irritated that she found herself momentarily tongue-tied. "I'll be in touch."

She wasn't sure, but it seemed he looked long at her for a minute, studying her features intently like it mattered to him that he remember her.

Chapter 7

If Seth Langford said he was going to do something, there was no question whether or not he'd make good on it. Keeping his word was like breathing to him, something that seemed to surprise people on a regular basis.

Maybe it was the fact that he didn't write much down, no matter how intense life got. For years, he'd shucked calendars and planners, even sheets of paper torn from tablets, all offered up by friends and colleagues who were more anxious about his memory than he was.

He knew he probably looked absentminded, but truth was, he never forgot anything. Not dates or times or birthdays. And never the details of conversation. He stored everything in his head, and up to this point, his system was near failproof.

He assumed his renegade looks didn't help him out much. A clean-shaven suit in Armani attire looked far more credible than a shaggy-haired guy in faded jeans and Rockports. But Seth didn't work in the ebb and flow of Chicago commerce, and he felt no particular need to look influential or powerful.

To the contrary.

He'd long concluded that anyone set on getting to know him would figure out his eccentricities had nothing to do with the steadfastness of his nature.

Very little got under his skin, he took almost everything in stride. But the *Tribune* columnist and her priest friend were an odd match he couldn't shake. When Meranda Kaine had called, she'd said the paper was planning a possible series on Wings Like Eagles. Would he toss around a few story angles with her? And while they were at it, could he talk with her friend about Taize?

He'd been glad to do both. The shelter had relocated, expanded its scope since the newspaper last covered it, and somehow, the long-ago treks to Taize lingered, still fresh and sweet in his mind.

But the encounter produced a twist he hadn't expected. A nagging question he couldn't answer.

Was she or wasn't she involved with the priest?

Seth knew it was ridiculous. He didn't know either one of them. But Jack Frasier seemed connected to Meranda in a more than friend sort of way, and she was about as easy to decode as Mona Lisa's smile. So he had no idea what the arrangement was between them, and it bugged him that it mattered at all.

One thing was sure. He planned to call her before she got the chance to track him down. He had the feeling she thought he'd wanted to shake loose of her last weekend, though the truth was he was looking forward to seeing her again.

And he was particularly glad her friend would be back in Boston.

No doubt, Jack Frasier seemed sharp enough. Smart, conventionally good-looking. But there was something about him that rubbed Seth the wrong way.

Alice Pike thrived on the details of working for a staff of obsessive wordsmiths, but without question, Mera was the secretary's favorite. Perhaps it was because she wasn't as moody as the other columnists. Or it could have had something to do with the biweekly Starbuck's decaf lattes the young columnist brought by for her.

Whatever it was, Alice liked Mera—so much that instead of letting her phone messages pile up with the rest of the City and Region staff's, she made a habit of personally depositing the pink memos in Mera's chair.

After lunch today, Mera found the typical little mound, with one of the slips attached to a note from the messenger.

"Nice note, your majesty." She stopped in front of Alice's desk and waved the rosy paper. On it, the secretary had sketched a cross-eyed happy face with the words "see the queen" situated on a bad rendition of a throne. "What's up?"

Alice allowed her fingers to cease flying over the keyboard while she peered over the top of her horn-rimmed glasses.

"I'm supposed to *personally* catch up with you now that you're back." She shrugged. "Seth Langford's orders."

"Really?" Mera said carelessly, though she was all ears. "Since when is he giving orders around here?"

"He said he was following up from the weekend. Wanted to make sure you knew he'd called."

"Oh."

"He's like that you know," Alice baited.

"You know him?"

"Just from working with Sally. She used to cover his shelter when she did a regular column."

"I know. I saw everything she did when I was sifting through the archives."

"Have you met him, yet?" Alice's maroon lips, usually confined to a droopy pout, turned up a little.

"Last Saturday."

"What did you think?"

"Interesting."

Alice rolled her eyes and gestured dramatically at Mahmoud Nasir, who had stopped by to retrieve his stack of messages.

"Interesting . . ." Alice groaned to Nasir, "our friend here, our brilliant and beautiful and single, I might add, friend, meets Chicago's most intriguing bachelor three days ago. And what all does she have to say but, 'he's interesting.'"

Nasir scratched his balding head. Adjusted his glasses.

"My wife used to think I was interesting," he deadpanned, then disappeared.

"C'mon, Mera, you had to think something." Alice returned to her little questionfest.

"Passionate. That's it. There's no lack of passion in what he's doing, that's for sure."

"Did you see him with the folks in the shelter?" Now Alice was smirking like she had something to add.

"The staff?"

"No. The residents."

"I just saw him with a few staffers. They were getting braced for that last Canadian front."

Alice pushed up her sliding glasses. "You should see how he handles the people who come through that place," she winked at Mera. "I know he looks like something out of *West Side Story*, but he's got a heart of gold."

Mera let a discretionary few seconds pass. She liked Alice. A lot. But she had no intention of even hinting how many times Seth Langford had crossed her mind since she and Jack had left Wings Like Eagles three days ago. And the fact that she'd decided he was probably the reason artists paint was most definitely her secret.

"Well," she pretended to muse, "if his heart is anything like his shelter, I'd say he's a lucky guy. Because that shelter's like nothing I've ever seen."

"You know, he's got a reputation . . ."

"So does Nasir," Mera cut her off, "and most days we don't boo him. Except maybe his wife since he's not interesting anymore."

Alice ignored the smug comeback.

"Well they say he's got the memory of an elephant, the eye of a tiger and . . ."

"What? The wings of an eagle?" Mera quipped, hoping Alice couldn't hear her heart pounding in her chest.

"Smart mouth." Alice shook her head in mock defeat as Mera walked away. "Anyway," the secretary lilted after her, "he said if he hadn't heard from you by four, he'd call again."

Staring at Alice's pink message back in her office, Mera was annoyed with herself. What difference did it make whether

Seth Langford lived in infamy or was dubbed a saint? Whether he could recite the Nicene Creed backwards or couldn't remember what he'd eaten for breakfast? None of it was any business of hers, and the fact that she'd let anything about him matter, even for a minute, aggravated her.

~

She intentionally hadn't returned his call; for some reason she was curious what he would do next. So far, he seemed replete with contradictions. Busy but unhurried. A proper renegade. She figured the list went on, but in all, he just didn't seem like the type who concerned himself with too many loose ends. And it wasn't like his shelter needed more good press. So she figured his message amounted to nothing more than a final, obligatory follow up to Saturday.

But he proved her wrong when the phone rang at four thirty sharp.

"Meranda, Seth Langford. This a good time?"

"Sure, I'm just finishing up."

"Your column?"

"Yeah, one for later this week."

"You know, I like your work," he said easily. "It's honest."

The thought of him reading what she wrote made her feel awkward. Exposed.

"I hope so. I like yours, too, from what I saw last weekend."

"I'm just sorry we had to cut it short." Then, changing the subject, "Did your friend make it back okay?"

"I took him to the airport yesterday. He really appreciated your help."

It wasn't the complete truth. But she didn't feel bad telling the lie.

"Well, if he's measuring life change at Taize by what it can do for others, I hope Wings Like Eagles said something."

"It did."

"Hey," he interjected, like he was ready to move on to the next thing, "you said you wanted to toss around a few ideas for your column."

"I do. I'm thinking about a series. Maybe highlighting someone from the time they come to your shelter to when they re-enter the community."

Seth was quiet, like he was mulling over the idea.

"That'll probably work. Let me chew on it and we'll talk some more. Can we meet up for lunch early next week?"

"How about breakfast this Saturday? I'm headed out of town Monday."

"Saturday's good."

They decided on a time and place, and hanging up the phone, Mera had no idea why her heart was beating hard again. And she certainly had no way of knowing that just a few miles away, Seth was staring out of his window, retracing the curves of her face from memory.

It was one o'clock, and they'd been at the stuffy diner since ten. The food was good, just the basic eggs and bacon with toast. But from the time they'd slid into the red-glittered plastic benches and ordered coffee, the conversation hadn't stopped.

Seth had carried in a canvas briefcase, which he opened almost immediately. With heavy weekend crowds streaming in and out of his shelter, Mera assumed his plan would be to get down to business and get out quick. But after he passed her three paper-clipped files and offered thirty second highlights on each, Seth crossed his arms and leaned back in the booth. Then smiled.

"What?" She feigned a frown. "Why are you laughing at me?"

"Who's laughing? I'm just thinking."

"About?"

"*A Dirty Golden Halo.* Your Boston story."

"That was years ago."

"I know."

"And *you* read it?"

"Are you kidding? I think every human rights advocate across America read it. You were a voice crying in the wilderness."

"That's probably an overstatement." She flushed with the open praise.

"No way. That story was incredible," he continued, animated. "The insight, the empathy. It was unreal . . ." He leaned forward like he was about to confide something. "You know, sometimes I couldn't tell where Harry left off and you picked up. Or vice versa."

"Mr. Langford . . ."

"Seth."

"Seth, that's the nicest compliment you can pay a writer."

"I know. I did it on purpose," he said, looking right at her. He hardly knew her, but she seemed somehow familiar. Comfortable and easy. Her sharp cheekbones, clear green eyes should have rendered him nervous. She was beautiful.

But there was more to her than that, he sensed. Without a doubt, there was an underlying authenticity about her that almost demanded him to see past her looks.

Then the waitress brought plates of steaming food. Between forkfuls of eggs and bites of toast, they talked. About Chicago and Boston. About Wings Like Eagles and the *Tribune*. And finally, it seemed safe enough to talk some about themselves.

"You miss Boston?" Seth wanted to know.

"Not really. I didn't leave much behind."

"What about your friend, Jack?"

"I do miss him."

He had to ask. The suspense was making him crazy.

"Are you and he . . .?"

"Together?" She finished the question when she noticed how awkward he suddenly looked. "No, not at all. We were best of friends for years, though. Practically from the time we were born all the way through college." She smiled at the memory. "So there's a whole lot there. But not like . . . not the way . . ."

"I get it." He did, and in this case, it was a welcome comprehension.

"But you know," she continued, pensive, "while he was here . . . well, actually, I noticed it on the phone before he came down, there was something different about him."

"How so?"

"You'd have to know him to get what I mean. But ever since I can remember, being a priest is all Jack wanted to do. Everything he did — his whole life — was always about either helping people or showing them something about God."

"So what changed?"

She nibbled a piece of toast then swallowed a sip of coffee before she answered.

"I'm not sure, exactly. Closest I can come to explaining is it's like a fire in him went out. Like he's been switched off and gone cold inside. It's hard to put a finger on it, but it's almost like he wants religious power more than he wants . . ."

"God, Himself?" Seth laughed, a slight snicker. Then pulled a cigarette from his parka. He took his time lighting it, watching the thin paper glow orange and wither as he inhaled.

"Exactly! It's like this new ambition has suffocated his love for God."

Seth was quiet so long she thought he might not answer.

"Man, I'm really sorry," he finally said. His voice was gentle like he understood exactly what she meant. And cared. "Glory's a cheap substitute for passion."

"Wow. That's well said." She grimaced slightly then looked away to trace the bluish tendrils of smoke rising from his cigarette into the air. "And definitely worth pondering."

"Hey, it's probably none of my business, but if you're really that good of friends, why don't you say something to him? You know, friends do that sorta thing—tell you true stuff you sometimes can't stand to hear."

"I tried. I made this innocuous comment about his mentor, about something that didn't seem to add up," she started wryly. "Six or so years ago, this guy took Jack under his wing, and I swear, he might as well have cast a spell over him. But since he's supposedly some bishop over the biggest diocese in Massachusetts, he can do no wrong."

A quizzical flicker skimmed Seth's features and he leaned in closer.

"So what happened?"

"He got really mad, as in the, 'I'm holding it back, but I'm on the verge of hitting something' kind of mad."

"Did he defend the bishop?"

"Totally. The guy has Jack eating out of his hand. He's overseen all his work at EDS. And he's giving him some upscale parish once he's half-done with his dissertation. But if you ask me, the man's a fraud. And Jack's snowed. He just can't see it."

"So you know the guy?"

"No, just of him. But Jack's convinced the sun rises and sets in Thomas Kahlier."

"*That's* the bishop?" Seth's eyes widened before he made himself busy crushing his cigarette butt hard against the glass ashtray.

"Yes." She shifted nervously in her seat. "Look, I've talked too much . . . way too much, and I don't even know why. I hardly know you."

"I do. You're as comfortable with me as I am with you." He looked pleased with himself.

"That's a bold statement, Mr. Langford."

"Maybe. But can you tell me I'm wrong?"

"Let me look through these profiles, here, and I'll get back with you on one." She fumbled with the folders he'd handed her earlier, determined not to look up. "Like I said, I'm thinking about following a person's progress over six to twelve months, tracing the steps they take toward repatriation, as you put it."

Seth drummed his fingers lightly on the table, smiling. "Good idea. But you never answered my question."

"What question?"

Without meaning to, she looked up and his eyes met hers. River blue and intense, they were searching her, almost daring her. She looked away.

"Basically, I said we kinda like each other. But then you went and called me bold, so I asked if I was wrong." He smiled. "That was my question."

For what seemed like minutes, she didn't take her eyes off the folders she was buckling back and forth in her hands. Like one suddenly awakened from deep sleep, she kept blinking as if trying to decide whether or not this conversation was real. Then just as Seth figured she probably wouldn't answer his question, or that she'd counter his theory, she lifted her eyes to meet his.

"No," she said slowly. "I'd actually be lying if I said you were wrong."

Chapter 8

It was unusually hot for June, nearly a hundred degrees, and it wasn't much cooler in the shade. In four months, she'd made her way to Wings Like Eagles several times. And always, this little crowd of men caught her off guard.

Today, half of them huddled under the crimson of the shelter's awning while the others formed a loose congregation that glistened like black oil in the blazing sun. In all, there were probably two dozen of them, reed-thin giants that sometimes topped seven feet in height and gibbered loudly in an African dialect lyrical as song.

From a distance and in the day's gold light, their skin was flat black. Like ink. But up close and indoors, they turned the frosty blue-charcoal of a plum harvested mid-summer. Without exception, the insides of their hands and soles of their feet were the color of pink cotton candy, but it was their smiles that were most striking. Against the midnight of their faces, what teeth they had glowed florescent white like little blinding rows of interrupted light.

She'd exchanged only vague greetings with these natives, something probably due to the fact that they spoke little English, she spoke no alternative and they pretty much kept to themselves. But with every passing encounter, two things came clearer to her. First, these strangers sported the widest smiles she'd ever seen. And second, once the grins faded — and they always did — the solemnity that recast their features, the hollow that filled their eyes had to be mirrors from another world. A very dark world.

What they were doing here she didn't quite know. The few times she'd asked Seth anything about them, all she'd gotten were cryptic answers.

They were natives of central Africa. Refugees given asylum from a right-wing regime. They had fled across borders into Egypt, he said, before landing at the American Embassy in Cairo.

That was it. No other explanation other than the actions he took on their behalf.

But then what he did for them was pretty typical of how he handled everyone who passed through his shelter. Whether it was battered women with children in tow or the serial homeless with nothing but the clothes on their backs, Seth Langford was about one thing. Life change—the kind of change, he liked to claim, that's only possible when one person puts the weight of his life behind another's.

Pushing her car into park and fumbling with a few loose papers that had escaped her notebook, Mera mused again on Seth's part-desert father, part-economist, philosophies. Never, it seemed, did he fail to connect the dots between conviction and practical living. Smiling, she tugged a cardboard sun visor across the length of her windshield.

Siiiipp. Pause. *Awwwwwwor.*

She snapped to full attention. The guttural sound was coming from outside, from one of the three African men pacing and cradling their heads in their hands. The trio was clearly devastated.

Siiiipp. Another pause. *Awwwwwwor.*

It was the deepest inhalation possible. A sucking in of all life.

Then a wait while the air held in collapsed. Mutated into noise and sound that transcended words.

Finally the release. The torrid expulsion of many dark things held dormant too long.

Siiiipp. Pause. *Awwwwwwor.*

There was no language to describe the abysmal ululations that kept emitting like a low siren from the agonized native. Flanked by towering friends who sustained him on either side, the man's sucking in, then wailing, seemed like it might go on forever.

Now more concerned than alarmed, Mera quickly exited her Explorer and made her way from the stifling heat toward the shelter where Seth was expecting her.

This was definitely odd, she thought, casting a backward glance at the little assembly. Out of character. This community usually maintained a monarchical dignity. A decorum that bordered on stoicism.

They were meeting with Tad Ryan this afternoon, the ex-convict who had agreed to being featured in her twelve month *Tribune* series. Fresh out of prison, Seth had offered Tad a job at the shelter, and grateful for a semi-permanent address and the chance to hone his skills, the young man readily accepted. So far, it seemed a good match, and this was month number two.

But winding the corner into Seth's office, Mera stopped short. Seth was on the phone, his back to the door. Tad was nowhere in sight.

"I know, we heard about an hour ago. No, we don't *know* what it's gonna mean . . . not yet." Seth paused and let out a long sigh before he continued. "Worst case, they shut down borders. Best case, access gets restricted." He rubbed his forehead, then twisted around in his chair. Glimpsing Mera in the doorway, he motioned her to come in.

Then continued.

"Fine. He's fine according to reports, but there's talk now he'll deploy troops into that contested desert region," Seth explained, something more like worry than she'd ever heard edging his tone. "So here on out, we've got to worry about freedom between the borders. No doubt Cairo's gonna play it closer to the vest now. Things'll be tightening up and quick . . ."

Mera had no idea what he was talking about, but she noticed his right hand doing the tremor thing it seemed to do when he was anxious. He nodded a few more times, fished a cigarette out of an almost empty pack on his desk, then promised to call whoever he was talking to back later.

"Is everything okay?" She sank into the chair in front of Seth's desk.

"No, not really." His face was tight as he lit up and inhaled. "Hosni Mubarek was almost shot this morning going into Addis Ababa."

"As in the Egyptian president?"

A silent nod.

"None other." He breathed out a cloud of smoke, remembered she didn't share his habit, then tamped out the cigarette just enough to be able to re-light later.

Mera wondered why this news would hit Seth so hard, what the tedious politics of far-east Africa could have to do with his work here. But noticing the distraught expression had completely eclipsed his usually easy air, she opted not to probe.

"What was he doing in Ethiopia?" she asked instead.

"Attending an African Unity meeting. Information sources are tying the assassination attempt to the government of Sudan. Mubarek has no successor, no vice-president to step in . . ."

"I don't get it; what good would it do them to take out Mubarek?"

"Who really knows, exactly. It's a mixed bag over there, sometimes another world of warlord assassins that plan and hatch little terror plots like chickens hatch eggs. Anything to destabilize . . ."

"What were you saying about the borders?"

"Egypt's been neutral or better in aiding the refugees we've got here. They've all but looked the other way when immigrants cross their borders. Even more, they've worked with the embassies in Cairo to try and help relocate some of them."

"So you're thinking they might tighten border control?"

"Without a doubt."

"But with no proof yet?"

Seth's eyes flit to the doorway where Mike was passing by. Then back to her.

"It's a long story, but if Sudan's National Islamic Front was even remotely connected, they can't afford not to."

"I'm not following," she said, perplexed.

"Egypt is one of Sudan's nine border-states, obviously. But less than a decade ago, a military coup flipped the Sudanese government, installed itself. Even before that, figuring politics there was like programming computers without algorithms. But as you might imagine, this regime's downright hostile." He picked up his prematurely expired cigarette, looked longingly at it, then tapped it like a pencil against a stack of papers in front of him. "And knowing that, there's no way to tell the difference between a refugee fleeing for asylum or a terrorist planting himself for some future take 'em out mission."

Her eyes widened.

"Isn't that a little extreme?"

"No, Mera, I don't think so," Seth was patient, but she could tell her question had irritated him. "And neither do people who know what this government's capable of."

It dawned on her why the three dark men outside looked so grief-stricken.

"Some of your men from the African group were . . ."

"Pretty torn up," he finished the sentence. "They've got family in Egypt waiting to be deported to the States and our embassy in Cairo's been handling the papers."

"Will they still get out?"

"It's anybody's guess now. Egypt could crack down on all traffic, incoming and outgoing. After this, they're gonna be hypervigilant about domestic threats. And no one could blame them."

"So all your African residents are from the same place?"

"They're from central Africa." Seth shrugged noncommittally. "By the way," he switched subjects, "Tad couldn't hook up with us today. A meeting with his parole officer came up."

She nodded, trying to digest the past ten minutes.

"But I did something you should know about." He offered a half-smile.

"You did?"

"Yeah, especially since it involves you. You and me actually." He ruffled through the pile of papers he'd been tapping his cigarette against until he found a small white envelope. "I bought two tickets to *Madame Butterfly* for Saturday night. I was hoping you'd say yes."

"Saturday's your birthday," she said, trying to disguise her pleasure.

"I know. And I can't think of anyone I'd rather turn thirty-six with."

She tried picturing him in something other than his usual jeans and untucked shirts. But it was hard. It was like he was born to sport only ascetic, rugged basics. And any departure from that was inconceivable.

She thought for a minute.

"What if I try and scare up dinner beforehand?"

"No, I'll take a rain check, though. Besides, I've already got reservations."

"You do?"

"At 6:00 P.M."

"Where?"

She tried to sound curious, though it didn't matter whether he had burgers and fries in mind.

"Only if you say yes." He was smiling in earnest now, his eyes soft, and when he looked like that she had to look away. It was like he wanted more of her and was searching for where he might find it.

"I'd love to go, Seth."

She hardly ever used his name, but when she did, it made his stomach hurt a little. Against his own wishes, he really liked Meranda Kaine — more than any woman he'd ever met.

Chapter 9

Mera didn't know what surprised her most, the formal clothes or how he looked in them. When she answered her door, a copycat of Seth stood outside, this one clean-shaven in a tailored black suit and tie. A red handkerchief peered from his coat pocket and his hair, usually careless waves to his shoulders, had been coaxed into orthodoxy. Even the trademark earring in his left ear was missing.

She'd dressed up, too, a sleeveless black crepe with matching shoes. Then a strand of tiny pearls only because she wasn't brave enough to try anything more creative.

At least she was satisfied with her hair. Instead of its usual clean precision or neat ponytail, it was curled tonight. Pulled up on both sides and twisted, the rest cascading long and thick.

But staring at Seth now, Mera forgot about her hair, along with any thoughts of whether or not her dress was too boring.

He was beautiful, undeniably so. Rough-perfect, like he'd deigned to step off the cover of *GQ* to make his way here. And standing there trying to act as if looking at him wasn't a phenomenon made it occur to her that before now, she hadn't an idea of what an embellished version of Seth might be like. She'd assumed he had no interest in fleeting vanities like clothes and hair and smooth-shaven skin.

"Hey, I'm a few minutes early . . . and you're beautiful." He kissed her cheek lightly, something he'd never done before.

"And you," she took a deep breath, hoping her warming cheeks hadn't flushed red, ". . . you look fantastic." It was all she could get out without stammering.

"It's the missing earring." Winking, he tugged at his left ear.

Then, "I picked these up on the way here." He'd had his hands inconspicuously behind his back, hiding a bouquet of white roses twined with wild heather and eucalyptus. Now he handed them to her. "They reminded me of you."

"What, white and thorny?" she chided, touching his shoulder lightly.

"No. More like somewhere between exquisite and perfect," he answered, never taking his eyes off hers.

"They're beautiful . . ." she murmured, looking away. Like you, she wanted to add.

Once again, his candor had disarmed her, and as she tucked the flowers into a vase, she wondered how he could live so transparently. So unafraid of being really seen.

He never did mention where he'd made dinner reservations, so when they stopped to valet outside Ruth's Chris Steak House, Mera did a double take. She'd eaten here a few times on business, and though the food was exceptional, she remembered the prices could be, too. And Seth ran an inner city shelter, not the Chicago Stock Exchange.

"Something wrong? Is this not good?" He read her hesitant expression.

"No, I mean, yes. It's great. It's just, this is more than what I was thinking."

"How so?"

She lowered her eyes as the attendant made his way to open her car door.

"This is . . . this is extravagant."

He didn't answer until he'd made his way around to help her up the few steps, his fingers barely touching her waist.

"Then it's fitting," he said gently, "because so is being with you."

A few minutes later, they sat inside the softly lit dining room, amid the tinkling of crystal and china. An ivory candle on the table glowed between them.

"Happy birthday," she whispered after she'd slipped a slim package from her purse.

"What's this?" He looked surprised as she set it on the table's flawlessly pressed white linen. "You weren't supposed to get me anything."

"Says who? Besides, you've been wanting it."

"Wanting what?"

"Open it."

Seth untwisted the black and tan wrapping until he came to a hardbound copy of Fyodor Dostoevsky's *The Idiot*.

"You remembered," he exclaimed. Then smirking mischievously as he ran his hand over the cover, "Or else you're trying to tell me something . . ."

"Remembered what?" she retorted, mock-innocent.

Just a few weeks ago, Seth mentioned his mother's literary hero had been the Russian author, his *Idiot* her favorite. For years, he said, he'd intended to read the book and the fact that he'd never gotten around to it felt a little like unfinished business.

Their steaks arrived then, flame-grilled to perfection and served with tiny new potatoes. They ate in silence for a few minutes, enjoying the food.

Then Seth put down his fork. Hesitated a little.

"There's something I want to say." He looked serious, and even in the muted light she could see color creeping into his cheeks.

She stopped eating.

"Okay."

He took a deep breath. Waited a second.

"We've spent a lot of time together the last few months, work time, just hanging out. And . . . it's so easy being with you." He reached across the table for her hand. Squeezed her fingers lightly. "It's like . . . I feel like I've always known you."

Mera tucked a strand of her hair behind her ear, determined not to look away this time. Instead, she concentrated on his chiseled features and the candlelight shadowing the outline of the scar over his top lip. For one wild second, she wondered what it would be like to kiss him.

"But here's where the road might divide," he continued, leaning in closer. "I really like you, Meranda. I think you're beautiful and smart and funny. I like the way you write, and I love the way you care about people who can't do a thing for you. I even like the way you look away, like right now, and I love the way you say my name." Seth paused for a second. Took another deep breath. "Bottom line, whenever I'm with you, I feel like everything before you was just a rehearsal for this . . . for now," he lowered his voice, almost whispering, ". . . for us. And I'm saying all this because I'm hoping you feel the same way."

The sudden declaration should have been too much. Professing such emotion, such personal feelings, might be natural for Seth. But it wasn't for her. His frankness should have disarmed her, should have made her retreat somewhat.

But it didn't. She was getting used to his expressiveness, even if she wasn't quite comfortable with it. And she liked what he'd said, so much so, that she played it over in her mind while she gathered her own thoughts.

"I like you too, Seth," she started awkwardly, looking into the candle because finding his gaze would be too hard. "A lot. And what's more, you . . . you sort of amaze me." She glanced up, letting her eyes meet his for just a second. "And I'm not sure that's ever happened to me before."

That was huge for her and he knew it. Mera had always been kind, attentive. Even a little affectionate at times. But she threw up a wall when it came to talking about anything personal.

Up to now, he'd had no clue how she really felt.

They fell quiet then, her hand covered in his, both ignoring the food on their plates when two sets of triple *beeps* interrupted their silent conversation.

"Glad I at least muted the thing," Mera reached inside her handbag, silenced the culprit then squinted as she angled the small device beneath the candlelight. She frowned.

"What's wrong?"

She stared hard at the numbers like what she saw was confusing.

"It's Jack."

"That's not normal?"

She shook her head.

"He's never paged me."

Seth signaled the waiter, who came immediately and escorted Mera to a side room.

When she slid back into her chair fifteen minutes later, it was obvious that something was wrong. The kind of wrong that gets worse before it gets better.

"It's bad," she spoke after several seconds had passed to Seth's waiting, but inquiring, gaze. The effort of getting the words out seemed to be on par with sprinting a marathon.

"How bad?"

"Really bad."

More silence, though she seemed unaware of its passing.

"I'm a terrible guesser, probably the worst." Seth hesitated. "Is it . . . is Jack okay?"

She looked up, a sharp wince momentarily crumpling her features. "Jack's fine. Or I guess he's fine considering his mother died just a few hours ago."

"Wow," Seth shook his head as he reached for her hand. "I'm so sorry. I wish . . . I wish I knew what to say."

"Emily's been sick off and on for years," Mera explained. "With lupus. And apparently her system started shutting down over the last few weeks."

"When do you need to leave for Boston?" Somewhere in her semi-fog, she noticed he said when and not if. Something else she could appreciate about him.

"Tomorrow. Jack said he'd make my flight reservation for tomorrow and leave the details on my answering machine. I told him I was out with you tonight."

"Look Mera, if we need to cut the night short, I understand. We'll do this another time."

"No, really, this is fine."

"But you'll need to get ready and . . ."

"I want to be here with you," she cut in. Then feeling too exposed, she added, "I can get ready later and there's nothing to be done until morning."

The rest of the evening passed in alternating waves. One minute was the newness of Seth's shoulder against hers, her hand in his as the Joffrey Ballet Company twirled through the Auditorium Theatre, painting the tragic *Madame Butterfly* in a kaleidoscope of color set to symphonic scores of terrible beauty. The next was the chilling revelation that Emily Frasier was gone.

No longer here.

Somehow that reality wouldn't quite sink in.

To top it all off, she felt guilty, like she'd dampened Seth's thoughtful plans and cast a shadow on his birthday. Never mind he'd told her probably a hundred times not to worry — and at least half that many that things like this happen. It wasn't until they reached her front door that she found herself mostly convinced.

"I can't thank you enough for everything, Seth. For dinner, the ballet, for what you said . . ."

"I meant it, Mera. Every word of it," he said softly. "And when you come home, I hope we'll talk about what's next."

She looked down, avoiding his eyes. He took one of her hands in his and lifted her chin with his other one.

"You do want to talk about us?"

"I do, I'm just . . ."

"What?"

"I don't know . . . scared maybe."

"Why? What's scary?"

She didn't answer.

"What scares you about us?" he pressed gently.

She looked up at him. Then down again.

"I don't know, really. Maybe the us part. Maybe being more than friends."

The headlights of a passing car lit his face for a second, a menagerie of tenacity and tenderness, and something else she couldn't define, all entwined in one expression. Then the light was gone.

"Tell me . . . is this scary?" He tilted her face toward his and leaned down to kiss her. The fact that she kissed him back, tentatively at first, then like she didn't want him to leave, seemed to take him by complete surprise.

"Good night, Meranda." He pulled away abruptly. "I had an incredible time tonight."

"Me, too."

"Good luck in Boston."

"I'll need it." An almost crippling wave of sadness pulsed through her.

"And you'll call me when you get back?"

"Sure. And Seth?"

"Yeah?"

"Happy birthday again."

It was the best birthday, the most amazing night he'd ever had, and he thought about her all the way home.

Chapter 10

The flight into Boston was long and fitful, a waking dream of pictures from the past. She tried hard to fall asleep, but every time she closed her eyes, her mind chased a million thoughts, mostly about Emily. Thoughts she'd deemed long forgotten.

Like the time she was five, Jack was six and Emily harnessed them both on the Frasier's porch swing to pluck tiny burrs from their hair. All while they'd dripped orange Popsicle juice on the chipped gray porch and bickered loudly over who had rolled faster in the tall summer grass.

Or the night ten years later when she and Jack happened upon Emily and Mark swaying beneath the yellow of a harvest moon, leaves swirling about them like colored snowflakes. It was the first time she'd seen grown ups dance.

Or the sequence of pink cupcakes and cards and little surprises that had come from Emily on each of her passing birthdays. Birthdays, that sometimes, no one else remembered.

The images went on forever, one behind another, until Mera finally decided eyes wide open would be best, even if it did make the three hour trip an eternity. She couldn't wait to get off the plane, let the anguish take hold and start unraveling. Anything, she figured, had to be better than this.

But even before she'd taken ten steps into Logan International, she knew she was dead wrong. One look at Jack robotically propelling his way through the crowd and she knew the reality was going to be uglier than she'd imagined. And when he reached her just seconds later, she felt the weight of his pain fasten to her like iron shackles.

"Jack . . ." She dropped her purse and carry-on bag to hold him close. He wrapped his arms around her, held on tight and buried his face in her hair.

"God help me, Meranda . . ." The words clawed from this throat like he was being tortured. "I just can't believe this . . ."

She didn't say anything because words weren't required and it wasn't like there were magical ones that would relieve the hurt. Instead, she kept on holding him, feeling the warm of his body, the way his chest heaved up then crashed down like waves at high tide.

"She's been so sick . . . and we knew this was coming . . ." He nearly choked before he took another deep breath. "But I can't believe . . . I just can't believe she's gone." He breathed out a low groan. Squeezed his eyes shut like he was holding back the waters of Hoover Dam.

A quick stop to get a Coke so Jack could take two Tylenol and an hour later, they pulled up at the funeral home where, inside, Emily's body was on display amid an ocean of subdued flowers. About fifteen feet from her, Mark Frasier, now sporting a shock of snow-white hair and deep creases on his hollow face, was surrounded by endless sympathy coming from men in dark suits and women with stiff hair in pleated dresses.

"Mera, Mera. You're here." His eyes brightened and he smiled a little when he saw her coming. "How's our girl?" He wrapped his arms firmly around her.

Our girl.

For as long as she could remember, the Frasiers had called her their girl. Now the sudden reminder of that brought tears to her eyes.

"I'm good, Mr. Frasier, really good. I'm just sorry, so terribly sorry about . . ." She couldn't finish because an unobstructed glimpse of Emily's lifeless form brought back at once a thousand memories and all that went with them. Without trying, she pictured Emily making pot roast and cookies, Emily tilting her head back for a good laugh. She could see her holding Jack's hand in a white hospital room long ago, touching Mark's face for no particular reason.

Larger than life.

That's what Emily Frasier was, what she'd always been.

Now she lay cruelly thin, ethereally beautiful in a satin-lined maple box, where any minute, she would sit up, and tell them all to stop crying because everything was fine. And everyone would listen because Emily was almost always right.

But she didn't sit up. She didn't do anything at all, and the reality that she never would or could again was a hot wave that drowned Mera for a minute.

Like he had just remembered something, Mark started fumbling in his pocket until he pulled out a folded handkerchief. It looked lumpy.

"A few days ago, Em asked me to give this to you. She wanted me to tell you . . . to tell you that she loved you . . ." Mark bit back tears and carefully unrolled the handkerchief until two rings spilled into his palm. Emily's engagement and wedding bands. He thrust his hand toward her.

For just a second she stared. Then it registered what he was trying to offer.

"Oh no, Mr. Frasier, I can't take these . . ." Gently she closed his hand holding the rings with hers. And held it shut.

"Honey, these are yours. I . . . I promised her. It was what she wanted," Mark insisted, eyes pleading. "Em always said you were the girl we never had, the sister Jack always bugged us for." Somehow he managed a weak smile though he swallowed twice to keep his voice from wavering. "You're like our own, Meranda," he repeated.

She considered objecting again then thought the better of it. Instead, she leaned over, kissed Mark's weathered cheek and stayed beside him until Jack managed to untangle himself from the crowd of visitors some twenty minutes later.

"Come on, Dad, let's get you home. It's been a long few days and the funeral's tomorrow." Jack sounded almost annoyed as he took in his father staring dully at Emily's porcelain face.

"I don't want to leave her, son."

Jack nodded, more like there was business to attend than grief to be consoled.

"Right. But we both know she's not in that body anymore. We're just passing by the dragon."

"What's that supposed to mean?" Mera interposed.

"The dragon sits by the side of the road, watching those who pass," Jack recited like he was narrator in a play. "Beware lest he devour you. We go to the Father of Souls, but it's necessary to pass by the dragon."

Mera offered him a blank stare. "Jack, what are you talking about?"

"St. Cyril of Jerusalem said it. Basically, it means life takes some cheap, ugly shots at you, some fiery digs. But you should stay the course that leads to heaven. You know, don't buckle when it gets tough . . . keep moving . . ."

Glancing sideways at Mark, Mera noticed he hadn't heard any of the dragon talk or Jack's wanting interpretation of it. Instead, he was bent over Emily, stroking her hair and whispering something.

"I said come on, Dad. *Knock it off.* She's dead."

For what seemed like minutes, Mark half-gaped at his son and Mera wondered how, in the time between the drive from the airport to now, ice water had replaced the blood in Jack's veins.

Mark's face crumpled. "I know that, son," he whispered hoarsely. "I also know when we leave here, it's the last time I'll see her face."

Before Jack could answer, Mera slipped her arm through Mark's.

"Easy, Jack," she said as lightly as she could. "This is hard for both of you . . ." Then to Mark, "Come on, Mr. Frasier, let's go home and I'll try and whip you up something to eat. I'm still a scary cook, but I'm betting we can figure out something."

Without another word, Mark nodded like an obedient child,

and holding her arm, followed her away from his lifeless Emily to Jack's waiting car.

—~—

Her eyes hadn't been closed five minutes before a glowing teddy bear, crooked and mouthless, broke the thin black veil of new sleep. Then, as always, the whiskers moved in, cinnamon-salt whiskers that belonged to Father Duncan, though this dream priest had no face. But before the cold air and gossamer little girl and boy could take their places in this dark order, the dream gave way to something else.

"*. . . you were the girl we never had, the sister Jack always bugged us for.*"

Like the endless whisper of wind over a wide-open plain, Mark's quiet voice echoed over and over again.

"*Our girl . . . loved you like our own . . .*"

She tried to wake up, this variation stark enough to at least nudge her toward consciousness before she was sucked back into the vortex of it all.

Pink dress, shredded.

She could see herself again, clear as day. In a little pink dress ripped, ravaged, by her father—her own father—in a fit of drunken lust.

So very cold.

Frigid, the wintry air that night had been bitter. Needle cold.

Ruby-red stains. Silver-clear moonlight. White, frosty clouds swirling around Jack, around her. Swirling forever. And the pain . . . oh, dear God, the agony of just standing . . .

But it was the imperceptible anatomy of her soul freezing that had paralyzed her, simultaneously burning and icing everything inside her.

Glacial cold. Searing heat. Fused together. Never to be quite the same again.

It had been the night she'd shown up on the Frasiers' front

porch after Steve Kaine had finished up his first violation of her. His first of many.

"You're like our own, Meranda . . ."

Hadn't she wished? Wished with everything in her for a father like Mark who bought her messy ice cream cones and never touched her in secret places, a mother like Emily who could speak her mind and braid her hair and keep bad people from hurting her . . .

In the end, it was Mark and Emily who finally shattered the lies and secrets that had kept her long imprisoned to her horror of a father. It took years, the Lockwood system being what it was. And when that nightmare finally ended, another began.

Stephen Ray Kaine shot himself to death on an iron-gray February morning, one bullet to the temple. He'd done his two years in the local slammer, gotten out early on good behavior, then gone to a cousin's house where he scrawled a note, found a fifth of Jack Daniels and ended it all. Just like that — no remorse, no confessions. Not even any final words of love or regret.

Two days after his funeral, Mera turned fifteen, too young to make sense of the chaos that had ruled her last half-decade and plenty old enough to go crazy though that hadn't been her intention. But truth was, she just hadn't known how else to live. And she certainly had no clue how to ease the constant gnaw in her belly, no idea how to slay the shame dragons that kept her up nights.

So she gave into what came natural. Gave into large living, wild parties and, in general, any and everything that kept her from feeling pain, joy or whatever might be in between.

But that all changed May 25, 1981 with a high school graduation party that nearly killed her best friend.

Because that night, her revelry almost cost the person she loved most his life.

⁓

Heart hammering in her chest, Mera bolted upright as if the dream itself had catapulted her from the past to now. Taking in several ragged breaths, she wiped her damp face with the sleeve of her nightshirt and tried to sort out what went with what.

One thing was sure: she was safe now and so was Jack.

Jack was fine. She took in another breath and intentionally let it out a little at a time. *There was no one, nothing, that would hurt either of them now.*

She lay back again in the dusty light, waiting for the reality of that to sink in. Pulling the heavy covers up to her chin, she watched braided shadows playing chase along the walls. Behind the blinds, willow branches twisted and whipped in the wind, filling the room with flowing silhouettes that belonged to years long past.

She'd stayed in this room as long as she could remember.

After her twin brothers went off to college and her mother, Annalise, would sneak her out before going to work nights at a local diner.

When she'd creep from her bungalow window after Steve had slaked his lust with her small body before drinking himself unconscious for the night.

And finally, when the authorities carted her away from the sordid hell of 1042 Sierra Lane.

She'd come here to the Frasiers.

To this home, this very room where there were always hugs and Emily's lap, snacks and a quilt as warm and soft as it was beautiful.

Shivering at the memory, she sat up and sifted through her purse until she came upon the soft lump of Mark's folded handkerchief. It felt like a little pillow. Then tiptoeing across the wooden floor to the window framing a ghost-white moon, she slowly unrolled the bundle until Emily's two rings glittered in her palm.

Without question, this was the most excruciating gift she'd ever gotten and suddenly, everything inside her ached.

The rings hadn't just belonged to Emily Frasier. They *were* her. Solid and timeless. Invariably beautiful. And the reminder that someone so wondrous had lived and loved — and now passed on — was almost suffocating.

But as she watched the fiery colors flash and glow in the pale light, Mera realized the rings were also the loveliest gift, the most extravagant, she'd ever gotten — a fact that had nothing to do with white gold or carat weight. And before she tucked them away, she wondered if God ever whispered messages from those on earth to those in heaven.

Just in case He did, she thanked Emily for always making a place where a sad little girl could find sanctuary when she'd needed it.

Chapter 11

Throughout the eulogy, Mera never took her eyes off Jack, who never once shifted his gaze from Emily's casket as he spoke. The funeral was beautiful, as funerals go, a perfect commemoration of a life well lived. But as she sat beside Mark while Jack stayed as close as he possibly could to Emily, the raw and final truth of a life passing—especially a life like Emily Frasier's—produced a burning not unlike that of staring too long at the sun. Except this stinging wasn't restricted to the eyes.

"As most of you here know, Mother lived simply, first for God, then for others. In many ways, so many countless ways, her life epitomized His goodness and grace." Blinking hard, Jack stepped from behind the lectern, adjusted his heavy black cassock then inched even closer to Emily's closed casket. "But what you probably don't know is that she found her model in an ancient prayer, the *Simple Prayer* of St. Francis of Assisi."

The old Lockwood sanctuary was packed, its tired wooden pews crammed and overflowing with people. It was hot outside, stuffy inside and the acoustics were bad, but no one seemed to notice as Jack continued.

"*Lord make me an instrument of your peace. Where there is hatred, let me sow love, where there is injury . . . pardon. Where there is doubt . . . faith.*"

Mera's ears rung. The haunting words might have easily been written to describe Emily Frasier's life, whether she was the third-grade room mother passing out holiday cookies or the doting older woman kissing cheeks at their college graduation ceremony.

"*Where there is despair . . . hope . . . darkness . . . light, where there is sadness . . . joy.*"

Dear God, how many of these people here — *was it all of them* — had been moved and shaped in some way by Emily's unblinking belief in them? How many had been lovingly convinced that the best was yet to be, the future wide-open with promise?

"O Divine Master, grant that I may not so much seek to be consoled . . . as to console, to be understood . . . as to understand, to be loved . . . as to love."

Mera was crying again, and now Mark was, too. Quiet sobs cleaved through him without a sound.

"For it is in giving . . . that we receive, it is in pardoning that we are pardoned, it is in dying . . . that we are born into eternal life."

Like stiff silence after a storm, the air was motionless except for the ceiling fans chopping the thick air.

The old saint's prayer had so clearly lived on, incarnated centuries later in the humble life of Emily Frasier.

"Today, we're here to celebrate Mother's rite of passage into Heaven, into eternity, where she lives forever now with her Divine Savior," Jack broke the quiet. "So we grieve, dear friends, but not as those who have no hope. For all of us who are in Christ will someday join Mother in that place of unending joy and peace, where there is no pain, no tears . . . no more suffering."

Amazingly, Jack's voice hadn't faltered once, but as he rested his hand on the floral-sprayed coffin, Mera saw his chest swell, his eyes flood with tears. Next to her, Mark sat perfectly frozen except for the orbit of his thumb and forefinger rolling and unrolling a white handkerchief in his lap. Gently, she took one of his hands in hers as six pallbearers wearing dark suits and taut expressions encircled, then swept, the wooden chest from its flowery garden.

Then in a slow procession, they carried it outside — past the glassy pond and the old clearing to a waiting plot where the body that had housed Emily would be forever covered by insignificant, unfeeling dirt.

6 July 1995

The strange thing about belief, about believing, is that it doesn't happen at once. I wish it did, wish that mystery came clear to us when we needed it to. But it doesn't — not at all. So I'm left wondering, then, if we're not made to live between reality and this constant hope of something more.

I thought about all this again today, thought about heaven and Emily and God and faith. And as I listened to Jack making sense of death and promising an endless other world, it occurred to me for the first time that, really, there is no such thing as unbelief. We all believe in something, some worldview, some ideologies, outside of us. And we arrive at these faith forms or absences of them as deliberately as we do slowly.

I understand both sides of belief. The reality of doubt as faith and the hope of God as conviction make equal sense to me. But it wasn't until I saw them lay Emily into the ground this afternoon that I realized how complex belief is and just how much our faith stories have to do with what we see in other people's lives.

Through her closed door and over the nip and scratch of her pen on paper, Mera could hear Jack puttering downstairs in the kitchen. The *click-clump* of shoe heels on wood and staccato *clinks* of silver against china told her that he was still up, still pacing the floor and stirring excessive sugar into far too many cups of coffee. Despite the fact that it was after 1:00 A.M.

I know exactly when, even where, I first contemplated the possibility of God and I know without a doubt that it had to do with what Emily and Mark and Jack did and didn't do.

She pictured the days immediately following that May night Jack nearly died. The blinding white and flashing mirrors of the OR, the endless plastic tubing that poked through bandages or hissed air or fed IV ports with dewy drips that channeled into Jack.

But it was the way Mark and Emily treated her that still made her throat tighten, her eyes water.

It wasn't like Mark and Emily didn't know how Jack had gotten there. Because they did. They knew everything. How stoned I was, how wild the party had gotten and exactly what Louis Creech and I were doing in Mr. and Mrs. Creech's bedroom. And the fact that their son had almost lost his life trying to defend an honor code I didn't have, should have made them want to kill me.

But they didn't. Instead, they did the most damning thing of all. They loved me. Without ever once pointing a finger my way. And looking back, that, I'm convinced, is what made me think there could possibly be a God.

Like it was yesterday, she could see Jack's face bandaged where two of Louis' smashed compatriots had crushed his left eye socket bone. Orbital fracture, the surgeon called it. And the newly sutured carotid artery, gashed open via switchblade, lay protected beneath thick gauze and tape. Then there had been the broken collarbone and a bruised spleen . . .

Even now, I remember everything about that day. Jack's worn out Bible open by his bedside, the thick-set little nurse with black curls and stubby fingers who kept limping in and out of that stock-still room. I can picture the wind slapping maple leaves the size of hands against Jack's window, the ray of gold light on the wall clock that never got tired of clicking off seconds. I can see the cards, the flowers, the balloons.

And as I took it all in, I remember thinking how powerful one life could be, be it for good or for bad. Because my life, my selfishness, had done this to someone else.

Mera tucked the pen in her journal, rubbed her temples and walked to the window. Outside the sky was inky and starless, thick with humidity. Just a few feet below, Mark paced the length of the porch and his footsteps on the hollow planks made the creaking shuffle of a very old man. It made her heart ache.

She was tired. Suddenly so exhausted and sad and aged that maybe fifty years had passed in the last thirty minutes. It certainly seemed so.

She undressed, pulled on cotton pajamas and switched off the lamp. In the veiled light, she twisted her hair back into a knot then stretched across the bed. It was late and sleep was a good idea.

But when she closed her eyes, the rest came back in a flood: Reverend Duncan's wagging beard, his twinkling brown eyes. The glowing teddy bear she'd imagined from the mosaic of stained glass in the church's east window just the morning before her father had raped her.

Her father had raped her. Her own father. Then.

And later.

For years.

And in her mind ever since.

Sitting up, Mera set her jaw. Collected her thoughts and shored up her will. Like she always did when her past volcanically erupted.

She had had Jack, though, she reminded herself. Always Jack. After that first terrible night and all the ones that followed. And the ones years later, too, when all that was familiar was late nights, cheap booze and clandestine dope offered by blank-faced guys who used her body like a fire hydrant to sate their lusts.

Jack, who'd warned her ten thousand times over that all that could come of her short-sighted jaunts was disaster . . .

She leaned over and twisted on the light. Then picked up her pen before flipping her journal open again.

I think the strangest thing about that day wasn't reliving the pain, though that wasn't in short supply. It was this half-knowing, half-hoping sensation that something else should follow — something more, maybe even something good. I don't know why I thought that, but I did, and if anyone would have suggested God, I would have laughed, probably told him where to go. But I was all alone that day, except for Jack sleeping in the background.

All alone with the open Bible and verses Jack had highlighted and scribbled notes beside. Notes penned in messy scrawl that

obviously meant something to him. She'd memorized the words
years ago and she murmured them out loud now as she wrote:

> "... *If you do away with the yoke of oppression, with the pointing*
> *finger and malicious talk and if you spend yourselves on behalf of*
> *the hungry and satisfy the needs of the oppressed, then your light*
> *will rise in darkness and your night will become like the noonday.*
> *And the Lord will continually guide you and satisfy your needs*
> *in a sun-scorched land* ..."

For a split second, she remembered how she'd felt when her eyes
had fallen upon the alien words.

I wouldn't have thought much of it, really, though I remember
being a little intrigued by how the words sounded. Lyrical and definite
at the same time, they almost seemed like a promise. But since I didn't
put much stock in promises back then, I started closing the book. That's
when I saw another sentence Jack had written in the margin.

Like the page was in front of her, she pictured his slanted
cursive:

> "... *And how can they believe in Him whom they have not heard?*
> *And how can they hear without a preacher?*"

Before she could wonder what the verse meant, she had noticed a
date and two words next to it: "*10/9/79 — my calling.*"

That was it, she thought even now. No other explanation.

That's when it started to happen for me, though the revelation came
more zephyr-like than gale force. Nonetheless, it was something real,
something that made me sure that I couldn't go on like I had.

As I looked at Jack and thought about how he was so ridiculously
sure that he was made for more than just living and dying, I craved
some cosmic chance that I was here for a reason, too. And I wondered
if God could possibly have something to do with things like meaning
and purpose.

So I thought some more and though it seemed a crazy option, at
least for someone like me, I got to thinking that even with my landfill's
worth of garbage, God still might want me to find Him. Despite all
I'd done ...

Then, just like that, I did it. I decided on something that wasn't quite faith, but it wasn't all doubt anymore, either. I figured if Jack's God were real, then just maybe there was such a thing as second chances and clean starts. So I told Him, Him being God, that I was a total screw-up with a ball and chain the size of Texas. But a screw-up who wanted to change . . .

She closed the book again, still awed a little by what had happened all those years ago. Because in the still of that immaculate hospital room, Meranda Kaine hadn't even finished her sentence before her confession was part of a dialogue, an odd sacrament intercepted somewhere she couldn't see.

Without another word she'd felt the raunch of her past start withering, not entirely, but enough to recognize that something, maybe even *someone*, bigger was moving forward. And whatever, whoever, it was, rendered her more alive, more hopeful, than she'd ever been.

Chapter 12

She hung up the phone, poured fresh coffee into a cup then picked up her plate of soggy pancake squares swimming in a lake of syrup. "That was Sally." She sank back down at the kitchen table where breakfast was still spread out everywhere.

"As in *Tribune* Sally?" Jack's eyebrows arched slightly as he lowered the morning paper just enough to peer over at her.

Mera nodded, stabbed a little stack of squares and ate them. She licked the syrup from the inside corners of her lips.

"Yeah. They need me back home. Mahmoud Nasir's out next week, Sally's in New York for three days and we've got two new series starting. So . . ."

"You need to go," Jack finished the sentence as he stood up then rubbed his calves like they were cramping from his five-mile, break of dawn, run. "When?"

Mera's gaze rested on Mark dozing lightly on the couch. The thought of leaving him made her anxious.

"Sometime tomorrow. Sally's getting Alice to try and get the first flight out. But we'll have to see. She said she'd call back later with more details."

Jack took a long drink of watery orange juice and gnawed on the dry toast he'd made after he had come in from running. Then he disappeared into the pantry.

"Too bad you can't stay longer," he said from inside the deep closet. "Dad'll miss you."

Mera hesitated. "Will you and your Dad be okay until you head back home?"

Jack was planning to leave for EDS on Sunday. But this was only Wednesday.

"Of course. Why wouldn't we be?"

He reemerged holding a jar of blackberry preserves, which he proceeded to open and slather on his toast before he sat back down and took up the paper again.

Mera pushed back her plate and looked evenly at him.

"Jack," she began, "you know what I'm talking about."

He lowered the paper. Shrugged nonchalantly. "I do?"

"You do. Ever since I've been here, all you've done is ride your Dad. If it hasn't been about what to do with your Mom's stuff, you're getting on him about how he parks the car or what he's eating." She lowered her voice, careful not to awaken Mark. "Look, this has been a week from hell. I get that. But these trivial things you keep swinging at are nothing. He's in pain, Jack. *You're* in pain. Don't you think it'd be a good idea if you realized you were on the same team and then just started acting like it?"

Jack pushed back his chair, a frown crossing his features.

"Nothing's wrong, Meranda," he bristled. "Everyone's just a little edgy, but nothing's changed and nobody is picking on anyone." He sounded phony, like it was an election year and he was promising to lower taxes.

"You know, if you were anyone else, I might buy it, Jack. But I know you. I know your family. And something's not right."

Jack folded the paper and all but slapped it down.

"Duh."

"Duh?"

"Let's see, Mera. What could be wrong? My mother just died, this dissertation is killing me and my father's acting like he's ten instead of pushing sixty when he's not all up in arms about something I'm doing wrong." He stood up, drained the rest of the juice from his glass and grabbed his keys. "But don't worry because everything's fine."

Mera met him at the door.

"Please, Jack, that's not what I meant. I'm just worried about leaving, that's all. I want things to be okay between you and your

Dad. Like they've always been." She lowered her voice again. "I . . . I guess what I mean is I don't want to head back home knowing there's friction between you."

Jack's features softened a little but Mera heard the same insincerity in his tone that she saw in his eyes.

"Really, Mera. You're imagining things." He smiled coolly as he opened the door. "Like all good writers do."

As she watched him climb into his Jeep, the sunlight glinting mercurial gold over his head, Mera decided one thing was sure: there had to be a reasonable explanation for Jack's epic change. And before she left, she intended to at least try and sort through some of that.

~

Her opportunity came later that night, less than twelve hours before she was scheduled to head back to Chicago. Mark was upstairs sleeping, the first good rest since the funeral, and Jack was alternately browsing another newspaper and flipping the TV remote. It was hot inside, muggy outside and at 8:00 P.M., Mera abandoned the idea of reading a book. The sticky air made concentrating impossible.

"You want to get out awhile?" Jack stood and pulled at his perspiration-soaked cleric's collar.

"Sure." Relieved, she creased the page she'd only been staring at and closed the book. "Where to?"

"You name it, I'm game."

Mera thought for a minute.

"What about a few of our old haunts?" Maybe revisiting familiar places might loosen him up a little. Get him to talk.

Outside, the humidity wrapped them like thick sticky wool. The forecast had predicted a downpour all day, but so far, the bloated clouds just threatened. Like Jack's features, Mera decided as they wound through sloping hills in his black Cherokee. Both the skies and the visage of the friend beside her loomed heavy and ominous. On the verge of splitting open.

What sort of thing, what kind of phenomenon, could possibly have moved him to be like this? At times, he wasn't even the same person . . .

His internal tug-o-war had to be exhausting. Jack stayed so agitated now, so constantly on-edge. He spent uninterrupted hours at the kitchen table sifting through his research, slept only when exhaustion claimed him and drank way too much coffee as if to stave off rest.

Maybe though, in fact, surely, some of it had to do with losing Emily . . .

She hadn't noticed where they were going until he pulled the Jeep in front of her old house and clicked off the engine.

"Can you believe it? It's still empty," he scowled, surveying the tangled vines and weeds that covered the Cape Cod cottage. Several windows were shattered and the paint was peeling so badly, it looked like snowflakes in the moonlight.

"It's no wonder. Just look at it," she finally said, trying to keep the quaver out of her voice, the look of shock off her face.

Why here? What on earth had possessed him to come here?

"I forgot, how long ago did your mother sell it?"

"I think around five years ago."

"Oh yeah, I remember. She unloaded the place right before she settled on Walden Pond with Devon whatever his name was."

"Kilpatrick. Devon Kilpatrick." Mera tried to smile at his reference to Annalise and her longtime boyfriend's preference to Tennessee's backwoods over the big city.

"Right." He thought for a minute. "By the way, whatever happened to them?"

"Your guess is as good as mine. Devon's so possessive, I haven't talked to Mom since I moved to Chicago. I guess they're fine, though, probably collecting Social Security and living off the proceeds of this place." The old Kaine house looked tiny and innocuous in the dim-lit darkness, but Mera cringed when she thought of the hell that had happened behind the nailed-shut doors.

"It needs a paint job," he commented after a few more seconds had passed.

"Actually, I was thinking something a little more extreme."

"Such as?"

"Lighting a match to the place."

"Want me to? You never know, maybe I'm a priest by day, pyro by night . . ." Laughing, he pretended to strike a match, and suddenly he was his old self again, the imposter completely gone. He put his arm around her shoulder and pulled her close to him.

"I'm sorry, Mera, I shouldn't have stopped here," he offered sheepishly. "Let's bolt."

They did, driving all over Boston, by Lockwood High and Boston University, past the Freedom Trail and the Ritz-Carlton. On a whim, they got out and strolled beneath the midnight moon through The Commons sprawling gardens. Then, they stopped at an all night drugstore and bought turtle fudge ice cream before driving to Lockwood Church where they ate it with plastic spoons in Jack's Jeep.

"I love this old place," Mera said, taking in the whitewashed structure's shadowy outline, its pert steeple that was a long black spindle in the dark. "I can just see Reverend and Mrs. Duncan standing at that door, her clucking over everyone, him telling all us kids to get ready to race him by the pond." The church sat on five forested acres that touted a peanut-shaped pond just a quarter mile from the sanctuary's back doors.

"Weren't those the days?" Jack said wistfully before it occurred to him that this church and his house were the only places she'd ever felt safe back then. "I mean . . ."

"It's okay, Jack. Really."

He didn't say anything for a minute, just scooped and scraped his ice cream carton until there was nothing left in it.

"That was good," he finally said. "How was yours?"

"Too good. I'm stuffed." She took a final bite and tugged at the waist of her khaki shorts.

"You don't look stuffed." He sounded admiring, almost seductive, and Mera decided now was probably as good a time as
any to talk.

"Jack, since I'm going back tomorrow, there's something I
really want to talk about."

"Is it about us?" He sounded hopeful.

"Not really."

"Then what?"

"Jack . . ."

"Is it about that Taize fairy you've been seeing?"

"That's rude, Jack. Seth's an incredible person."

"Seth's an incredible person," he mimicked in a mocking,
high-pitched tone. Then, noticing no response from her, he
rolled his eyes. "You really like this guy, don't you?"

"I do," she said quietly. "We have a lot in common."

"So do we, Meranda. Like a lifetime. As in I was always there for
you the first twenty-five years of your life."

"This is what I want to talk about. These . . . these seismic
personality shifts that just show up for no particular reason."
Mera shook her head, looking evenly at him. "I noticed it when
you came to Chicago. One minute you're fine, the next, it's like
you're someone else . . ."

"Are you doing Langford?"

She gaped, not sure she'd heard correctly.

"What . . . what are you talking about?"

"Langford."

"What about him?"

"Is he doing you, Mera? Like Kurt did, like Rocco and Creech
did?"

For a minute, she couldn't catch her breath. His words cut like
a knife.

"Jack," she said, steadying her voice, "this is more than just
a little disturbing. Why are you saying these things? What's
wrong?"

"Just answer me. Or should I just rephrase the question now that you've half-answered it? How long have you and Langford been at it?"

The twisted accusation unleashed an avalanche of emotions, more than she could bear. In one motion, she flung the Jeep door open and started running, first across the parking lot then into the sprawling grassy field. She kept on for what seemed like miles, passing the old church and the pond before she tripped and nearly fell on a moss-covered stone at the edge of a wide clearing. The only light came from Jack's distant headlights; the starless sky was black with only a haze of moonlight to tinge the wooded darkness.

Winded, she sank down on a thick tree stump not ready or able to think about Jack's stinging words. Instead, she made herself take in the ebb and flow of wet breezes fanning through the trees, short air bursts that whistled whiny little songs.

Seconds passed, then minutes, before she was surprised to feel someone stoop beside her. Jack had made his way the almost quarter mile to where she sat.

"It's going to rain, Mera. We should go." He sounded almost penitent as a sudden gust of wind whipped through the trees behind them. A deluge of dusty leaves filled the air.

"Jack, what made you say that? What have I ever done to make you so mad at me?" She tried to choke back tears.

Jack reached down and skimmed a handful of leaves from the ground. Then crushed them.

"I don't know. Things are just different now," he said sullenly. "We're not kids anymore."

"Of course we're not. But aren't we still friends?"

"I need a wife, Meranda, and there's nobody for me but you. It's always been that way."

She waited to answer.

"Jack, we had this conversation almost eight years ago."

"I know. But if I'm going to get this parish, if I'm ever going to be a bishop, I need to get married . . ."

The religious politician was back now, no hesitation whatsoever in his voice.

Mera tried to disguise her horror as she answered.

"God help us both, Jack, listen to yourself. *Listen.* This is all about you, *your* ambitions, *your* career. And you're using marriage as a means of . . . of what? And for what?" She felt sick. "It's not right, Jack . . . it's just not and you know it."

"You're not getting it, Mera. The hierarchy looks at a married priest's credentials over a single . . ." Jack was completely beyond reach, reciting facts from a trance.

"The *hierarchy*?" she snapped. "You mean Thomas Kahlier, don't you?" At the mention of the bishop's name, Jack reeled like he'd been slapped from his daze. "He's reduced the church to a corporate ladder, an institution to be exploited until everyone but God cashes in on the returns."

"Shut up, Meranda. Shut up and leave him out of this. You sound just like my father."

That was it. The reason for the gulf between Mark and Jack. Mark, too, must have tried pointing out the bishop's greedy ambition.

"No, I won't shut up, I *can't* shut up. I've loved you my whole life. And I have no idea what I'd be like now if it wasn't for you." She reached for his hand, lowering her voice. "You showed me faith, Jack. You showed me that it was something real and good, something that matters . . ."

He set his jaw hard as she continued. "But you've changed now, and I can't figure why."

"What you mean is I'm not the Wings Like Eagles loser you're screwing."

She kept quiet a full thirty seconds.

"I'm not sleeping with him. There hasn't been anyone since . . . before you were . . . in the hospital fifteen years ago."

Jack slumped his head in his hands but she could still make out his profile against the misty fog rolling in. Even in the murky dark, he was so handsome to her, so much like a brother, and yet something more she could never put her finger on.

"Do you love him?" he finally asked.

"I don't know."

"You like him, though."

"Yes," she admitted. "A lot."

"You want the truth, Meranda?"

"About what?"

"About you. About me. About where I am in all of this."

She waited for him to continue, feeling his gaze bore into the side of her face.

"I want you, Meranda. I don't want him to have you."

She faced him squarely, her cheeks hot.

"Look, all my life, I've loved you, Jack. Ever since I can remember," she said brushing the side of his face with her fingertips. "I think you know that."

"Then marry me."

"Please. This isn't funny anymore."

"It was never meant to be funny."

"Even if I wanted to, Jack, you want me for the wrong reasons. Nailing down a parish isn't the right reason to get married, and you know it."

"*You're* going to preach to me about ethics and morality? I don't think so . . ." Another bitter quip, like he couldn't keep it from spilling out.

"I love you," she repeated, "but not like you want me to. And honestly, you're scaring me. It's like I don't know you anymore. Like a part of you isn't even real now."

"You loved Creech and Turner and Wilson enough to let 'em have at you . . ."

"Stop it. You know I didn't love them. That was a long time ago when I was messed up and afraid. I made mistakes . . ."

"You loved Daddy enough to let him keep on you, didn't you?"

Oh, God . . .

She felt a bomb go off inside her, its nuclear heat detonating everything. For what might just as easily have been hours as seconds, all she heard was the black noise of a million demons past. And somewhere amid the raging pandemonium of unleashed secrets, blistering memories, she felt the bridge she'd built from her past to here utterly collapse.

Like nature was syncing up with human tempests, the wind whipped wildly and rain started falling in heavy drops. A second later, two silver streaks skimmed the clouds and thunder clapped in the distance.

Mera tried to get up and run, but Jack grabbed her wet arm and she slipped back down to the ground.

"Why, Jack . . . *why* are you saying these things? You were *there* . . . you know what Papa did . . . you know how I hated it all . . . how I hated myself. You *know* that . . ." She was yelling between sobs, the driving rain blinding her.

"You know what I'm remembering right now?" he shouted back. "I'm thinking just about everyone has gotten a shot at you but me, the person who wanted you the most. And now, Langford's up in the batter's cage." The lights from his Jeep had dimmed, but through the storm she could see him pulling his shoes off, unzipping his pants. He was still squeezing her arm, a vise grip, but it didn't occur to her that he might hurt her.

"Jack, what are you doing? We need to go. You're upset and crazy, and we need to get out of here." She tried unsuccessfully to break free of his grasp.

"Oh, we will, Meranda. We will. But first I'm gonna show you just how real I am . . ." One-handed, he squashed her wrists together, while he kept peeling off his soaking pants with the other. Then, he yanked at the buttons on her shorts, ripping them wide open in a single jerk.

"Stop it, Jack. You know you don't mean this . . ." A sharp adrenaline surge made her heart a pounding drum but the knowledge that this was Jack calmed her enough to keep talking sense to him. *This couldn't happen . . .*

"For once," he rasped, grabbing to force down her shorts, "it's about me . . . before anyone else gets another chance with you . . ."

Locking his arms under hers and squeezing her flush against his torso, he swept his right foot behind her legs so as to knock her off balance. Panicked now, Mera realized the time for reasoning was past. Reeling backwards but still knotted in his grip, she attempted a sharp kick. But Jack blocked the blow and fastened his legs like ropes around hers. Through the hammering downpour, she could hear sharp grunts as he struggled to overtake her. Overhead, radiant spears forked the skies and a groaning rumble made the ground tremble beneath them.

Then in a surreal nightmare, Jack hauled his full weight against hers, toppling her flat down on the soaking grass. With a dull thud, her head smacked the solid earth and she felt her ability to think enveloped by a numb blackness. But her body took over, inexplicably thrashing and punching until he pinned her arms then crushed his mouth against hers. Out of instinct, she bit his lips, hard, then grabbed for the collar at his throat when he inadvertently let go of an arm. She could taste sweat mixed with blood dripping into her mouth from his, enough to have to keep swallowing so she wouldn't choke, and for a minute, she was sure he would come to his senses. But that hope died as he wrestled her back down, her slender build no match for his long, muscular one.

A violent roll of thunder shook the ground below them just before a flash of lightning outlined his face. Horrified, Mera realized she didn't even know the man glaring down at her.

This villian-stranger had confiscated Jack's body to do evil things. Things her Jack would have never done.

As she felt her shorts being peeled away, she tried again to think rationally.

This still couldn't happen, there was no way. Jack loved her, he always had. He would never hurt her.

Any second now, this ludicrous dream would end and she would wake up and wash the sweat from her face.

But the wet drenching her face wasn't perspiration. It was rain pounding them. And the nightmare wasn't about to end, she gradually realized as the deluge pelted their slippery, half-naked bodies. Then struggling to breathe as his brawny frame crushed hers, she knew the scenario was sickeningly real when his body betrayed hers, the reality sharper than a knife.

It seemed like hours passed before something in her snapped, repelling and cooperating at once as if by default.

She had been here before, she reminded herself. This wasn't new and she knew what to do because God only knew how many times she'd done it before.

Her body was helpless, but she wasn't.

Concentrating on the rainfall's steady cadence, the musty-sweet stench of dry earth drinking in water, she made herself disconnect from the rhythmic force rocking her body. Eyes squeezed shut, she blocked out the needle-like scratches that came from every direction. Sharp cold rain from the heavens above. Tiny jabs from the earth beneath every time she slid back and forth with Jack's motion. The wet grass was filled with tiny burrs.

Pedora, think about Pedora. What was her fat yellow cat doing right now? She was eating, wasn't she . . . sometimes she wouldn't eat if she was left alone . . .

Jack's panting grew heavier, quicker and more shallow, matching the tenor of the night storm. Tiny rivulets of water trickled from his soaking ringlets onto her face.

She concentrated harder.

Was it raining in Chicago, too, and would Sam remember to pick up the mail? Last time, her next door neighbor had forgotten and left half of it soggy and crushed in her mailbox . . .

She had no idea how long his weight suffocated her, how long it was before she felt a deep shudder pulse through him. Sometime later, his breathing slowed, returned to normal, and suddenly, her body was hers again. But the euphoria of being freed was cut short as she felt something slap the side of her face, gale force. It never occurred to her that it was Jack's hand.

Doing her best to hide her body, she sat up. The rain had faded to a mist that made Jack's headlights long, yellow funnels in the distance. Eyes that had seen everything.

"Get dressed." She felt the sopping weight of her muddied khaki shorts hit her.

She couldn't think straight. The moment was a scene from a movie. Or someone else's life.

Had this really happened? Did Jack just rape her or was it a dream?

"Come on, get your clothes on," he repeated, unable to see her numb stare.

It had to be a dream, really, because Jack was a priest . . . is a priest.

"I said, get dressed, Meranda."

No, it had to be real. She was half-naked and bruised, and there was Jack, saying things about getting dressed. But still, this couldn't have happened because rape is violence. Violence. And Jack couldn't be a rapist because he was a priest . . . a good priest . . .

Her endless questions were interrupted by a surge of nausea that ended in a deep gag. Teeth chattering, she realized the metallic taste in her mouth was Jack's blood, and looking down, she saw dark stains shadowing her drenched shirt.

"Jack?"

He didn't answer; he was trying to pull on his clothes. Shaking, she tried getting into hers, too, but the wet weight of them made the task go on forever.

"Why . . . why did you do this . . .?"

He didn't say anything for a long time. When he did, though, his answer was an icy dagger.

"Why should I finish last?"

That was it. He stood up and started walking toward the Jeep's glowing lights. As she reached for one of her missing sandals, Mera noticed his cleric's collar was still clutched in her hand, muddy and torn from his shirt. Numbly, she shoved it in her pocket, not sure what else to do with it.

Then she limped across the hazy field, her footsteps sinking deep into the marshy grass until she reached Jack and the Jeep.

Chapter 13

It started on the flight home from Boston. At twenty thousand feet and climbing, she drifted off, only to be wrenched awake seconds later by a graphic replay of the night before.

Rain like tears soaking everything.

Gritty earth beneath human flesh that slipped and slid before final force made two bodies fuse. Merge.

The salty metal of blood, the musky odor of sweat mixed with summer rain.

Paralysis followed by a wave of nausea cut through her and everything inside came up. The air turbulence bag had been less than an arm's length away.

That was the beginning. For the last week, she'd sat huddled in the corner of her couch, clad in flannel pajamas and covered in thick blankets that never quite warmed her. She knew she wasn't technically sick, no aches or fever. But she couldn't stop the bitter tastes and odors that kept her gorge rising and spilling over like a too-full cup.

The worst part was she knew she needed to get off the sofa and get on with life. Sally Noble had been more than understanding, but bills certainly didn't pay themselves and there were plenty of people who counted on her to make things happen.

But when she wasn't hung over a toilet or the kitchen sink, all she wanted to do was stare and hold Pedora, who was eating again now that she was back home.

~

Sam Wiesel was her first step toward reentry and he didn't even know it. He had shown up to bring the mail, banging in loud, staccato raps on her door until the clatter rattled her so badly that she'd finally opened it.

"Oh, it's you." Mera's sweaty forehead glistened like the rest of her grayish face. Just the trip to the door had exhausted her. "Hey, Sam."

"What the . . . what's wrong with you?" Sam narrowed his eyes, then ran a short fat hand over his fuzzy auburn curls. "You look awful."

Mera pulled her robe tighter around her. Moved a wisp of hair out of her eyes.

"A brash statement of the obvious."

"What's up?"

"Sick, I'm sick. That's all."

"Chick, you're lookin' like a ghost just hightailed it after you." Sam glanced sideways back and forth. A supersleuth taking in the atypical mess of her apartment. "Oh, here . . . I brought your mail from last week." He thrust a thick stack of papers and envelopes at her. "Been meanin' to get it to you for a coupla days now." He looked at her skeptically. "By the way, how long you been back?"

"Almost a week."

"How long you been like this?" He scratched his lower left arm where a tattoo of a suspicious leafy plant peeked through peach hair.

"A few days . . . look I need to go . . ." Another sick urge crested through her and she bolted for the kitchen sink since time was of the essence.

Sam followed a few steps behind.

"Hey girl, this here's some serious puking." He wet a dish towel and handed it to her. "You been eatin' anything in between?"

She shook her head and flopped back onto the couch.

"Nothing's staying down."

Sam folded his arms in thought. Then perched them atop the dough of his belly.

"I'm goin' home right now and calling Sabitha. She'll get you somethin' that'll stop this crap." He was so determined his round glasses shifted beneath his furrowed brow. His girlfriend, Sabitha Rajani, was a tiny bookish-looking internist from Bombay; he was a saxophonist in a start-up jazz band that landed most of its gigs in New Orleans. Mera never really saw the two of them together, but right now she was glad they were. Anything, anyone, who could help stop the vomiting was akin to an epic hero.

A few hours later, Sam beat on her door again, holding a bottle of pills.

"Phenergan," he announced, looking proud of himself. "Mother of all abdominal cease-fires."

"Thanks, Sam, you have no idea how I appreciate this . . ."

"It's nothing," Sam said magnanimously with a careless wave. "Can't have my best neighbor kickin' the bucket and smellin' up my bedroom." Then noticing Mera's blank stare, he explained. "You know, your den wall's my bedroom wall. And if you keel over . . . you know how they say rottin' flesh is the worst . . ." Another glance at Mera's mortified face and Sam opted to quit while he was ahead.

"Well, anyway, Sabitha said to take one of them pills, stay in bed and drink when you can. These things'll knock you out, but you need 'em."

"Thanks," she said, starting to shiver.

"She said to call her if you don't quit by tomorrow. She'll stop by and check you." He looked at Mera, taking in the drawn face, her fragile frame swathed in a quilt. "All I can say, girl, is this must be one wicked flu. Sometimes you're funky lookin', but you ain't never looked this bad." Sam shook his head. Handed her Sabitha's card as he turned to leave.

The medicine worked like a charm. Besides making an end to the vomiting, it cast a groggy stupor over her, and for the first time in a week, she crawled onto her couch and drifted into a stretch of dreamless sleep.

Hours later, she woke to the sound of her answering machine picking up a call. She'd forgotten to turn down the volume the last time she checked messages.

"Mera . . . Mera?" It was Seth. "If you're there, pick up the phone. You've got me worried. Sally just told me a few minutes ago how sick you are . . ."

Disoriented, Mera jumped to her feet. Immediately, bile gathered in her throat. She swallowed hard and prayed nothing would come up.

"You had no business calling Sally . . ." Another forceful swallow as she picked up the phone and talked into it.

"Thank God, I haven't heard from you in two weeks." His tone was terse and relieved at once. "There's been no answer, you're not returning calls . . ."

"You had no business calling Sally . . ."

Silence to the count of five.

"I've known Sally for almost fifteen years, Mera." He didn't say, "That's longer than you've known her," but she could read between the lines. Seth wasn't someone who could be ordered around.

"No harm done," he continued. "She knows you're working on the series with us." He paused for a second. "Look, I just wanted to see what I can do to help. Can I head to the store for you, get you anything?"

"No, I'm fine."

Another short pause.

"Can I come by and see you? I've missed you," he almost whispered.

"No, I'm sick. And you don't want this." *Like he could catch it anyway.*

"Look, I've got to make a benefit across town tomorrow. But after, I'm going to swing by and . . ."

"No, Seth, don't," she pleaded. "Please don't come by."

He hesitated like something unpleasant was registering.

"You . . . you don't want to see me, do you?"

"I'm . . . I'm not well."

"But that's not it, is it?"

"Seth, I was too hasty before I left for Boston."

"What's that supposed to mean?"

She took a deep breath and closed her eyes.

"I've had more time to think and some things have . . . well . . ."

"Changed?" he finished her sentence.

Without trying, she felt Seth's soft kiss on her lips, but it somehow morphed into Jack's mouth crushed into hers. And at once, sweaty rain mixed with blood filled the back of her throat, the air became sharp with the muskiness of wet earth.

She dropped the receiver and gagged so violently that vomit splashed everywhere, over the phone, into her lap, spilling onto the floor.

On the other end, Seth heard the deep retch, the watery rush that came up behind it. Then nothing but silence.

Which led him to a quick decision.

He'd run by and check on her. If Mera had been this sick for a week, things could be bad. Besides, she never came back to the phone, and that wasn't like her.

*

It took him a second to regroup when she opened the door because the woman standing behind it was definitely not the same one who had left for Boston holding his heart two weeks ago.

This version of Mera was some dark spirit, some ashen-faced, dead-eyed form who had given up expression for numbness, connection for detachment. Besides her hair clipped back in a careless knot, her pajamas hung on her, too, like eating had become a thing of the past. Worst of all, though, he could tell she wasn't glad to see him.

"You never came back to the phone," he started lamely.

"I forgot. I got really sick that time . . . everywhere." A slight grimace traced her features. "In fact, I just got through cleaning up the mess."

"Can I come in?" Through her half-cracked door, he noticed the couch was a disaster, and Kleenex and bottles of various sizes crowded a nearby coffee table. Propped against her barstool was a partially open suitcase that still hadn't been unpacked.

"I don't want you to catch this." The lie was bitter in her mouth, but it wasn't like the truth was an option.

"I'll take my chances."

She blocked the door so he wouldn't come in.

Even through her sleepy haze, she noticed how rugged his good looks were, how clean and defined he looked in just worn jeans and a long-sleeved t-shirt. But instead of the familiar safe feeling she had when he was around, panic sliced through her.

What would it take to get him to leave?

"What's wrong, Mera?" Like it was instinctive, he went to touch her face, which bore the expression of a deer caught in the headlights. She intercepted the gesture with a quick swipe of her hand.

"I think it's best you go," she said flatly.

He took a step backward. Blinked like a thousand thoughts had lit through him at once.

"Something's wrong. This isn't just about you being sick. What happened up there?"

"I had time to think."

"Yeah, so did I," he lowered his voice. "And the more I thought, the more I'm sure of what I want to say to you."

"This isn't going to work," she cut him off.

"What isn't gonna work? What's wrong . . ."

"I'm in love with someone else, Seth. Someone in Boston. And we're trying to figure things out." She forced herself not to wince at the look of raw shock, then hurt, that crossed his features.

It was another lie because, again, the truth couldn't be deployed. How could she tell him that she'd spent most of her life as a sperm bank or a whore depending on how you looked at it or who was doing the deed? Seth might be offbeat and unconventional, but she knew by now that he did things the right way. And she couldn't stand the thought of him knowing just how often she'd played the tramp.

"It's Jack, isn't it?" His voice was hollow with hurt.

"It doesn't matter who, Seth. The fact is, it's not you and me." The words felt scorching even as they came out, but they created distance. Now he would go away, and hopefully, any decent memories of her would remain preserved. Uncorrupted by the truth.

"You liked me, Mera. I know it . . ." He wasn't giving up.

"I did, but I love him."

"Who's him?"

"It doesn't matter. I'm just sorry I led you on. We'd broken up . . . awhile back . . . and when I was up there, we decided to try again." The look on his face was about to kill her, but she continued the charade. "I'm sorry . . . really."

She watched him breathe in slowly like doing so was imperative to his maintaining composure. Seth had a temper, he'd once confided, but nine times out of ten he controlled it. This appeared to be the one time he didn't want to, based on the brittle way he was holding himself, the manner in which he kept curling and releasing his fingers at his sides.

"No problem," he exhaled loudly, "I'm outta here. No love triangles for me."

"Honestly, I didn't mean for things . . ."

"Hey, it's best to cut your losses while you can, right?"

"Seth . . ."

"We could've been good together, Mera." His eyes met hers for a second, an indictment in them. "But if this is how you want it, I guess I'll see you around."

He shrugged carelessly, and as he turned to leave, the pain of him going gripped her so hard she couldn't breathe. He was walking away, no doubt thinking how fickle and shallow and cold-hearted she was. He probably felt used, even betrayed . . .

The universe spun in cadence to the roaring jet overhead, to the blinking of a million jewel-colored city lights, to the measure of hot summer breezes stirring the air.

A fool, that's what he'd been. Fodder for every self-serving joke in the anthology of human history.

As he slammed the door of his Bronco shut, Seth spit out a cache of choice words. He could feel the blood rushing in his ears and his head throbbed like he'd been pounded with a sledgehammer.

An idiot, that's what he was. A total fool.

Mera cared for him, he'd convinced himself, maybe enough to head toward something permanent.

Moron.

While she rekindled some old flame, he'd been down here counting the days until she came home, eager to say three words he'd never said to any woman before . . .

Through her slatted blinds, she watched him pull away, sobbing as the fiery glow of his taillights faded into the night. How could he know, how would she ever know, that he was the closest she'd ever come to really loving someone?

She felt her stomach heave, twist inside out, but this time, she made it to the bathroom. Reaching for another pill, she decided no matter what, she was going back to work Monday.

It was time to start moving on.

Chapter 14

If her life would have read like a paperback novel in a drugstore, she might have cried a few more tears, grit her teeth and decided to just get a grip. But since this was real life and she possessed few heroine-like tendencies, she decided moving and breathing at the same time would have to be enough for now.

So for the past few months, that was what she'd aimed for.

In the morning: up and out of bed. Into a stinging shower and clean clothes.

Moving.

Then out the door to another day of decrying human injustices on paper.

Breathing. At least of sorts.

She was playing with an ironic hand of cards, there was no doubt about it. If only everyone, or even anyone, knew what a sham her life was . . .

⁓

One more month, that was it, Sally Noble decided as Mera skulked past her office. If that girl kept on like this much longer, she'd either disappear like a vapor or simply expire from lack of life.

It was a toss up and Sally knew it. Either ignore the evidence or confront it and deal with the consequences.

Whatever was wrong had to be big—and it was becoming worse with each passing day. Ever since she'd been back from Boston and the stomach virus hiatus, Mera had pretty much mutated into an antisocial anorexic. With the exception of mandatory meetings, she hovered behind her shut door, producing still impeccable work with almost no human interaction.

Now it was her clothes. Which made Sally even more suspicious. On top of the dysfunctional behavior and new emaciation, why would Miss Dress for Success suddenly don skirts and blouses that were dark, frumpy and three sizes too big? Mera had always dressed to the nines — smooth hair, polished makeup, the works. In the last few days, though, she'd traded her svelte apparel for sacks. And personal maintenance didn't seem to include much more than brushing her teeth and pulling a comb through her hair.

It was all odd. Very strange and out of character. Maybe Mera really had taken the passing of her friend's mother hard. This was certainly a possibility considering she'd mentioned on more than one occasion that the Frasiers had been closer than family.

But the rest didn't add up and Sally knew better than to do nothing.

No, another few weeks and that was it, she told herself as she heard Mera's door close behind her. Then she'd say something though it wasn't in her nature to interfere.

Mera's clothes were different because she'd gotten rid of almost everything in her closet. She started by lugging her still-packed suitcase from Boston out for trash pick-up. There could be nothing in it that she would ever want or need . . .

Then to the mall after surveying her closet. Her clothes were provocative, maybe even slutty, she decided.

Why else would a priest, an honorable man of God, ravage her body?

There was one explanation and one only: if she'd managed to move Jack to this, she must look like she was asking for it. And the fact that he'd recited the roster of names that had gone in infamy before him was a sordid reminder of just how trashy she'd always been.

So she bought new things. Long, baggy skirts. Prim collared blouses to replace her tailored clothes and jeans.

As for the weight loss, the explanation was simple. Since that night, she hardly ate. Nothing more than sips of Seven-Up, maybe the occasional piece of toast with orange slices, sounded decent. Her mouth kept a constant tinny taste now, something she tried to assuage by keeping her teeth brushed and swishing mouthwash several times a day.

Seth was particularly glad for the milieu of demands waiting when he walked in every day. The shelter kept pretty constant traffic, some highs, occasional lows, depending on the weather and new immigration. But between a sweeping proposal to clear out inner-city housing and the publicity from the *Tribune* series, Wings Like Eagles was suddenly the homeless place of choice.

He welcomed the hotbed of activity, especially now. All the meetings and obligations and demands on his time were blessed distractions that kept his mind occupied, all the while reminding him just how lucky he was to be helping others.

Lucky, even if the last thing he remembered at night was clenching back hot tears.

He hadn't expected the whole thing to hit him this hard. Seth Langford was no lightweight; Sally Noble had summed him up five years ago in a feature article when she dubbed him "a steed of a man, self-bridled into semi-conformity, perhaps, for the sake of the powerless." He wasn't easily affected, and he surely wasn't ruled by emotions.

But something about Meranda Kaine had gotten under his skin and nothing seemed to change that.

From the start, she'd been something of a paradox. Kind but elusive. Beautiful, yet somehow tangible. She'd been willing, even glad, to forge a friendship, though equally vigilant to make sure it never became something more.

Until that night before Boston. The night he'd decided to take his chances and just tell her how he really felt. Until then, he had no idea what she thought of him, of them.

He tried hard not to think about her and he was usually successful until late at night. Then, he couldn't help but wonder what happened. Had she just been stringing him along? What was it about the other guy that made her choose him?

But as he tossed and turned, he couldn't help remembering her echo his affections. He felt her kiss on his mouth, warm and sincere, and he wondered how she could've convinced him so fully with just half her heart.

That's when the tears would come, and thank God, no one knew how many there had been. The only saving grace was he hadn't told her what he'd planned to say when he showed up at her doorstep.

At least he'd been spared that humiliation . . .

It had been three months now, and thankfully, they'd talked just once—to make arrangements for the rest of her series on his shelter. Conveniently, they planned it where meetings would be with Tad Ryan and a few other staff members. Only the final article would include a sign-off and photo shoot with Seth.

Five more months, that was it. Then Meranda Kaine could start fading into a memory that would eventually dim and vanish.

The thought was comforting, especially for a man who wasn't prone to mourning anything as silly as unrequited love.

~

Mera's hands shook non-stop and her heart pounded like a drum between her ears. The bathroom was a mess, pale green bile splattered on shiny white tiles, small threads of reddish debris floating about on top.

She'd been too sick after her shower to clean the latest expulsion that missed the toilet.

At least it was Saturday. She could take a pill to stop the riveting nausea. Then she would sleep, and with any luck, feel good enough to clean it all up when she awakened.

That's the way it worked lately. Violent queasiness that gave way to racking heaves. A pill to get it under control if she didn't have to be at work. Then deep sleep, no dreams or interruptions. The medicine was a gift, a pathetic placebo for peace that was about to expire. Sabitha had called in a refill a few weeks ago, but Mera knew a third replenishment was out of the question. The four tablets she kept rationing were all she was going to get.

Somehow she had to get this under control. Reliving the sounds and smells of that rainy night in Boston had to stop, if for no other reason than to keep from going insane. And she needed to start doing normal things again — mingling with people, eating real food without throwing it up. Somehow, she had to undock herself from the couch and move toward the periphery of things again. Even if it was just little by little.

How, though, this was supposed to happen she didn't know. Just existing now was taking every ounce of energy she had when she wasn't hung over a toilet vomiting her guts out . . .

There now, she'd done it. It had taken a whole week to muster enough courage to dip the little white stick in her urine. But as she twisted it back into its plastic cap and laid it flat on the bathroom counter, she felt a curious peace.

In five minutes, she'd know one way or the other. In the meantime, she leaned over the toilet and gagged.

This time her aim was perfect.

⁓

The air had a definite chill, nothing extraordinary for Cambridge in the fall. But as he stopped, mesmerized by a gust of wind whipping a pile of leaves into a floating whirlpool, Jack knew the cold he felt had nothing to do with the weather.

He could pinpoint when he'd first felt the iciness. The eerie emptiness that went with it. It was the morning after that sweltering night in the rain.

The night that should—and still might—damn him entirely, if not eternally.

So like Cain now, forever sentenced to wander, far from God or anything good, Jack moved through the days, dead inside. He ached to confess his evil, longed to decant his transgression. But he had no idea how to do it.

He'd committed an irrevocable wrong, undeniably. But it wasn't like there was a way to make it right again. How could he un-rape his best friend? Or even ease her pain?

He had been the violator.

No, he reasoned, staring at the twirling kaleidoscope of foliage as he started walking again, this was his Rubicon and there was no going back.

Nothing could be done.

But for the millionth time, he felt his mind start searing with the hellish question that taunted him like a jeering demon.

Why? Why had he raped her?

Mera had been his friend, his closest confidant, since he could remember. They'd grown up just ten months apart, two streets between them. In school, they sat together from the first day in kindergarten, she clad in a little green and orange plaid dress with a maple ponytail, he in neat tan trousers with his curls combed to the side. They'd stuck together always, then and through long years that followed. Whether it meant digging mud trenches in the summer rain to play army or sitting on his porch swing while she cried because her father had done things to her he hadn't understood at the time, Jack Frasier and Meranda Kaine had been inseparable. Even after he'd almost lost his life hauling a stoned buddy off of her at a raucous party-turned-orgy, they'd only gotten closer. Then they'd gone away to college together, him to study more about his God, her to enter the world of story crafting. He'd been so proud of her, so awed by how she'd found the strength, the faith, to move past her hell of a childhood . . .

And then *he* had raped her, too.

It was almost too much to live with.

He knew he should do something, knew with everything in him that he needed to blow the whistle on himself. But Nottingham was his in just a few short months. And after more than a decade of school and studies and waiting, he could wait no more.

No, he decided, it was done now, and confessing his sin would only complicate matters. Maybe even keep him from the work God had made him to do.

As for the rape, he knew Mera wouldn't say anything. Maybe she wouldn't marry him, but their lifetime of allegiance to one another would undoubtedly keep the deed concealed.

Which made his guilt all the worse. How could he have taken advantage of her, said the cruel things he had, and just let her leave? These last few years had changed him and the metamorphosis wasn't all good.

If only she knew how sorry he was now. How horribly he regretted it all.

His last image of her had to be an archetype of Cain's damning mark; branded into his thoughts, it glared constantly at him from his mind's edges.

When they'd pulled back into the Frasiers' driveway, Mera had tumbled from the Jeep, tiptoed upstairs and dragged her suitcase down. Then she'd called a cab and waited alone on the porch until the taxi's lights cut the pitch-black and finally pulled to a stop. Without a word, she'd stolen into the night, stopping just once to look backwards at him in the doorway. Mortified, he noticed her clothes were torn, her face swollen and pale in the moonlight.

Just like the first night she'd shown up at his house after her father did to her what he just had.

～

The room was spinning and she could hardly breathe as she stared at the test strip.

A clear window meant safe. A blue window, pregnant.

But this was wrong. It had to be.

The aqua blue stain beneath the test window had to be a mistake.

No way. There was absolutely no way.

Mechanically, she tried calculating the days since her last period though she knew the effort was in vain.

She couldn't remember starting since she'd been home.

Worst part was, she hadn't paid attention. Just trying to cope was taking everything she had and demanding still more.

And the nausea certainly hadn't clued her in considering she'd felt sick even before she pulled her clothes back on that terrible night. Since, she hadn't gone more than a day or two without throwing up.

But counting backwards now, it made awful sense.

She'd been in Boston the first week in July. It was mid-October now, nearly four months since she could remember having a period. Which totally explained the constant trips to the bathroom. The ever-distending belly despite a twenty-pound weight drop.

She was pregnant with Jack's baby.

Pregnant.

Why she decided to take the test was still a mystery to her. She hadn't thought once, at least consciously, that she might be pregnant.

But something inside her must have suspected otherwise.

Maybe it was her bloated stomach and swelling chest, both stark contrasts to her otherwise skeletal frame. Or maybe the vomiting had gone on too long, far too violently to be normal. Whatever it was, she'd bought the test a few days ago then waited, praying she wouldn't need it.

But the days passed and still nothing.

Until now. Until this tiny blue casement offered another window into the truth.

She was going to have a baby she couldn't explain. An essentially fatherless child.

Mindlessly, she stared at the little stick. The little secret-keeper and truth-teller. The crystal ball that mirrored her past and glared into her future.

What now, what was she supposed to do?

For a second, her mind flitted to the red brick Planned Parenthood building she passed on the way to work. Bright pink and purple flowers bloomed year round in its window box and a wide scalloped green awning flapped effortlessly in the wind.

She made herself take a deep breath. The idea wasn't unreasonable. In fact, it felt more like fresh wind, chains unfettering. A neat and professional out no one would ever know about.

She kept her eyes closed, trying to squeeze out a swelling thought from the periphery.

God.

Damn it. Could she never escape Him? The same deity who had witnessed the mosaic hell of her past would watch her intentionally excise an unwanted life from her body.

He'd be there to see it all.

Holding onto the stick like it had guide-on properties, she shuffled from the bathroom. Then collapsed in a heap onto her bed.

This was so crazy, it couldn't be real. This was someone else's life. Somebody else's dark dream.

Any second now she'd wake up, grateful for the nightmare's end, thankful that a single act of violence didn't really have the capability to yield a child who could think and feel and live.

Suddenly, little tremors made her legs twitch before she started shaking all over. She was crying, too, though she never associated the wet staining her pillow with anything spilling from her eyes. Rolling onto her side, she squeezed herself into a ball.

Minutes passed, maybe hours; she couldn't tell.

Then her gaze fell on the nightstand.

People would talk, it was only natural. Sally. Alice. Other colleagues and acquaintances, they'd all wonder about a baby with no father. Oh, they'd feign neutrality, but truth was, Meranda Kaine was pretty much known as a quiet professional, not an impulsive adolescent driven by whimsical feelings and hormones.

And what would Seth think?

He was sure to find out, there was virtually no way he wouldn't. Maybe not now, or even anytime soon, but eventually he would know the truth.

And all the while she would say nothing.

Because she couldn't without condemning Jack.

This whole thing was sadly ironic, she mused. Her once greatest ally nearly died years ago trying to rescue her from much of the very fate he'd now brought on her.

She was going to have a baby. Jack's child. Despite her will or her preferences and without her consent. And she wouldn't be able to say a word in her defense.

Unless she took matters into her own hands.

Reaching across her bed, she opened the nightstand drawer and pulled out the Colt Defender she kept buried. It was loaded, the safety catch on, but she could fix that.

She twirled the barrel aimlessly.

A single shot, that's all it would take.

Then the vomiting would stop forever. The cold numbness would go away.

Just a pull of the trigger.

Then her secrets would die with her and she'd never have to face the shame of this pregnancy.

Slowly, she released the safety catch and laced the pistol through her fingers. Slats of muted light angling through her blinds made the silver barrel a metallic reflector. Mesmerized, she stared at the blue test window next to her bulging stomach, feeling the weight of it all—the lies, the truth, the Colt balanced in her hand.

Then oddly, she felt nothing and the weight of no thing at all seemed heavily absent and constricting.

Pull the trigger, one tiny missile can end all this . . .

She couldn't quite agree with the notion, not because she knew it wasn't the best option, or even the right one. Besides even if it were wrong, wouldn't God understand?

Wouldn't He?

More minutes passed before she realized she already knew that question didn't belong to the answers she was really seeking — inquiries about whether or not she'd have the courage to see this through, ponderings about where the strength, the dignity, to live through this would come from.

Without answers to anything, she glanced again at the test strip. Hesitantly, she reached to touch it like it just might belong to her.

Then she flipped the Colt's catch back on and tucked the gun back beneath the papers and junk that covered it.

Chapter 15

Christmas in Chicago was something she'd never gotten used to. Never mind this was her third holiday season here; the transformation from thriving metropolis to dazzling winter wonderland still took her off guard, still convinced her something magnificent was bound to happen.

"Even this year," Mera marveled under her breath as she treaded through a glittering white universe trimmed in golds and silvers. Across the street, Lincoln Park was aglow in braided ropes of holly and evergreen lights that went on forever.

It was all breathtaking. Majestic. And in the presence of such wonder, even the worst circumstances seemed to stand a chance.

She needed the charge more than ever right now, needed to believe something good might finally break her string of awful luck. But as she noticed swollen gray clouds cloaking the sun, she couldn't help worrying that they were perched there as an omen of how her conversation with Sally Noble would go.

Lingering for one last look at Michigan Avenue through falling snowflakes, she stepped into the *Tribune* Tower and took a deep breath. She'd put this meeting off long enough.

Sally was in her office, coffee in hand, phone perched against her ear. Already she looked weary and it wasn't even 9:00 A.M.

When she glimpsed Mera in the doorway, the older woman rolled her eyes and dangled the resonating receiver in the air. Someone on the other end was yelling at full lung capacity.

"Ross Dryden at the Merc Exchange." Sally finished a minute later, shook her head and moved a stack of papers to the left side of her desk. She stuck a yellow Post-It square on the pile and scribbled something. "Didn't like Nasir's latest column.

But get in here and let's talk about you."

Mera had liked Sally from the time she and the editor had met in an old café near O'Hare three years ago. Making the most of a quick layover and wrapping up shop talk in less than fifteen minutes, the two had sipped tiny cups of steaming expresso and talked theater reviews and classical literature until Mera realized she had just minutes to dash back to the airport.

Sally Noble was enchanting, Mera had decided even before her plane roared into the cold evening sky. With her warm energy, silvery cropped hair and bifocal glasses, the editor was more a character out of a Dickens or Dumas yarn than a journalist . . .

                  ~

Sally grabbed her coffee and closed the door before she joined Mera on the couch. She put down her cup on the table in front of them, folded her hands and leaned in toward Mera. Then she waited.

Mera shifted uncomfortably. "Sally, I was hoping . . . I mean, I was thinking you might help me decide who we'd reassign the Wings Like Eagles series to."

Sally blinked twice. Picked up her coffee and sipped it.

"That's a curve I wasn't expecting."

"I know, really. And it's one I never planned on throwing."

"Why though? Since you've started that series, we've gotten some of the best reviews we've had all year . . ." The editor's gut had told her this meeting would shed some light on Mera's situation. But so far, this wasn't it.

"Honestly, I'm just swamped. And since we added the investigation of Judson's child labor snafu, I can't seem to dig my way out."

"But we've got readers tuning into Tad Ryan's progress like '*Days of Our Lives*,'" Sally protested. "If I let this switch midstream, it'll be a huge hiccup."

Mera crossed her arms and pressed them close to her.

"I just can't do it, Sally. With everything else, it's more than I can handle." She avoided Sally's gaze.

"How often are you actually meeting with Seth Langford?"

"I'm not. I'm working with some of his staff. And, of course, Tad."

"I thought Seth was overseeing the series. He's always been involved in the past."

"He is. I mean, he was. He must've gotten busy and delegated it."

Not one to miss a trick, Sally blew lightly into her coffee, then took another sip. She'd known Seth since he was just out of college and founding the center and she'd worked with Mera three years now.

Never once had she bowed out of a project. And Sally knew for a fact that Langford had seemed concerned in a more than professional way when he'd called her a few months ago trying to track Mera down after the Boston trip.

"Mera, by any chance, does this have anything to do with Seth Langford?"

Again, Mera made no eye contact.

"No, really. I just thought since it's a series project, it'd be easier to reassign."

"Let me get this straight," Sally was cross-examining the defense. "Seth assigned the series to someone else on his staff and you're wanting me to help you reassign it to . . ."

"Someone else here," Mera interrupted. "And that shouldn't be a whole lot extra. There's just three or four more meetings before the final interview and photo shoot."

"Who's the interview with?"

"Tad and Seth Langford."

Sally thought a minute.

"I thought you said Langford reassigned the series."

"He did. All but the final interview and signoff."

Mera's pallid complexion, flitting glances, told Sally she'd been right. There was more where this was coming from and she was determined to scratch past the surface. She inched closer to Mera, touching her arm lightly.

"Look, we're off the record here," she began gently. "I know something's wrong. I've suspected it since the summer. And whatever's bothering you has only gotten worse." Mera looked further down, her eyes filling with tears. "What does Seth have to do with this?"

"Nothing."

"Did he do something to hurt you?"

Mera looked up. A rose flush crept over her cheeks. "Absolutely not."

The editor leaned back, studying Mera's face. "I didn't think so."

They sat in silence, Sally tracing the ring of her coffee cup, Mera looking out over the city from the office's picture frame window. Below, was a world magically suspended by smiling Santas, Christmas shoppers and shiny tinsel.

The baby kicked and without thinking, Mera rubbed her distended belly, pressing her skirt against it.

Shocked, Sally watched Mera's hand travel inadvertently over her stomach. It was bulging softly, a definite anomoly from the pancake-flat tummy of a few months ago.

"Mera . . . are you . . .?"

Mera looked straight into Sally's gray eyes, her face a mixed mask of relief and terror. Her secret was out. For better or worse, Sally knew — and before long, so would everyone else.

But studying the older woman's face revealed no trace of disgust or condemnation or even pity. Instead, Sally sat quietly, gaze lowered, while a warm empathy seemed to emit from every pore in her body.

"Yes . . . I am . . ." She tried fighting it, but the dam inside her broke. Hot tears coursed over her cheeks like she'd turned on a faucet.

"Oh, no," Sally recoiled. "Don't tell me that you and Seth . . . is that why . . .?"

"No . . . no. Definitely not." The words surged out like Mera was mortified for even a second that Seth might be connected with this. "It's not Seth's . . . it wasn't like that with us," she stammered, grappling for composure as Sally reached for her hand.

"Then what does he have to do with this? You have my word, I won't say anything. But I can help more if you clue me in."

Mera took another deep breath and bit her lower lip. "Okay, here's what happened. But I need to know you'll keep it between us."

"On my honor." Sally held her fingers up, a Girl Scout pledge.

"Well, several months back, Seth and I had gotten to be good friends. But early this summer, it changed, like it might be headed for something more." As if she needed a distraction, Mera looked down and started rubbing her fingernails with the pad of her thumb. "We were going to talk when I came back from Boston. But it never happened."

"Did he change his mind?"

"No. When I was home, I met up with my old boyfriend, someone I grew up with, actually."

She fell silent. Like either the gravity of the situation or the effort of explanation was too much. Or maybe both.

"So what happened?" Sally asked after a minute.

"We decided to try and work things out. I don't know, it seemed like there was potential. Possibilities. And while I was there, I got pregnant." The words were stones falling on ice, lies ricocheting in every direction. "Seth doesn't know."

"About your boyfriend or the baby?"

"The baby. He has no idea."

"And you don't want him to know, right?" Sally was patient, trying to place facts that still didn't add up.

"Right," Mera whispered.

"Does the baby's father know?"

"It didn't work out. More than likely, I'm going to place her for adoption."

"It's a little girl?" Sally smiled; she had two grown daughters of her own.

"I just found out last week."

"When's she due?"

"End of March."

"And the last of the series finishes first of April."

"Right."

Sally sighed. "Why don't you want Seth to know?"

Mera let her gaze meet Sally's.

"You know, I'm sure he'll eventually find out. It's inevitable. But I guess I'd like to put it off as long as I can. And between you and me, I don't want him to see me like this." She looked down again.

Sally didn't want to interfere; it wasn't in her nature. But she knew Seth fairly well and the despair on Mera's face was pathetic.

"Maybe it's not too late for you and Seth to try again," she said, choosing her words cautiously. "I've known him a long time and I know he's tough, but he's got a great heart. My guess is if you talked to him, he might understand."

"I can't do that." Mera was definite.

"Why?"

"I just can't."

Sally sighed again. "Sure you can."

"It's not even an option, Sally."

"It's not an option because, if you ask me, you're afraid of hoping there could still be another chance that you wouldn't know what to do with." Sally squeezed Mera's hand then let it go. "But stay with me, sweetie, play this out. What would happen then? What would happen if you and Seth talked and found that there was a way to pick up the pieces and get this to all make sense again?"

"That *won't* happen. Because he'd *never* understand." Mera had grown even more pale, her expression taut. "And he shouldn't have to. I was the one who made this mistake . . ."

"And don't we all do that?" Sally's eyes flashed. "Are we not all human?"

"Look, I revisited something I should have left alone. And now, I'm living with the consequences." She patted her stomach wryly. "That includes losing Seth."

"Is there a reason you aren't keeping the baby, a basis for not telling your boyfriend he's a father?"

"On both counts, it's just better. Trust me."

Sally let a minute pass before she spoke again.

"Mera, answer something for me."

"I'll try."

"Do you love Seth?"

Whatever memory cut through her must have had a rapier edge because Sally watched a half dozen emotions play across Mera's features—angst, longing, emptiness, fear, etc.—they were all accounted for and present before Mera bit her lip as if to compose herself.

"It doesn't matter anymore," she managed to choke out.

Sally was silent again, deep in thought. Maybe it was three decades of investigating leads that ended up opposite where they'd started. Bottom line, Mera's story didn't add up.

Couples making a fresh go of a relationship are optimistic. Hopeful. But the young woman who had returned from Boston was little more than catatonic, withering into an antisocial skeleton. How often did rekindled romance have *that* effect?

And what about the baby? So maybe the relationship hadn't panned out. But was that reason enough for Mera to pass on motherhood and keep the man from knowing he was a father?

Sally was fifty-four, and while she didn't have all the answers, she guessed fairly well at some. Meranda Kaine was hiding something and she knew it. But her instinct told her to lay low, help the girl where she could, and wait. She'd lived long enough to know that time was always the biggest break in any case. Almost all truth was eventually revealed in its passing.

"I'll send a letter to Seth letting him know I've reassigned the series to Rachel Curtis," she finally said. "If it's got to be handed off, she'll do the best job."

Mera stood up and stared out the window.

"Thank you, Sally. I can't tell you how much I appreciate this." Her voice trailed off as she looked out over Michigan Avenue watching tiny people scurry past the Salvation Army Santa who kept ringing his monotone bell, decreeing Christmas cheer.

Chapter 16

It was after 11:00 P.M. and he knew he should head home, but the warm air and rich coffee smells made him linger. A downtown Starbucks on a weekend night was usually a mixed bag of entertainment and tonight had proven no exception.

For starters, a blind man with his guide dog had stopped in for a latte, but the canine got wind of a passing bull terrier and tried to bolt, landing master and beverage on the concrete floor. Seth had just helped man and beast get settled when a drag queen in black lace sporting a red feather boa pranced in from the snowdrifts. Noticing Seth, he flipped the boa, flashed what had to be his most alluring smile and followed it up with a subtle wink.

Seth decided now might be the best time to call it a night.

He drained his cup and picked up the *Rolling Stone* he'd halfway perused for the last hour. Then offered a polite nod as he passed the posing queen and almost slammed into Sally Noble making her way inside.

"Seth Langford, what a surprise!" Smiling broadly, Sally cleared the doorway then reached up to hug him. "How *are* you?"

"Sally Noble. Wow, it's good to see you."

"It's been a while, hasn't it?"

"A couple years, at least." He looked sideways to get the latest on the queen's geography. Coast was clear — he was busy chewing biscotti and talking into a cell phone.

"Come on, join me while I recharge with a Venti Mocha."

Seth had adored Sally from the time they'd met fifteen years ago. At first, it was her quirky, intelligent sense of humor that made him think she was the coolest older person he'd ever met.

But as time passed, he realized it was something both more and less than that. Sally definitely had a sprite-like air to her, a capriciousness that made her seem more mythological than human.

This fascinated him.

As the years rolled on, though, Seth realized that past the whimsical veneer lay the heart of a woman who cared more deeply about people than anyone he'd ever known.

And for that he loved her.

Glancing sideways again, Seth decided the queen must have lost interest. A long-legged young woman in fishnet stockings with spiked hair and talon-like nails in shades of violet had joined him and they seemed to have plenty to talk about.

"Sure, I'll get us a table."

Minutes later, Sally sat down with her cup just as a swarm of theatergoers ducked in to warm up and rehash the evening over countless java options.

"Love the dress." Seth brushed his fingers over Sally's black wool sleeve. "Did you catch a show?"

"*A Midsummer Night.*" Her gray-blue eyes danced behind little round rims. Silver like her hair.

"Shakespeare sucker." Seth shook his head, smiling. "I guess some things never change."

"I can't help myself. I see something new every time."

"Probably because you weren't paying attention the time before." He'd always teased her mercilessly, and getting warmed up again was fun. "Hey, where's Hal?"

"Left him home. Girl's night out."

"You mean you ditched your old man to sit with a bunch of hens and swoon over Shakespeare? Sally . . ."

"Hal can't hack Wills thithers and the thous, so after thirty years, I leave him home to watch basketball," she retorted, mock-indignant as she sipped the steaming coffee.

Seth pulled a box of Marlboros from his jacket and lit one.

As if on cue, they both fell silent, watching the smoky threads twist then vanish like one of Dickens' Christmas spirits.

"You look like a cigarette ad with that thing hanging from your mouth."

"That supposed to be a slam?" He took a drag, held it for a minute.

"Are you kidding? You're beautiful."

"I am?"

"You are. James Dean with long hair. Brad Pitt on a noble mission." She paused to smile at the young couple settling in at the table next to them. "Need I go on?"

"No, but you could." He grinned, shot her a playfully seductive look.

"Little narcissist. Remember what came of Chanticleer's preening."

Seth rolled his eyes. Sally's insatiable drive of making literary parallels to life was something he'd long been used to.

"Who's preening? I'm just sitting here, minding my own business and enjoying a nice cigarette."

"Which will kill you if don't quit. You should, you know."

"Should what?" He feigned ignorance.

"Quit."

"So I hear, but I figure I've got plenty that'll finish me off before these things do."

"Ouch, I caught that."

Seth looked puzzled. "Caught what?"

"That 'I'm not going to be easy to read but I'm hurting anyway' look that just flashed across your face."

Seth shook his head. "I'm fine. You should get your glasses checked. You're seeing stuff."

"Wrong. I'm old and I know when something's up. And I know you."

Seth closed his eyes and let out a sigh. "I'm good, really. Just a lot going on."

"Like what? Tell old Sal . . ."

"Oh, just the general insanity . . . work, life, the likes," he said nonchalantly.

Sally quirked an eyebrow. Pushed up the glasses that had slid down her button of a nose.

"Would the likes happen to include anyone special?"

"Now, what would make you say that?" He flicked ashes into an empty cup on the table then twirled the Marlboro box in his other hand.

"Nothing. Just wondering."

"Oh."

Sally sipped her coffee again and waited. She had the unfair advantage of a longtime journalist. Time passing in silence never made her uncomfortable.

"I got your letter a few weeks ago," Seth changed the subject. "The one where you mentioned the *Tribune* had reassigned our series to Rachel something or other."

"Right, Rachel Curtis. I figured you'd want to know before the January edition. Did you meet her when she came out?"

"No, I got a few other staffers following this deal. But I guess I'll meet her when we do the last thing in March."

"I thought the wrap-up was set for April. Mera said . . ."

"No, it's March," he cut her off. "By the way, how is Mera?"

He sounded entirely too casual. And Sally hadn't been born yesterday.

"Okay," she shrugged, watching the tension line his face.

"Just okay?"

"Yeah. I think."

"You think? She works for you."

Ten seconds of silence, deliberate on Sally's part.

"She's swamped, I know that. A lot of work, some personal things, too."

Seth tapped more ashes into the cup then rubbed his chin.

"How long have I known you, Sally?"

"Fifteen, sixteen years, something like that. Why?"

He leaned in close, propping both elbows on the table. "Did Mera ask you to reassign the series?"

"Why would she do that?"

Seth knew Sally, knew how she used rhetoric to get her questions answered or deflect the ones she wanted to duck.

"Did she?" he pressed. "Was she the reason you switched writers?"

"Reporters, Seth."

"Yeah, right, reporters. Whatever."

Sally picked up her coffee, hesitated, then put it back down. "Okay, I can't stand it," she exclaimed.

"Can't stand what?"

"That confused, sad puppy dog in a kennel look on your face. It's not like you." She clicked her fingernails on the table. "Are we on the record or off?"

"C'mon Sal, what'd *you* think?" He ground his cigarette butt inside a black plastic ashtray he had procured. Then flicked it into the cup he'd been feeding.

"Yes," she said softly. "Mera asked me to reassign the series."

He dropped his head into his hands, raked his fingers through his hair.

"I know what you're thinking," Sally said after several seconds had passed.

He looked up.

"You're probably wondering what the hell happened and I can't say I blame you. Ever since I've known you, you've been some kind of magnet that lures women your way. They love you, almost without exception . . . your quirky antics, your bohemian good looks. But from everything I've seen, and I sure don't claim to have the whole story, nothing meaningful has really clicked for you. Until maybe . . ."

"Sally," he interrupted, "can we drop the diplomacy for a minute?"

"I didn't think we were being all that diplomatic."

"Please?" He sighed. "Can we talk?"

"Sure, babe."

"Did she say why?"

Sally laid a hand on his arm. "Sweets, you ought to give her a call. Maybe you two could talk." Her accent was reminiscent of earlier years in New York, something indistinguishable unless she chose just the right words.

"What's there to talk about?"

"Maybe nothing. Possibly plenty. You'd have to take your chances."

"All I know is she and an old boyfriend got back together."

"Is that so?" Sally reached into her purse and pulled out a tube of lipstick. Then opened it and traced the salmon color over her lips.

"So she said. You know, we'd gotten to be pretty good friends before she left for Boston last summer. In fact, we . . . well . . ."

"I know."

"You do?"

Sally nodded.

"She told you?" His eyes widened.

"A little. Just a little. She's pretty private."

"How well I know." He picked up Sally's cup and swallowed a mouthful of cool coffee. "Do you know if they're getting married or anything like that?"

Sally waited to answer.

"Definitely no plans for that," she finally said.

"Really? She sounded so sure the last time we talked."

"When was that?"

"Right after Boston, when she had that flu or whatever it was."

"Have you talked since?"

"Only once, about the series."

"You should call her again," Sally repeated.

"You think?" He took out another cigarette and struck a match.

"I do."

"Maybe I will."

"You really like her, don't you?"

"Maybe . . . I don't know . . ."

"I know I do," Sally thought out loud. "She's brilliant and thoughtful, she's funny when she's not so sad . . ." She stopped suddenly, like she'd accidentally given away a secret.

Seth pounced on this immediately.

"Sad? Why is *she* sad?"

"Recant. I didn't just say that."

"Sure you did." He breathed out a swirling cloud of lavender smoke and flicked some more ashes. "Unless you're planning to blame Shakespeare's ghost for leaking it."

"Come on, Seth, Mera works for me. You can't let on we had this chat."

He looked mildly annoyed. "You ought to know me better than that. Does that even sound remotely like something I'd do?"

"No." Sally looked sheepish.

"Tell me, Sally, what's up with her?"

Sally started, like she wanted to say something then decided against it at the same time.

"You know, I really can't." She brushed her hand over his. "But I'll say this. I don't think it's what it seems."

Seth rolled his eyes, exasperated. "Wow, that's so cool, Sal, so helpful . . . I just love mind-benders . . ."

"Come on, Seth. It's the best I can do . . ."

"For crying out loud, what's that supposed to mean?"

"Just that. I think there's more going on than she's letting on."

They sat in silence again, Seth sucking his cigarette, chewing on the riddle, Sally sipping coffee until it was gone. The shop was almost empty, and through the window, the snow was a white falling curtain, nothing unusual for January.

Chapter 17

He'd tried catching her at the office twice, once at home, but both places only proved she had voice mail. And he definitely hadn't planned on stopping by. After so long, that just seemed too awkward. But something about the night, plus the fact that he was just minutes from her flat, compelled him to drop in and see if she was around.

As he rapped a second round of knocks on her door, though, it occurred to Seth that she was probably working late. She tended to do that early in the week and today was just Tuesday. Still, he persuaded himself, he had nothing pressing for once and it was unusually pleasant and warm for February.

He could afford to hang out, maybe wait awhile.

Brushing off the dusty steps of her landing, Seth took a quick look around before sinking onto the cool damp concrete. Then he did something he wasn't accustomed to doing.

He just sat.

For what seemed like hours, he sat and watched people coming and going—alone, in pairs, in packs—until finally, they all dissolved into shadows moving in the amethyst twilight. Off in the distance, he heard dogs baying, horns droning. Chicago settling in for another night.

More time passed, enough for the streets to quiet and the air to turn as cold as it was dark. He stood up to leave just as two short silhouettes stopped in front of him.

"Hey, dude. I know you." It was Sam, peering suspiciously over two sacks of groceries.

"Yeah?"

"Yup. You're Mera's old pal."

"Right." Seth wasn't sure he'd ever done more than pass the guy.
"Sorry, I don't remember the name."

"Sam. Name's Sam Wiesel, Mera's neighbor. And this here's my girfriend, Sabitha Rajani." Sam thumped Sabitha's shoulder proudly, like he'd won first prize.

"Seth Langford," Seth knew he sounded short, but he was in no mood for small talk.

"What brings you out here, man?" Sam barely hit Seth's shoulders, but he wasn't letting stature differences dampen his investigation.

"I was in the neighborhood. Thought I'd drop by and say hey to Mera."

Sam nodded as if he wasn't sure about the answer.

"I used to see you around a lot. Then you vanished, like, into thin air." Sabitha went inside the flat next door and Sam joined Seth on the steps.

"Mera's busy, I'm busy . . ." He wished Sam would go away.

"Lies, dude. All bunk." Sam's smirk was confident. "So what hit the fan?"

And Seth thought he wasn't one to mince words.

"Nothing. It just didn't work out. That happens sometimes, you know."

"Sure does, dude, and it reeks, huh? But hey, I'm telling you, man, she's gettin' a rap."

"A rap?"

Sam made a clucking sound.

"Yeah. For good love gone bad. And it sure ain't pretty."

It was Seth's turn to probe.

"You care to translate that?"

"She's been actin' weird for months now. You know, we're neighbors, so we talk and stuff. And between you and me, she's definitely not on the top ten list of chicks lovin' life."

Seth wondered if Sam ever communicated in anything other than code. He sat back down. A second later, Sam plunked beside him.

"That sucks, really. What do you think's bothering her?"

"Dude, it's more like *who*. I'm telling you, the whole thing's bogus." Sam was warming to his subject. No more watchdog persona.

"What do you mean, *who*?" Sam had his full attention now. "Her boyfriend?"

Sam pulled a deformed stick of gum from his shirt pocket, which he proceeded to unwrap and start chomping.

"Boyfriend? Buddy, there ain't no boyfriend."

"Well, if he's not the problem, who is?"

Sam scrutinized Seth's face. "You really don't know?"

"Know what?"

"You plannin' to hang out 'til she gets home?"

"No. I'm heading off now. It's getting pretty late."

"Aw, you should hang on. She'll be along any minute now. Usually pulls in between seven and eight." Sam stood up and ferociously slapped dust off his backside. "Gotta hit the sax now; band's got a gig this weekend."

"Hey, before you head off . . ."

"Sorry, dude, I really gotta jet."

"*Who's* bothering her?" Between Sam and Sally's riddles, Seth thought he might lose his mind.

Sam quit grinding the gum long enough to purse his lips and let out a long low whistle. "Dude, one look at her and you'll figure it out."

~

For some reason, Mera missed him more than usual today and she couldn't figure out why. By now, she'd conditioned herself to keep reminders of him at bay, a practical discipline considering no good ever came from dwelling on the past.

But that hadn't happened today. Instead, she'd let images of Seth seep through her thoughts since she had gotten up this morning. And the memories were like live wires that shot fiery sparks through her.

She had changed so much she wondered if he would even recognize her now. Her face had sunken into itself, gone sallow and splotchy—and her expressionless eyes belonged to a POW.

If that wasn't enough, her body had ceased looking human, mutating into something that looked more like a life-sized ant in a bad sci-fi movie. Stick-thin little extremities showcased her ever-growing belly, a globe so vast and swollen, she couldn't even see her feet over her front girth. And it was still six weeks out from delivery.

She was glad it was almost over though she knew parts of the agony would never end. Already, the lies had taken their toll, especially at work where the raised eyebrows and cool stares were wordless indictments:

Where on earth did Mr. Right go?

Fine predicament he's left her in.

What was up with adoption? It wasn't like she couldn't afford to keep her baby . . .

But she'd decided months back that she couldn't worry about what everyone thought. Her objective had to be to simply get through this . . .

And that she was doing. Not anything more—or less.

As for Seth, any fleeting thoughts or notions of what might have been got scribbled into a journal she kept by her bed, a safe harbor incapable of causing more pain.

Now as she turned the corner onto her street, she couldn't wait to get inside. The night was still early, she was exhausted and the gingery aroma wafting from her bag of Chinese take-out was making her mouth water.

She smiled a little at her perfect plan: go inside, kick off the three inch-high pumps that felt four sizes too small, wriggle her aching toes and eat lo mein with egg rolls. Then she'd edit her column, shower and hopefully be in bed by eleven.

The form settled on her stoop made her heart lodge in her throat. Just last month, Sam had had to come out and persuade an intoxicated vagrant off her landing.

But as she locked her car door and hiked herself onto the sidewalk, she knew immediately that the figure wasn't one of a drifter. Even in the vague moonlight, she recognized the familiar cleft of that chin, the rough-perfect outline of those features. And as he turned his head and watched her waddle closer, she wished the earth would split open and swallow her whole.

~

At first, he was sure it was an optical illusion. Depth perception was easy to skew at night, especially in the dusty light of just the occasional lamppost.

But as the misshapen outline grew clearer, there was no denying it. Even through her long wool coat, it was obvious Mera was pregnant.

Very pregnant.

And as she stopped in front of him, it occurred to Seth that he didn't have a clue what to say.

"I . . . wow . . . I was in the neighborhood. I . . . I thought I'd stop by and . . ." he stammered, taking in the enormous orbit of her belly despite the thick coat.

"What? See how I was doing?" she interrupted tersely, seemingly oblivious to the shock, then pain, that contorted his features. "Bet you weren't expecting this."

He stood up. Shoved both hands into his pockets.

"No. You're right. I wasn't."

"Well then, you can say you've had your surprise for the day. Unless, of course, something else has already trumped this." She whacked at her belly the way high school football players thump each other's behinds for good luck.

"No . . . no. This definitely wins out." He shook his head. Shifted back and forth on his feet. "I had no idea."

"And you think you do now?" Mera snapped before siphoning in a long drag of frosty air.

"What's that supposed to mean?"

"I told you. We decided to work things out."

"And this is working things out?" He hadn't meant to sound so sarcastic.

"Behold," she rested a hand on her belly, "the working out of all things."

The comment didn't line up with Sam's missing person charge or Sally's inference of a player boyfriend. But he didn't say anything.

"I didn't know you were having a baby," he repeated, a little more composed now.

"She's due next month."

"Oh. That's soon." Then, "It's a girl?"

Mera nodded. Said nothing.

"Sally has girls," he offered. "Grown girls."

"Sally who?"

He looked at her like she should know what he was talking about.

"Sally Noble."

"Yeah, you're right. Betsy and Briane."

"They're twins." He had no idea why he was pursuing such feeble conversation.

"No, they're a year apart."

"Oh."

"And this is just one girl."

He didn't know what to say.

"Girls are good," he finally offered.

"I guess. We're giving her up for adoption, though."

Her use of *we* made a strange ache pass through him.

"That's a curve ball."

"We're not quite ready for the parenthood thing yet."

That *we* again. It set up two land masses with an ocean between them. Her and another on one side, him on the other. And nothing to close the space between them.

"So you get an A for grasp of parental obligations, an F for failure to prevent conception, and what, maybe a C for damage control? That's at least one and a half out of three, right?"

She scowled. "Congratulations. You may have just set the new world record for most biting rhetoric."

"Unintentional, really. I just meant that you're a little short on planning if you didn't want a kid." He nodded at her voluminous belly. "Are you marrying him?"

"It's an option."

She was hiding something. Sam had said the guy was nowhere to be found. If that was the case, why was she lying and where was the seed-spraying phantom who had left her like this? It was a long shot, but he decided to press past the cavalier façade.

"Why didn't you tell me?"

"About?

"This," he said, shaking his head. "About this whole thing . . ."

"You never asked. Besides, it wasn't any of your business."

He'd had enough of her flippant attitude.

"Don't be so glib, Mera," he snapped. Then lowering his voice, "When you left here last summer, you were almost my business. We had a good thing starting and you know it."

"For the love of everything beautiful, Seth, I told you that I said things I shouldn't have. Things I didn't really mean."

"I don't believe you."

"Why?"

"I'll tell you why," he pressed. "You spent months playing it close to the vest, seeing if you could trust me. You think I didn't notice how you dropped your guard, a little at a time, until that night . . ." he waited to finish, "that last night when . . . you kissed me."

She winced like the memory of that evening cut into places she needed shut tight and sealed off.

"It was a kiss, Seth," she lashed out, "not sex. Don't make anything more of it."

"Well Mera, that's all it would've ever been with me." He was stinging all over, but hell would freeze over before he'd let on. "Unlike whoever got you into this predicament, I would've married you before we slept in the same bed."

"Noble, Seth, very noble." She said it like she felt a strange triumph watching her callous words stun him. For seconds that seemed hours, he just stared at her.

"You . . . wow . . . you really had me fooled," he finally rasped out. "Or maybe I just duped myself because I totally missed this side of you."

"Well here's Mera!"

Immediately, the caustic retort registered. He looked sick and deflated, like someone realizing at endgame that all prior moves had been futile because the rules had been rewritten but never communicated.

"Look, Mera, I'm sorry." Seth stepped backwards, away from her. "I owe you an apology. I honestly had you for someone different . . ."

Mera bit her lip, tracing the outline of the hazy lamppost shadow on the sidewalk. She never looked up as hot tears spilled down her face onto the pavement.

Out of the corner of his eye, he watched her expression soften as a glittering trickle slid down her cheek. Without trying, he heard Sally's voice echoing in his head, "I don't think this is what it seems."

Maybe it wasn't, but he had no idea how it all added up. And now a baby was part of the equation, a clear indication he had no business hanging around.

"I'll leave you alone, Mera. You have my word." He turned and walked away, and as the shadows claimed him, he wondered how long she would stand beneath the cold moon, alone and crying.

Chapter 18

The phone rang just after she'd wrapped up a 9:00 A.M. conference call, gone to the bathroom and sat down with another cup of decaf coffee. It was Rachel Curtis, long-distance, and she sounded either out of breath or in pain. But with the bad connection, it was hard to tell which.

"Mera, what's going on out there? I've been trying to reach Sally for the past twelve hours at every number I have and all I'm getting is voice mail."

"Sally's got meetings in New York for the next couple days, remember? She left us inmates to run the asylum."

Rachel usually loved to quip; her scatty sense of humor kept her and everyone around her in stitches. But she didn't so much as snicker now. Instead, all Mera could hear between the wild crackling on the phone lines was what sounded like labored breathing.

"You need me to tell her something for you?" Mera coaxed.

"Yeah. I'm history for a few days."

"History?"

"It was supposed to be a quick ski trip, a last minute weekend thing for a friend who's getting married next month." Rachel took five full seconds to catch another breath. "So we were all in Keystone having this great time until late yesterday when I got a little too ambitious."

"This can't be going anywhere good."

"It's not. I hit a slope I shouldn't have and . . . well here I am. It was a pretty bad fall."

"How bad?" Mera looked at her watch, wishing she wasn't so pressed for time. But between the mile-long checklist Sally had left her to handle, calls to return and a nine thirty meeting to make, she hoped Rachel would hit the high points and hang up.

"That's why I'm calling." She faded in and out with the static. "I got to the ER at seven last night and they just set the cast on my leg an hour ago."

"Cast. ER. Rachel, this is sounding worse by the second."

"Tell me about it. I broke my right leg in two places. Fractured my left wrist."

"You're kidding . . ."

"I wish. The Blue Northern that dipped down last minute dropped the most gorgeous fresh powder I've ever seen. The slopes were as packed yesterday as the ER was last night."

"Ouch," Mera said with feeling. "One break's bad enough, but two?"

"Worst part is, I won't be home for a few days."

Alice was at the door of Mera's office motioning a time out charade to which Mera held up her forefinger and nodded. Alice disappeared again.

"Look, I've got to run, Rachel. Sally's out and it's a zoo around here this morning. Don't worry about anything. It'll all wait until you're back."

"That's just it, Mera," Rachel persisted, almost petulant, "I'm in the middle of something that *can't* wait. The final Wings Like Eagles article runs this week."

Mera's heart stuck in her throat. Rachel had no idea why Sally had given her the series. No idea at all.

She waited for a second so as to choose her words carefully. It was important that she sound calmer than she felt. "Today's just now Monday. When do you think you'll be back?"

"Earliest, Thursday or Friday. The orthopedist who set my leg says it needs to be elevated a few days. So my friend, Kate, is taking me back to her place in Denver until I can fly out." She heard the wince in poor Rachel's voice as she breathed in again.

"When are you scheduled to meet with Wings Like Eagles?"

"Today at four."

Mera's stomach knotted and her tongue was deadweight in her mouth.

"Who were you meeting with?" she choked out.

"Tad Ryan and Holly Greigenbeck."

"Not Seth Langford?" It felt weird to say Seth's name aloud.

"No. Mike Zimmer said Seth Langford was scheduled to be out of the country when we did the final sign-off. So I'm meeting with Tad, of course, and Holly."

Just before she left for Boston last year, Seth had appointed Holly director of the shelter's public relations. So having her step in for the wrap-up was a logical alternative.

"Never mind, Rachel. I'll cover for you." She breathed easier knowing Seth wasn't part of this afternoon's line-up. But she couldn't help wondering what business he had out of the country. "You just get well."

"Remember Shari Flitner's going, too. To do the photo shoot."

Now she was really grateful Seth wouldn't be there. Arriving at the shelter with her freak show-sized belly was bad enough, but having Shari along to snap a thousand pictures while she tried to act inconspicuous would have made the trip unbearable if he was around. She thanked God for small favors.

And thanked Him, too, that the last link to Seth would be expunged, hopefully by five or six this evening.

⁓

Downtown traffic turned out to be bad, a combination of heavy showers, low visibility and a downed power line. March rains being what they were, the precipitation was typical, but besides the cold blinding sheets and rising water, this squall had spun off flash floods and a series of power outages across the city.

Nonetheless, at 4:00 P.M. sharp, Mera pulled in front of the shelter, pushed up the economy-sized umbrella on loan from Alice and waded through the swelling river in the street.

Just inside, Mike Zimmer caught wind of her courageous waddling. Grabbing a towel from behind the kiosk, he rushed to the door and opened it just in time for the deluge's trajectory to slant in the equivalent of a shallow pond onto the lacquered concrete.

Another gust of wind slapped a fresh curtain of rainwater their way before slamming the door shut with a resounding thud. For a few seconds, they stood in front of the kiosk, drenched and taking in the mess.

"Hey, I'm really sorry about the floor." Mera shook her head regretfully. "Much more of this and I think we'll need an ark."

"No big deal. The whole place'll be wet in a few hours. We got folks pouring in like the rain."

She took the towel he handed her and though it was largely saturated, attempted to blot water from her soaking shoes. But balancing over her mountainous stomach made the ordeal too cumbersome, so she straightened and smiled at Mike instead.

"You meeting with Tad or Seth first?" Mike said, adjusting the wet cap on his head.

"Tad, I think, then Holly."

"Oh," Mike furrowed his brow, "Seth told me he'd be meeting with the *Tribune* this afternoon. Said he was expecting Rachel somebody for the final thing the paper's doing."

Mera felt the room start to spin. Seth was supposed to be out of the country, far from Chicago's windy rains, far from the logistics of finishing this miserable series she wished she'd never started in the first place.

"Rachel's in Denver," she explained, trying to stay calm. "She had a skiing accident yesterday. That's why I'm here."

"That's rough," Mike empathized. "Here, go ahead and have a seat. Let me tell them you're waiting." Before she could protest, Mike had paged Seth and was working on catching Tad over the intercom.

Just then, the doors flew open and another spray of water gusted in, along with the most towering giant of a man Mera had ever seen.

He was enormous, over seven feet tall with the lean bulk of a linebacker and quick stride of a point guard off court. His head was massive and his skin was the same purple-black as Seth's center residents from central Africa. Unlike them, though, this man was unmistakably cosmopolitan, with the superior air of someone who knew and worked the inner machinations of systems few even realized existed. In his huge ebony hands, he clutched a black leather briefcase and his shoes were scrupulously polished black-winged tips. He wore a charcoal trench coat open at the collar with a gold serpentine chain about his neck. Noticing Mera seated a few feet from him, the giant offered a reluctant nod, no expression.

"Right this way, Mr. Barekhandi." Mike rushed to his side like a bellhop attending a celebrity at a five-star hotel. "Seth's expecting you down here."

Down here proved to be down a winding corridor which the lumbering guest traversed with Mike as escort. From the back, Mera noticed the younger man didn't even clear the giant's shoulders.

"He looks like a basketball player," Mera said when Mike returned a few minutes later. She was half-hoping to learn who Mr. Barekhandi was.

Mike nodded. "He's colossal all right, but he's definitely no ball player." Abruptly, he switched subjects. "Hey, when's your baby due? I didn't even know you were having a kid."

"Two weeks." Mera was again grateful that no one at the shelter had known she and Seth were seeing each other.

Mike turned his attention to the ringing phone and Mera started flipping through a folder, when out of nowhere, Seth appeared in frayed jeans and an untucked army green t-shirt. He stopped dead in his tracks when he saw her.

"Hey, Mera." He was formal, stiff, before he turned to look over his shoulder at Mike.

"Mike, let's get Leo to mop these floors asap. Someone's gonna slip and break their neck."

Right away, Mike was on the intercom again.

"Hello, Seth." Mera felt herself stammering. "Rachel's in Denver with a broken leg. Ski accident."

"Bad news." He set his jaw and kept his gaze roving.

"She said she was meeting with Tad and Holly today for the wrap-up." Mera needed him to know she wasn't here hoping to see him. "You were out of town, she said . . ."

"I was. Got home a day ahead of schedule." He turned to greet two residents, soaked from the storm, before he continued. "Listen, I was gonna do this since I'm back, but I just had a meeting land in my lap. So if you don't mind, I'll let you wrap up with Holly after Tad. Okay?" He was working hard to be polite but every word set up more distance between them.

"Sure."

Though he didn't look at her, she noticed the whites of his eyes were pink clouds with squiggly red lines tracing all through them. It was obvious he hadn't slept much in days, if at all. With his wavy hair in a damp ponytail and darkly stubbled face, she thought again that he looked more like Tarzan than an inner-city entrepreneur.

Then he was gone, leaving her to meet with Tad and work with Shari as she snapped what seemed like a million pictures. Tad in front of a computer. Tad tutoring a few residents. And finally, Tad shaking Holly's hand and holding up an envelope that contained a job offer for an assistant manager from a nearby restaurant.

It all went smoothly, no snags at all. Right up to Holly's signoff on the final column to run Friday.

"Thanks for everything, Holly." Mera was so pleased to be leaving this shelter and Seth and all that went with it that she didn't have to feign sincerity. "This place is really amazing, and we've enjoyed working with all of you here."

"Our pleasure, Ms. Kaine." Holly grinned, and for the first time, it occurred to Mera how pretty she was. Her strawberry blond hair was twisted into smooth ropes, her creamy skin had just a smattering of nutmeg freckles and her amber eyes tilted up when she smiled. "As you saw by following Tad this last year, we really do want to see our people thrive when they reenter their communities."

"Everything you do here attests to that, Holly." Smiling, too, Mera closed her file and stood up slowly. She reached to shake Holly's extended hand. "Before I leave, would you mind pointing me to the nearest bathroom? You know, I still get confused on these long hallways."

"Me, too, sometimes," Holly confided. "But go straight past the reception kiosk, fifth door on the left. And be careful, the floors are still wet."

They said final goodbyes before Mera teetered down the long hallway, wondering why she'd never noticed how beautiful Holly was. Surely, Seth had to notice, too, she thought, feeling more than a little jealous. Then she forced herself to part with the notion.

Outside the rain was falling heavy again, but she missed its steady drum as Seth's muffled voice echoed from behind a door she was passing. A deep lyrical brogue cut in, no doubt belonging to the towering man who had blown in with the storm.

Somewhat curious about the animated conversation, but even more intrigued by who the black giant was, Mera reluctantly moved past the door and settled herself in the tiny bathroom where she stayed much longer than she intended. Her stomach had been achy all day, and now the cramps had turned vise-like. She hated the thought of driving home.

Ten minutes passed, then fifteen, before she finally mustered enough resolve to head back out.

Wobbling down the corridor again, she heard Seth's voice, this time slightly raised. The door was now ajar.

"Come on, Onesphore, be realistic . . . you know I don't have a venue for 'em all," Seth resisted, though his tone suggested he'd drawn no final conclusions. "When we're talking fifty or so it's one thing. But pushing four hundred through is another story."

Five seconds of stilted silence.

"Kenya cannot handle the traffic. You know we cannot make the move through Cairo, now." The black man spoke slowly, words deliberate with no contractions in his heavy accent.

"I realize that. But . . ."

"We can split the transport three ways; this will at least spread them out geographically. But I need an answer now."

"This is crazy, there's no way we can do business like this."

"So what are you proposing?" The man's voice chilled.

"What I'm suggesting won't help us out right now. We've got to take this one on the chin, but next meeting, we're gonna revamp this railroad, take another look at our border options." Seth was quiet again for what seemed like minutes. "Go ahead, push 'em through," he agreed, half-heartedly. "I'll figure it out as we go along."

From behind the door, a chair creaked wildly, like someone had risen to stand. Heavy footsteps followed, a pacing of sorts.

"The rainy season begins soon now. This will buy us time. And we are lucky this year."

Seth snickered. "Yeah, since tomorrow is St. Patrick's Day, we can kidnap one of those little green genies that bounce around. That oughta do it for us."

"You speak nonsense, Langford, but I am telling you of some genuine good fortune this year," the black man said soberly.

"Well so far, I'm not feeling any of it."

"Forecast calls for more rain in the next two months than they have had in the last two seasons."

"The rain could be good," Seth agreed. "And God knows we'll take all the obstacles we can get."

"Ground warfare is not likely with the storms and crude roads. You know that. So that just leaves the aerial campaign." Depending on the words, the stranger's accent lilted up and down, a rich song.

"What's the latest on the northern retrievers?"

"Bedouins?" The man spit out the word like it was toxic. "Like you, I do not trust them. At best, the cash changing hands is only fueling the militia effort. Worse case it is building a secondary slave market . . ."

"Which only widens the north-south divide," Seth finished the sentence.

"Bingo."

Mera stood frozen outside the door, spellbound by the conversation. Words like railroad and transport and slave market, all in the same few sentences surely couldn't add up to any good . . .

Mind racing, she tried inching her way past the door. But another cramp seized her belly and this one was so sharp, she lost her balance. Before she could catch herself, her heels slipped beneath her and she landed squarely on the wet floor.

Outside the door, Seth heard a sick *plop*. Without thinking, he rushed into the hallway, the mysterious giant just a few steps behind him.

"What on earth . . . what happened, Mera?"

She couldn't talk. Another wave of pain had clamped her stomach and she felt a wet gush spill from under her dress.

"Bathroom. Had to go to the bathroom." It was all she could get out between the cramps contracting her belly.

"Are you hurt?"

"No." She managed to shake her head. "Just . . . have . . . pain."

"She will have her child soon," the black man explained evenly as he stepped forward to push Seth out of his way. "That is the look."

She wondered what look he was talking about and how and

what the stranger knew about women and childbirth. But she hurt too badly to ask. Besides, he had to be right. Whether or not the fall had caused it, her water had broken and was now forming a small puddle beneath her.

Without a word, the giant scooped her up as if she were feather-light and carried her down the long hallway, past the reception area until he'd wound his way to the center's living quarters. It was obvious he knew his way around.

A few seconds later, he stopped in an empty room and deposited her on a cot-like bed. Seth was just behind him.

"Mera, I'm going to call an ambulance. It'll be much quicker this time of evening, especially with the rain."

"Can't go to the hospital without my papers." Getting words out was about to kill her. "Got to have the papers, they told me."

"What papers?" For a second, his eyes met hers.

Another contraction squeezed her abdomen, a steel grip, and she held her breath until it passed.

"My pre-registration papers for the hospital. For the anesthesiologist, the whole thing."

"Where did you register?"

"Rush Presbyterian St. Luke's. It's just . . ."

"About five miles west of here."

The giant had disappeared, calling the ambulance Mera guessed. Meanwhile, another leak from beneath her was spreading a murky greenish stain over the white sheet.

"I'm so sorry, Seth . . ." The pain had subsided long enough for her to feel completely humiliated.

"Forget it; we just need to get you to the med center." A crimson flush crept over his cheeks. "Look, I'll go get your papers and meet you there."

"No, really. They can probably look me up in the system."

"Where's your apartment key?" He handed her the purse she'd dropped back in the hallway and she dug around until she felt her keys.

"It's this one." Though she hated the idea of imposing, she held up the key in question.

"Okay. Where are the papers?"

Another wave of pain crested through her and this one took full possession of her nervous system. At once, her whole body started shaking and her teeth chattered uncontrollably. Like he wasn't sure what else to do, Seth tucked a thin blanket over her.

"Can't remember." She could hardly talk and she was thankful for the soft wail of an ambulance siren in the distance. "Think they're either by the phone in the kitchen or the top drawer of my nightstand. In my journal."

He nodded. "I'll be there as soon as I can."

Chapter 19

He figured the storm would make the evening traffic crawl, but he definitely hadn't expected it to take an hour to inch the fifteen miles to her flat. Lightning was the culprit, he eventually discovered. A wayward bolt had struck a nearby transformer and surrounding electricity was out, traffic lights and all.

So he sat in the metallic sea of inert cars, chain smoking as he replayed the awkward, yet somehow not offensive, scene at the shelter. Remembering the strange stain on the sheet, the agonizing look that had convulsed Mera's face every few minutes, Seth hoped she was okay, hoped for some odd reason the baby wouldn't come until he got to the hospital with her papers.

Just before dark, he opened her front door, not expecting the stale air that wrapped him like wet ropes. Obviously, the power had been out awhile, but out of habit, he flipped a light switch. Nothing happened. A second later he tripped over Pedora on his way to the kitchen. The fat cat hissed her displeasure before bolting out of sight.

The countdown was now and he knew it, both in terms of the waning daylight, as well as the impending baby debut at the hospital. Trouble was, he wasn't quite sure where to start foraging first.

Three neat piles, each about two inches high, were stacked beside the kitchen phone. Figuring this was as good a place as any to start, he plunged into the first one.

Bank statements. A few bills.

Seth tackled pile two then three. A couple *Lands' End* magazines, a collection of travel brochures and halfway down stack, there was a few of her past columns slashed with red edit marks.

Nothing even remotely resembling a packet of medical papers.

Next on the list would be her bedroom, which he figured had to be somewhere off the only hallway in the apartment. Navigating the shadowy corridor, he turned into the first of two rooms just as the lights blinked backed on.

Everything was pink. Or shades of it.

The walls. The floral comforter and pillow shams on her four poster mahogany bed. Even a robe lying across the foot of her bed was the color of pink lemonade.

He knew he shouldn't have, but Seth picked up the robe. Pressed it to his face. It smelled clean and warm the way lingering soap did on skin after a shower. Before he put it down, he saw two long hairs on a fuzzy collar.

Her hairs.

For a minute, Seth tried picturing her in here, moving around, crawling into bed, reading books, going to sleep.

Then he stopped himself.

Mera Kaine was at the hospital right now having some man's baby.

His only mission here was to get what she needed and get out.

Based on the books piled atop one of her two nightstands, it was easy to figure where she slept. Mentally crossing his fingers, he sank down on the bed and started pulling stacks from the drawer—a few *Money and Investing* magazines, stray papers and an old address book. A well-worn Bible and half a bag of jelly beans.

A little more fumbling and he felt a lump of cold metal that turned out to be a .45 caliber pistol. Without meaning to, he laughed. The thought of Mera brandishing a Colt was like the idea of him sleeping in an endless world of pink.

He was just about to declare this search and rescue mission pointless when his fingers happened upon something thick and rectangular. It was lodged at the very bottom of the drawer but he pushed and tugged until a red canvas book emerged. A large envelope was stuffed inside it.

The journal. It had to be.

"Bingo," he said aloud, pulling the envelope from her book. At the same time, a frayed muddy cloth fell out.

Puzzled, he picked it up off her bed. Turned it over. It looked like a collar torn from a shirt.

Strange souvenir, he thought as he opened her journal to stuff it back in.

Absentmindedly, he glanced down. Then gaped in horror at the single word burning up at him.

"*RAPED.*"

It was scrawled in huge red letters, a journal entry dated July 1995.

After Mera's return from Boston.

Eyes riveted to the page, Seth read on.

RAPED! Again, damn me. Guess I didn't log enough time feeding my father's sick appetites. Now Jack's done it, too. Can't believe this, oh, God, I can't believe this is my life. I keep thinking maybe it's not real, maybe I'm crazy. But the pain is definitely real, I'm sure of that because it's about to kill me.

Why? That's all I want to know. Why? Jack spent half his life saving me, shielding me, from what he just did. What in God's name happened to him? And when did his priest's collar become a godforsaken mask to hide behind?

Please, God, help me. Help me! Jack wore the damn thing the whole time . . . I still can't believe it . . . one thing's sure, though. I must be trash. Filth. Why else would this happen twice in a lifetime? First my own father, then my best friend . . .

Seth twisted the tattered collar over and over again in his shaking hands, half-grasping, half-trying to wrap his mind around the enormity of it all. But the more it all sank in, the more loathsome the truth seemed until it was so vile and sharp he felt his stomach heave.

What kind of madness, what brand of evil would reduce not one, but two, human beings to such depravity?

He knew he shouldn't have read Mera's secret and it wasn't like he'd meant to. But now, he had to look one more place. Flipping past several pages, he found another entry, this one dated a few months later.

I'm pregnant. Pregnant. I should have known. All the signs were there. Maybe I just thought they'd go away. Like I want to go away . . . Oh, God, what's next? What's next and what am I supposed to do? You know, I might've loved Seth. In fact, I think I must have because nothing I do rids him from my thoughts. But that's another story. Because now there's another intrusion, another damning twist . . . Oh, God, a baby. A little secret baby I don't get to explain to anyone. Not Jack, especially not Jack. And not Seth, though he'll have me for a whore before too long. So what? Where do I go? What do I do and how do I keep the aloneness from swallowing me whole . . . or maybe it should and then all this would just end. I would end . . .

He was kneeling now, inadvertently crushing the torrid cloth between his fingers to the cadence of his pounding heartbeat.

He should have known. He should've figured it was something like this . . .

He hadn't deceived himself after all. Mera's cold incivility had been nothing more than an act. A charade to protect him from the truth and keep herself from anymore pain.

Oh, God . . .

Numbly, Seth shoved the collar back into her journal. Then closed the drawer. As he did, the full weight of what he'd read hit him.

Her own father . . . how morbid, macabre, was that? Then after witnessing her torment, after fully understanding the magnitude of her suffering, her best friend had followed suit.

It was beyond sick. Past lecherous.

And outside of what seemed forgivable.

Alone in the room, Seth slammed his fist against the mattress, though it did nothing to abate his rage.

Jack Frasier needed to pay.

And he needed to pay big.

But he'd have to think about that later. Right now, he had to get to Mera, to the hospital with the papers that had already done much more than clarify medical information.

Silently, he thanked God for the strange chance of being back a day early. For the odds of Mera coming to the shelter because of Rachel's delay in Denver. He thanked Him for being the one to go find her papers and stumble onto the truth she'd kept so diligently hidden.

Then tucking the packet under his arm, Seth made perhaps the greatest commitment he'd ever made and he did it without any hesitation.

No matter what it took — highs, lows or anything in between — he would spend the rest of his life loving Meranda Kaine. Somehow, he would take her fragmented ruins and help her build something real and good if it took everything he had.

And he'd start right now.

Chapter 20

One look at the lead paramedic's face and Mera knew something was wrong. Really wrong. And if she hadn't been completely debilitated by the titan clench wringing her belly, she would have resorted to a string of questions. Instead, she balled her hands into fists while the pain crested and made herself focus on his resolute Asian features as he lifted her from the shelter cot onto a narrow gurney. Noticing the growing olive stain on the sheet, the lead started barking choppy orders.

"Move her out, *stat*." A second later, another medic was at her feet and the two navigated the hallways in thundering footsteps that ended at a waiting ambulance. "Okay, let's get her hooked up." Then to a third technician helping transfer her inside the vehicle, "C'mon, McDougal, move it. We got a fetal distress here."

"Ma'am, can you tell me how long ago your water broke?" The lead turned his attention back to her, calmly connecting a monitor around her ballooned abdomen. A couple of *snaps* and a *click* later, he flipped on a switch. Instantly, she heard the *swoosh swoosh* of her baby's heartbeat.

"Less than an hour ago."

"Okay. Tell me about the fluid. Was it this same color at first?" He pointed at the still-morphing shape beneath her.

"I don't know, maybe. But, I don't think so." Another contraction squeezed her like an iron hand.

"When's your baby due?" He split open a packet containing a sterile IV needle. The sharp jab stuck like a knife as the ambulance careened through the side streets.

"Two weeks. She's due in two weeks. But tell me what's wrong . . ."

Suddenly, McDougal interrupted, "Heartbeat's down to 115."

"Tell me *now*! What's the matter with my baby?" she screamed, half with worry, half in pain.

"Ma'am," the lead began firmly, "I really need for you to stay calm. Your baby's distressed but we're working to get a handle on things." He started shifting her as he explained. "So I need you to relax while we move you onto your left side. This'll optimize blood flow and oxygen to the fetus."

Within fifteen seconds, the monitor echoed progress; the baby's heartbeat went up considerably. But as she glanced at the readout, she knew something still wasn't right. On the thin strip of paper was a series of erratic red and black spikes with no predictable pattern. Meanwhile, the second technician was calling in her vital signs over a radio.

"How far are we from Rush Presbyterian?"

"Just a few miles. And we got a team waiting for you, ma'am." The paramedic's slanted black eyes were sympathetic, and he wiped the perspiration from her forehead before he adjusted the belt around her stomach again.

~

The rain was a steady drizzle, but even with the wet streets, traffic was already clearing. Groping for the envelope in the seat beside him, Seth shook his head, still trying to make sense of what was happening.

Or what had happened.

Was it just a few hours ago that he'd been surprised, and not pleasantly so, to see her in the reception area? Then, she'd been merely the figment of what he'd dreamed of in a woman, though empty of the virtues he'd first fancied in her. He had looked at her swollen stomach, her pale, sad face. And suddenly, he'd been more saddened than repulsed by how casual she was about monumental things like life and love and what should be lasting.

But for the first time, he'd been glad he had learned just how different they were, how far apart they'd probably always been. There's a reason for everything, he thought as he'd walked away to catch a meeting. Holly would handle the wrap-up just fine.

Now he knew better and he was furious with himself for not getting it straight in the first place. This was the one time in years he hadn't gone with his instincts, hadn't stayed the course he sensed was right. Sure, Meranda Kaine had an aloofness about her, an almost wordly air. But it was like she exploited that veneer so as to protect someone far more fragile and vulnerable.

He'd known that, almost absolutely, from the beginning.

Gripping the steering wheel so tightly his knuckles burned, he pictured her outside her door last summer.

She'd been cool, meticulously so. Calculated, too, obviously to keep him from tracking the scent of her lie. But all the while, she'd never once looked him in the eye.

Then there was the night he'd waited outside her flat. Waited in the cold purple darkness, hoping against hope that there could still be something between them. Instead, he'd run headlong into evidence that offered the final verdict that he was odd man out.

She hadn't cracked then, either. Though the deceptive sham must've been both exhausting and agonizing, her heartless tramp act was so believable, he'd bought it and written her off for good.

And all the while, she'd been protecting Jack.

He struck his hand hard against the steering wheel. Let out a word he always asked his center residents to omit from their vocabularies.

He should have known better . . .

As he turned onto West Harrison and wound toward the medical center, Seth knew that the toughest times had to be ahead. Mera had already lived through a lifetime of abuses — and at the hands of people she'd trusted most.

Which brought him to a stark reality.

Trust had to be meaningless to her, now, a hypothetical ideal that belonged always to other people.

But never to her.

Why and how could it be anything different?

Thinking again about the ragged cloth and scarlet letters scribbled onto pages no one would ever see, Seth felt himself understanding why she'd decided no one was safe, why she had been hoodwinked into thinking she was a magnet for disaster.

His hands were tied, though. He might know her secret, but what could he do about it? If Mera even suspected he'd read her journal, it would only relegate him to traitor status in her mind. Someone no different from the others she'd wanted to believe in.

Just the same, there had to be a way back for her.

Turning into the hospital's parking garage, Seth felt himself smile a little. He had a proven track record of long commitments in the same direction. And this was a course worth staying, he decided. Even, if in the end, there was nothing in it for him.

~

The last thing Mera remembered with any clarity was the synchronized *thump-bump* of the paramedics' footsteps as she floated past the glinting steel and glass of the ER doors into a blinding white hall that went on forever. True to the technician's words, she was passed off at corridor's end to a waiting team who whisked her to labor and delivery. There, more questions followed as two RNs hooked her up to monitors and another IV bag.

Then something changed, though she was too dazed to know what. Everything had been moving fast, so quickly that the world had become a miscellany of morphing faces, flashing lights, amid stark white and endless *beeps*.

But now time stood stock-still as the monitor shrieked a high-pitched plea for help.

As if by magic, she felt the cool wind of a doctor's long white coat waft air up into her face. The breeze smelled of starch and antiseptic.

"We're losing the heartbeat," a faceless nurse was reading from Mera's chart. "Fetal reading first came in at 110, got up to 125, and started dropping. EMT recorded meconium staining."

"When did the water break?" It was a gravelly voice. Brusque and confident.

"Over an hour ago."

"Cord compression. Get her in the OR, stat." Before she could make sense of his features, the doctor vanished. The nurse pressed her face just a few inches from Mera's.

"Honey," she began patiently, "that was Dr. Simmons . . ."

"Simmons . . ."

"Dr. Simmons," the nurse repeated reassuringly. "He's chief of obstetrics and gynecology. And he needs to do a C-section."

"But . . ." Mera tried to sit up but her body was lead. So were the thoughts trapped inside her head.

"Ms. Kaine, your baby's umbilical cord is compressed. What that means is she's not getting oxygen. That's why it's critical we get her out as soon as we can."

Mera was almost a universe of her own now, everything else miles outside of her. Only pain held her here, warm, sleepy waves that made her want to giggle and cry at the same time. Some part of her wanted to ask a million questions. But all she could do was give into it all and nod.

The nurse injected something into her IV that made everything go black.

⁓

Seth caught Sally on her cell phone, fresh off the plane from New York. He knew it was a long shot, but he hadn't known who else to call. Mera had no family to speak of, no close friends or colleagues as far as he knew. But he figured a woman, especially a rock like Sally, might be helpful when the time came.

As she stepped into the waiting area a half-hour later, though, it occurred to him that he probably needed her just as much.

"Does she know yet?" The older woman held him close before they sank into the waiting room's worn blueberry-colored chairs.

"No, she's still in and out." Seth raked his fingers through his hair. "They're waiting to tell her."

"Poor girl." Sally shook her head sympathetically. "Every time I think her luck's bound to change, another disaster strikes." She straightened abruptly. "By the way, how did *you* wind up here?"

"Long story, lotta details."

"Never mind," Sally patted his arm, "I'm just glad you're here. Did the doctor give you any specifics, any clue what caused . . .?"

Seth's eyes were wild in his face, like he'd been eyewitness to the paranormal.

"I was the only one here, so he probably said way more than he should've."

The waiting room was almost empty, just an older couple huddled in a far corner, playing cards to pass the time. Nearby, a big screen television blared the ten o'clock news and every now and then, the whispery *squish* of white-soled shoes signaled the advent of a snow-clad nurse. Off in the distance, a thin balding man heaved a mop to and from a rolling, yellow bucket. His efforts left behind glistening white floors and a faint hint of lemony antiseptic.

"So what did he say, sweets?" Sally broke his daze.

"Remember, I told you she fell back at the shelter?"

Sally nodded.

"Well, her water broke, and I saw this funny-colored stain on the sheet where we moved her. Since I don't have a clue what's normal, I didn't think anything of it." He rubbed his forehead like it hurt. "But apparently, if a baby's distressed, it passes this waste-like stuff into its little sac. That's why Mera's water was green."

"What caused the distress?"

"Supposedly, her umbilical cord was compressed, so she, I mean the baby, wasn't getting oxygen. Her heartbeat spiked and dropped all the way here. Then they got a flatline just before the C-section." From these last few hours, Seth knew more about childbirth and traumatic delivery than he'd learned in his almost thirty-seven combined years before.

"Oh," Sally winced.

"Simmons, that's the doctor, said they did all they could. They tried resuscitating her, but it was too late."

Just then, a paunchy little nurse with slightly bowed legs and bifocals motioned Seth from around the corner.

"She's awake, Mr. Langford. Dr. Simmons is getting ready to go in."

"Does she know yet?"

"No, but she's asking questions." The nurse pushed up her glasses and scratched a scaly spot on her cheek. "I thought you might want to be there when we told her."

"I do."

He stood then followed the woman's short stride, stopping just outside Mera's door.

"Hi there," he said softly. She looked tiny beneath the hospital blankets and her face was nearly as white as the pillow she was propped against. Under the covers, her stomach was smaller than it had been, but still swollen.

"Hi, yourself," she whispered.

"Can I come in?"

"Sure. Did you see her yet?"

He wanted to hit something, preferably Jack, and yell at the same time.

"Ms. Kaine, we have some bad news." Dr. Simmons squared his broad shoulders, handed a clipboard to a passing intern and passed from the doorway to her bedside in two long strides. Looking grave, he rubbed his gray-stubbled chin so hard it sounded like sandpaper scraping wood.

"I know I told the agency I'd give her up in the delivery room. But I can at least see her once, can't I?" Mera pleaded, her eyes beginning to fill with tears.

The doctor shook his head slowly. "I wish it were that easy. But your little girl died during delivery, Ms. Kaine. Her umbilical cord was compressed and wrapped around her neck. We did all we could to try and save her." Simmons paused for a minute, letting the news register. "I'm so sorry."

For what seemed like hours, she didn't say anything. Instead, she pulled the cotton tufts on her blanket and watched the fuzzy little flurries lifting into the air. When she looked up, it was at Seth.

"Is that . . . is this true?"

He nodded slowly, then took her hand in his. She didn't pull away.

"Could I see her?" The nurse shook her head yes, looking long at Dr. Simmons as if to cue him.

"Mr.," the doctor began.

"Langford. Seth Langford." His tongue stuck to the roof of his mouth.

"Mr. Langford, would you mind if we had a few words with Ms. Kaine before we bring in the baby?"

"Of course. I'll be in the waiting room if you need me."

He was still holding Mera's hand, and he could sense that she didn't want him to leave. But Simmons looked tired and like he had some weighty details to cover, so he gave her fingers a squeeze then touched her cheek before he turned to go.

"Seth?"

He stopped at the doorway, his back to her. "Yeah?"

"Her name's Emily. Emily Kate. In case you were wondering."

Chapter 21

She was glad the day dawned crisp and clear, grateful the sun had burgeoned from a glowing crescent into flaming splendor. Color and beauty, noise and movement, somehow distracted, if only for seconds, the cold gray shadow she couldn't shake.

Emily Kate Kaine...or was it Emily Kate Frasier . . . is dead. Dead. As in not breathing. Not alive.

Mesmerized by sunbeams cutting through the glass windows and spilling in every direction, she said the words to herself. But the veracity of them wouldn't belong to her. Instead, they beaded up and rolled away like raindrops on a newly waxed car.

She tried again, wincing as she shuffled down the gleaming white corridors. At least she could feel the searing ache where her belly had been sliced open. That pain was real and she was strangely glad for it.

Baby Emily's waiting family would never get her.

Still wouldn't compute.

Finally: *Jack Frasier's little girl, named after his mother, was laying cold and stiff in a tiny casket at St. Luke's hospital chapel.*

That did it. A hot wind and fiery sword crossed hell's threshold to stab and burn her at once, an indescribable agony that made her knees buckle as she sank beside Seth and Sally in the chapel's hardwood pew.

She hadn't cried until now. In fact, considering the heartbreak of the past year, she'd hardly cried at all. It was like she and sadness were one and the same, so any expression of it only confirmed its presence, not relieved her.

But that last thought made everything inside her shatter into a million pieces.

Taking in the cool quiet of the room, the white doll-sized coffin positioned just a few yards away, she began to sob uncontrollably. She knew she should try and compose herself, but she didn't do it. Instead, as deep heaves racked her gaunt body, she gave into them completely, not even caring what Seth or Sally or any of the other few people here for the service might think.

Somewhere in the middle of it all, she felt an arm drape across her shoulders, a leg press lightly against hers. Seth had moved close.

She meant to pull away immediately, meant to will that this pain was hers to face alone. But more agony cleaved through her and his warmth was so soothing she let herself keep it, even if his comfort was nothing more than pity for her. She remembered once that Sally had bragged on his great heart, and just for today, maybe it was okay to take what she could get . . .

Now the cold air rippled with words and sounds, but she couldn't make sense of what the chaplain was saying. The liturgy was a labyrinth of ideas stringing together, mixing, echoing in a tunnel:

This new life . . . precious little one . . . Emily Kate Kaine . . . these things we don't understand . . . our heavy hearts . . . these tears we cry . . . another time, another place . . . into the hands of a loving God . . .

She tried hard to listen, tried to imagine that the ricocheting words would eventually congeal themselves into a picture that made all things clear. She knew she needed to understand these sounds, these ideas, because they had to do with her. And her baby. But then it was too much and all she could concentrate on was the sliver of Emily's profile peeking over the casket's white satin trim.

Her hair was dark and wavy. *Like Jack's.*

Her nose was sharp and tiny. *Like hers.*

Her delicate lips were a rosebud, perfect and baby-pouty.

This still doll was her daughter. Her beautiful little girl.

Oh, Emily . . . sweet little Emily Kate, I'm so sorry. So sorry for how you were conceived, but not that you were. I loved you, Emily. Even if I knew I couldn't keep you . . . please know that I wanted you. I wanted you to giggle and eat hot dogs and ride piggyback on the shoulders of someone you'd call Daddy. I wanted you to sit high and tall on a red tricycle and then go inside and bake cookies with a woman you'd call Mommy. I knew there would be clowns at your birthday parties, roses at your ballet recitals. But more than anything, I prayed you would be loved. Loved and safe. Oh, my sweet baby . . . my little girl . . .

Two waves of pain simultaneously washed over her. Her still-bloated abdomen throbbed where the incision was, a pulsing life of its own. Then the sharp realization that little Emily Kate would never have a favorite color, never eat cotton candy or play hopscotch, made her almost scream.

A thin-lipped organist with a helmet of flaming orange hair was piping an old hymn now, no words to accompany it. Mera knew its melody, had intermittently heard it all her life. But she couldn't place it.

"When peace like a river attendeth my way, when sorrows like sea billows roll . . ."

Weren't those the words to it? It was coming back now. Big rolling sorrows, the composer had written about. Indescribable, drowning pain.

Like she somehow needed to, she struggled to remember the rest.

"Whatever my lot, Thou hast taught me to say, it is well, it is well with my soul."

Well, it surely wasn't well with her soul. How could a soul tormented by rape and betrayal, shrouded in lies, and now, death, find peace again?

"Though trials shall come, let this blessed assurance control . . . that Christ has regarded my helpless estate, and has shed His own blood for my soul . . ."

The words had broken loose in a deluge. Floated across time from the old Lockwood choir loft to here. And suddenly, she knew why she needed to remember.

There was Father Duncan's craggy eyebrows, his cinnamony beard peering out from her childhood lockbox.

This time, though, his face was somber, his eyes red-rimmed.

She was just twelve years old when the priest and his wife lost their baby son, a stillbirth. Even now, she could feel the tension of that first Sunday morning after they had buried their baby. As usual, Father Duncan had taken his place at the lectern and then in a broken whisper, he'd told the story of the ancient hymn.

A successful attorney by the name of Horatio Spafford had lost nearly all his real estate investments in the great Chicago fire of 1871. Attempting to lift the spirits of his wife and four daughters, Spafford decided his family should vacation in Europe. But when he was detained on urgent business, he sent his family ahead, planning to join them.

Halfway across the Atlantic, an English vessel struck the S.S. Ville du Havre, and it sank, along with all four of Spafford's daughters. He learned of the tragedy when his wife telegraphed him from Wales, just two words—"Saved . . . alone."

The grief-stricken man stood hour after hour on the ship deck carrying him to Europe where he'd join his wife. When the ship came upon the place where his girls had drowned, Spafford had penned, "It is Well With My Soul."

You could have heard a pin drop in the little church as Father Duncan recounted the old story, seeming oddly sustained by the anguish of another father who knew what it was like to love, and lose, a child. Then in a voice that trembled, the priest implored his parish to trust God, to embrace a faith bigger than pain and greater than circumstances. "God doesn't stop being sovereign in the midst of human suffering," the priest said in a hoarse whisper. "In fact, it's only at the center of our crucibles that all of our ideas, our notions, our images of Him burn away. And then miraculously, we best see Him for who He is."

Mera couldn't remember another sermon he'd given. Just that one. Somehow, that one had encrypted and stayed with her all these years.

It was time. They were moving back the wilted pink rose sprays and closing the box with the tiny doll tucked into it. Now, they were lifting it, featherweight, and carrying it away.

Jack should be here . . . Oh, God, he should suffer this, too.

But she didn't belong with Jack; he was a stranger now. And Emily didn't really belong to him. She'd merely found her genesis in him, in a wretched moment of violence.

She felt weak now, so tired. Just this morning, the nurse had said a cesarean section was major surgery.

Pressing her belly as if to confirm that it was real, that this was all happening, she conceded that the pain definitely felt major. But she couldn't lose sight of the little coffin, either. For the first time in nine months, her baby was going one way and she would go another.

This is the final stake, the summit of dying. The living go on and out, the dead go out and under. Oh, God . . . no, please no. Emily!

She tried to cry out and stand up at the same time, but a black wall closed around her and she collapsed, a rag doll in Seth's arms.

Chapter 22

He'd been helpful the last few months, though he wasn't sure to what extent. Her layers of grief were like a thick onion, one endless segment beneath another. The past several weeks had confirmed this, with days on end of her huddled on the couch in the same mismatched pajamas, refusing most food and content to lapse into protracted silences complete with zombie-like stares.

But Seth was in no particular rush of any kind. Even if he hadn't happened upon those few telling pages in her journal, it was easy to see that Mera was dealing with pain so dense and exorbitant that no amounts of goodwill or cajoling would combat the shadows that seemed to keep her. He knew a repository of words wouldn't be helpful, though there were some he'd really like to say. And given the circumstances, the normal expressions that conveyed tenderness — flowers, dinners out — seemed superficially out of context.

Instead, he was convinced that consistency was what she needed most. Basic kindness with no strings attached.

So he had offered that, careful to make it clear that he knew they were in no way picking up where they'd left off before the ill-fated Boston trip.

Meranda Kaine was simply his friend, or really, he was her friend.

Lately, though, he had noticed a slight change. Nothing to hang his hat on or get excited about, but in the last week, Mera had almost seemed to brighten a little when he stopped by. And in the last couple of days, she'd even attempted snippets of conversation before she numbed out again.

Now as the bells on the deli door jingled behind him, Seth realized her maternity leave was almost up. Just two more weeks. Ruefully, he pondered the *Tribune's* whirring activity, its breakneck pace. And he worried that someone so fragile and spent might easily get sucked under and spit out like waves at high tide.

Mera almost ignored the bleating phone. Anything that disrupted her television trance was unsettling and annoying. But since it was next to her and Seth tended to call this time of afternoon, she picked it up.

"Hey, I took off a little early." The connection made every few of his words echo. "Thought I'd pick us up a bite at Ed's Deli."

"Seth, you just brought by Chinese last night . . ."

"So you'd prefer Italian?" he quipped.

"No. What I mean is I don't want you to . . ."

"Pick up Limburger on pumpernickel? Okay, then, put in your order."

She hesitated. She would have to get off the couch, get showered and put on clothes, an effort that was Herculean right now. But . . .

"Well if you insist . . ." she heard herself saying.

"I do. Or else it's liverwurst and sauerkraut."

She smiled. "Okay. Turkey and Swiss. On wheat if you don't mind."

"I don't."

"And Seth?"

"Yeah?"

"Thanks."

He cleared his throat and that echoed, too.

"Sure thing. I'll see you in about an hour."

Seth's heart sank when she answered the door. He knew the past year had taken its toll on her, and while the thought of that was hard, it was easier than facing the raw culmination of it.

Up to now, she'd given into hair scooped back in a messy knot, rumpled pajamas and no makeup. In some ways, he had liked it that way. It kept the truth at bay, the reality of where she was mostly a possibility. Cloaked in mourning, there was no need and no way to really measure the consequences of the last several months.

But now she'd made an effort to look nice. For the first time since she had been home from the hospital, her hair was clean and dried straight. She'd even put on makeup though, in his mind, this was a mistake. The light color and shading only called attention to her listless eyes and jutting cheekbones. If that wasn't enough, her jeans and black blouse thinned her already emaciated frame to refugee status.

Trying hard not to stare, it hit him that it wasn't only that he missed her good looks. He'd learned years ago the complexity and dimensions of real beauty. It was facing up close that she'd suffered beyond expression that gripped him like an iron hand.

But she was trying again, he told himself, and that was a step toward something.

"You look really pretty, Mera," he said, making himself sound more like he was commenting on the weather than paying her a compliment.

She smiled wanly. Motioned him to come in.

On her kitchen counter, she'd set out glasses, soda and a bag of jalapeno chips. He put down his paper sack, bumping a flat box with a raffia bow slipped around it.

"That's for you." She pointed at the box.

"What's for me?" He wasn't sure whether she was talking about the waiting glasses or the box.

"This." She picked up the package. Handed it to him.

"Why?"

She shrugged.

"No particular reason. It just reminded me of you."

She motioned again, so he picked up the box and started unwrapping it. When he opened the lid, his breath stuck in his throat.

Lying beneath the tissue was a brown tooled-leather journal.

Surely, she couldn't know that he knew, he told himself. There was no way . . .

"I loved the way it looked," she broke his thoughts, "though I have no clue if you even keep a journal." She shrugged again. "But you've always struck me as someone who might. I actually got that for you a . . . well, a while back."

He ran his hand over the dark rawhide cover and smiled at her. "This is so cool. And you're right. I've kept one since Taize."

She looked mildly interested, progress from her usual listlessness.

"You started one at Taize or after?"

"At," he smiled. "If you can call it that. All I had with me was a little two by five notebook, half-full of ideas I'd been tossing around for a term paper. But when I got up there, something happened and it was like I had to get it all down somehow." He shook his head like the memory was still fresh. "It looks like a bunch of chicken scratch, especially now. But that's how I got hooked."

"I think I started one halfway through college, mostly to stay sane. But for some reason, I kept at it." Her voice wavered and for a distraction, she picked up one of the glasses and watched silver frost spread outward from the warmth of her fingers.

Trying to feign normal while staying on this topic was exhausting him.

"Well, you know what I've been thinking?" As the words came out, he felt the too-brightness of them. Like a 100-watt bulb where a fifteen would have been sufficient.

"Let's see. Maybe something along the lines of a missing boyfriend?" She'd said it casually, but he could hear dread weighting the words.

"Well, I'm not gonna lie and say that hasn't crossed my mind. But for now, I was just wondering when I'd see you eat more than a bite or two. You need to start doing that, you know."

Clearly relieved, she cracked open two cans of Coke and poured them over tiny ice pebbles that filled the glasses. The carbonation hissed and foamed for a few seconds. Then stilled.

"Now's as good a time as any."

"Great." He pulled the sandwiches from the deli bag and they ate for a minute with nothing other than the sound of chewing and swallowing.

"I meant," she started again, "this might be a good time to talk."

"About?"

"Everything . . . you know . . ."

"That's not necessary, really. You don't owe me any explanations."

"I know, but I want to talk."

About what?

Was she planning to suddenly come clean with the truth? Given her unflinching loyalty to Jack, that wasn't likely. So what, then, could she possibly say that would protect her secret and clarify the last ten months?

He didn't want to know. All of a sudden, the thought of her digging herself into a deeper hole sickened him. But it wasn't in his nature to be unkind.

"Sure," he said lightly. "But you gotta promise to eat first."

"Just say it, you think I'm skinny," she teased.

"Well you're no candidate for Weight Watchers, that's for sure," he bantered back. "And I figure if you don't start choking down more than bird rations, I'm gonna be forced to have a truckload of those healthy little canned shakes dropped off at your door."

She rolled her eyes. But she was smiling, and for a second, she looked almost pretty.

Then came an awkward silence that made the background murmur of CNN in the den seem like a live concert.

"What did you do today?" He opted for some small talk.

She swallowed a bite of sandwich, sipped from her glass. "Pretty much the usual. Hung out, watched the news."

"Any interesting headlines?"

Until today, she'd forgotten the suspicious conversation between Seth and the black giant at the shelter. In fact, it was only in the last few days that the events of that terrible afternoon were coming clearer.

But late this morning, the distinct likeness of the stranger's accent to some high-ranking east African officials in the news had triggered a sudden recall of the sketchy dialogue she had overheard. Since, she hadn't stopped wondering what Seth and the lumbering dark man were up to.

"The UN Security Council's planning to impose sanctions if Sudan doesn't turn over the men they suspect of trying to kill Hosni Mubarek last year . . ."

"They'll never do it. Sudan, I mean."

Her eyes widened. "How do you know?"

"I just do."

"Is it something you've been following?"

He laughed wryly. "Maybe if things were easier to follow, I could. But tracking the troubles over there is like chasing rabbits." He took a long drink of soda. "And Sudan will never fork over the suspects because last week, one of 'em fled the country."

"So?"

"A couple days later, the U.S. announced the Sudanese government abetted the fugitive. And just after that, we expelled one of their UN diplomats."

Mera watched his expression carefully.

"The speaker of parliament they elected was on."

"Promising world peace and lower taxes, I'm sure." He was sarcastic. "And since his impeccable track record makes him so trustworthy . . ."

"Makes who trustworthy?"

"Hassan al-Turabi," he said without hesitation. "The guy you saw. For all intents and purposes, he's head of Sudan's National Islamic Front, the real muscle behind Omar al-Bashir."

She pictured the man's beady eyes glittering behind thick black ovals. She saw his silver-bristled brown face, the stark linen turban that topped his head like a crown. He looked more like a Bedouin than a government leader.

"Oh. Well, he, al-Turabi, I mean, and a few other officials were on. Making counter-statements and swearing their innocence."

"Of course they were." He made no attempt to conceal his disgust.

"And I got to thinking . . ." She hesitated.

"About?"

"Well, these guys definitely looked Arab, but some of them had accents just like that man at your shelter."

"The man at my shelter," Seth repeated slowly, like he was thinking about it. "Right now, we've got a lot of men at the shelter with Arabic brogues lacing their tribal languages." He was referring to the immigrants although he knew she wasn't.

"No, not them," she persisted. "I'm talking about the man with the briefcase. The one who picked me up after I fell."

He polished off the rest of his sandwich, chewed a few chips before he answered.

"Wanna go sit down?"

"Sure," she said, picking up their drinks and carrying them into the den. One handed, she flipped off the television then set the glasses onto a low table in front of her couch. Straightening the cushions, she sank down on one end and pointed Seth to the other. As if on cue, a purring Pedora sprung into her lap.

"You're wondering who he was, aren't you?"

"You could say that." Mera shivered like she could feel the enormous muscled arms that had effortlessly lifted her up and away.

"He's an old friend. A buddy I met in Taize introduced us seven or eight years ago. Name's Onesphore Barekhandi."

"Does he live here?"

"No. His folks do, though. His dad is actually from southern Sudan, Juba to be exact, and his mom is from Asmara, Eritrea. But his family moved to Chicago from Eritrea when he was a kid."

Her eyebrows shot up. "From Eritrea to Chicago?"

Seth smiled at her expression. "His Dad was in oil and gas way before energy was an agenda item in most of Africa. He came over here as an engineer with Pelos Oil. The family went back and forth for years, from what I know, then finally settled in for good about the time Onesphore headed off to School of Mines in Colorado."

All this said, she wanted even more to ask about their stealth venture. But the idea of doing so seemed a little audacious.

"Why are you looking at me like that?" Seth's blue eyes pierced hers.

Without meaning to, she'd been studying him.

"I'm sorry, I was just thinking."

He swung forward as if he might stand. Then as if a conflicting thought had crossed his mind, he sank backwards, put his head in his hands and ran his fingers through his hair.

"Seth, are you okay?"

He wasn't. His mind suddenly burned with the crimson words in her journal, the angst of Emily Kate's death. And now, there was the wisp of a person she'd become. He thought about Onesphore's list-filled briefcase, about the immigrants at his shelter.

And the roiling combination of it all made the air turn to lead in his lungs.

He cared for Mera. A lot. But between her tormenting secrets and the complex maze of his own work, things were just too complicated to sort into something concrete. At least right now.

"Look, I should go, Mera." He stood and fumbled in his pocket until he found his keys.

"Please don't, Seth. I need to tell you something."

He didn't want to hear it. Not tonight and not in light of everything he knew. She would need to lie, that was the only foreseeable option. The thought of that sickened him even though he understood why she'd do it.

"Listen, I'll give you a call tomorrow . . ."

"No." She was adamant. "I don't want that. What I want is for you to hear me out tonight. Please."

Reluctantly, he sank back down on the couch. Braced himself.

"Seth," she began, trying to keep her voice steady, "I'll skip the details since they're not important, and I'd rather not relive them. But last summer, when I left here to go to Emily Frasier's funeral, I didn't plan what wound up happening."

Now words were erupting from her as if she couldn't hold them in.

"I met up with an old . . . well . . . for lack of better words, an old boyfriend. And I guess my guard was down. I was upset, not thinking straight. Long story short, you can add up what happened from there."

"And without a degree in biology," he answered more lightly than he felt.

"It was a mistake. A terrible mistake," she whispered, tears welling up in her eyes and spilling down her cheeks.

A white-hot anger twisted in his gut.

Damn, Jack Frasier.

Here she was attempting to be as honest, as vulnerable, as she dared. But *she* was taking full responsibility for the violation as if she'd become convinced it was *her* fault.

Damn him . . .

"Did you try and work things out with him?" Seth asked, if for no other reason than to keep her from figuring he knew anything.

"No, Seth. I knew we'd never work out." She wouldn't look at him.

"That day at the door . . . you said you loved him."

She glanced up for a second.

"I lied. Like I said, it was a big mistake. We haven't talked — not even once — since. After we . . . after that . . ." She didn't finish the thought.

"What about the baby?"

"I never told him about her. He doesn't know she existed. Or that she doesn't anymore." She grimaced like pain was shearing through every part of her. Then closing her eyes, she leaned back into the red denim of her couch.

"Wow. So he knew nothing at all?" Seth hated playing dumb, but he kept up the questions because he knew that certain ones dignified the course of her revelation.

"Nothing," she repeated softly.

She looked so drained and miserable he offered a diversion.

"Tell me . . . did you ever think about that last conversation we had?" He lowered his voice. "The one right before you left?"

If only he knew how many times she'd relived that night. Beginning with the damp ivory roses he'd handed her to the crisp white of the tablecloth between them. From the flicker of candlelight shadowing the crescent scar above his mouth to his fingers lacing through hers . . .

But it was the probing innocence of his gaze, his lips lingering gently on hers that always made everything inside her twist and ache.

"I . . . I did," she stammered, "and like I said, I didn't mean for what happened to ever . . ."

"Was it Jack?"

Seth shocked himself. It wasn't like he was guessing. He knew. Considering that, he wondered why the singeing edge to his voice.

"Really, Seth, it doesn't matter who. The choice was mine to make and now it's mine to live with." If she was surprised he'd guessed right, it wasn't obvious. "Things might have been different now if I hadn't screwed up."

He wasn't sure what to say, but he was glad he hadn't left ten minutes ago. Maybe this friendship, or whatever it was, wasn't supposed to be easy or predictable. But something reminded him any effort invested wouldn't be in vain.

"You know," he began slowly, "I can't guess what might have been anymore than you can. All I know is life is full of detours that sometimes land us back in a story we thought was long finished."

She blinked. "So what are you saying?"

He leaned over and lifted her chin until their eyes met.

"Bottom line?"

She nodded.

"I have no idea what happens from here. But I know one thing: I'm not willing to walk away from whatever this is."

"I don't know what this is, Seth. I really don't."

He shrugged. "Then that makes two of us because I don't either."

"But why? How?" She stared at him, bewildered. "How could you not want to run the opposite direction?"

He moved close enough to rest a tentative hand on her shoulder.

"That's an easy one," he said, never taking his eyes off hers. "I guess I'm a believer in second chances."

"I don't get it." She looked away, bit her lower lip. "I know what I did to you, how I hurt you. And that kills me . . ."

"The past is just that, Mera. If we can let it stay there . . ."

"But I still cringe when I think about that night you were waiting on my stoop . . ."

"That was a bad night," he agreed. "But . . ."

" . . . what must've gone through your mind when . . ." She was consumed with the memory, tormented by it.

"Hush." He cut her off then did something he hadn't planned. He reached over and pulled her to him. Held her close and kissed the top of her head. "No one's perfect, Meranda."

The way he said her whole name made her stomach tighten.

The fact that she kept her head on his shoulder made everything inside of him tense.

"I'm so sorry, Seth," she said thickly.

He rubbed his cheek against the top of her head, breathing in the sweetness of her hair. Then seeing more tears trickling down her face, he offered his shirt sleeve.

She sat up and breathed out a long, low sigh.

Looking at her gaunt face, her red-rimmed eyes, everything inside him wanted to proclaim that he knew her truth: she wasn't guilty, she never had been — and she was free to drop the charade.

Instead he brushed a hand over hers.

"Like I said, Mera, I have no idea where we go from here. I think this whole thing's banged us up and left some pretty ugly scars. But we've got it out in the open now." He lowered his voice. "And I'm not afraid to try again."

She took a long time to answer.

"I *am*, though." She bit her lip again. "I don't deserve another chance, and even if I did, I wouldn't know how or where to start."

Of course you don't, he wanted to yell. Your whole world has been subverted, and the gag in your mouth keeps you from screaming about the hell in your heart. That would mess with anyone's head . . .

He thought for a long time, careful to choose the right words.

"Look, let's do this. Let's give ourselves some room, some time. We shouldn't be defining anything right now, anyway." He offered a reassuring smile. "We're friends again, and that's a good place for both of us. We'll deal with later, later."

"Could I ask you something?" She needed to change the subject.

"Sure."

"That day at the center . . . you know, right before I fell?"

"Yeah?"

"Well, I passed your door on the way back from the bathroom and I overheard you and Onesphore talking."

"That's all we do when he's in town." Seth shook his head with a smile at the thought of Onesphore's brittle countenance. Then he froze, remembering their last conversation.

"So, I heard something really bizarre." She hesitated. "Something about a railroad and moving things across borders in installments."

Seth's eyes shifted from the couch to the cat. Then he looked straight at her. "Mera . . ."

"Seth," she leaned forward a little, "please tell me you're not part of some black market deal. Tell me those immigrants at the shelter have nothing to do with all this."

He was quiet for so long that he knew she was thinking he probably wouldn't answer.

"I'm guessing you can handle this," he finally said.

Her eyes widened and a frown traced her features.

"Handle *what*?"

"First, I'll tell you what it's not. No black market of any kind. No high stakes shadowy underworld stuff. No drugs, porn, arms sales."

"Then what are you moving in mass quantities?"

He took a deep breath. "People. Refugees. From the south of Sudan."

"Refugees?"

"From Sudan," he confirmed calmly.

That's crazy." She stared at him, incredulous. "Why?"

He tightened his jaw, groping for a springboard sturdy enough to clear him of what could be gross misunderstanding. A question fit the bill.

"You're a prominent journalist. What do you know about Sudan?"

Mera thought for a minute.

"Okay, it's the largest African country, around a million square miles, if I remember right. The land is divided into north and south, north being primarily Arab Muslims, south being black Christians and animist religions. I'm not quite sure, but I think it shares eight border countries . . ."

"Nine," he interrupted.

". . . and the national language is Arabic, the capital, Khartoum, the president Omar al-Bashir and the population around thirty million."

He smiled.

"Man, that's pretty good for impromtu. Tell me what you know about the social and political climate."

She shook her head.

"Not much. I know Sudan got its independence from an Egyptian-Great Britain co-dominion in 1956 and it's been pretty bad ever since. Political unrest. Factional infighting. Civil skirmishes and a rigid government." She took a deep breath. "I think that about covers all I know."

"Here's some more. Since eighty-three, about six years before the right wing junta flipped the helm in Khartoum, there's been an unrivaled civil war going on. Nothing new, the north and south have been divided for decades, since before the country's independence in fifty-six. But in the last fifteen years, the northern militia's killed well over a million civilians in southern Sudan." Mera was looking at him like he'd lost his mind, but he continued anyway. "I know it sounds crazy, it sounds impossible. This whole thing's basically been kept under wraps . . ."

"But what . . . why . . .?"

"Trust me, there's a definite blueprint behind the north's tactics."

"Such as ethnic cleansing? Come on, Seth, this is insane. There's no reason . . ."

"Actually you're right. There is no *one* reason. There's a profusion of them. But to keep it from getting too complicated, at least for the moment, I'll stick to a few major ones." He twined his fingers together before stretching out his arms and giving his knuckles a good crack. "The government's all about two things. On the surface, it's this conversion mission . . ."

"Conversion to what?"

"Like you said, southerners are usually animists or Christians, both beliefs that run contrary to the radical sect of Islam they're advancing."

"So?"

"So the north sees it one way: the southerners are infidels. And they can either convert or get wiped out, though there's more to that, too, once you start digging deeper."

"Wait a minute, you're talking modern day Crusades in reverse . . ."

"*Jihad*, pretty much the same thing," he confirmed. "Islamic holy war against non-Muslims."

"I'm missing something, here."

"As in?"

"Well, the government of Sudan is the National Islamic Front, and while I'm not a follower of Islam, I can't see where Muslim disciples are assassins."

Seth swallowed then cleared his throat.

"That's not what I'm saying. I don't believe all Muslim disciples are assassins anymore than I think all Christians blow up abortion clinics. But this militia's part of an extremist faction ready to overthrow anyone who doesn't swallow their theology whole."

"You said the north was up to two main things," she pressed.

"Here's the other. The southern regions are oil-rich. Primitive, but steeped in crude. People there live in tribes, mostly farmers tending what little crops and animals they have. The fact that there's oil under their villages has never come into play."

"Until?" Mera anticipated his next words.

"Until fairly recently when an international oil giant got the ball rolling on tapping into the south's reserves. Another multinational based here in the States had pointed it out back in the seventies, but they sold their interests following some bad blood with local guerillas." Seth rubbed his forehead like the act was helping him think. "Still, there's a major basin that runs through the south, the largest of the Central African rift basins, and proven reserves are huge. Which means on top of the *jihad*—which was already bad enough—the quest for crude's spelled pandemic disaster for the south."

"Explain disaster."

He shook his head in disgust. "Destruction beyond anything imaginable. Villages burned and pillaged. The southerners, especially the Dinka tribe, are cattle farmers. So the government's been killing the men, slaughtering the livestock. Women get gang raped and maimed while they watch their land and their families gunned down or go up in flames." He rubbed his eyes and forehead again. "The raids start just after the rainy season, when the few graded dirt roads they have dry out. And nine times out of ten, the latest conquest is a village on top of reserves. So the militias move in, do their shock and awe thing, and then deport any survivors back to the north to be made into slaves."

"Seth, this is insane!" Mera couldn't believe her ears. "It's the end of the twentieth century and what you're telling me sounds like the Holocaust all over again . . ."

"And not unlike the Hutus snuffing out nearly a million Tutsis in Rwanda a few years ago," Seth added.

"Exactly," Mera agreed, "that's why the UN would never let that happen. Not again . . ."

"In a perfect world of foreign affairs, you'd be absolutely right. But unfortunately, just like the Third Reich's earlier days, this whole scandal is going all but unchecked by the world at large."

"So what you're saying is the north is getting by with scorched earth campaigns and ethnic cleansing policies all to lay hold of southern land that may or may not be oil-rich. But then what? Do they have the sophistication, the technology to produce the oil?"

"Nope."

"So they siege and murder their own people for being religious infidels and burn villages for oil they can't get their hands on?" Mera was trying hard to follow the logic of it, but so far, there wasn't any. "This really makes sense."

"The government knows exactly where the oil is," Seth explained patiently, like he'd had experience doing it before. "Some years back, after the American multinational sold its interests to a Canadian company, the Sudanese government entered into a cooperative that would move production ahead with oil giants in Canada and China and a few other countries. But it's a pretty twisted win-win."

"What do you mean?"

"Well, the companies do the dirty work for a price. They export a huge portion of the reserves. But Sudan benefits too, at least the north. The government keeps about ten percent of the revenues."

"And that translates into . . .?"

"Millions annually. But not for the south, though, technically, it's theirs. The northern government collects it, then goes next door to Russia and Yemen, and, of course, China, to buy yesterday's aircraft and artillery—grounded Antonovs, AK-47s . . . whatever they can get their hands on. Then, they come back and try out the new toys on the villages supporting their habit."

Mera pushed Pedora, who was mewing for attention, off of her lap.

"Wait," her eyes narrowed, "you were talking ground sieges, guerilla warfare. Are you saying the government's running aerial campaigns as well?" The more she heard, the more preposterous the whole thing sounded.

"Routinely. In fact, aerial's their top pick since aircraft's not affected by the weather like ground maneuvering is."

Without meaning to, she laughed out loud, something that startled Seth since he hadn't heard her do so in a year.

"No way, this can't be right," she said like a teacher explaining the history of the world religions to a first grader. "The UN's a stopgap for crimes against humanity. If this is true, nothing's more criminal than genocide at the hands of your own government."

"I hear you. But this hasn't been formally classified as genocide. Just gross human rights abuses, crimes against humanity . . ."

"Whatever you want to call it, it's ludicrous. Any government with this kind of systematic destruction policy would be on the radar screen of every leader in the free world. This is a threat to international security."

"You'd think, huh? And the UN keeps slapping the government's hand, like you heard today. But with the infighting between some of the southern tribes, the north's able to pass off its brutality as tribal wars and quelling rebel insurgencies. Sometimes they'll chalk some of the tyranny up to southerners resisting the state religion. And everyone keeps buying it."

"But what if that's true?"

"It's not."

"How do you know?"

"I've been there several times, witnessed it firsthand. And the refugees and humanitarian aid teams I've worked with report the same things I've seen."

"Like?"

"Human Rights Watch, CARE International, to name a couple. Then there's Save the Children, Freedom House . . ." His voice trailed off.

She sat quiet for a minute, mulling it all over before a thought struck her.

"So you work with Onesphore to get these people from Sudan to where? Here?"

"Sometimes. It's hard to tell how many have been dispersed since the war started. But like I said, well over a million have been killed, and we figure at least two to three million have been displaced. Those are the folks we're transporting."

"But how do you find them? Or maybe I should ask, how do they find you?"

Seth gave his knuckles another crack and reached for the almost empty soda glass on the table. He looked at the inch or so of remaining liquid, noting the clear and brown stratum where Coke had separated from the melted ice. He downed it in one gulp and was still thirsty.

"A lot of times, they filter over the borders into Egypt. Some wind up in refugee camps in Kenya or Uganda, sometimes Ethiopia. We don't have hard numbers on those. Our aim's been working with the embassies in Cairo and Nairobi when they've shown up seeking asylum."

"But hundreds of people at a time wandering into our embassies? How likely is that?"

"That's where the railroad comes in."

Mera squinted, shaking her head again. "And that sounds . . ."

"Really bad, I agree. Even illegal," he finished her sentence with an impish smile. "But it's not, I promise. The State Department's behind it all, thanks to one of the few good recommendations the UN's made in all of this. So even though we do a lot of working the system, it's completely straight up."

The magnitude of what he was saying was far more complicated than she'd imagined and, suddenly, Mera felt like she'd swum the English Channel.

This was the first demanding conversation she'd had in weeks. The first diversion in maybe months. And for the last few hours, she had all but forgotten her baby's death.

Now the break was over as a fresh spiral of grief threatened to reclaim her. Familiar, paralyzing tentacles simultaneously stung and wrapped her as she pictured Emily Kate's still little body for the zillionth time.

This time, though, she did something different. She decided not to let the anguish control her. Maybe later she would, but not now. She needed to hear Seth out.

"I'm part of a relief operation working with the government opposition," he was explaining, "a small band of rebels fighting the Government of Sudan's mercenaries, though before you start thinking in terms of good guy/bad guy, it's smart to remember that these guys are far from angelic martyrs. But they're fighting a brutal regime, so when we can, we get humanitarian aid in, pressure Washington officials to stop turning a deaf ear. On a local level, though, we're helping the south move their refugees to safer regions until they can be repatriated."

Repatriated.

That word again, this time, not for Chicago's downcast. But for distant Sudan's persecuted.

"So how are you doing that?"

"Carefully," he smiled and she couldn't help noticing how perfect his teeth were, how the tiny lines at the corners of his eyes were like little smiles of their own. "Point men in the southern army get their people across borders into refugee camps. Often the camp conditions are heinous. They're squalid, there's little food or water, sickness runs rampant like an angel of death. But some of these camps are in places where we have nearby embassies. And it takes some work, but from there, we get visas based on need for sanctuary. Other times, we move in with relief planes when we're notified of large refugee pools under siege. Those we fly out on emergency status."

"What happens after that?"

"Different things. Some folks get visas to the States, others head to Europe, or get absorbed by border countries. The embassies and reps at relief sites give them options, though most of them don't really care where they go, so long as they're with people they know. So we usually try and settle them in communities, like the group at my shelter. It eases the transition." Seth paused like he'd had a sudden thought. "Funny though, almost every one of them leave planning to return someday."

Mera brightened, remembering something.

"A few months ago, I read an article about a population of boys wandering for years in the Sudan. They were mostly orphans, I think . . ."

He shook his head fervently.

"The Lost Boys, that's what the NGOs and SIGs and media's coined them. Back in the eighties, when this all started, the kids were left to wander after their parents were murdered during village raids. So for years, they just walked, the blind leading the blind, not understanding what it was all about. A lot of 'em died, got killed by wild animals or drowned. Some crossed over into Kenya or Egypt or Ethiopia and settled in temporary relief camps. But that didn't last long, either. In just the last few years, we've been able to bring close to two thousand of them into the States."

She looked like her mind was buzzing with a million facts going in a hundred directions.

"But what does Onesphore have to do with all of this?"

Seth squared his shoulders like he was bracing himself for something big.

"I met him in Canada at an Operation Aid Sudan meeting. I learned about this whole fascist nightmare from a Taize buddy, Regis Devereaux. Regis was already involved with the opposition, and for several years, I kinda patronized him. You know, heard him out, never really intending to do more than that. I was busy enough holding the fort down here."

Out of habit, Seth groped his top shirt pocket for a cigarette, a gesture that ended with his hand falling empty on his lap once he remembered she didn't smoke.

"One day, Regis called me from Paris. He'd been working with another situation in Mauritania and he bugged me until I agreed to show up in Montreal for this meeting about the hell in Sudan. That's where I met Onesphore."

"But what's his role in all of this?" she repeated.

"At the meeting, he was like a regional representative of the Sudan. He's fluent in Arabic, Khartoum's native language. And he speaks both Dinka and Nuer, which are two major southern tribes. But here's the caveat: Onesphore's something of a switch hitter."

"And that means what?"

"Well, he works for the Canadian oil giant who signed the agreement with the northern government. A few years ago, Spectrum — that's the Canadian company — started drilling in the south, and Onesphore's the engineering field superintendent."

"So whose side is he on, the north or the south?" This whole story had the makings of a great movie. Somewhere between spellbinding and exhausting.

"He's an expatriate with Spectrum, the Canadian company spearheading the consortium. But since the production blocs are obviously in the south, southern labor does the on-site work. So on one hand, Onesphore oversees it all. On the other, he uses his position to collude with the south and the SPLA."

"The who?"

"The SPLA, Sudan's People's Liberation Army. The band of rebels resisting the northern government," Seth said simply, like vigilantes cracking down on corrupt regimes was normal.

"So what does Onesphore do with you?"

"Well, since he's got expat status, he's back and forth a lot, usually between southern Sudan and Vancouver, where Spectrum's based. But he flies into Chicago a few times a year with the cover of seeing his folks. And while he's here, I get updated lists and information on new refugees."

"Why you?"

Seth let out a long sigh before he glanced at his watch. It was nearly midnight, and he wondered if an out for the night would be his best bet. This was a lot to absorb, especially given what she'd been through.

She was staring at him like she expected an answer.

"How straight do you want it?" he asked reluctantly.

"Pretty darn."

"Okay, here goes: I'm the point person here."

"The point person," she repeated.

"Right."

"In Chicago?"

"In North America." He thought she might pass out as he scrambled to explain. "But it's not like running for Congress, Mera. There aren't multiple candidates on this ballot ready to rally to these people's cause. I just act as a central clearinghouse. Get the lists, call a few key folks in other cities. Then I get things rolling when the Sudanese head for the U.S., check in with the embassies and so on. Onesphore finagles the more complicated details."

If the last hour had triggered sensory overload, she wasn't letting on. Despite the unexpected twists and turns of this conversation, she had managed to stay right with him.

"Isn't that risky? I mean, keeping a double life collision-free sounds extreme, at best, with a constant chance that things could head south — and quickly."

"True, though his background, his family, even his education, buys him a great cover. But yeah, if he got busted helping out the south, the Sudanese government would have him on a couple counts. Collusion and conspiracy at least. Probably espionage on a really bad day." Seth traced his finger around the perimeter of a small hole starting in his jeans. "In just the last few years, he's helped thousands of refugees find sanctuary and resettle, both here and overseas."

"That would definitely make him a wanted man, at least in some corners of the world."

"No doubt. Particularly the one he works in."

"Impressive, though, especially since it runs counter to his day job." She was half-joking.

The wall clock struck midnight, twelve like chimes that cast a moment of dead silence in the room. Then Seth continued, his words more reflection than anything else.

"First pass, Onesphore seems a little odd, but you've got to know him. Once, we had a group of refugees getting immunized before deportation. Onesphore was there, explaining that one of the shots was to prevent polio." Seth smiled and shook his head at the memory. "Of course, the guys had no idea what polio was, what it could do. So one kid speaks up and asks what folks do when they get the disease. And Onesphore explains that best hope years ago had been the iron lung, a machine that would breathe for them since they were too weak to do it on their own."

Seth paused again, reliving the reaction in that stifling little room just outside southern Juba. Red dust and mosquitoes had filled the air and the vinegary stench of unwashed bodies shoved closed together made breathing almost impossible. The Dinka chatter had sung on and on, indecipherable music to him. But he knew he'd never forget the expressions that crossed their dark faces following Onesphore's explanation.

"Seth, what is it?" Mera's hand on his shoulder broke his thoughts.

He rubbed his cheek with the heel of his hand then pulled his fingers through his hair.

"It's what the refugee said when Onesphore told them about the iron lung."

He was quiet as if grappling with the memory.

"What did he say?" she asked after a few seconds had passed.

"Well, before Onesphore even finished answering his question, the guy ran forward and just dropped at his feet. I mean dropped." Seth paused again. "Then he started chanting something over and over, this beautiful, crazy-sounding jingle . . ."

"What was it? Did you know what he was saying?"

"Yeah. A nurse . . . she was one of the aid workers, she told me. He was saying the north tries to cripple us and we are weak. But you, *sahib*, you are our iron lung, you keep us breathing." Seth swallowed hard. "After that, no one ever called him Onesphore again. All the southerners call him Iron Lung."

Mera said nothing for the better of a minute.

"What an incredible picture . . ." She finally choked out.

He nodded and they fell quiet again, the stretching silence broken only by occasional cars passing on the street below. Next to her, Seth sat with his shoulders slumped forward, elbows on his knees.

For the first time in months she felt strangely satisfied. Almost full inside. Watching him deep in thought with the knowledge that he contemplated life so fully made something inside her warm.

He must have sensed her studying him because he looked up, his eyes soft.

"What is it Meranda, what are you thinking?"

"How good you are."

"Don't I wish."

"Then how do you explain the shelter, the help you give these people halfway across the world?"

"No different than how you hunt down, expose injustice in your work. You champion the good, hate the evil on paper. I just hit it from another angle. In the end, though, we're mostly doing the same thing. Trying to help folks who can't do it for themselves."

"Did you always want that?"

Seth snickered. "Are you kidding? I started this journey opposite of here. I had no father to speak of, and I saw my Mom suffer enough for two lifetimes before she died young. The last thing I wanted was to do anything for people who weren't useful to me."

"Really?"

"Absolutely."

"So what changed?"

"Do you remember that first conversation at the shelter?"

"The one about your trek to Taize?"

He nodded. "Yeah. I guess Taize kind of kicked off the domino effect for me. Things started making sense up there, things I'd wrestled with for years. And as they did, I got this clear view of God for the first time in my life. It was crazy . . . amazing. Because when that happened, it was like I was given a glimpse of what I could be if I'd just knock the chip off my shoulder and quit making everything always be about me."

Mera would have investigated that thought further, but Seth kept talking.

"When I saw how passionately that community lived, how seriously they took things like loving your neighbor and being your brother's keeper and just caring, in general, about what's good and right, I knew I wanted what they had. Keep in mind, I grew up around enough religion to choke the life out of Mother Teresa. But until Taize, it never once occurred to me that what I'd seen had nothing to do with God."

"You don't think they're related, religion and God?"

He shook his head to the contrary.

"I'm not saying that at all. I've grown a lot since then and I've known some amazing followers of Christ in local churches. But at the time, all I'd seen was people manipulating His name to get what they wanted." He shrugged. "I figured if that was serving God, heading toward heaven, I'd take my chances and risk the flames."

She winced a little, like what he'd said had hit closer to home than was comfortable.

"But getting a no-frills picture of the Christ, Jesus without all the cheesy add-ons, is what did me in," Seth continued. "My whole worldview flew out the window when I saw . . . really saw how far God's love drove Him."

"What do you mean?"

He thought for a second, a slight smile tugging at his lips.

"Well, I don't usually have a problem loving folks. In fact, sometimes I even think I'm okay at it."

"Better than okay. You're better than just okay," she said awkwardly.

"But I'm under no false notions about my love limits."

"What do you mean?"

"Well, let's just leave it at I'd never let a bunch of ingrates tack my kid to a cross, no matter how much I loved them. No matter how much good it might bring about."

Mera smiled. "That's the most offbeat explanation of the crucifixion I've ever heard."

Seth chewed his thumbnail like he was thinking hard.

"What Jesus did *was* offbeat . . . and radical. Which made me get to thinking that if He could do that to clear my record with God, I could start living on purpose, doing things that mattered. At the time, though, I had no clue what that meant."

"Do you feel like you're doing that now?"

"Mostly. Though, I have to admit there are times when I wonder. I guess it's like my life is this constant tug-o-war. Like I've gotten myself into this corner where everything I do — the shelter, the immigrants — boils down to who lives and who dies, who survives and who gets lost in the shuffle. And with no margin in between, it gets tiring. And, if you want to know the truth, scary."

"I can't even imagine."

"And sometimes, I question whether the stabs I take at these things do any more good than trying to irrigate a desert with a sixteen ounce bottle of water." He looked at her, hoping to find some kind of affirmation. "You know what I mean?"

She did, completely. And for just a second, she let her gaze find his.

"You mentioned most of the refugees want to go back home." She switched the subject. "Does that happen?"

"Like I said, they love their land, their people. But going home's not really an option until the civil war ends."

"And what would make that happen? From everything you've said, there's no silver bullet here, no easy answers."

He didn't flinch. "You're right. In a country where there's no rule of law, no checks and balances that restrain corruption, justice is pretty much a hit or miss thing. But the answer is this: war could end when both sides work out a fair peace that they'll stick to. And for starters, that'd mean the north quits sabotaging the south and its resources." He reached down to pick up his keys from the floor before he stood. "But in the meantime, we're at least getting them some education and training, a few political venues. So when they go home someday, they're hopefully set to make maximum impact."

Mera breathed in sharply, like she wanted to say something but then changed her mind.

"Mera, you okay?" Without warning, her whole countenance had shifted. Now she looked so pale and drained, Seth was sure he'd said too much, stayed too long.

"Fine. I'm good."

He wasn't convinced. "Look, you need to get some rest so I'm gonna head out now. I won't see you for a few days but . . ."

"Why?" She was alert again.

"I've got some business on the East Coast. I'll be back midweek."

"Oh."

"I'll give you a call from . . . while I'm there." He was vague, knowing how curious she could be. But the intensity of the last several hours had exhausted her, and she seemed content knowing he cared enough to call from wherever he was going. And he was grateful she hadn't asked where that was.

Chapter 23

Summers in New England had always cast a spell on him, even when he was very young. Maybe it was the sudden burst of all that was lifeless and subzero into pulsing color, warm air. Years ago, it was probably the promise of langorous days, unmarred by homework and ringing tardy bells. Whatever it was, Seth had never gotten used to the majestic wonder of summers on the northeastern seaboard.

But until now, with the silvery Charles River threading into and out of the horizon on his left and the sunrise spilling copper over Boston's skyline on his right, he'd forgotten how picturesque home was.

Home.

An odd thought after living so long in Chicago, a world away, a life far from where he'd come.

A life away from what?

He wound through downtown and though the morning was brand new, people buzzed through the streets looking frenetic as race cars warming up at the Indy 500. Men in suits talking into cell phones, women simultaneously smoothing windblown hair and swinging briefcases. Even tourists stirred along the Freedom Trail looking obvious in sunglasses and Bermuda shorts as they snapped pictures and studied folded maps.

Not much different than he remembered. Like Chicago, Boston never really seemed to sleep.

Sleep. Think about sleep now.

He hadn't so much as even dozed for the last twenty-four hours. There had been too much to do.

Make sure the shelter was covered. Priority calls returned.

This isn't an ordinary trip . . .

Wash some jeans, a few shirts, toss them into a duffel.

Head to the airport. Park.

Stay focused.

Board the plane.

Try hard to get some sleep.

Like rain to the desert, he craved it, but it was beyond his reach. Instead, there were images, one after another . . .

So he'd opened his eyes. Stayed awake to keep the demons at bay, which was no minor feat. Three hours had been like three years.

In the car now.

Think about sleep again.

He would check in at the hotel. Crash for a few hours.

Please let it be deep, dreamless.

Then a hot shower, something to eat. He'd already decided on coffee and bagels, maybe some juice. Isn't that what people did when they stayed in hotels? Sleep, clean up, eat. Normal things he did on autopilot back home.

Oh, God, why is this so hard?

Stuffing back his Tarbela Dam of recollections was about to kill him.

How did Atlas balance the world with all its imposing memories on his shoulders . . . when did he sleep . . . and what if he shrugged?

A random thought and he knew it, though the absurd image of Greek brawn and stamina offered a welcome distraction.

But before he even pulled his rented Honda under the Hyatt's porte cochere, he knew he wasn't going to sleep or eat or do anything until he went to whatever room he was staying in and wrestled with more than the purpose of this odyssey.

The last time he'd been back to Boston was to bury his mother, the person he'd loved more than anyone in the world.

He figured the trip here wouldn't be entirely productive, but even with the latest blow, he refused for it to be futile. For days, he'd run through a mental checklist of what was and wasn't most likely to be accomplished in this journey. And he'd already braced himself for how complicated things could get as his plan unfolded.

What he hadn't anticipated, though, was Jack's absence.

Zigzagging off I-95 onto the smooth ribbons of Highway 117 just outside Boston, he choked back the suffocating anger. He'd already pounded the steering wheel so hard his fist was numb.

Just stay cool, he admonished himself for the hundredth time. Figure out the options.

But it was hard, especially since he'd made this stupid appointment a month ago, four full weeks to the day.

He'd called Nottingham at 5:10 P.M., an hour later than he'd intended because he hadn't been able to see his way clear to a phone before that. Surprisingly, Jack Frasier's secretary had answered on the first ring, and after only seconds of turning on the charm, Seth had the woman putty in his hands.

His name was Father Roger Tilburn, Seth had confided, and he was a rector in the Missouri diocese — St. Louis to be exact. Business had him in Boston next month, a pre-delegation meeting, and while he was in town, he had hoped to check out the acclaimed Nottingham parish. Maybe even meet briefly with Father Frasier.

In a deep southern drawl, Marilee Monaghan, who had gladly volunteered her name, and seemed to want to share much more, asserted that Dr. Frasier would *shorely* be glad to visit with him. And within the hour, she'd called back to confirm a meeting between Roger Tilburn and Jack Frasier on May sixth at 5:00 P.M.

Feeling only a twinge of guilt about the alias, Seth said his thank you, wondered what Marilee Monaghan looked like and mentioned he also planned to take Jack out for a bite.

He left out the part about wishing it could be the priest's last supper.

Without meaning to, he'd rapped his knuckles against the steering wheel until they felt bruised.

Dr. Frasier. Esteemed rector of Nottingham standing behind holy lecterns delivering God-messages to unassuming parishioners.

Bastard, that's what he is. Literally. A spiritual bastard.

No child of God would do what Jack had done, then live with the travesty, the heresy, of it all. If God were at all the priest's father, wouldn't his conscience be a searing flame that demanded remorse?

Another surge of anger.

Now his chest was throbbing as he turned into a gas station for a fresh pack of cigarettes and a Coke. Inside, a girl with dyed black hair and a pierced tongue took his money for a pack of Camels and a hot Tab.

They were out of Marlboros, she explained, and the cooler had been restocked just fifteen minutes ago.

Why not? Everything else has gone wrong today.

He climbed back into the car. Lit the filterless stick before he popped open the can of warm soda. Then, despite his intentions, he headed east, the sun setting behind him as fresh air whipped through his cracked windows.

"I'm so sawry, Mista Tilbun," Marilee had apologized with a seductive smile when he arrived at Nottingham's sprawling campus. "Docta Frasia's fillin' in foa conference speaka in Dallas, a last minute thang." She really had the accent working, right along with the big hair and double D cups, fake or not. "He tried callin' yew, but yo phone was outa network."

She'd let another sympathetic smile slither over lips that looked collagen-injected. "He asked me to give yew this, though." It was a glossy folder adorned with a host of smiling people from the church. The inside was no doubt full of useless Nottingham publicity. But since there was nothing else to do, Seth had thanked Marilee as politely as he could, not believing his pathetic luck.

He'd used the last few months to decide what this trip might look like. As he planned, Seth found himself using a centuries-old method the early church fathers practiced as they had sorted out what the Christ was like.

Via negativa, they called the ancient principle. A backward way of figuring out who Jesus was, what He was like, by determining who He wasn't and the things uncharacteristic of Him.

Since he'd first learned of it in Taize, Seth had been compelled by the idea and its practical wisdom. And the older he got, the more it seemed that things really were as much defined by what they weren't as what they might be.

So he'd started a mental list of what *wouldn't* be accomplished while he was here.

To begin, there would be no accusations. At least not outright. Jack had too much at stake and he'd just deny them anyway.

And no talk of his stumbling on Meranda's journal. Which also meant there could be no mention of little Emily Kate or her death.

No. The only stunning moment needed to be the revelation that Roger Tilburn was really Seth Langford. From there, the tryst needed to be subversive.

So the plan was pretty simple: he would just let the priest know that something corrupt and leveling had happened to Mera. Something excruciating enough to keep her a lifetime prisoner of pain. Then perhaps an insinuation that Jack might know a thing or two about it.

The end result: Jack's conscience, if he had one, would start wearing him down.

In the meantime, knowing that someone in Mera's corner had something on him should be enough to keep Jack far from her should a case of sudden regret get the best of him. And considering Mera's frailty, that made Seth breathe a little easier.

But now, it wasn't going to happen, at least not according to initial plans.

Startled, he jumped as a fiery sting burned his lips. Lost in thought, he'd sucked the Camel to a tiny butt. But leaning over now to flick it into the empty soda can, he felt a new wave of determination wash over him.

If there was a distinguishing mark of his life, it was this: once Seth Langford set his mind to something, it would happen, regardless of the obstacles.

The sky glowed a grand finale of pink and blue, last embers of the day's blazing sun. Glancing at his watch as he turned onto a suddenly narrow road, Seth siphoned in a long breath.

His timing should be perfect.

Following the forested path's graceful curves and bends, he couldn't quite remember how long the melee of pebbles popping and crackling beneath his tires would go on. Was it one mile or six? He used to know . . .

The gravelly path kept winding and firing little rocks for another five minutes before it finally emptied into a wide clearing, where set back on impeccably manicured acreage were two structures. The first was a sprawling old English church that looked more like a castle than a house of worship. With its thick stone exterior and arched cathedral windows hooded in heavy-planked wood, it looked more home to Geoffrey Chaucer's friar and monk than a late twentieth century parish.

A smile tugging at his lips, Seth noted the stained glass was more beautiful than ever in the late evening sun. He'd forgotten how the patterns of interlocking circles flashed and glinted like fiery jewels before the dusk claimed their brilliance. The solid wooden doors were the same as he remembered, though. Meticulously arched and adorned with cast iron hardware, they looked as if they were the collaborative opus of a medieval carpenter and blacksmith. Off to the left sat the small priory, aged, but all the more beautiful for it and atop the parish sanctuary stretched the Celtic-style steeple, a needle that got momentarily lost in tall pines before it reappeared about ten yards later pointing heavenward.

The other edifice was a quaint, but good-sized rectory, a Tudorish house situated a few hundred yards away. It was surrounded by tangled gardens of dark creeping ivy and honeysuckle twisted about lilac shrubs in full bloom.

Scanning the length of the idyllic landscape confirmed his hypothesis. Parked in the driveway of the rectory sat an old blue Chrysler.

All he'd need to do was wait.

⌒

Thomas Kahlier was winded. Just walking downstairs from his office left him breathless and lightheaded now. He knew it was the pipe; too many years nursing it had done more than stain his fingers and teeth.

But it was too late to quit even if he'd wanted to.

Anyway, home was just across the campus, and at almost 8:00 P.M., the sky was flushed with dimming color and a pleasant breeze rippled the air.

As the parish doors thudded behind him, though, the old man felt himself tense.

Not another vagrant . . .

Just twenty or so yards ahead, a shadowy form sat slumped on a stone bench beneath two bark-brindled tallow trees with canopies so thick, only the gustiest breeze persuaded sunlight to break the green awning. The figure didn't turn around, didn't so much as move. Not even as the bishop shuffled close enough to nearly choke on the acrid haze of tobacco that made the twilight a lavender and silver paisley.

"Can I help you?" Kahlier started like he usually did. His Cambridge parish was wealthy and these drifters were usually content with a little transportation fare and a bag of non-perishables from the church pantry. Though he really wished the bum had wanted charity while his secretary was here . . .

"I don't know, can you?" Seth stood and faced the bishop. The dusk muted his features but the voice was familiar. Kahlier reeled backwards like he'd been struck.

"What in God's name . . . what do *you* want?"

"Which way you headed?" Seth dropped his cigarette and ground it with his heel. Then fell into step with the old man. "Out, or to the rectory?"

"Rectory." They walked in silence, the sunset spreading pinkish gold light over Seth's chiseled face. "Scar on your mouth's new."

"Good observation."

"Where'd you get it?"

"Selling Girl Scout cookies." Then noticing a look of premature irritation on the old man's face, he relented. "Actually, breaking up a fight at the shelter."

They walked on until they reached the front porch where Kahlier checked his mailbox before unlocking the door. Without invitation, Seth followed him inside then into the kitchen, which was littered with stacks of paper and mismatched dishes cluttered on the countertop.

"Want coffee?" Seth asked, opening the refrigerator and taking out a red can. It was sticky with little purplish clots of what looked to be dried grape or raspberry jam.

"Why not?" Kahlier settled at a badly nicked oak table in the adjoining breakfast room and fished a pipe from his coat pocket. He started digging tobacco from a small tin.

Seth moved about the spacious kitchen easily; within a few minutes, he had steaming coffee dripping into a glass pot.

"So, you just decided to drop in, see how things are going?" Kahlier was sarcastic.

"Something like that."

Kahlier cleared his throat but this only gave way to a coughing fit that took the better of a minute to subside.

"Cut the crap, Seth," he finally ground out, "and tell me what you want. By the looks of you, you've run out of money."

"Well . . . well. Some things never change. I see you're still breaking your back jumping to conclusions."

"And I see a man on the fray who isn't getting a penny more of my cash."

Seth put down the two coffee cups he'd wrangled from the far corner of a cabinet.

"Any *more?*" He approached the old man with a cool stare. "What's that supposed to mean?"

"Think, boy. Think real hard."

"Actually that's not necessary because I could think from now to the end of time and still end up at the same place."

"And what place might that be?" The bishop clicked his teeth against the pipe before sucking in deeply.

"The locale of I've never taken a penny of your filthy money. And you know it."

"No, of course not. You had nothing to do with duping me out of your mother's estate."

Seth took a deep breath. He'd been down this road before and he had no intention of traversing it again. Careful to keep his hand steady and even more vigilant to guard what came out of his mouth, he poured coffee into two mugs. He set one in front of the old man.

"You know as well as I do that Mother made her own choices. That she believed in me long before she ever believed in Wings Like Eagles . . ."

"Asinine project," Kahlier hissed, any remnant of civility giving way to disgust. "You were just too lazy to get a real job, a real ministry that meant you had to work."

"Like yours, you mean?"

"I'm a bishop, Seth. With jurisdiction over this entire region. And I train rectors to . . ."

"To what?" Seth's eyes sparked blue fire. "You train them to what . . . to be like you, Dad? To drown themselves in so much religion they forget who they're serving in the first place? To collect religious titles and institutional status, even if it means divorcing their wives and kids?"

"I never divorced your mother."

"Didn't you?"

"You fool, what are you inventing now? I was married to your mother until the day she died."

Seth sighed. Checked the volume on his voice.

"On paper, yes. But why is it I don't have a single memory of you showing her basic decency, let alone love? Why did I always find her crying over anniversaries you forgot and making excuses for promises you never kept?" With two fanning strokes, Seth parted the opaque smoke curtain the bishop had exhaled at his face. "When I was little I used to tell everyone how brave Mother was. How nothing and nobody ever scared her because she was like God. She could handle anything." He dropped his head for a second. Then looked up evenly at the old man. "But it wasn't that she was brave. It was that she had nothing to lose. And it wasn't that she could face anything, though she probably could have. It was more that if she didn't keep showing up, whatever that meant, no one else would do it for her, no one else ever had her back."

Kahlier said nothing. Just sucked his pipe and puffed out silvery smoke bands.

"So maybe you never left her on paper," Seth almost whispered, "but you were as gone as it gets."

"I don't owe you a thing, boy, least of all an explanation. This is a hard line of work, a calling that few ever understand. Overseeing and shepherding people is . . . ."

"Something you know nothing about," Seth interjected, not caring that he'd interrupted. "You call playing church, living in the limelight, service to God. But what about the bigger things? Things like integrity, like what you do when no one's looking? What about loving your own wife, your kid . . .?"

Kahlier took the pipe from his mouth and sat up straight.

"Okay, you want it straight? I outgrew your mother, that was the problem. She wasn't interested in the church. And that was my life. As for you, well, you've never been anything but trouble to me." The bishop's words were venom-laced. "You! You and your half-assed ideas and . . ."

"Go right ahead and say what you want about me. But hell's gonna freeze over before I let you lie about Mom." Seth deliberately lowered his voice again. "You didn't outgrow her, you sorry excuse of a man. You just found a new edition. And Mom knew it years before she ever caught you two in that office over there . . ."

A crimson stain flushed the old man's cheeks, but Seth knew the color had nothing to do with embarrassment. The bishop was incapable of shame.

"Your mother loved to speculate," Kahlier defended himself. "She could never prove anything between Louise and I."

Seth shook his head in disgust. Gulped a mouthful of coffee. It was strong and hot and it burned his mouth and throat. "Sure. Right."

"Don't patronize me, boy . . ."

"Then for God's sake, quit lying."

"Lies? You're going to talk to me about lying? After what you finagled out of your mother?" the old man rasped through clenched teeth. Thick blue veins bulged in his forehead. "And *you're* going to call *me* a liar?"

Seth mentally counted to ten.

"When I came home from the Rome Center and told Mother I was skipping law school, she understood," he said with an icy steadiness. "When I told her what happened to me in Taize, she got that, too. But not you, definitely not you." Seth shook his head. "Why is that, I wonder?" he said more for effect than thinking he'd get an answer.

"Why's what?"

"You'd think a bishop would be happy when his kid tells him he's finally made his peace with God. You know, I hated Him for years."

"Hated, who?"

"God."

"That's your problem."

"You're right, it was. I just had Him mixed up with you. Once I got it straight He was nothing like you, it's all been uphill."

The bishop sniffed haughtily.

"What are you getting at, what's your point? Running that ridiculous shelter's turned you into a moron. Look at you—when was the last time you shaved or cut that hair or even bought a pair of jeans?" He feigned a shudder. "God save you, you look like the freaks you think you're helping."

Seth counted to twenty this time.

"Look, I wonder if we can keep the digs to a minimum. I know how you feel about the shelter, about the fact that I didn't follow your lofty climb. I just thank God Mom understood. And that she believed in me."

Seth took a deep breath and leaned across the table.

"But so far as money went, you knew I never asked for anything. I didn't even know what she had until Jake Pennington read her will."

"You think I believe that?"

"You think I care if you don't? Mom left the money to me because she knew I didn't care about it."

Kahlier reached for his tobacco tin and re-stuffed his bowl. Then struck a match and pulled hard on the stem three times before a dingy cloud appeared.

"And since then? You can't tell me that in the last ten years you've lived like an Essene in the desert with no thought of worldly goods. That you haven't enjoyed the untold millions that belonged as much in my account as yours. Little huckster . . ."

A hundred ways to answer chased through Seth's head. Half of those he knew he'd regret even as they came out.

"Sir," he said icily, "you're free to check with my steward board. I have no secrets. I also have no particular wants which I suppose makes me unusually lucky." Seth took a swig of his coffee then wanted to spit it out because it was growing lukewarm. "So with the exception of using some of the interest to fund the shelter, that money's been in trust for nearly a decade." He looked squarely at the bishop. "She knew you didn't care if she lived or died. But for the record, we never once talked about money."

The air-conditioning unit kicked on and its sharp hum startled him. "I loved Mom, you should know that. More than anybody else in this world. I would've never hurt or used her like . . ."

"I did? Say it, boy, go ahead," the old man bellowed as he stood up and shifted his bulk. "You'd love it if the whole world knew what an ogre you think I am. Nothing would thrill you more."

Seth drew back and lowered his voice until it was nearly a whisper.

"You're wrong, Dad. I'm way past hating you. Truth is, I forgave you a long time ago. For how you treated me. For how you trashed Mom, though that was a lot harder . . ." He trailed off momentarily. "No . . . I don't hate you. I just feel sorry for you."

Kahlier rolled his eyes and resumed his place in the chair. "Please. Spare me the pitiful diatribes. And answer this: if you've got nothing against me, what's up with using your mother's name?"

Seth didn't blink.

"Kahlier didn't work anymore, not that it was ever a fit."

"And what's that supposed to mean?"

"You want the real story?"

"Your stories suck, boy. They always have. How about just sticking to the question."

"Do you know that I actually believed that freakin' lie my whole life?" Seth shook his head. "But you're wrong, man, dead wrong. You want to know why?"

Kahlier shrugged. "You obviously plan to tell me."

"Because there's no such thing as bad stories or good stories. Maybe bad art or good art. But not good or bad stories."

"What the . . ."

"By virtue of the fact that someone has a story, that they've got something to say, it's real and good and valuable. I just wish I'd figured that out three decades ago."

"And when you're done ranting, I'd like to know what all this has to do with you shedding your name."

"No, Dad," Seth contradicted the old man, "I dissed *your* name. For two reasons. One, we both know I was never the son you wanted. You made that clear. Two, after you tried suing me for Mom's money, I needed peace, and that sure wasn't happening while I carried your name."

"You little . . ." Shaking his head, the old man muttered a colorful expletive then returned to nursing his pipe.

Seth ignored the outburst and switched subjects.

"So . . . now that we're warmed up, let's get to why I'm here."

Thomas Kahlier dreaded hearing what came next. Though he hated to admit it, Seth had never been one to exaggerate.

"I can't imagine why you've graced me with your presence after ten years."

"Jack Frasier. The name ring a bell?"

Kahlier crossed his legs, leaned over to hike up his left sock. Then blew out a veil of smoke so thick it made Seth's eyes water and the bishop lapse into another coughing fit.

"What do you know about him?" the old man finally said.

"I figure he's your latest protegee. Your rookie priest who looked me up last year wanting the scoop on Taize." Seth swigged some more coffee then dug into his shirt pocket for a cigarette. "For some doctoral project he was working on." He struck a match, lit the stick and breathed in as deeply as he could.

"He told you I sent him?"

"Didn't have to. A blunder in the introductions gave him away. But it wouldn't have taken a rocket scientist to add it up. You and Doc Vernon have been friends since I can remember. It would have been a cold day in hell before you told any of your cronies at EDS that your son headed up some organic street ministry, compliments of a Taize gig." Seth offered a careless smirk. "You gave Frasier the wrong name to drop."

"What makes you think I told Vernon you had anything to do with the project? Don't flatter yourself. Frasier needed a topic to get his parish and the media's been all over Taize lately. That's the only reason you were in the loop." Kahlier looked bored.

"Well, he's done more than his self-serving paper."

"What's your point?"

"Jack has an old friend, a woman in Chicago he grew up here with. To make a twisted, long story short, your boy raped her last summer. Here in Boston after his mother died."

Seth watched the blood drain from the bishop's face. The accusation was all but a confirmation. For months now, even before he'd assigned Jack to Nottingham, the old man suspected something wasn't right. But with nothing to go on, he'd done his best to ignore the signs.

Kahlier reclined as best he could in the rigid kitchen chair while he dragged on his pipe. He appeared to be in no rush to answer until something came to him.

"What makes you think if something did happen, that it wasn't mutual?" He offered Seth a cunning smile. "You know, women have a thing for men wearing collars."

"For God's sake, and I mean for *God's* sake, don't you ever get tired of hearing yourself lie?" All Seth could think of was Mera's slanted red words with the torn collar crammed next to them. Without trying, he could see baby Emily's tiny form in her casket. "Or are the lines so blurred you don't know the difference anymore?" Seth clenched his jaw. "You know, I'm not even swinging at that one. Let's just leave it at I could scare up enough evidence to land your priest in jail. And that wouldn't look so hot for a stud bishop like you."

For once, Seth could see the old man sweating something out. Literally. Tiny beads of perspiration glistened on the bishop's forehead and he arched his neck in a slow rotating motion that betrayed otherwise perfect composure.

"What do you want, Seth? You've got money . . ."

"Money," he spit out the word like it was poison. "You can torch the money for all I care. What I'm after is a promise, an oath you'll keep like your life depends on it. Because if you don't, you can bet I'll be back with details gruesome enough to . . ."

"I said, what do you want?" Kahlier cut him off.

"Frasier to keep clear of Meranda Kaine. For good. I've no reason to think he'll be looking her up again. But in case he gets the itch, I want some insurance. Get my drift?"

"Your friend's a big girl. If this whole saga's true, why didn't she turn Frasier over to . . ."

"Maybe your priest is just a lucky guy. Or maybe Meranda's in a world of hurt you know nothing about. Whatever the case, Frasier's gonna keep his distance."

"Jack's a grown man . . ."

"Is he? Is this what your grown men do?"

"Damn it, boy, lighten up. What am I supposed to do? Put a homing device on this kid under the guise of sedition when all he lacks is a little mettle?"

"Come on, Dad, we both know how this works." Seth wasn't cutting the old man any slack. "Jack's your boy on a string and you know it better than I do. You got him jumping before you even say how high. Just like you do with all your boys . . ."

"Stick to the point."

"Frasier'll do what you tell him. And you're gonna make sure he doesn't go near her again. You'll let him know there's hard evidence ready to leak if he so much as picks up a phone to call her."

Kahlier stretched before he pushed his chair back from the table. Through the back screen door, crickets were chirping, a night song answered by a whispering breeze through the lilac trees. The air in the house was thick and heavy. Outside suddenly sounded like a good idea. He shuffled to the door, letting it thump behind him as he stepped onto the porch. He didn't have to look up to know Seth had followed him.

"You know, your mother loved the smell of these lilacs." The bishop breathed in the perfumed air like he was savoring it. "They were her favorite flower."

Seth shook his head and half-smiled at the old man's theatrical gesture. "No, Dad. The lilacs actually gave her headaches this time of year. And white roses were her favorite flower."

They stood on the porch overlooking the lush acreage of Kahlier's parish. Neither said a word. After what seemed hours, the bishop turned and faced his son.

"I'll see Frasier keeps his distance."

"Permanently," Seth added.

"You said it yourself." Kahlier raised his eyebrows like he was letting Seth in on a secret.

"Said what?"

Kahlier winked at him. "We both know how this works."

"Good," Seth nodded slowly. "I'll be going now."

Then without another word, he sauntered down the moonlit path to his parked car. As he went, the lilt in his step reminded Kahlier how much Seth liked skipping when he was a boy, especially when he was anticipating a promise kept.

Chapter 24

He finally decided he'd have to live with the depressing thoughts and harrowing doubts. At least for now. They were the temporary side effects of seeing his father after ten years. The fallout, he realized as he wadded his pillow in an attempt to get comfortable, of witnessing that nothing had changed.

Nothing.

It was his age-old story. Little Boy Blue blowing his horn at the Man in the Moon praying to God that the elusive Man would just for once smile on him.

Or even half-smile, Seth told himself years ago. That would have sufficed since he had jockeyed, not so much for Thomas Kahlier's affection, but for something of his approval. Early on, he'd learned love was out of the question. The bishop gave that to no one.

But Kahlier had never been any different than he was tonight. The immutable Man glowering coolly, intangibly, at the suspended world of a little boy below. A boy-turned-man who, even after all these years, still longed for some eleventh hour declaration that his father felt the tiniest bit of warmth toward him.

Exasperated, Seth yanked the stubborn pillow from under his neck and kicked off the stiff sheets and flimsy hotel comforter. It was insane to let it eat at him like this and he knew it. His father was sterile. Incapable of human connection.

So why, after thirty-seven years, was it still a splinter in his heart?

Reaching over, Seth switched on the light and glanced at his watch. Only 11:00 P.M. Which meant it was just 10:00 P.M. in Houston and David Brantley never went to sleep before midnight.

He didn't waste any time pulling the phone onto the bed and dialing the number from memory.

David answered on the second ring.

"Dave, dude." Long before David was a pastor, he'd been Seth's college roommate and best friend. It was a relationship that had endured mutual highs, lows and just about everything in between for the better of two decades.

"Hey, man!" David was clearly pleased to hear Seth's voice. "I was just thinking about you the other day. What's up?"

"Things are crazy, but it's all good. I'll have to catch you up when I get back."

"Back? You in Africa again?" David had followed his work in the Sudan years before he had agreed to be Seth's key contact in Texas.

"I wish. That'd be a whole lot easier than this." Reaching for the remote, Seth flipped on the news, hit the mute button. He stared at the anchor broadcasting late night news with such gusto that her nostrils flared and her eyebrows knit together in a semi-permanent line. "No, I'm sprawled across a bed at the Hyatt in Boston. Can't sleep."

"Boston?"

"Boston."

What's happening there?"

"I paid Dad a visit tonight."

That was all he needed to say. Seth heard David breathe in quietly before he spoke.

"How did that go?"

"The truth?"

"What else?"

"I feel like someone took me out back and beat the crap out of me."

Silence, for nearly a minute.

"I'm sorry, Seth," David said. "I really am."

"Brantley?"

"Yeah?"

"Remind me. Please remind me."

"Of?"

"That real pastors, real priests, are still out there. That some men behind pulpits and lecterns aren't using God to make names for themselves."

They fell silent again, this time even longer, and suddenly Seth wished he could see his friend's face, sit in the same room with him like old times.

"You know, Seth, my hunch is your Dad probably started out with a genuine call from God. And intentions for the greater good." David paused, choosing his words with meticulous care. "Most of us in the ministry do, you know."

"You know, Mom used to say that," Seth sighed. "She used to tell me stories of when he was in school and they were first married. Stories about how he loved Rosa Parks and how he once saved money to go to St. Jude's Hospital to see the little boy of one of his seminary buddies. Mom said the poor kid had been in a car fire. He had burns everywhere and looked like a little gnome. And when Dad saw him," Seth's voice trailed off for a second, "he was perfect. He just laughed and played cards and checkers and everything the kid wanted until visiting hours were up. And then he and Mom went back to the hotel, some cheap little dump, and Dad cried all night because he knew that kid's life would never be the same."

"See what I mean?" David was almost reverent. "He began well . . ."

"But I never knew that man. And while it's all well and good to score right out of the starting gate, it's the finish that's most telling." Seth leaned back on his flat stack of pillows and yawned.

"I don't disagree."

"I just wish I knew what happens, what makes a real boy end up a wooden puppet."

"That's a good one, buddy. Sad, but good."

"What is it about divine work that chokes the life, the passion, out of someone supposedly marked for God's service?" Seth continued. "What turns a compassionate lover of people into a megalomaniac who doesn't give a damn about anything but his image?"

David waited to answer, like offering a full measure of devotion to his response was of supreme importance to him.

"That's a tough one," he began, "one I've wrestled with for years. And the only thing I've been able to figure is that some of it must have to do with our titles . . ."

"What?"

"Take your pick. Preacher, priest, rabbi, pastor . . . it doesn't matter. Just those names give us a certain amount of influence."

"True, but that's not all bad."

"Heck, no, it's not bad. I mean, aren't we supposed to be the ones our people look to when they're trying to figure out what it means to follow God?" David was on a roll. "But here's where it gets dicey. Pretty soon our congregations put us up on pedestals. They do that, you know. They get to looking at our titles and forget that we're human, too. And you know the worst part? If we're not careful, we let them. We let 'em roll out the red carpets and treat us like we're up for an Oscar. We let them think that, unlike them, we've got it all together, all figured out, that we somehow live above the grit and grind of this life. And you know why we do it?"

"Keep going."

"Because it makes us feel a little like God, Himself. And whether or not we admit it, we like that kind of power."

For a split second, Seth was stunned by David's frankness.

"Man, Dave. That's brutal."

"Maybe, but it's true."

"You ever wrestle with that?"

"Seth, when I started this whole ride, I asked God to keep my heart from growing power-hungry hands." David paused again like he was looking for the right words. "You know better than me that there's enough religious faking and clawing and just plain greed to scare the hell out of sinners long before they get a chance to hear about heaven — or get a close up of the Jesus who hates the sham worse than they do."

Seth swallowed hard. "Isn't that the truth . . ."

"And I don't want to add to it," David continued, dead serious. "I never want to be a reason someone looks at God and says, 'David Brantley was a fake or a liar or an egotistical pig. And he claimed to follow Christ.'" He paused thoughtfully. "You know, Langford, I'm convinced people look at our lives and decide whether or not Jesus is worth following . . ."

Seth shook his head. "Brantley, after twenty years, you still blow me away."

"How's that?"

"You've stayed so real and I don't know how."

"That's easy," David volunteered. "I don't have an ivory tower."

"Did they tear it down again?" Seth joked.

"I'm serious. There's no king of the hill, here. No lord of the castle. Don't get me wrong, we're anything but perfect." David cleared his throat. "But God's made it pretty clear to me that leading these folks is more about entering their stories and loving them in Christ's name than it is about using my title to get my way. The latter is just spiritual bullying marketed as God's will."

Seth smiled at David's typical intensity.

"Profound, dude. As always." Then changing the subject, "How *is* the church doing?"

Seven years ago, David had taken a pastorate at Timbers Community Church in Houston, Texas. Since, the sleepy little congregation of just a couple hundred had mushroomed to more than three thousand members.

"Good. A few growing pains right now. But on the whole, it couldn't be better."

"You still doing three on Sundays?" Seth was referring to the sequential sermons his friend preached.

"Yep. And we started a Q&A thing on Saturday nights. For folks trying to figure out what the whole God and church thing's all about."

"If you somehow get it nailed down, let me know, will you?" Seth quipped. "I could use the help."

"Yeah. Like Michael Jordan needs help sinking three pointers."

"Hey, we all need a little steering every now and then. That's why you're on the other end of this phone right now, isn't it?"

"All I'm saying, buddy, is that you do church better than anyone I know."

"Right."

"I'm serious. In a culture that's re-imagining almost everything, especially faith and the church, we got folks debating and dialoguing and basically slogging it out about whether to have a church or *be* the church. Whether belief gets fleshed out better in the shape of institution or the organism of community." David paused for a second. "But not you. Your whole thing has always been about sticking to the point, dropping the vial . . ."

"Vial?" Seth was confused.

"Figure of speech, Langford. You know, the alabaster vial . . ." David paused as if he expected Seth to grunt his understanding. When he didn't, David kept explaining. "The one the woman broke open and lavished all over Jesus' feet while everyone else griped about the price and called her crazy."

Seth snickered. "Dude, I know that story and I know I drop a lot of balls. But I'm not tracking with your dropped vial motif."

David gathered his thoughts.

"Here it is: day in, day out, you break out the best you have and spend it on the least of these. You love folks who might not ever give a flip about you, lavish help on people who may or may not choose to embrace life and faith. And when the right moment comes, you've shown them so much of who Jesus is, there's no need to convince them that He's real and that He cares about whether they live or die." David took a deep breath. "How many people can you say this about in a lifetime?"

Seth was at a momentary loss for words.

"Our Father who art in nature . . ." he finally began.

"What?" David interrupted. "What are you talking about?"

"John Steinbeck. He said this thing that goes something like, 'Our Father who art in nature, who has given the gift of survival to the coyote and the common brown rat, etc., etc., must have a great, overwhelming love for the no-goods and the blots-on-the-town and the bums . . .'"

"So is this your latest manifesto?" David wasn't daunted by the quirky digression.

"No, but I like it. I like the idea that God steers nature toward survival. And then he turns an even more fierce kind of love on the down and out."

"And this is what I'm saying, Seth. I may preach four sermons a weekend. And I love it and love what I'm made to do. But your life is one uninterrupted sermon that makes knowing God and following Christ look like the most honest and noble thing we can do with our lives."

Seth didn't know what to say. Too many compliments made him uncomfortable and David had always been liberal in the praise department.

"I'm gonna need a root canal by the time we hang up," he jested. "You're ruining me with this sweet talk."

"And you're killing me by keeping me on the phone 'til all hours of the night. I hardly sleep anymore, you know."

"And why is that?" Seth asked, flipping the remote until he saw silvery porpoises slicing through lapis waters, a *National Geographic* special.

"Oh, just church stuff. Staff meetings. Hospital visits. Studying . . ."

"Then you need to get a handle on it," Seth interjected sharply, "before it winds up owning you. Promise me, Dave . . ."

"I know . . . I know what you're thinking. But I make sure I catch enough time with Lerryn and the boys."

"Play ball with 'em man, don't miss their games . . . hug 'em so tight they can't breathe . . . tell Lerryn she's beautiful and mean it . . ."

"I know . . . really. Seeing what you've been through has been a freaky reminder of how *not* to order my priorities."

A surge of emotion cut through Seth, and this time he didn't bother to stuff it back. It was Dave, his best friend. There was no need to hold the line with him. David, who had flown up with him when his mother died and did what he could to diffuse the bishop's raucous assaults even as Lucy was being lowered into the ground.

"God, I'm just so mad. So sick at what he does, what he gets away with . . ."

"What he gets away with or what you *think* he's gotten away with?"

"Both, maybe. I don't know."

"Seth, you know this, but I'll say it for the record. Men masquerading behind God for their own gain *will* answer for their charades. They'll get called on their heresies. Bottom line, buddy, there's a pay day someday, and everything done in His name, good or bad, gets tossed on the scales."

"I know. I guess it was just seeing him again, and finding that . . . that . . ."

"He was no different than the time before?" David finished his sentence.

"Yeah." Seth felt the ire inside him cooling, the tight coils in his belly loosening a little for the first time in days. "And maybe knowing for sure that there'll never be anything between us. You know, I think I spent my whole life wanting him to notice me, to say just once, 'good job,' or 'I'm proud of you.' I guess it was too much to ask."

"You've got to know that it's not you, Seth. It wasn't thirty-something years ago and it's not now. Somewhere along the way, your dad sold short. And I guess when he did, he decided making a name for himself was more important than people. Even when those people were his own family."

"Maybe that's true . . . maybe that's exactly what happened. But the older I get, the more I can't figure why. Because when it's all said and done, what could matter more than what you invest in a life?"

"You're preaching to the choir here," David agreed. "But your Dad's obviously in a different place."

"Yeah. Like the dead zone."

"Sadly, that may not be too far off the mark. Sure, he's got the vestments and the collar and the bishop's ring, but we both know the icons aren't enough. Think about it like this, Seth: he's on empty, spiritually bankrupt. So how can you expect more than what you got tonight?"

Seth let David's words sink in. "Your parish is lucky to have you, Brantley. Really."

"*Congregation*, Kahlier. How many times do I have to tell you?" David teased.

"*Now* who's forgetting? I haven't been Kahlier in ten years. And whatever they are, those Timber folks are way lucky to have you. You should tell 'em I said so."

"I'll do that next time someone hurls a spear my way."

"I'm serious, Dave." Almost like magic, Seth felt the weight of the last few weeks melting away. "You're a great guy."

"And, as usual, you're two fries short of a Happy Meal. Go to bed."

Seth could picture David's brown eyes dancing in his still youngish face. He could see him wrestling with his boys, twirling a strand of Lerryn's hair in his fingers.

"Thanks, buddy. For everything."

They said goodbye and hung up. For a long while, Seth stayed right where he was, staring at the glinting porpoises and twisting the phone cord around a pen with *Hyatt* printed on it. Then without any explanation, he felt a peaceful hush fall over him like a warm blanket. Without question, he knew David was in his Houston study, doors closed, on his knees praying for him.

Chapter 25

The weekend was a success, at least on paper. The delegation in Dallas had hosted more than a thousand Episcopal priests across the country — young, spiritual potentates set on leading their parishes from the oft-predictable highways of the twentieth century right on over into the cultural free fall of the twenty-first. It must be God smiling on him again, Jack figured, because there he was, younger and far less experienced than most of them, a keynote speaker on *"Helping Your Parish Find God in the Postmodern Church."*

Climbing the steps to his Nottingham Parish, he took his time looking around. As always, the view made his pulse quicken.

Beauty everywhere.

The late afternoon sun splashed gold over gardens of fiery poppies intermittently choked by honeysuckle and lavender gone awry. A hundred yards out, a granite fountain of a dove amid flames burbled softly, the water sheathing from the bird's wing span into a kidney-shaped pond bordered by heavy flint stones. Even from the steps, he could see the spray of connecting waters mist the air in a rainbow of glittering diamonds.

Majestic. Absolutely stunning.

He breathed in slowly. Tasted the sweetness that hung in the air.

These few acres of New England charm weren't at all sprawling like some parishes. He'd known that long before he came here. But the century-old sanctuary had been restored just months before his appointment and he loved that the classic architecture had been preserved despite expansions to accommodate the parishioners flocking here in droves. His own rectory was a spacious cottage directly behind the parish.

Twisting a key into the door that led to his office, Jack couldn't help thinking how good life was. It was good to be home, even if he did have a mountain of paperwork to tackle before tomorrow. Good to have calls to return and hospital visits to make.

All welcome indicators that added up to one thing: he was back.

He'd wrestled in solitude, a penance of sorts, for what he'd done. For months, he'd grappled with just how lurid human nature could become, how dark and carnal it had surfaced in him. But that was hopefully behind him now, replaced with God's favor. Otherwise, why would he have been the one Thomas Kahlier picked to fill in at the conference?

Another gauge of divine esteem: if God were still grieved with him, He surely wouldn't have let nearly every priest there offer the adulation he'd gotten.

It's good to be back in the game. Thank you, God, for second chances.

But stepping into a hallway of stale brown air, Jack knew he was fooling himself.

Because the ghosts were back. The haunting images of earth and wind cooperating with water and human fire made his spine tingle, his gut wrench.

He closed his eyes. Blocked out the visuals and tried forcing the legion back into submission. But they were many and though he was used to them now, once these demons showed up, they played like hell.

And they never left until he was worn out.

Thomas Kahlier never minded waiting. In fact, postponement was so much a part of his method in shaping others, he actually enjoyed the discipline of delay. It made the outcome all the more powerful.

So he'd sat for the last two hours, perusing a couple of magazines, then a book, and finally, yesterday's edition of *The Wall Street Journal*. Then he switched off the overhead light. But he wasn't restless at all, even as he heard the tread of light footsteps growing more distinct, keys jingling in the door.

Jack Frasier's office was comfortable. He'd seen to it himself that it would be. And with his feet propped on the desk, pipe in hand, all he had to worry about was what expression he'd wear when the young priest opened his door and found him there.

He'd barely cracked the door before the rancid odor hit him like a brick wall. He swallowed twice, mostly to keep from gagging, and though his eyes had yet to adjust to the darkened room, Jack knew Thomas Kahlier was perched somewhere nearby. He had to be. That sickening reek of tobacco, whatever it was, was his trademark.

Stepping tentatively into the slowly churning fog, he breathed in again. Felt his chest twist with the mixture of terror and anticipation that stench always evoked.

"You're back, son." The controlled monotone greeted Jack from the shadows. Trembling inside, he flipped on a light, rounded a short corner and faced the stock-still sight of Thomas Kahlier.

With his feet propped on the desk, hands folded behind his head, the old man was the picture of Sabbath. He couldn't have appeared more at rest. In fact, had it not been that the smile he was wearing was, upon closer examination, a forced smirk, he would have epitomized the benevolent reformers of old. But Jack felt his stomach lurch when he noticed the bishop's eyes. They were Arctic ice.

"Why yes, sir," he stammered, attempting to keep the quaver out of his voice. "I got back a few hours ago. I . . . I had a few stops to make . . ."

"I understand the conference went well." Jack didn't wonder how he'd found out. By now, he'd decided Kahlier was either omnipresent or he had connections just about everywhere.

"It did. We had more than a thousand and . . ."

"I know." The bishop cut him off again. "Sit down, boy." The invitation had a counterfeit warmth, but knowing it wasn't optional, Jack sank into a navy winged-back chair in front of his desk.

He tried inhaling slowly, anything to calm his nerves. But the dusty haze from Kahlier's pipe settled in his throat and he gasped out a sputtering cough.

"Nasty cough." Kahlier's gaze locked his. Then held as the old man pursed his lips and aimed a stream of smoke at Jack's face.

A sudden buzz of the phone on his desk split the air. Relieved by the distraction, Jack stood to answer it. He wasn't expecting the bishop to knock it out of his hand.

"Not now, son." His voice was a viper's hiss as he clamped it back on the hook. "It's Saturday. Whatever they want can wait."

Jack felt dread start to swallow him. Kahlier's molten anger was a gathering tsunami just minutes from breaking shore.

But it wasn't like him to show up, unannounced . . .

"Wondering what I'm doing here?" Kahlier read his thoughts.

"No . . . actually, yes. I'm not sure to what honor I owe this visit."

"Or to what disgrace." In one move, Kahlier swung his feet off the desk and sat up straight. "I know what you did last summer, Jack." He put the pipe to his lips and sucked.

"I . . . I . . . don't know what you mean," Jack stuttered, feeling the forces of nature crush him from every direction. For the moment, he was a rat trapped in a maze, a dreamer stuck in a nightmare.

"No, Frasier, no games."

"Now, sir . . ."

"Don't you 'sir' me, you lying fool." The bishop bared his teeth like a rabid dog.

Now that the steely composure had melted, Jack knew anything was possible.

"Please, Dr. Kahlier . . . please. I don't understand . . ."

"Then use what's in between your ears, boy, because I know what you've been using between your legs. And you're in knee deep."

Jack felt himself become the center of a spinning universe. A world of hearts pounding like snare drums and ears full of birds chirping and blood rushing and silence ringing. A cosmos of lost men facing dark gods in collars and bishop's rings . . .

Oh, my God . . .

He blinked back at the ancient verse burning at him from his mind's eye: "*Do not be deceived, God is not mocked; for whatever a man sows, this he will also reap.*"

Damned. He was damned now and he knew it. Being remorseful for last summer hadn't been enough . . .

"What are you asking, sir? Jack tried to collect himself. "What do you want to know?"

"What do you have to tell me, boy?"

"About what?"

He couldn't say it. He hadn't up to this point, and somehow, saying the words would make his evil real.

Kahlier leaned forward, his gaze a cerulean frost. "You know I'm a patient man, Frasier. But I'm giving you thirty seconds to come clean. And if it comes and goes, this is the last you'll see of me, the last you'll see of Nottingham, and the genesis of a whole new world behind bars." He arched an eyebrow. "And there's plenty to back it all up. Your choice, son."

He knew. Thomas Kahlier knew. Like he did everything else.

Oh, God, maybe he's Lucifer. Maybe he's your age-old Enemy garbed in a cassock. Is that how he knows so much?

Jack tried to steady his runaway imagination. The old man was human, he calmed himself. And besides, didn't Jesus once say something about Satan not being able to cast himself out since a house divided couldn't stand?

If the bishop was the Enemy, he would be celebrating evil, not reckoning with it.

"I . . . I slept with," he choked out, the words dry as desert sand on his tongue.

"Try again, Jack," Kahlier countered through clenched teeth.

"I . . . I . . . I . . ."

"You what? Out with it now or I'm out this door."

"I . . . I raped Meranda last summer. After Mother died. I didn't mean to, I swear, I never meant to hurt her . . ." His shaking voice faded to a whisper.

Kahlier set his pipe on the desk, folded his hands together and reclined back in the chair. For what seemed like hours, he sat motionless save the barely detectable grinding motion of his jaw.

"You sick, sad moron," he finally scraped out. "Tell me, what were you thinking . . . that she'd enjoy it?"

Jack felt his mouth fill with acid saliva.

"Oh, Dr. Kahlier, I don't know. I don't know what's happened to me. I loved her. I love her still." Jack slumped forward until his elbows folded onto his knees. He dropped his head in his hands and sighed before looking up to meet the old man's gaze. "Help me, sir. Please . . . help me."

"Help you what? Rewind the clock? Undo the deed?" Kahlier shook his head in disgust. "Tell me you knew better. Tell me . . ."

"I did. I do." Jack's eyes begged for understanding. "But it's like there's this otherness to me now, like some part of me has its own agenda. And when whatever it is takes over, I do and say these things that are like . . . like evil." The truth felt good even though he had no idea what the outcome would be.

The bishop said nothing for a full sixty seconds.

"Jack . . . Jack, part of you *has* changed." As if controlled by a switch, Kahlier's tone was silk-smooth now. Priestly enough to assuage the guilt of a converted mass murderer. "You've embraced your calling, my son, and God knows the little nuances and compromises we have to make to keep it all together."

Jack exhaled loudly.

"I don't know, maybe so. Maybe that's true. But none of that changes the fact that what I did was wrong. How . . . who told you?"

"Does it matter?"

"I swear I'll go make it right with her, sir. Or, at least, I'll try."

Kahlier laughed out loud, a sinister jeer that made Jack's skin crawl. "I don't think so, son."

"Don't think so, what, sir?"

"No apologies, my boy. And you can bet there'll be no confessions. Not on my watch."

Jack was confused. Was Kahlier outraged at his sin or was he just hacked that the deed had been leaked?

It had to be the first. He'd betrayed a friend in the most wretched way possible and the bishop wouldn't stand for such depravity. Any minute now, he'd get his penance, then counsel, how to make this right.

"Listen to me, boy, because I'm not repeating myself. Far as I'm concerned, your ass is history. Any fool stupid enough to pull the kind of stunt you did deserves what he gets. If you're that hard up, go get a girl."

Jack heard the bishop through a channel. Or maybe, he wasn't hearing right at all. It seemed Thomas Kahlier was furious about one thing: that he had been found out. Not that he'd sinned against God or hurt another person. Just that he'd been caught.

For a minute, Jack thought about tearing the collar from his throat and catching the next plane to Chicago. He longed to see Mera, ached to beg her forgiveness. For a split second, he could leave all this behind — the throngs of approving people, the command of towering behind a lectern. Like a dehydrated pilgrim staggering through a desert, he craved more than a mirage.

"I've covered for you this time, Frasier. But there won't be a next. Another stunt like this and you're out on the streets or wherever you land." Kahlier glared at him. Ran a papery hand over his shiny head. "I won't have you making me look bad. Do I make myself clear?"

Like a dark magic, the other self eclipsed Jack, at once absolving all doubts about Father Kahlier and his yearning to see Mera. Shoving back a final chard of uncertainty, Jack forced himself to remember all the bishop had done to get him where he was.

"Yes sir, perfectly."

"You don't talk to her again." A command.

"What?"

"You heard me. Any contact with her and you're out of here."

"But I need to tell her I was wrong," Jack objected, "that I didn't mean to hurt her."

"You know what mortal error number one was." Kahlier pointed to his equipment and heaved his girth upward, a rusty thrust. "And number two won't be happening."

Jack hesitated a second. "And what is number two, sir?"

"Fessing up to number one."

Jack felt the room spiraling around him. He didn't want to believe what he was hearing. Worse, he dared not contemplate the sincerity of the man saying it.

Kahlier puffed a few light clouds then stood up.

"By the way, Frasier . . ."

"Yes, sir?" Jack felt more spent than he could ever remember.

"You got six months to get hitched."

"To do *what*?" he said incredulously.

"To find Mrs. Right." Kahlier didn't flinch. "Mrs. Jack Frasier."

"That's crazy . . . impossible . . . I don't even know anyone I'd . . ."

"You should've weighed all this out before you unzipped your pants last summer." With a nefarious grin, Kahlier ambled toward the door. "Sorry, son, *you* raised the stakes. This is just part of remediation, now."

"But . . ."

"Six months, my boy. Nottingham's cream of the crop and I've got guys who'd walk through fire to be here. Show me how bad you want to keep it."

The bishop looked back one final time to wink at him. Then as he shuffled down the long corridor, Jack recognized a familiar tune drifting backwards, and horrified, he realized Thomas Kahlier was whistling "Trust and Obey."

Wiping cold sweat from his forehead, Jack realized, too, that the heresy of the hymn's timing was no coincidence.

And that he really didn't have a choice.

Chapter 26

It was past midnight for the fifth night in a row, and still, she had more questions than answers. At first, the epic task of grasping for something that resembled understanding had felt a little exciting, a quest of sorts. But the further she read, the more tedious and complicated it all got because each quandary seemed to be predicated on countless earlier ones that had cropped up only to be swept aside without any lasting resolutions.

Mera pushed aside a foot-high pile of papers and magazines. Then scooted Pedora off the couch.

Rome. That's what this cyclonic tragedy reminded her of. Julius Caesar's Gallic campaigns. His brutal conquest of 800 cities, 300 nations. All in the name of Rome's "expand or die" philosophy.

Letting out a long sigh, she dropped a paper-clipped stack of *New York Times* and *Washington Post* editorials onto the pile, pulled on her bathrobe and headed to the kitchen to make fresh coffee. After the last five hours, she needed the diversion, needed to think of something other than signatory nations and Hague and Geneva Conventions.

But now her mind was racing at near Olympic speed.

This whole thing was next to impossible, she informed herself for the hundredth time.

Distracted, she spooned out an excess of sable Arabian grounds, filled the water chamber to the half mark and switched on the coffee pot. Then she pulled skim milk from the refrigerator and a little Tupperware container of brown sugar from the cupboard. Anything to keep her mind off this wrenching saga.

No, she decided as she toasted half a blueberry bagel, some of these articles, at least part of this information, had to be skewed. Genocide or anything even remotely close to it wasn't possible in this day and age.

Not after the Third Reich and the still recent Rwandan ignominy. Not on the heels of the Bosnian war crimes and human rights abuses in Liberia and the Congo.

She thought again about the Roman dream turned empire. About how it was forged on the anvil of bloody conquest and human sacrifice.

But in antiquity, *nunquam iterum* had yet to be ratified into the 'never again' of the twentieth century because there had been no United Nations stopgaps in place.

Pouring the viscous brew into a mug, then warming her hands over the steam, she did a mental scan of the metrics.

A million and a half southern Sudanese dead, two million displaced. An Arab Islamic government in the north, a black agrarian community of animists and Christians in the south. North and south divided by the near-impassable Suud swamp, split sideways by the endless Nile River.

North and south polarized by issues and worldviews that were as intricate and copious as the sands of the Sahara.

North brutalizing the south in a no-holds-barred military campaign not unlike Caesar's eight-year conquest of Gaul.

Swigging a gulp of the searing liquid, she realized that she'd forgotten to add milk and sugar. Normally, she would have choked on the sludgy aftertaste, and depending on where she was, spit it out. She did nothing of the sort now, only tilted the mug and downed it to near empty.

Ludicrous. Impossible. Or was it?

Her head was spinning, not so much because the data was bountiful. It was more that it was all verifiable.

***

When Seth had dropped off a box of magazines and news clippings on his way out of town, Mera had all but bet that she'd find his

Sudan assessments exaggerated. Civil skirmishes were one thing. But the full-scale brutality he had described belonged more to early empires and emerging civilizations than the decorum of the twentieth century.

She was wrong.

An unprecedented civil war really had resumed more than fifteen years ago, even before Omar al Bashir and his National Islamic Front had mounted a coup for Khartoum's helm.

As Mera sifted through more than a decade's worth of articles, a staggering account unfolded, one with a dizzying mishmash of religious clashes, power struggles and wealth-sharing battles that stretched back centuries, perhaps milennia.

For almost the last week, she'd occupied herself with intricate history, not so much because it was interesting, but because of the chain effect. One thing in this nation was inexorably linked to another. And it was harrowing to follow. Tracing Sudan's origin from ancient Cush to Meroe to independent nations under Ottoman-Egyptian rule in the north, then a short-lived jihadist state compliments of Islamic Mohammed Ahmed's nationalist revolt, kept her jotting down notes every few minutes. Even after Ahmed, known as *el Madhi*, seized Khartoum in 1885 and lost it just four years later to Anglo-Egyptian rule, following the divided north/south politics was like trying to nail Jell-O to a tree.

The more she read, though, the more she realized how deep-seated the issues were and how oversimplifying them could only jeopardize hopes for a lasting peace process. True, Sudan had achieved independence from Egypt and Britain in 1956. Yet only a decade of harmony had ensued since. Otherwise, broken promises, corrupt government and militant religious demands had made power and wealth sharing impossible.

But the worst was triggered in 1983 when former President Gaafar Nimeiri reneged on a 1972 peace agreement and imposed *shari'a*, or Islamic law, throughout the entire country.

The south and its Nilotic people revolted.

Under former Sudanese army colonel John Garang, southern rebels formed the Sudan People's Liberation Army, or SPLA, as Seth had called them. Meanwhile, the better-equipped north embraced a tyrannical campaign that included everything from bombings and guerilla sieges to aerial attacks, scorched earth policies and enslavement of surviving natives.

It was all-out civil war.

Back on the international scene, mum was the essential word. Like Seth mentioned, the UN had slapped the NIF's hand a few times, the U.S. State Department had listed Sudan as a sponsor of state terrorism and the current administration was embroiled in talks about comprehensive sanctions against the country. That was about it.

Then southern-seated oil hit the radar of a Canadian energy giant.

But alas, no alarms sounded. Not as Canada's Spectrum forged a multinational energy consortium and not when one of the key players proved to be a Government of Sudan affiliate. And no alerts pealed when the NIF started signing off on exploration and production agreements that outlined oil situated beneath populated southern villages.

So with a perpetual green light, no accountability and even less intervention, the north had turned the oil-rich southlands into killing fields. Ant beds slated for extermination.

Sabotage was passed off as tribal infighting.

Rape and torture was chalked up to the religious agenda of converting infidels.

And just as often the government outright denied any clashes at all.

She took a final drink of coffee and dusted bagel crumbs off the counter.

If this whole debacle were true, why, for the last decade and a half, had nothing been done to neutralize the Khartoum administration? Where had the media been?

And why had this travesty not warranted an international response?

Chewing her thumbnail, Mera padded back to the couch where she sank down amid a sea of old newspapers. She started sifting again, this time through pictures.

Then she stopped.

It was a photo of a naked little girl, probably just four or five years old. The article beside it was ragged and yellowed, but the tiny, malnourished form collapsed on the desert hardpan was painfully clear. So was the hovering vulture positioned in wait behind her.

Glancing at the caption explained more: it was March of 1993, the child was on her way to a feeding center somewhere in the Sudan. A free-lance photojournalist there was snapping pictures.

The helpless little figure glared up at her, and for a split second, it was Emily's body, stiff and tiny in her doll-casket. But before the memory could debilitate her, Mera turned over the photo. It was stapled to another article.

This one was a world brief, a few paragraph blurb torn from the *Houston Chronicle* dated July 29, 1994. Reported from Johannesburg, it cited "Pulitizer Photographer Commits Suicide."

The article was about Kevin Carter, the same man who had photographed the starving Sudanese girl. A South African himself, Carter won the Pulitzer for his gut-wrenching depiction of the region. Later he'd been found dead, apparently of carbon monoxide poisoning. He was survived by a daughter of his own, the article concluded, though the fate of the little girl in his prize-winning picture remained unknown.

Staring at the montage of tiny words, Mera was overwhelmed at the power his single image had wielded. The photographer was dead, just thirty-three years old. He had lived and died and somewhere in between contributed something compelling enough to perhaps save lives.

Letting the loose pile slip from her fingers, she leaned back. Maybe Kevin Carter had no idea how convoluted the politics between Sudan's north and south were. Then again, maybe he'd known exactly what the situation was. In either case, what mattered was his picture might have made a difference, might have catalyzed change for others suffering like that little girl.

Then a certainty hit her.

What one person does can matter.

Kevin Carter had helped summon awareness of what was now being called the world's worst humanitarian crisis.

Day after day, Seth Langford helped Chicago's underprivileged while teaming up with Onesphore Barekhandi to aid persecuted Sudanese refugees.

One life. That was all it took to make a difference if the right moment is seized.

The reality wasn't brilliant.

But it was newly staggering.

Listening to the thrumming wind against her window, the whir of passing cars below, Mera traced her finger along the caesarian scar still healing beneath her pajamas. She thought about little Emily Kate and the life she'd never have. She thought about Jack, too, this time as he'd once been—good and honest and loyal.

Then she thought about her work. Her years of winding facts into story, and often, stories into a public action call. That was what she did, what she'd done with passion and purpose.

But what if everything she'd done up to now was leading her to this? To this scandal against a people in the Dark Continent oppressed by authorities deftly suppressing crimes against humanity?

Skimming her past like a book, Mera felt hopeful for the first time in months.

No doubt, she had a colorful history. Trouble had a way of finding her like she'd been somehow marked for it. And while that left a lot of unanswered questions, she sensed something else. Something new.

God just might use someone like her to help those people.

It was an appealing thought.

Maybe she didn't know the cacophony of air raids or shrapnel shearing through her flesh. To be sure, she'd never watched humans get gunned down like toy soldiers. But with her lifetime of losses, Meranda Kaine wasn't afraid of pain. Not her own anymore — and certainly not the plight of others.

In fact, sitting in the stillness of her den, the idea of choosing apathy under the guise of pacifism suddenly felt like treason.

What would happen from here, she didn't know. Exactly what would be required of her, she had no idea.

But as a light summer shower brushed raindrops against her window, she was sure of one thing: if and when the right moment arrived, there was no question whether or not she'd seize it.

PART II

Ergo

"Come, my friends,
'Tis not too late to seek a newer world.
Push off, and sitting well in order smite
The sounding furrows; for my purpose holds
To sail beyond the sunset, and the baths
Of all the western stars, until I die.
It may be that the gulfs will wash us down:
It may be we shall touch the Happy Isles,
And see the great Achilles, whom we knew.
Tho' much is taken, much abides; and tho'
We are not now that strength which in old days
Moved earth and heaven, that which we are, we are;
One equal temper of heroic hearts,
Made weak by time and fate, but strong in will
To strive, to seek, to find, and not to yield."

Ulysses, Alfred Tennyson

Chapter 27

It didn't matter it was hours past dark. The air was stifling like it was midday and a thin, rising mist made the earth an equatorial sauna.

They had been walking just ten minutes or so, ten minutes that seemed more like ten hours. But lagging behind now to unkink the spasm that gripped her back and traveled down her legs as copiously as the perspiration soaking her skirt and blouse, Mera studied the yet unnamed attendants hauling the remainder of her luggage.

They were semi-miracles of nature.

Moving like there was no time to waste, the shadowy figures in their little caravan forged on, undaunted by the airless night or the oppressive weight on their shoulders or the fact that only a single lantern lit the unfamiliar path. A reed-thin man who stretched infinitely toward the sky led the way, followed by a cloaked female version of him. The lanky giant wore a headlamp, but its crude funnel of indigo light had gone out almost immediately after he'd switched it on. They didn't seem to notice that as they walked, the ground beneath them crunched out a steady rhythm, almost melodic.

Fifteen minutes later, a long row of flat buildings surrounded by a mud brick bastion appeared out of nowhere. Adobe-like, the squatty structures rested behind a heavy entrance gate and a weak candlelit flame at each door split the darkness. Identical and adjoining, the straight line of them continued one after the other until they were swallowed into the inky horizon.

The angular man stopped abruptly, his dark features anxious and glistening with sweat in the jaundiced light. A quick look around and he pulled a key from his torn shirt pocket. Then he worked it into the iron-barred gate before he opened it wide enough for Mera and the quiet servant woman to slip through.

"This way, madam, we are not far now," the man said above the low moan of the passageway clamping shut. His English was broken, tinged with an accent.

Mera nodded and shifted the heavy bundle in her arms. She felt suddenly nervous but it was too late for that now. There was no going back. Because after more than a year of planning and praying and finagling, she was finally here.

In Africa. In the Sudan.

Looking up at the hazy pearls glowing beside a veiled moon, she marveled that the universe's ceiling looked far different in the savannah woodlands of southern Sudan than it did in Chicago. From what she could see, though, the company compound didn't look at all unlike the government wards of the Windy City . . .

They walked on, no sound but the dusty gravel's snap beneath them and the labored breathing of the two native workers. Like the towering man, the woman next to her was tall, nearly six feet, and waif-like. But unlike him, she was swathed neck down in a *jilbab* that finally ended at her sandaled feet. Her head and throat were covered, too, in a *hijab*. Only her face and hands were visible.

A minute later, the woman breathed in sharply then buckled under the weight of the luggage she carried. Stepping up her pace, Mera swept to her side then groped in the shadows to take a bag from her. She didn't expect the woman to jump like she'd been spooked.

"No, madam," she resisted staunchly, "your belongings are mine to carry." She reallocated the bulk, refusing Mera's help. "You must let me."

Just then, the man stopped in front of one of the identical doors. In a jerky move, he lifted his sleeve to his dripping face and mopped at the rivulets coursing down his face. Then he fished another key from his pocket, pushed it into the door and wrangled with it until red dust misted everywhere. The jams and seals had completely crusted over and now thin sediment crumbled away from the door's blue-chipped paint and filled the air. Panting heavily, the man jimmeyed his way into the black void then used Mera's bulkiest bag to force back the door enough for her and the woman to follow him inside.

"You are home, madam." He sucked in a deep breath then let the luggage drop from his hands before he flipped on a light switch. Then he stood upright, and free from the weight he had carried, the guide looked to be nearly seven feet tall. He was the color of midnight. "Welcome. Welcome to the Sudan. I am Abdullai. This is Mashada and we are both here to assist you."

Abdullai returned to the door. He carried the rest of what she and Mashada hadn't gotten inside before he pointed to a wooden bassinet set beside a long bulky sofa the color of dried oatmeal.

"Mr. Wellington requested the bed. Separate for your son . . ."

"My nephew," Mera clarified quickly, "the child is my deceased brother's son." She looked down at the sleeping toddler curled in her arms.

"Of course, madam. I am sorry for your loss." Abdullai's gaze met hers, deep and somber. "But if all is well now, I will take my leave. Mashada, though, will remain with you." The woman still hadn't spoken, other than the few contesting words over Mera's bags.

"For the evening?" She didn't understand what he meant.

"Of course. For all evenings. And for all days," Abdullai explained with a sweeping sort of dignity that conveyed that he took pride in the order of things. "She is your attendant while you are working in the Sudan with Spectrum."

"There must be some mistake. I didn't ask for . . . a . . . for any help other than someone to oversee Donovan during the day . . ."

"Of course, madam. But it is custom here. In the compound, every company worker has an attendant, sometimes many. During daytime, a girl will come to help Mashada care for the son of your brother."

"But that won't be necessary," Mera insisted. The thought of four people in the cramped rooms was overwhelming. "I'm sure this kind woman will be enough."

"Indeed, madam. But this is how it is done here." He offered a polite nod toward the woman. "You will find Mashada a very faithful servant and her helper . . . how do you say . . . adequate. Good evening, now. And welcome." Abdullai bowed slightly, the light casting a powdery sheen over his ebony features. Then he closed the door behind him, leaving Mera alone with the silent Mashada and her sleeping Donovan.

Her mind had no intention of shutting down for the night, at least not yet. She was too wired, way too restless.

In the little bed beside her, Donovan was sound asleep, gauzy moonlight from a window across the hall painting his baby face silver. His rhythmic breathing matched the metronome of her ticking clock and the two familiar sounds together made her forget, at least for a minute, how far away home was.

It must be well after midnight, she figured, though she hadn't checked the time. Considering the past few days might as well have been years ago now, gauging time in minutes and hours felt newly meaningless. Even as she had unpacked Donovan's little clothes and put away her own belongings, she felt Chicago's bright lights and noisy bustle already belonging to another world.

Then she climbed into the narrow bed that was hers now. Hers for only God knew how long . . .

She didn't realize she had drifted off until she woke with a start drenched in briny sweat. Sitting up and peeling her sticky nightgown from around her legs, Mera realized the compound's generator had kicked on the air-conditioner, a strident thump followed by a long, shrill whine. Such clanking and clatter seemed superfluous considering the dusty air was anything but cool . . .

Wide-awake again, she checked Donovan, who lay beside her since the bassinet had proved undersized for his chubby toddler body. Seeing all was still well with him, she headed into a tiny bath off the hallway where she splashed filtered water from a basin over her face. Through a crack in the second bedroom door, Mera heard the rustle of bed sheets and Mashada's even breathing. At least someone was getting rest.

Without making a sound, she navigated the semi-darkness, opened the front door and slipped outside. A weak breeze fanned her hair as she sank onto the two by five concrete landing that doubled as a porch.

She looked around in the heavy silence. Tried to take it all in. But everything was so new.

The baby sleeping soundly inside.

This line of tiny barracks lit by a full moon in an uninterrupted sky.

The rusty-butterscotch hardpan beneath her feet that seemed to go on forever.

What a difference a year could make . . .

~

It started last summer though it was impossible to pinpoint what went with what.

There was work and Seth and the refugees at his shelter. The omnipresent ache of losing little Emily. And, of course, the lies to hide the truth of it all.

As a little time passed, there came, also, the fact of two undeniable things: she would give almost anything to help relieve the Sudanese plight — and nearly whatever it took to interrupt the collision of emotions that somehow went with the re-forging of her friendship with Seth.

Then an explosion killed almost a thousand natives near one of Spectrum's southern production blocs. The catastrophe registered only a few seconds in the world news, but not one account linked the devastation to the pursuit of oil in the region.

Two days later, though, the media was up in arms. Terrorist training camps outside Khartoum had been identified and early reports linked them to NIF sponsorship.

"I want to go," she told Seth one night over dinner. It had evolved into a semi-routine with them shortly after she'd gone back to work. Once the shelter was mostly settled for the evening, they slipped out to eat burgers at Ike's, a little hole in the wall just a few blocks away from Wings Like Eagles.

The place was empty except for Ike and the 10:00 P.M. headlines booming out the Sudan terror camp story.

"Go where?" he said between bites of his burger.

She pointed at the big screen suspended in a corner.

"There. Sudan."

He shook his head. Slurped the foam off his root beer. "It's really bad there. You know that." He sounded like he was admonishing a preschooler.

"I know. But I wish there was a way to work over there. A way to get close enough to the politics to do something."

He studied her carefully. "Like what?"

"Like what?" she echoed, deep in thought. "Hmmm, okay . . . I guess something that lends itself to a sort of reconnaissance. Like what you and Onesphore do, except different."

"And what would that look like?"

"Like being so entwined in the daily operations, you just naturally close in on the golden ring. And then at the right time, you blow a whistle on it all."

His eyes narrowed a little and he shook his head.

"I don't like the idea of that."

"I do," she answered impishly. "And you know you could help make it happen if there was ever a chance."

He didn't answer. Instead, he stabbed French fries and burger with his fork, dragged it through ketchup and put too much in his mouth.

Two weeks later, though, it was final: she was Spectrum's Sudan-based public affairs rep in the concession fields north of Bentiu. With censure from the explosion, plus the terrorist camp scandal, Spectrum said her background was just what their sagging image could use.

The only snag: she needed to be on location in just six weeks. And she needed to tell Seth.

"Sit down." Mera was nervous as they locked up the shelter nearly a week after she'd firmed up her plans. It had taken her that long to muster up the courage to tell him, and it wasn't until they stopped at the front kiosk for Seth to sort through phone messages that she blurted it out. "I have something to tell you."

"What, you won the lottery and I get half?" He looked up with an unsuspecting grin.

"Funny."

"Yeah. But it's a fun thought, huh? We could run away, live happily after." He made a wry face. "Whatever that means."

She looked around. Then at him. "It means this." She gestured at the surroundings. "What happens here is the chance of a lifetime for some folks. The realistic version of happily ever after. So no getaway plan for you."

"Aw, man . . ." He feigned disappointment but his cheeks flushed with her compliment.

"Seriously, it's about a call I got." She took a deep breath. "The call I got last week."

Seth blinked. "What call?"

"Spectrum."

"Spectrum?"

She nodded.

He sat down behind the kiosk. "They called last week?"

She shook her head, willed herself not to look away.

"And?"

"They want me."

Silence stretched between them for several seconds.

"They want you," he repeated, like his mind had gone blank. She nodded again.

"Right. Of course they do. They'd be stupid not to." Though matter-of-fact, the words sounded leaden, as if he was forcing his tongue to produce them.

"Next month. They said November's a good time to go."

"Right," he said in an almost inaudible whisper. "The rainy season's past." He leaned forward, elbows to his knees. For a long time, he said nothing.

"Seth, what's wrong? Isn't this what we hoped for?"

"No," he said, raising his head to look straight at her. "It's not."

"Then what . . ."

"What we've wanted is healing for these friends. We've prayed for intervention and a fair peace. We've lobbied for change, worked for reconciliation. But never for an instant have I pictured you parachuting into a war zone with no rules other than win or die . . ."

"It's not that bad, Seth."

His eyes sparked. "You haven't been there, Mera. It *is* that bad. When you've got a crammed garrison of dehydrating fourteen and fifteen year-old boy soldiers gagging on the stench of their nineteen year-old commander's rotting corpse while they wait out the latest mortar round and pray the shelling doesn't tear up their buddies in the outpost fifty yards away . . . when you pick up a tiny kid who looks two but is said to be five and his thigh is this hollow hole of oozing gel and bloody maggots because two weeks ago, a government solider tried to finish him off in a village raid, but he lived for the time being . . ." Seth's voice trailed off.

She looked at him, horrified. "But you called Onesphore for me about this job . . ."

"You're right, I did. But I called him because you practically asked me to," he answered shortly, "because it's something you said you wanted."

"But Onesphore . . . he doesn't even like me. If he thought for a minute that you weren't behind me going, he would've never agreed to recommend me. You know that."

Seth shrugged like the movement might somehow lighten the weight he was carrying.

"What I know is Onesphore's just a quirky kind of guy, Mera. No one ever figures him out. And I called him because it was what you wanted," he repeated, a hollow edge to his voice.

She let several more seconds pass.

"Seth?" she finally said.

He looked up.

"Are you not hopeful about what this could mean?"

He stood up then. Took her face gently in his hands. The half-wild, half-tender look in his eyes momentarily unnerved her.

"Look, Mera, I totally get what you're saying. And while I appreciate your intentions, I don't share your sentiments. You treading into 'access denied' territory is actually the last thing I want." He swallowed. "Ask me why."

"Why?"

For a second he looked satisfied. "Okay, here it is: I know what we agreed to, what we decided last year. We're friends . . . good friends. That's supposed to be it." He tilted her face toward his until just a few inches were between them. "But somewhere in this whole thing, it's all changed . . ."

"Seth . . ." She wanted him to quit looking at her like that because it made everything in her hurt and want more at the same time.

"Let me finish," he said almost roughly as he pressed his fingers against her lips. "I'm not sure how to say this, or even if I should . . ."

"Then don't." She moved his hand, realizing where he was headed.

"If you're flying out of here, half a world away, I'm gonna say it."

She pulled back and tightened, but he drew her close and turned her face again until her eyes locked into his.

"I love you, Meranda. I've loved you from the first time you sat in my office and listened to me ramble on about Taize."

"You never ramble." It was all she could get out. Her ears were ringing, her stomach had no bottom and more than anything, she wanted to echo his words. But they were so far back in her, she knew they'd never come out.

"I love you," he whispered again, "and I can't let you leave here without knowing." He reached for her hands, threading his fingers through hers.

Then he pulled her against him, so close she could feel warmth coming through the thick cotton of his shirt, his heart beating in her ear. And this time she didn't fight him. Instead, she'd lost track of the minutes standing there, holding on like it could never be time to let go.

~

The business of leaving came next. Resign from her *Tribune* post. Fill out reams of endless paperwork that went with getting a visa and passport. Then medical documents, immunizations and the records to go with them. The red tape was unending and at the finish of it all was still more paperwork.

That's when the call from Annalise had come. And the news was bad.

Kyle, one of her twin brothers, and his wife had been killed, her mother wailed over the phone. A terrible car accident. Within the hour, Mera was at O'Hare booking the first flight out of Chicago to Boston.

She was gone for three weeks. When she returned, it was with an unexpected bundle. A toddler she explained as Kyle's youngest child.

Little Donovan was beautiful, with wide, green-gray eyes and dark, curly hair. Only eighteen months old, he had the disposition of an angel and a smile to match his sweetness. One look at him, she later told Seth, was all it took for her to decide she'd take the child and give him the best life she could offer.

And as she had toted his small plump body aboard the plane back to Chicago, she felt the razor-sharp anguish of Emily's death soften a little.

Chapter 28

It was Mashada that made the cramped quarters a reality. Dappled morning light warming her face was common enough and the drab walls with cowering ceilings did little to jog her sleep-fogged memory.

But the silhouette of a willowy dark woman was something new. Something different.

Maybe in a dream, but perhaps half-awake, Mera opened her eyes and tried to decide whether the colorless linen and wiry frame were reality. Either way, she was so groggy . . .

Then came pacing, maybe from a dream world, maybe from the kitchen — and a tune that belonged to another universe. It floated about like incense, this aria, filling the air with arabesque flutings that had some secret power to tranquilize and possess at once. At attention (at least her mind was fully alert), she worked hard to wake up, determined to will herself from the vortex of it all.

No luck. Somehow her sleep-trance was tied to the melody. And it wouldn't break until Donovan wailed.

Then the tall dark ghost wafted by her open door to collect him.

Now she knew it was real.

The trip from Chicago to London. The flight from Heathrow into Cairo. Then finally, the journey from Khartoum into the newly verdant southlands.

Without a doubt, it had all happened, and if nothing else made it real, Mashada was the proof.

Now, as filigreed sunlight—compliments of a yellowed lace curtain hanging in her tiny bedroom window—cast florid shadows on her walls and down the hallway, Mera strained to get a better look at the woman holding Donovan. This was an easy feat considering space in the quarters was minimal. The entire bungalow was a mere two tiny bedrooms off a single narrow hall-path attached to a small living area and minute kitchen. Mashada stood there now, in plain view.

In the day's white-gold light, Mera noticed again how unusually tall the woman was, and from the way her cheekbones jutted, stick-thin. Like last night, she was swathed in a featureless linen *hijab* and *jilbab*, but the morning's rays revealed truths the evening had kept secret.

Her eyes. It was her wide haunted eyes that did her in. Two dark pools, they seemed to take in everything yet promise to say nothing.

Otherwise she was all tranquility. All plum-black lines and etchings that angled upward, as if to say that despite a perpetual threshold of angst and tension, she had chosen to embrace life. When she moved, it was a graceful glide, almost queen-like. And though her hands appeared leathery-rough and worn to a shade lighter than the rest of her, she cradled Donovan close, the way a mother would her child — one hand buried in his curls, the opposite cupping his chubby bottom.

Fully awake now, she sat up, pushed back the stiff white covers and breathed in the rich aroma of fresh brewing coffee. The curious sweet-spice that hung in the air was almost intoxicating.

"You are awake, madam." Mashada lowered her eyes and bowed slightly as Mera stepped into the kitchen a few minutes later.

"Good morning, Mashada." Then reaching for little Donovan, "Hello, sweety, how did my big boy sleep?"

The child fastened his plump body tight against Mera and dug his stubby fingers into her newly combed ponytail.

"Bibboy, bibboy." *Big boy, big boy.* "Donban pay Meerie." *Donovan play with Mera.* He looked as emphatic as a toddler possibly could.

"Okay, little pal." She kissed his pink fleshy cheek, tousled his ringlets and breathed a silent word of thanks that it was just

Saturday. The long travel had caught up with her and Donovan could use some extra attention before another week got underway.

"Pay aowpanes." *Play airplanes.* He wriggled free from her arms and spread his own like two wings, flying through the tiny rooms.

Mashada watched, her wide eyes solemn.

The day passed quickly, without event. Donovan was tired and napped twice, two hours both times. True to his word, Abdullai reappeared like a bellhop in a hotel, checking the order of things. He also passed on a message that Jake Wellington, Spectrum's Sudan-based general manager, would be by tomorrow.

But Mashada was the twist Mera had least expected. The woman was so quiet that sometimes only her breathing signaled she was in a room. She stayed close to Donovan, like she was learning to anticipate his every move. She changed his diapers, though Mera protested, and she returned his toys to neat piles almost as quickly as he scattered them.

Twice, the woman disappeared without notice into the barrack's tiny kitchen. Both times, she had reemerged to set the table with prepared meals. The first time it was rice and beans, the second, a kind of rice and meat dish that tasted as good as it smelled.

Several times, Mera tried making conversation with her, but the woman was either painfully shy or had no interest in idle chatter. Since she couldn't figure which, Mera let the silence hang between them and tried hard to ignore its awkward weight.

For now, she told herself, she could be grateful that Mashada seemed to enjoy Donovan and that she didn't mind cooking. There were no fast food stops in southern Sudan, and she'd never been much of a cook . . .

But she couldn't help wondering as she tucked Donovan into bed that night why Mashada had seemed mesmerized by his toy helicopter. All day, she'd stolen dark glances at the child's little fist, which had been invariably wrapped around the coal-black plane.

The behavior seemed odd. Spectrum's mud and gravel landing strip was just a few miles from the compound. Surely the woman had seen her share of company jets and helicopters coming and going.

But with the taciturn wall between them, there was nothing to do but wait and see what time might tell.

Chapter 29

Onesphore was waiting for her outside the compound gate at 7:00 A.M. sharp in a battered Land Cruiser, probably chalk white ten years ago. Now it was lacquered in thick red dust, just a few gaps of tainted ivory peering through. The engine alternatively whined and clicked, threatening the heresy of quitting once and for all.

Mera climbed in, pulled the door shut and half-shouted a greeting over the vehicle's rattling machinations. Onesphore's reply was a terse nod, no eye contact.

"Did Wellington stop in?" he finally inquired after he'd shoved the groaning vehicle into drive and proceeded toward a crude road-path. For some reason, the Cruiser quieted a little as it rocked over the graded dusty trail scythed five feet on either side from knee-high brush and tall soft grass.

"Yesterday, about noon."

"He said to take you to the fields first."

Mera nodded. "He mentioned something like that."

"But that is not where you will work," Onesphore said, a disdainful edge to his tone. "Wellington just figured you should see the operations."

They drove eastward, silent for a few minutes as the low morning sun stretched, then burst, into orange-pink flames over the shrub-scattered horizon. Watching the blazing color awaken the pale-lit morning, she felt her breath catch in her throat.

"I had no idea it was so beautiful here."

Onesphore glanced sideways at her, his rigid features unmoved.

They chugged along, past a cluster of acacia trees and over plains of billowing grass and scrubby bush that seemed partial to clinging close to the rusty earth from which it proceeded. In the distance, Mera watched a pack of slender-horned gazelle grow smaller and thinner until the vast expanse swallowed them. Like a wide-lens camera, she took it all in — the artistry of endless skies, the crystal dew blanketing everything green, the unfamiliar wildlife that dared to move and breathe alongside humanity — one image after the other, ones from every direction, declared the pride of Africa.

"You have met Mashada?" Onesphore's question broke her thoughts.

She shook her head. "She's very kind. Wonderful with Donovan." The thought of the chubby child made her smile.

"Mashada is one of the best in these compounds."

Mera hesitated, then decided to ask the question anyway. "The servants here, they're hired mostly from the north aren't they?"

Onesphore shrugged. "Why do you ask?"

"Mashada . . . Abdullai . . . they seem to practice the northern customs. You know, their clothes, the way they bow . . ."

"Bowing is not uncommon here, Meranda," Onesphore interrupted her. "It is protocol. But to answer your question, the help is government recommended, mostly from Khartoum. Spectrum cannot afford the risk of employee disloyalty."

The last statement was vague but she knew what he meant.

They drove on, the uneven ground beneath them thick with gummy mud clumps that pitched the Cruiser back and forth every few feet. As far as the eye could see, there was nothing. No buildings. No housing. Nothing at all reminiscent of civilization. Just intermittent lime-green patches and brambly brown expanse that eventually fused with the flushed horizon.

"How close are we to the oil fields?"

Onesphore gestured lightly with his head. "The one I will show you is past the landing strip where you flew in Friday night."

A few minutes later, she made out a lone Cessna Caravan sitting on a long red-dusted stretch of earth. Another thirty seconds and she saw two men hauling wooden crates off the little aircraft.

Three other workers waited nearby, deflecting powdery clouds that kept whipping off the landing strip. When they got close enough, Mera recognized it as the plane that had carried her and Donovan from Khartoum to here.

They kept driving, and suddenly, a production bloc rose out of nowhere like it had sprung from the earth's center. Surrounded by vast nothingness, the site wasn't big, not more than a few square miles, but it was covered with heavy gray equipment as foreign to her as an instrument panel on a Learjet. Only the drilling rigs, which seemed deceptively benign as they pierced the earth, were familiar.

"This is it. Halig field." Onesphore pulled the Cruiser to a smooth stop. He shoved the door open on his side and a warm sticky wind and host of mosquitoes gusted into the vehicle.

"Do they all look like this?" Squinting, she stepped out of the vehicle and fell into stride with the giant.

"More or less." Onesphore shrugged as he kicked at a mound of reddish dirt. "Some smaller, some bigger. But they all have the same kind of equipment, several operators running them."

They walked on in silence for a few minutes then stopped to watch as several men in yellow hardhats and crude-soiled clothing grappled with the heavy machinery. Even from a distance, their skin was the same blue-black as Mashada and Onesphore's, though a number of them weren't as tall and agonizingly thin. Like there was no time to waste, they heaved and hoisted and bustled about in unison, never pausing to look up.

"These are some of your men?"

"That is right."

"Where do you find them?"

"My workers are locals. They need the money, I need their labor." Onesphore was smooth, the proverbial company man, and for a second, Mera forgot he did anything other than oversee Spectrum's operations. "Later, we will drive into Kadugli so you can see where the school will be. This is where you will work first."

"I'm really glad to be here," she said sincerely, noticing again Onesphore's brittle expression.

What had she done to warrant his contempt?

"The board is pleased you are here," he answered stiffly. "Seth is, too, though for different reasons. He thinks you will do good things."

"And you?"

"Me?"

"Are you glad I'm here?"

Onesphore studied her face.

"Whether or not I am glad, as you say, is of little consequence. I recommended you because of Seth." His eyes narrowed. "I trust him."

She thought for a long time.

"I see. And what would it take for you to trust me?"

Onesphore laughed, an irreverent jeer echoing across the infinite savannah. He looked at her squarely, his glance shooting a sub-zero chill through her. "An inconvenient sacrifice."

She felt her breath leave her and the expanse suddenly press in from all sides. But she said nothing as they resumed walking again, only the drone of the hot wind, the steady cadence of footsteps in her ears.

Then they climbed back into the Cruiser and drove east toward Kadugli. This time, Mera didn't bother to make small talk and Onesphore never took his eyes off the rutted mud road that just kept winding.

Chapter 30

The work wasn't at all what she expected, but the fact that most of it happened outdoors and away from company head-quarters made it more like a Peace Corps assignment than a corporate job. The exception was biweekly trips into the office to field press calls and sift through paperwork that seemed to have the multiplying capability of rabbits.

Other days she spent in a village outside of Kadugli. Spectrum had commissioned her there first since the site was just a few miles west of the last explosion, a catastrophe that had pretty much leveled and dispersed the two thousand-member community.

Now, what little glory or grandeur had belonged to the settlement was gone, reduced to rubble and crumbled mud-brick buildings that lay scattered over scorched grassland.

Most of the locals were gone, too, several hundred of them massacred in the explosion while another thousand fled to the nearby Nuba Mountains. Just a few hundred remained and half of those were orphans.

The tallest purple-black natives were Dinka, Mera learned, members of the largest ethnic tribe in Sudan. Scattered over the swampy Nile Basin in southern Bahr el Ghazal, the Dinka were longtime cattle and goat farmers who lived in *tukuls*, small mud huts thatched with umbrella-shaped roofs made of dried grass and bamboo. Each *tukul* was built to shelter a family, and extended relations constructed the little huts within feet of each other. Inside, there was no running water, no electricity, no modern conveniences, whatsoever.

Deng, the old village chief who had stayed behind with the remnant of his people, explained in near-perfect English that there were no crops anymore, either. Did she know that the north sometimes salted the land during a siege, he asked in an atypical moment of curiosity. Or that they randomly buried mines to make sure there could be no harvest?

She hadn't known how to answer.

So their once fruitful terrain that, for years, had given up groundnuts and cassava, sorghum and wild yams, was now a parched and barren wasteland. The exception was a single stream among the *tukuls* that ran full after the rainy season. It was in this tributary from the upper portion of the Western Nile where the village children played, rail-thin and naked little innocents who had no idea what their cool watering hole harbored. Splashing and swatting flies as they dunked their grimy jerry cans before heading home, the laughing little creatures had no clue that merciless parasites might, at anytime, render them delirious with fevers and faint from dysenteries before they died.

Hands down, there was nothing worse, Mera decided the first time she watched a tiny writhing body fall limp and still. The sight of a skeletal little form, convulsing and whimpering before it finally gave up its spirit was something she knew she'd never get used to if she lived here the rest of her life. The guttural ululations echoing across the infinite prairie, the despairing wails that came from a mother's deepest parts; these things could never seem natural. Even if death's regularity was like that of the morning sunrise.

She'd been here six months now, a half-year of hell-hot sun, unending dust and sweat-coated natives focused on the non-stop work of building a small school. The labor had been back-breaking at times, constructing earthen kilns to bake clay bricks, piling up tall mounds of mud and bamboo grass. Then came the mixing and actual baking beneath a fiery sun that made the air shimmer and buckle as if atomic particles were suspended everywhere.

Little by little they'd carried out the project and now the mud and straw building was coming along so well, the village elders had decided just a week ago that the school would double as their church and meeting hall.

But early one morning, it was a chance conversation with Deng that gave Mera her first glimpse into how the locals saw their dilemma.

She'd packed up the Cruiser and arrived at the village just before dawn. By 10:00 A.M., the heat was typically at or past the 100°F mark, a fact that often roused her early so as to get a cooler head start. This morning, the horizon stretched charcoal on all sides and the skies still twinkled with tiny lights. The last thing she expected to find was the proud chief sitting propped against the new building, legs crossed, head bent.

"Deng, is that you?" Though the reverent posture was familiar, the form was mostly eclipsed in shadow.

A gentle wind gusted and the *tink tink* of the Cruiser's cooling engine punctuated the silence.

"Yes, Miss Meranda."

Switching on her headlamp, she unloaded a box of building supplies from the back of the Cruiser. Then she stooped next to him and snapped the bright light back off.

"Are you okay?"

Deng didn't look up.

"Yes, miss."

"What are you doing?"

He waited to answer like time was of no consequence at all.

"I am praying," he finally said. In the inky light, she saw his palms were upturned like he was expecting something to be placed inside them.

"So you are." She squinted in search of his worn features, and though they were shrouded, she could picture the rows of Dinka tribal markings etched into his creased forehead. "May I ask you something?"

"But of course, miss."

"Who is it you pray to? Is it spirits or gods?"

"Spirits or gods . . ." His words were a faint echo as he turned his face to the first streak of color illumining the sky.

"Or is it one God?"

For the better of two or three minutes, the chief said nothing, and Mera wondered if she had offended him. But then his shaking hands groped the earth until he found something and he grappled with his find before the morning's first rays fell on his answer.

He had made a clearing in the dirt, a canvas of sorts. There, he'd laid two twigs crossed in the center.

"This One." The old man pointed to the twigs. "I pray to this One, miss."

"I see," she said staring at the crude little cross. For a second, she couldn't breathe. "And this God . . . you think He hears these prayers, these thoughts, of yours?"

The old man lifted his shoulders, a sort of shrug.

"Do you hear my words now, miss? Can you see my face?"

"Yes."

"I am real to you?"

"Very."

"I pray to this One, this God," he pointed at the sticks, "because I am real to Him. He sees my face."

She stared at him, speechless, as he continued.

"This God, Miss Meranda, He is alive." He shook his head slowly. "And out here, we need a living God."

Everything inside her wanted to cry out. Here he sat, a crippled old man left in the wake of yet another rubble. For years, he'd watched his people starved and maimed and killed with no tangible hope that the future would be any different. Despite this, he had fastened himself to a bewildering God who had yet to intervene.

"Me too, Deng," she whispered. "Sometimes I'm not sure why, but that's my God, too."

The old man nodded.

"I know, miss," he said, softly. "We all do."

She was surprised. She hadn't once mentioned anything personal to the Dinka other than she had a young nephew here with her. "How?"

"God." With his lyrical accent, it was a one-word song.

"God?"

"God," he repeated. "He told us you were coming. Just before the rainy season ended."

"But I wasn't here during the rainy season."

"No miss, of course not." His consent was grave. "He said you would come to us and help."

Mera did the math in silence. Their rainy season ended late October; she'd gotten the call from Spectrum that first week in October.

Before the rainy season was over.

It sounded crazy, but the aging chief was far from capricious. He liked facts, preferring the obvious and practical over anything sentimental. But now in the early morning light, he recited his convictions as if there were no question about their credibility.

"God . . . He told you I was coming . . .?" She said it slowly, making sure he understood the question.

"Yes. Two elders, too."

"And you . . . believed Him . . . when He told you this?"

The chief looked puzzled. "But of course, miss. God does not lie."

"No. I didn't mean that. But how did you know that it was Him speaking?"

A slight smile tugged at the chief's lips, something rare. "You ask many questions today, Miss Meranda. But here is your answer. You are here. He said you would come to us. And now you are here." By his expression, Mera could tell he had nothing further to say, so she changed the subject.

"Deng?"

"Yes, miss?"

"Besides the school, besides helping rebuild this village, what would you ask of me?"

The chief's hand traveled over the ash-silver hair tufted close on his ebony head. "You miss, or Spectrum?"

"What I'm able to do comes through the company." His question had been shrewd, but she dared not offer any hint of what she really hoped to accomplish here.

"No, miss," Deng countered respectfully. "I have watched you this half-year. There is you and there is your Spectrum. But you and your company are not the same."

"You don't think so?"

Deng breathed in deeply.

"Sometimes you are doing a job here. You help us with construction, order and bring what we need. You will help us with our school, our hospital. That is Spectrum in you. But when your duty is done here, you do more. You hold our sick babies. You sit with our village women when you should be back where you belong. You bring things we do not ask for, special things to make our people happy." He leaned forward to pick up a stick and his arm was so thin it bore the reed's likeness. "That is not your company. It is you."

This time, the insight left her speechless.

"Then, Deng, what would you ask of *me*?" she finally said.

The sun was a ball of orange fire, cascading liquid color over the wide-open plains. In the distance, Mera heard the *bleating* of sheep, the sing-song laughter of a few village children. She could smell the acrid odor of burning wood and refuse, morning fires that would cook rice or bean rations that had come via UN or NGO aid.

"Onesphore, he told us you are like a storyteller, yes?"

"That's a good way to describe what I did before I came here."

His lips threatened to smile again. "I like stories."

"Me, too." She thought about Donovan and how he adored *The Three Little Pigs* and *Mother Goose* and *Goodnight Moon*. She thought about the stories she loved and the ones she'd written.

And it occurred to her that perhaps all people loved them, too, if for no other reason than the fact that humanity couldn't be separated from the stories they live in.

"We have a big story here," he confided with the dignity of a statesman.

"In Kadugli?"

"In the Sudan. Our people, they have suffered much and the north government keeps the world from knowing the truth."

"So I've heard."

"Long ago, I went to university in Khartoum. Before the war. I learned much about our people and the government." Deng reached for his makeshift cane, a long stick that supported his limp, before rising to his full height. "I know I look old and poor to you, miss. But I am no fool. I know why the planes keep coming and dropping bombs. I know why north soldiers bring guns and kill our people, take our women."

Deng looked down at her, his torn t-shirt flapping in the wind. "They have hate for us. For our color, for our faith. But it is our oil that makes them rich and we live on the earth covering it. So they kill us." He looked out at the vast spread of land past the village clearing. Two young men, naked with the exception of cloth tied over their privates, prodded a thin herd of cattle into a patch of waist high grass near the gray-brown river.

"But we try, miss, we don't give up," he continued. "We must never give up."

"I know." She knew Deng was talking about the SPLA.

A dark shadow crossed his face, like whatever he was thinking suddenly had a life of its own. A second later, the vise was gone and Deng's weathered features stilled.

"If someone who cared about us understood our story, it could be told, yes?"

"Yes, of course. But that wouldn't guarantee who would listen."

The chief let this sink in.

"One day something will happen in the Sudan," he offered.

"Something different in the south because of the north. Many more lives will be lost."

"But hasn't that happened before?" she feigned ignorance.

"Indeed. But when this . . . this disaster comes, it will be different."

"Why do you say that?"

He raised his chin, an almost imperious gesture.

"I know," he said. "And when it happens, the world will be ready to listen. But the story, it must be told if it is to help our people."

She scrutinized his face, the chiseled jet angles, the gullied creases and parted rubbery lips that revealed gapped amber teeth. "So you want me to . . ."

"Please, miss," he brushed his worn hand over hers, "tell what you learn here. Tell the truth because that is what will free us."

His eyes met hers and for a second, the encounter was bare, painfully so. It wasn't Mera the journalist and Deng the village chief. It wasn't even an exchange between two people. The connection cut it was so deep, and as his gaze held hers, Mera felt something of his people become her own.

Chapter 31

Mera could tell by the look on Mashada's face that something wasn't right. By now, the predictable serenity of the woman's countenance was a respite she had come to anticipate all day, and after a year in the same quarters, Mashada's tranquility was a soul-anchor that somehow made the punishing heat and endless skies of the Sudan home.

But this evening was different. Waiting by the unit door with Donovan tethered to her hip, Mashada appeared more like a caged animal than the placid woman who took nearly everything in stride. Clearly possessed by whatever angst was plaguing her, she was pacing back and forth across the tiny landing, oblivious to the fact that Donovan had managed to untie her apron and was now chewing on the loosened strings. She jumped like she'd been stung by a wasp when the child squealed and tried to wriggle from her grasp so he could run to Mera.

"Good evening, madam." Mashada allowed the squirming toddler to fling himself on Mera who met the gesture with a little kiss on each of his cheeks and a long bear hug.

"What is it, Mashada, what's wrong?" As they went inside, Mera noticed the distraught expression was only amplifying. Mashada's black skin had a gray cast, and her eyes, now frighteningly wide in her face, kept darting back and forth. She looked freshly alarmed as if bad news had touched down like a tornado.

"Bombings today, madam." The woman dropped her head. "Past the oilfields outside of Bentiu. They say many are dead."

"Dead. Dead. Dead," Donovan chirped merrily. "I hungwy. C'mon, An Meerie. C'mon My Shada. I hungwy." He patted his round belly then lifted his arms for Mera to pick him up.

"Hush, sweetie," she said gently as she hoisted him up and gave his cheek another kiss. He put his head on her shoulder. "Mashada needs to tell me something." She turned to face the woman again.

"Bombings today, madam. And . . . it is very bad," she choked out as though ejecting the words was akin to climbing Everest.

The news didn't surprise Mera because it wasn't a first. In the twelve months she had been with Spectrum, she'd routinely seen and heard government planes patrolling air space around the oil fields. Sometimes, too, brilliant orange and crimson-red fire fall would set the purple night sky aglow.

It was distant rocket explosions, she learned. Detonations followed up with machine gunfire that pretty much resembled Fourth of July Roman candle displays back home.

What was eerie, though, was Spectrum's explanation to the press, which was incidentally the same one the Sudanese government offered.

Infighting, they both claimed. Intertribal insurgencies between southern tribes that had somehow acquired sophisticated weaponry.

As for aerial activity, aircraft was a necessary peacekeeping presence and a mitigator of anti-government tyranny. There was never any mention that planes carried artillery or bombs — or that they sprayed them like confetti.

But if Mashada knew what happened outside the compound walls, if she had any idea what the Spectrum-government alliance generated, she'd never let on. In fact, the woman was so reserved, so elusive, that it had only been in the last few months that Mera had begun to splice together fragments enough to offer some insight into the mystery of Mashada. Even still, the only semi-definite she had was that the woman had come from Khartoum about two years ago — and she'd left her family behind.

"I know, Mashada. I heard about them just before I left Kadugli." Mera set down Donovan and made her way over to the woman's side.

"A runner from a village between the two towns came to see Deng." She pictured the wiry midnight limbs of the runner, the glistening sweat-soaked brow as he and Deng quietly conferred. "Apparently, he had run since daybreak, right after things had gotten really bad." Mera had heard from Deng that casualties were near four hundred and climbing. But she said nothing of that to Mashada.

A *crash* sounded from the kitchen, followed by a loud wail and instinctively, Mera and Mashada followed it. Donovan was standing on the burnt satillo tiles, surrounded by chards of pink and white pottery that had been a pig cookie jar just minutes before. In the rubble lay broken cookies of all shapes and sizes. In each of Donovan's little hands was a whole one.

"Donbon sowwy, An Meerie. I hungwy." With a sheepish pout, he held up his two prized cookies. "I hungwy."

Mera waded through the colorful debris and whisked the child up. She held him close. "Never mind, baby. I'll get this in a minute."

Mashada smiled at him despite herself. "Little *sahib* . . . little *sahib*." She shook her head. "Such a busy boy." Then looking at Mera, "Madam, please, I must beg a favor of you." She began bowing repeatedly like a buoy in a storm-tossed sea.

Mera put her free hand on Mashada's shoulder.

"Anything, Mashada. Ask me anything. Just relax. We're friends now, not strangers."

"I must go." The woman traded bobbing for hand wringing.

"Go?"

"To the fields."

"The fields?" Mera echoed. "Why would you do that?"

"For short time only, madam."

"But, why? You don't know anyone near the Union fields, do you?"

"Yes, madam." This was the single challenge in dealing with Mashada. In often broken but endearing English, the woman's answer to every question was always the bare minimum. Details or explanations were always omitted.

"I thought your family lives north of Khartoum," Mera pressed.

"I have two family members near Bentiu," Mashada explained with almost no expression.

"And you're afraid . . ." Mera didn't have the heart to finish the question.

Mashada folded her hands over her chest and breathed in deeply, an indication that she intended to maintain the barrier she kept erected between herself and the rest of the world. She stood motionless in the room's warm light, unflinching as she held her exposed head and neck arrow straight.

Her head, her neck . . . they were completely bared!

It was a first, and as looked closer, Mera was as much struck by the woman's delicate beauty as she was by the absence of her traditional head covering.

Without the *hijab*, Mashada was a sculptor's dream. Though well over forty, her face was clear and strong with sharp high cheekbones that swept under wide eyes. Haunted eyes. Her broad nose was small, hooked slightly at the end, and her lips were full and rosy against the midnight of her skin. Even with the sheer terror that had settled her features into distorted angles, Mera couldn't help thinking she looked more like hewn art than flesh and blood.

"Yes, madam. I am afraid." It was the first time the woman had admitted to any emotion. "I am much afraid."

"But, who . . . who do you . . .?"

"The people past Bentiu, they wait today for food at a relief site," Mashada interrupted, avoiding her question. "Landmines around the villages have kept many from having food. This you must know."

Mera nodded.

"And the people today, they think the planes are bringing food. But . . . but they only bring bombs . . . and guns . . ."

Mashada's voice trembled, cracked a little, and though Mera wondered how her information was so accurate, she decided not to ask. If Mashada needed to leave, whatever her reasons were, she would let her go. The only risk, and it was a minimal one, was someone from Spectrum might drop in looking for her. And while that wasn't likely, Mera still wondered how she'd explain it.

"Iron . . . Onesphore, he will come to take me to Bentiu. Kyla will attend you and Donovan in my absence." Mashada must have been reading her mind.

"Onesphore?"

"He will go to Bentiu to look at damage for Spectrum. For me, he tells Mr. Wellington that I have family from Khartoum who may be part of north army there now."

How and when had she made contact with Onesphore?

"The northern militia's closing in on Bentiu?" All day, Mera had heard talk of the catastrophic air raids, but there had been no mention of government troops occupying the land. The city was south of the north-south divide line, supposedly governed by the SPLA.

"Madam, I cannot know the plans of the north." Mashada was careful not to blaspheme the inner workings of the regime. "My business in Bentiu is to make inquiry for my family."

Mera waited to answer.

"Go then, Mashada. You need to go . . ."

"Thank you, madam." Without thinking, she bowed again, and when she did, Mera gasped at a heinous collection of scars that started above the base of her neck, disappearing somewhere inside the *jilbab* that covered her. It was hard to tell in the muted light, but it looked like there were at least a half dozen of them. Deep, angry cuts that must have taken months to heal.

For a split second, Mera wondered why she'd never noticed before. But as Donovan raced about the room, a makeshift cape flying behind him, she realized he'd confiscated Mashada's *hijab*, the scarf that normally cloaked her secret.

Chapter 32

Mera sat up straight in bed, eyes wide open like she hadn't slept at all. The cramped room was dim-lit and still. Completely silver and silent save Donovan's soft breathing and the placid tick of her alarm clock.

She looked at the ceiling above, at its far right corner where the thick cottage cheese texture was shadowed by a water stain in the shape of a four leaf clover. Then at the cotton skirt and pale blue blouse on the chair by her bed. She'd been too tired to hang them up.

No. It was just a dream. It had to be.

After all, she was here. Here, in her bed covered with stiff sheets so white in the moonlight that they burned her eyes. Here with Donovan just an arm's length away and the stout hands of her clock to confirm it all.

3:35 A.M.

Just three hours since she'd gone to bed.

It was just a dream.

Quieted, she leaned back and tried to settle into her pillows.

But the harrowing image flashed again, and this time it was so vivid, she felt an adrenaline surge jump start her pulse. And she hadn't even closed her eyes.

Now she was spooked, really spooked, and before her skin had a chance to start crawling, she untangled the nightgown from her legs and swung her feet to the floor. There was no use trying to go back to sleep now.

In the kitchen, she filled a pot with water and waited for bubbles to sprout and dance. Hot tea sounded good, the strong black kind that always required her to cut the bite with too much sugar.

Trying hard not to think about anything, she sank into a fraying bamboo chair. The quiet of the little quarters was a deadening ring in her ears cleaved only by the water's gentle hiss and the *bump-boom* of her heartbeat in her eardrums.

A dream, that's all it was.

Another one of her weird dreams.

Lost in thought, she stared out the tiny window into the night sky and tried again to make sense of the apparition that had jolted her from a sound sleep.

Only no matter which way she looked at it, it wasn't logical . . .

Mashada had slipped out just after midnight and Mera crawled into bed almost immediately thereafter. The day had been long, she was tired, and since Donovan was already asleep, she decided to see how Edmond Dantes would secure his release from the infamous Chateau d'If in *The Count of Monte Cristo*.

But she woke with a start right after midnight when her book slid off the bed and crash-landed on the floor.

Seconds later, with the novel rescued and set atop her night-stand, she'd switched off the light. Then snuggled deep under the covers grateful for another six hours of sleep.

What came next was bizarre. Anything but typical.

Sometime later, whether it was minutes or hours, an erratic dream gripped her, one that started with moving pictures playing on a film reel of an old projector. The backdrop was grainy and blurred, the black and white figures not at all unlike Charlie Chaplan's stilted antics in pioneer cinema. Even in sleep, she'd felt herself straining hard to distinguish who was who. It was to no avail, though. She didn't recognize any of the characters.

After several choppy frames, she was finally able to make out one person. It was a younger version of Mashada dressed in what she somehow knew was a tribal rendition of wedding attire. Surrounded by a crowd, the woman's face was painted. She was smiling broadly, something Mera had never seen her do.

Then came more natives in the dream-film, all of them strangers except for Mashada when she randomly appeared. In every image, she had on the same dress, wore the same expression.

Next, came the frame of a tall ebony man, garbed in fatigues. He braced a rifle across his chest, a fierce warrior as he stood sentry about a campfire encircled by people. Half the throng was swathed in bright-colored native attire, the other half outfitted like him.

Then another image, this one more vexing than hostile, but when it appeared, Mera felt a death-like cold creep through her.

The soldier was looking down at Mashada. Now, her dress was shredded and bloodstained. Her face was bloated and gashed like she'd been repeatedly bludgeoned. With a numb expression, the man merely stared into her face like what he was seeing couldn't be real.

Somewhere deep in the dream, Mera felt everything inside her simultaneously tighten and recoil.

Who was the man and who was he to Mashada? And what kind of tyranny had left her so disfigured and devastated?

But it was the final frame that wrenched her fully conscious.

Like it had been paused for a film edit, this image was frozen and hazy about its black and white periphery. Slowly, though, it grew clearer, and as it did, it morphed into full color.

It was a picture of Mashada, somewhat older and cloaked in her customary *jilbab* and *hijab*.

The soldier was there, too. He was much more spare and grave now, though, as if youth had come and gone and left him bereft of all but a beating heart. He stood beside Mashada, stoic, but close enough for their arms to touch at the elbows as she cradled a tiny naked boy in her arms.

A little corpse.

Probably just over a year old, the child's lifeless eyes were wide open in a blank stare, his jaw slack as a scarlet ribbon drooled from the corner of his mouth. His swollen stomach was speared open and bluish jelly organs shaped like skinny fingers dangled from a jagged gash that eventually hooked into an arc.

Suspended at the top of the frame was a hovering necrotic-black helicopter.

It was like a picture from *Time-Life* capturing the horrors of war and human injustice. There wasn't another way to describe it. But what made it most vilifying was the fact that Mashada had been a progressive part of the images.

Sitting at the table with her hands wrapped about the unfilled tea mug, Mera tried recounting everything she knew about Mashada. What she'd heard through the compound grapevine certainly seemed to have no correlation to these random, hellish images.

Mashada had grown up north of Khartoum. Her family served a line of northern officials, and though her parents were dead, she had brothers and sisters. She had never married, which meant under Muslim law, she would have no legitimate children.

The image couldn't have anything to do with Mashada.

But something about the whole dream or vision or whatever it was, felt real, even tangible. Maybe it was cryptic, but it seemed more like an equation to be solved than a riddle to ignore.

Drowsy, but too agitated to go back to bed, Mera got up, switched off the stove where the forgotten boiling water had all but evaporated and headed to the bedroom to check on Donovan. The advent of morning offered streaks of pale light, but she tripped anyway, landing hard on the floor.

Sharp pain sheared through her, and for a minute, she sat sprawled out and stunned. Then rubbing her throbbing left knee, she noticed the culprit.

It was thin, whatever it was. Net-like and twisted around her feet. Now it stretched long and filmy as she unwound and lifted it into the dusty light.

It was Mashada's *hijab*.

The woman had left her hijab behind. Something she never dared leave off, especially outside their barrack.

Before she could think more about Mashada and the forgotten scarf, another image seized her with a leviathan force.

It was Mashada again, crouched next to the soldier in fatigues. He was holding the dead child while she dangled her *hijab* over an open fire, feeding the gauze-like material to the hungry flames. Both of their eyes were squeezed shut, their mouths wide open like they were trying to purge themselves of an indescribable grief.

Chapter 33

It was pitch black when they turned into a clearing just inside a stretch of thick brush. Mashada had dozed off, a combination of the Land Cruiser's drone and the jostling over rugged terrain enough to lull her to sleep. But even before that, she hadn't said a word.

Onesphore was glad she'd slept. It gave him time to think without the pressure of forced conversation neither of them wanted in the first place.

Not that she required attention. Mashada was maintenance-free, a mistress of disguise. In all the time he'd known her, Onesphore had yet to see her show emotion or reveal anything personal. It was just the way she was and he knew it was a gender thing. There was a definite veil between the inner thoughts of Sudanese men and women.

Still, he wondered how she was dealing with the possibility of finding her husband and brother dead. So far, casualty reports outside Bentiu had passed the four hundred mark and they were still climbing. Out here, there were no guarantees.

Which made it all the worse. He'd long gotten used to the rending anticipation as he made his way to these sites. In fact, the lead weighting heavier in his gut as he drew closer was always transitional, edging him over disaster's brink to the stark face of carnage, from knowledge to knowing.

But he had never gotten used to what he might find.

That was an unknown, always a variable. Even before the full-blown quest for oil. Initial reports might cite one thing, but the reality of razed villages still smoldering amid endless black smoke and fiery embers was a frequent occurrence that never failed to shake him. And all the demolished little huts strewn with mutilated corpses wearing expressions like they'd tasted hell before death contributed to an anxiety and sorrow that only deepened with each passing year.

Glancing back at Mashada's still features glittering with heavy perspiration, Onesphore wondered what the woman had said to convince Mera that she needed to leave. What would she do if they got to Bentiu only to find the worst?

Even as the questions crossed his mind, he knew they would go unanswered. Mashada would reveal nothing, neither in words or in countenance. It was just the way she was.

He stopped now, pushed the Cruiser into park and let the engine idle. The sudden absence of unbroken turbulence awakened her. She opened her eyes and they were round white orbs in the rear view mirror. But true to her nature, she said nothing, only sat there in the stiff air and blinked.

Onesphore tried to ignore the dread wringing his belly like an iron hand.

"We are here," he said in Dinka a minute later. He knew they both needed the practice before daybreak.

"How far to the village?" she countered quietly. Her accent was perfect like she used it all the time.

"Maybe two miles. I could not get any closer because of the brush. So we will have to walk." He twisted the ignition off and for a minute they listened to the engine's *tink tink tink* breaking the silence.

"Dawn is near." She nodded toward the tarp of infinite black fading into bands of blue-gray.

Onesphore stepped from the Cruiser and went around back. He started lifting overstuffed bundles through the cargo window. Though she couldn't see, Mashada knew what he was doing, knew what came next. Without a word, she joined him, filling her arms with as much of the load as she could. They both knew better than to leave anything suspicious in the abandoned vehicle. Even for a short time.

The open-plain horizon was barely visible over swaying shadows of waist-high grass but they walked on anyway, Onesphore in front, Mashada several steps behind him. Her load was heavy, but she was glad for the weight's miserable ache. The distraction kept her from mulling over the relentless possibilities that might otherwise drive her to the edge of madness. So she willed herself on slowly, never once entertaining the thought that he didn't know where he was going. Everyone knew no matter where he was in these parts, Onesphore's instinctive radar did two things: let him navigate flawlessly and helped him track enemy presence with the precision of a bloodhound.

Like a light switched on behind a curtain, the sky glowed softly, cool shades of lilac and silver. A minute later, the brambly vines that lashed at their ankles were visible, and at the next clearing, Onesphore stopped to readjust the freight on his back. Sweat had soaked his shirt through and it stuck to him the way matted grass clung to the earth after the rains. Now he shifted the huge duffels he carried in both hands. Though tempted, Mashada didn't follow suit since she knew that she might never get moving again. Instead, she tried blinking away the sweat that kept dripping into her eyes as she watched Onesphore's huge biceps flex and strain beneath the bulk as he continued breaking path for them.

Out of nowhere, a towering masculine figure interrupted the predictable scenery. Easily the height of Onesphore, though much more spare, the form was about a hundred yards away and approaching. But even with the distance between them, Mashada knew him immediately. And though she was easily ten yards behind him, Onesphore heard her choke back a sob before she picked up her pace.

The man, too, had seen them coming, and that was all it took. Strapping a huge rifle around his neck, he broke into a lithe sprint, moving easily through the soft grass. As if in response,

Mashada let the bulk she was carrying slip from her shoulders and hands. Onesphore merely kept walking, saluting, as the loping soldier passed him.

The soldier stopped just inches from Mashada, staring at her delicate saddened features, at the tears streaming over her cheeks. For a long time, he said nothing and neither did she. Then, he took her face in both of his hands.

"You should not be here." He, too, spoke in Dinka. "It is not safe . . . and you could be found out." His charcoal features were warrior-like, but his eyes were tender.

"I had to know, Francis. I had to know."

"Who told you . . ."

"Iron Lung." She could say that name out here, away from Spectrum's confines, away from anyone who might be connected with the north.

"I cannot believe he let you come."

She looked mildly indignant.

"The choice was mine to make. I will stay back, back with you and our people while he looks at what happened yesterday." A vague shudder passed through her. "I have not seen you in two years."

"We will be busy with him here. He has much to tell us."

"I know this." She was undaunted by the fact that Francis was careful to disguise his pleasure in seeing her, even if she was his wife. "I am just glad to see you, to know you were not killed." Her face clouded with a question she feared asking.

"You want to know if John is alive?" He anticipated her thoughts.

"Yes."

Francis brushed a hand over one of Mashada's. "More than four hundred died yesterday," he whispered. "Another hundred are hurt."

"Is John dead?" Mashada asked flatly.

Francis closed his eyes like he was trying hard to forget something that demanded to be remembered.

"Your brother is hurt. Badly. But we think he will live if God is willing." He reached down to collect the heavy bags she'd lugged, swinging them effortlessly over the tight wire of his shoulders.

"I will go to him and help."

He stopped her, a light clamp of his hand on her shoulder. As he lifted his arm, a breeze carried the pungent smell of sweat and body odor coming from him.

"The village, it is worse than the first time, Mashada. Worse than . . . when they took us away." Noticing her faint expression, he clasped her elbow.

The haunting images of a night nearly ten years ago made her dizzy and she was glad for Francis' steadying grip. For just a second, she closed her eyes. Then opened them.

She wouldn't—*couldn't*—remember such things now. They were long ago, and dwelling on them could bring about no good.

Besides, her brother needed her back at the camp and so did the countless suffering others.

"I am here to help, Francis," she said, more stoutly than she felt. "Iron Lung has medicine and supplies in some of these bags, food and perhaps ammunition in the others. Just as he always does." Speaking their native language was an intimacy of its own, and she realized just how much she missed the lyrical sound of it.

"The army, we fought hard yesterday."

"I know."

He looked at her, quizzical.

"Iron Lung," she explained. "He tells me."

"Many from the north who came in trucks and tanks are dead." They were walking toward the waking village, the sun a perfect, pink circle behind them, the lacelike outline of a few acacia trees just yards ahead. "We captured some."

"But you could not fight the air raids," Mashada answered sadly as she breathed in the familiar scent of wood burning with animal refuse, "and the north knew that."

"That is true. That is why so many of us died." For a second, he look defeated, like he was weighted by what he couldn't change. "They dropped bombs from the sky," he sighed.

"God help us." She touched the whittled art of his cheekbone.

"He may yet." He moved her hand away, nodding his head in a light gesture. "He may yet."

Without another word, their gazes rested on the massive frame of Onesphore in the distance, busy unpacking supplies that were only pipe dreams five years ago.

Chapter 34

As he slammed the Bronco door shut, he wasn't sure what was worse, the shearing wind or the blinding white of another blizzard. In all his years in Chicago, Seth couldn't remember a more unpredictable winter. Clear and cool one day, frigid, amassed in snowdrifts the next. As he sat letting the truck's engine warm, he was grateful it was already February. Spring was just around the corner.

Glancing at his watch, he was glad he'd left the shelter early. The trip to O'Hare would be a slow crawl since the city's fleet of snow plows hadn't been able to keep up with the latest drifts. Which meant Interstate 90 would be an exercise in patience.

He figured he should call the airport and find out if Onesphore's flight had been delayed or rerouted, but he didn't care to camp on a cell phone. Worse case scenario, he'd sleep at the airport if there was a hold up.

Two hours later and a few miles from O'Hare, his cell rang, but just as he picked it up, the driver in front of him slammed on his brakes. Seth swerved wildly for a second, barely avoiding collision and a patch of black ice.

"Where are you?" Onesphore's accented voice thundered.

"I stopped off for a quick eighteen holes," Seth said, ignoring the rush from his near miss. "But go figure, I just can't seem to get my chipping right today. Maybe it's all the ice . . ."

"Funny, Langford . . ."

"I'm a mile from the airport. Been snaking your way for two hours."

"I caught an earlier flight. Plane got in at two."

"Just in time for that last avalanche."

"Definitely a change from Sudan." Onesphore cleared his throat. "We hit the hundred twenty degree mark last week."

"Scorching, man. But hey, I'm coming up on terminal parking now. Where are you?"

"Passenger pickup. International Terminal."

"Give me ten, traffic's clearing a little. But the roads are slick."

—

"You look bad." Onesphore was studying Seth's face, something he usually had no interest in.

"*Look* bad? Dude, I *am* bad," Seth quipped sarcastically.

Onesphore rolled his eyes. "You look bad," he repeated.

"Yeah?"

Onesphore quirked an eyebrow as Seth continued.

"Bad, how? Sick, bad? Up to no good bad? You're a little sketchy on specifics."

They were a mile past the airport, waiting for their food at Sam's Diner. The blizzard had stopped pelting Chicago, at least for the moment. But with traffic stacked up for miles and temperatures plummeting further with every passing half hour, dinner and a warm waiting place had sounded like a welcome alternative.

"Ugly, bad," Onesphore said, mock-definite. "As usual. But you cannot help that. You can never be as pretty as me." He grinned, his straight white teeth a stark contrast against his ebony skin.

"You're right, that would be a losing battle."

More derision was on the tip of Onesphore's tongue, but the waitress brought their food, a cheeseburger and fries for him, chicken fried steak with mashed potatoes for Seth. She refilled their mugs with steaming coffee and disappeared.

"I am serious now." Onesphore's eyes were suddenly grave. "You do not look well."

The truth was he didn't and he knew it. He was thinner, red-eyed from endless nights of just a few hours sleep and, to add insult to injury, his clothes were a disaster. But he was spread way too thin, that was the problem. For the third time in the last five years, he was expanding Wings Like Eagles, this time to accommodate the growing epidemic of homeless teenagers. Fortunately, the dilapidated warehouse next to his shelter had been on the market for over a year, a fact that motivated the owner to sell it last month well below appraised value. That done, Seth had hired a crew to start renovating. Even still, the project was taking more of his time than he'd anticipated.

In between all this, he'd gone back to law school. This was something he was keeping under wraps, though. Especially since he didn't intend to practice and he wasn't at all sure what he'd do with the degree.

"I'm busier than usual, that's all." He made the extra effort to sound noncommittal.

"Doing what?" Onesphore shot back evenly.

"I got the shelter expansion going, I'm working on a conference for the Lost Boys this summer . . ."

"Maybe this is so. But you are not telling me something."

Seth took his time polishing off another bite of chicken fried steak. Then dug into the mashed potatoes before he answered.

"What do you want me to say?"

"You will not look at me." Onesphore was smug. "That is not like you."

Shaking his head, Seth put down his greasy fork and wiped his hands on a flimsy paper napkin. His friend knew him too well.

"Okay, you win. Stupid as it sounds, I went back to law school last year."

Onesphore gaped. "What?"

"I went back to law school," Seth repeated.

"Why?"

"You won't believe it."

"Try me."

Seth knew what Onesphore would say, but he plunged in anyway.

"Okay, here it is. There've only been a few times in my life that I absolutely knew God wanted me to do something."

"Oh no, not the godspeak again . . ."

"Hey, you asked." Seth shrugged and held both hands up in a surrender gesture.

"You are right," the giant consented. "Continue."

"As I was saying, I've only been sure a few times that I was supposed to do something. First, it was starting the shelter. And then it was this impression that I needed to be Mera's friend . . ."

"And *now?*" Faith matters quickly exhausted Onesphore's patience.

"Crazy as it sounds, I think I'll need this law degree. It's like it's part of some future thing I've got to do."

Onesphore chewed his burger then drained his coffee mug. He looked out the glass window at the light snow falling again.

"You are right," he conceded, "it is crazy. And if there is a God, I cannot believe he would want forty year old men with insanely busy lives to go back to school."

"I'm not forty 'til the summer." Seth was used to Onesphore's skepticism. After a decade they understood each other well. It was time to change the subject. "When you called from Canada, you said something was up. What's the deal?"

"Later," Onesphore brushed him off. "What are you studying at this law school?"

"International law . . . human rights . . ."

Onesphore's rumbling laughter cut him off, lyrical guffaws that rose from his gut and shook his huge frame.

"You are a pit bull, Langford. Just say it . . ."

"And you're a pain in the neck." Seth feigned a look of disgust.

"Say it . . ."

"Okay . . . okay. Fifteen years later and I'm back to war crimes."

Onesphore's eyes met Seth's before he looked away, the image of that last massacre outside Bentiu suddenly clear again. Without trying, he saw Mashada's gaunt form gliding slowly through the open cemetery of slaughtered bodies. He smelled the fetid-sweet odor of decomposing flesh hanging in the same air as the cries of the wounded. Pictured the blackened acres of scarred earth, pocked and cratered where air raids had scorched crop fields, leveled villages. Then as he closed his eyes to block it all out, he felt the metal of tarnished shotgun shells beneath his feet, some still hot and wet with blood.

The conference room was stifling, an odd phenomenon since it was freezing outside and set well below the 80°F mark on the shelter's inside thermostat. Coming back here to talk had been a mistake, Seth decided as three hard raps broke his concentration. Especially since the place always hovered near capacity during subzero weather.

He and Onesphore had been interrupted four times and now Mike was at the door again. But this time, Mike repeated himself twice before Seth heard over the ringing in his ears.

What Onesphore was saying couldn't be true. But if it was . . .

"Come on, man, quit obsessing," Seth sounded almost paternal, speaking to Mike's furrowed brow and sequential intrusions. "You *run* this place when I'm not here. Why are you picking now to second guess yourself?"

"In a couple hours, that blizzard's bringing in feet, not just inches," Mike practically whined as he pulled the bristly start of a goatee at his chin.

"And it'll bring another Ice Age if that's what it brings. But in the meantime, you're letting it make us both crazy." Seth noticed Mike looked like he was on the verge of hyperventilating. "C'mon, dude, you know what comes next. You can do this. You've *done* this."

"Right, but . . ."

"Okay," Seth relented, realizing Mike's little emotional crisis wasn't about to pass until someone told him the bases he'd already covered were, in fact, covered. "Let's talk possible landmines."

Mike relaxed visibly.

"Food, a possible shortage, but Krause Grocers called with a huge donation to drop off. And that doesn't include the brisket and beans Lanier's brought by this morning. Blankets could be a problem, but I've got the Midway workers going through the supply and pulling from storage. Next door isn't ready for business yet, but it'll sleep an extra hundred fifty. On the concrete, but it's better than the streets."

Seth stood up and rubbed his chin like he was thinking so that Mike could be sure that he'd been double-checked and found satisfactory.

"You got every angle worked except staff, and I bet you're already on that." Seth clapped Mike's shoulder as he escorted him to the door. He wanted to finish his conversation with Onesphore. "Just hang tight, now, and pretend this door doesn't exist unless someone's bleeding to death."

Mike shrugged and readjusted the backwards cap on his head. "A little edgy this afternoon, aren't we?"

"Blame it on my better angels. They didn't show up today."

"Touchy."

"Don't let the door hit you on the way out." Seth motioned at the open door. Mike shrugged again, rolled his eyes and disappeared.

The room fell completely quiet except for the muffled noise on the other side of the door. Swift footsteps tread up and down the hall and Mike's casual whistle fluted in the background.

"Run the numbers by me again." Seth sat back down and ran his hands over the rough wood of the table. Little splinters snagged at his fingertips.

Like he was in no rush, Onesphore stood and looked out the window. Across the street, the dingy buildings were draped in dazzling white and glittering icicles. A few straggly wanderers with scant clothing and brown-bagged bottles in hand edged their way toward the shelter's front door. It was always a toss up for some:

forego the booze, enter the shelter and avoid freezing to death or just hang close by and swill from the bag while praying another blizzard wouldn't force a surrender. It was well known in these parts that crossing the Wings Like Eagles threshold meant discarding intoxicating or reality-altering substances at the door. Shaking his head slowly, Onesphore turned away and took up pacing the length of the conference room.

"The latest?"

"Yeah."

"We are at two million dead now, close to four million displaced. And those are just the ones we can account for."

Seth cracked his knuckles, doing a mental tally. "When did we go up a million or more on each count?"

"Keep in mind, until the last eighteen months, the mission was not nearly so complicated . . ." Onesphore quit walking and turned to face Seth.

"Right," Seth interrupted, "it was just warlords with caches of weapons on a medieval quest to wipe out infidels like mosquitoes unless mutilation and trafficking worked better for the moment. And maybe on the side, doing a little land clearing here and there. That was all good enough for a day's work, right?" He shook his head in disgust.

"Which is not to say things were not bad. But the timing was not critical." Onesphore's brogue was particularly heavy, a trait that surfaced only when he was provoked or disturbed. "What difference did it make whether they blew up a village today or two months from now?"

"But now that they've got the lines laid and the oil's actually flowing . . ." Seth hesitated.

"What do you think?"

"The stakes just got higher . . ."

Onesphore nodded slowly. "I do not think they can climb any higher. And Bentiu was just the beginning. The Union fields were the latest war zone."

"How so?"

"The government dispatched a three thousand man militia to secure the pipeline region. Within a week, four surrounding villages were leveled."

"Leveled? As in . . ."

"As in wiped out," Onesphore finished the sentence. "The loss reports link it to explosions. Ignitions sparked by pipeline fissuring. But to keep the captive from tracking their scent, the last incident suggests sabotage. By the SPLA."

"Captive . . . as in the consortium's insurance subsidiary?"

The giant nodded. "These so-called risks are well insured. They must be, right?"

"What a crock," Seth jumped to his feet, outraged at the lie. "So they file for cash back on the other three while they sell the SPLA as nothing but a bunch of war-mongering savages?" He shook his head. "Did you see the damage?"

Onesphore pressed his lips together. "On all four. Precision was too exact for line ruptures. And every one of the incidents was identical. Right down to the fact that they happened at night. Or should I say after midnight?"

"So you're thinking it was helicopter gunships?"

"Mi-24s. Without a doubt."

"What did they drop?"

"Mostly cluster bombs, a few rockets."

"Did you talk to any witnesses?"

Onesphore let out a long sigh.

"Every site was a wasteland. The woodlands were so dry they went up in smoke as the shells were on the way down. But the nail in the coffin was the incendiaries did not even wait until the corpses were cleared out before they seeded the land with mines. Survivors could not even come back to bury their dead. And we had to assess damage from the air." Onesphore pulled a yellow tablet from his briefcase and leafed through it. After a few seconds, he looked up like he'd remembered something.

"Francis said one of his men saw the first attack, the one they are writing off as sabotage." He was talking about Mashada's husband, a lead SPLA officer. "Said his soldier saw three government commandos firing into the ground until the line ruptured. Then they finished it off with the air raid." Onesphore shut his eyes, and for a second, his black face was an onyx sculpture. "That is the one they are taking the loss on."

"But the others?"

"I told you, the consortium plans to transfer funds back to the government. For their losses."

"*Their* losses?" Somehow Seth had never gotten used to the deception. "What did *they* lose?"

"The hundreds of natives they killed. The land they scorched." Onesphore was matter-of-fact, like war-zone injustices were just part of a day. "But for business purposes, property and casualty losses."

Seth sank back down into a chair and chewed on a pencil.

"Let's see if I got this straight," he said after several seconds had passed. "The north gets the empty land because they've magically cleared it with their clean hands."

Onesphore nodded again. "Right. Essentially it is buy one, get one free. Only in this case, there is no buying other than the munitions they take to the killing fields."

"Then there's the crude money and cash back for the loss of life they keep taking. And the fact that they're keeping the greenbacks in their one big, happy and dysfunctional family." Seth stared out the window, his temples pounding. Right now, he wished he hadn't given up cigarettes because a Marlboro sounded good. "Talk about sleight of hand."

"Worst part is, the government is building secondary militias," Onesphore added.

"Out of who? From where?"

"This is not new. The north has always fought by proxy. They will persuade, if you know what I mean, any local tribes not cooperating with the SPLA." Onesphore pulled out a chair and lowered himself into it. "Like the Baggaras from the west, the brainwashed Ugandan child soldiers forced into the Lord's Resistance Army."

Seth shook his head incredulously. "So once they've got 'em conscripted, then what? They train them to move in like shock troops and pelt the south with artillery . . ."

"*Government artillery*," Onesphore emphasized, "which, incidentally, will be turned on them when *their* location gets marked for drilling. It is all about who is in the way of the profits."

"That's pathetic . . . twisted . . ." Seth couldn't find words that articulated how incensed, how despairing and impotent he felt in the face of such injustice. "They have no clue they're playing right into the north's manifesto. No idea they'll either be forced into the regime or get blown away by the same munitions they're firing."

"This is true."

"And they can't know how high the stakes are . . ."

"A million a day," Onesphore cut in.

Seth's eyebrows shot up.

"Oil profits?"

"No. They are collecting two million in revenues. But a million of that is spent fueling the war effort. Every day. And Khartoum plans to keep deploying their *mujahideen* . . ."

"*Mujahideen?*"

"Protectors of the oil brigade. Essentially the government's special forces."

"Of course," Seth exclaimed bitterly, "the three thousand who were staked around the Union fields while the four villages around it magically went up in smoke."

"Exactly," Onesphore confirmed.

"How many barrels are they moving a day?"

"Over a hundred thousand, out of Port Sudan."

"I forgot. What are the coordinates again?"

"The pipeline runs 1600 kilometers, mostly from Halig and Union oilfields to the Red Sea."

"From the north-south dividing line," Seth remembered.

"What lines? There are no lines anymore. The boundaries move every time new production gets underway."

Seth seriously considered getting up and asking Mike to find him a cigarette. Or something stronger. The caustic metrics were driving him crazy.

"How much oil do they think is there?"

Onesphore didn't hesitate. "Anywhere from 600 million to three billion barrels. Enough to last fifteen years."

"That's crazy."

"Welcome to the new series of crazies."

"And, of course, Wall Street's gambling with their fortunes only cranks up the heat like a witch doctor sticking pins in a voodoo doll. Meanwhile, whatever we do is about as redemptive as slapping at windmills." Seth stood up again, deflated.

"Not quite." Onesphore sat on the table, facing Seth straight on. "Which brings me to why I am here."

Seth waited for Onesphore to continue.

"For years, the north has pulled out every stop. Land mines, AK-47s, tactical missiles . . ."

"Bombs shoved off folded Antonovs," Seth added.

"Right, these weapons are like toys to this regime." Onesphore paused. "But until Bentiu, a humanitarian site was the exception."

Seth felt his heart sink into his stomach. "And now . . ."

"Last week, they bombed the new hospital outside El Obeid. It was well past capacity when they did it. A meningitis outbreak had the place two to a bed, three or four if they were kids."

"No way," Seth felt his pulse surge like he'd been walking in a dark alley and someone had lunged at him from the shadows. The little hospital was a rarity in the decimated southern region that had almost nothing resembling health care. To think it had been a deliberate target was inconceivable.

Onesphore didn't answer.

"That's where Spectrum's refinery is," Seth added a second later.

"Convenient, yes? And to add insult to injury, you must remember the government recently set up one of its military bases there."

"So now, they're killing two birds with one stone . . ."

"Exactly. And it is all going off without a hitch. They clean up the crude and refuel the planes and armored vehicles with it. Then, they repack their arsenals, regroup, and head back to their southern mission."

"So you're saying . . ."

Onesphore swallowed. "I am saying anything goes now. Anything at all. They will resort to whatever it takes."

"Are they still moving the women and children to the north?"

"Like cattle." Onesphore reached over, grabbed a decanter off the table and filled a styrofoam cup with water. He drained it, then continued. "The northern women want slaves, the men want whores and if the captives know what is good for them, they pledge allegiance to Muhammad, work like oxen and lay on their backs with their mouths shut, even when master is beating them harder than he is doing them."

It was one atrocity after another, each worse than the next. Seth started to ask another question, but changed his mind. For just a minute, he welcomed the silence.

"What do you want me to do?" he finally asked. He knew the answer would be at least complicated, probably risky, too.

"It is going to get worse. One of our men captured two northern soldiers at Bentiu. Separately, they predicted the bombing at El Obeid a month before it happened. The humanitarian sites were next, they said. First hospitals, then food relief."

"But Operation Lifeline Sudan's a direct UN affiliate." Seth was talking about the UNICEF, World Food Programme and NGO alliance that routinely provided food and relief supplies to the south.

"True, but the government has a right to restrict airspace in the presence of enemy threat."

"*What enemies?*"

"You tell me. If they want to restrict relief, anyone is the enemy, UN or not. And an enemy on their screen gets taken out like one. Even if the planes are C-130 transports carrying in relief. In this case, *especially* if it is relief. Remember, my friend, starvation is a highly effective weapon of war."

"God help them. And we think the famine's bad now." Listless, Seth sank back into his chair.

"It is getting to the point where we cannot depend on traditional aid venues into the south. It is becoming too erratic, too dependent on the north's mood. We will have to start moving food and supplies in through Loki. On Caravans."

The city of Lokichokio was a once-barren trading post situated at the Kenyan-Sudan border. Now one of the UN's largest relief bases, it served as an important staging ground for much of the humanitarian aid going into the war-torn south. But the prospect of hauling supplies and people across the border on tiny planes and then over hazardous graded roads often occupied by government troops or rebel forces from northern Uganda, was overwhelming.

Seth didn't flinch though he knew what was at stake. "We'll do what we have to do," he said as he stood.

Onesphore pushed back his chair to leave. "I will be in touch." He glanced at his watch before extending his hand.

"Want a ride back to the airport?"

"No. I told the taxi to be here at four."

Seth clasped Onesphore's shoulder. "It's good to see you, man. Always is."

"And you, my friend." Onesphore offered a decorous nod. "We will meet again, soon." He turned to leave, his huge frame filling the doorway.

"Onesphore?"

"Yes?"

"You never did say. How's Mera?"

Onesphore turned back around to look at him, perplexed. "Meranda?"

"Yeah."

"Do you not speak with her, exchange mail?"

"Some, but it's not exactly easy."

Onesphore stared at him, examining his face closely. "When did you last see her?"

"Nearly two years ago"

"I see."

Seth drew in his breath. "Is she . . . the same?"

"No," the giant answered pensively, as if he were picturing her, "she is not. She is different now."

"How so?"

"Better than when she first came. Much healthier. Some say she is very beautiful. But . . . but there is more."

Seth was taken aback by Onesphore's elaboration. He wasn't one to offer details.

"She is shrewd in her dealings with the company. And I hear often that she has shown herself to be a very good friend to the people in the villages."

"I'm not surprised." Seth looked down, not wanting to catch Onesphore's eyes.

"Langford?"

"Yeah?"

"You said your God . . . He wished you to be a friend to Meranda . . . that is right?"

Seth nodded.

"If this is true, He had to know you would cross this line."

"What line . . . what are you talking about?"

"This one. This one where you stopped liking her and started wanting more."

"It's not like that . . ." Seth began.

"You love her," Onesphore indicted him.

Seth's eyes met his friend's unexpectedly, and neither of them said anything for what seemed like minutes.

"Tell me, Onesphore, what do you believe about love?" Seth finally broke the silence.

Onesphore chewed on the question.

"Langford, many people believe in a thing without saying so. And many say they believe in something though they do not at all." He fell quiet.

"Right," Seth replied cautiously. "So you're saying . . ."

"I do not believe love exists apart from how we live. My experience tells me the *idea* of love or the *idea* of sacrifice is what most people want. Because this costs little. But I imagine love or sacrifice at its best is something you do with everything you have in you." The giant cleared his throat. "My friend, you love Meranda Kaine."

"Maybe," Seth answered, everything inside him spinning at such a dictum.

"If I believed in a God," Onesphore continued thoughtfully, "I would not waste my time thinking Him small. He would have to be big . . . much greater than me, so that I would think Him capable of the extraordinary. Maybe even the impossible."

"Okay?" Seth had no idea where he was heading.

"You . . . you believe in this God. You follow him like He is real." Onesphore squinted at him, an inspection of sorts. "But I wonder sometimes . . ."

"Wonder what?"

"I wonder why you do not think Him vast. And why you must not ponder what may be His mysteries."

Seth was amused. Watching Onesphore contemplate spiritual matters on his behalf was something new.

"What are you getting at?"

"Your friend, she has suffered much, yes?"

"She has," Seth winced, thinking about Mera's past.

"Maybe she needed an ally, someone who did not expect anything from her."

"I've tried to be that for her."

"So you have. And in return, you have her trust," Onesphore hesitated, choosing his words carefully. "Maybe *this* was the greater plan of your God. Perhaps this is why He wanted you to show kindness to her."

"What do you mean?"

"Maybe you belong together," Onesphore said nonchalantly, as he opened the door and walked out, not bothering to look back.

Chapter 35

The squiggly symbols were starting to make sense, like an outline of a jigsaw puzzle. Arabic was a world away from the English she'd written and read her whole life and finding a common ground between the two alphabets had, at first, been an exercise in futility. There were no familiar gauges, she realized. Nothing to make it connect with anything she already knew.

But once she'd accepted that, the gist of it got suddenly clearer.

"You are doing well, madam. Try this now." Mashada pointed to more linear curls on a glossy travel brochure Mera had brought home from the office. It had come from an embassy in Khartoum, showcasing Sudan's developed northern regions.

"The Government . . . supports the people rights," Mera read slowly. "No, no that's 'rights of the people by fair considering'. . ." She slammed the garishing paper down, glad Donovan was sound asleep on the couch. "People's rights, fair consideration. What a sham."

"Sham, madam?" Mashada's eyebrows knitted together.

"Lies covered up. Pretending truth."

"I see." Mashada was placid, unmoved. "You are reading well for one who studies this language only one and one half years. It will not be long before you can read all things in Arabic."

"You mean all the lies." Mera didn't bother to hide her resentment.

"Madam," Mashada began, somewhat alarmed at Mera's atypical outburst, "you are angry. But you cannot think all writings in this language untrue."

Mera recomposed herself.

"Of course not. I'm just talking about this kind of propaganda and mumbo jumbo."

"Mumbo jumbo is . . ."

"Nonsense. Talking to inflate oneself. Conveniently leaving out anything self-incriminating." Mera pointed to the paper. "That's what this is—mumbo jumbo." She lowered her voice to a whisper. "To read it, you'd think a trip to the Sudan is an adventure in progressive African culture. Political tolerance and religious freedom for all, a transparent government . . ."

"Yes." Mashada wore the expression of a patient ox, a fact that only added to Mera's irritation.

"Yes to what? That this is the real Sudan?" She gestured at the foreign words. "This is our reality here?"

"No madam, it is different here," Mashada lowered her eyes and avoided looking at the brochure that had touched off this conversation. "This is not what we see."

"Of course not. They left out pictures of starving children and men with half a leg or arm blown off. They forgot to mention the Polish tankers and Russian airships bought with oil money or the chattel slaves beaten until . . ." Mera stopped short, suddenly realizing she was talking to Mashada.

Mashada, who, until the last few years, had lived her life in the north, practicing northern customs and the beliefs that had spawned so much of the south's predicament.

"I'm sorry, Mashada," Mera backpedaled. "I wasn't thinking . . ."

Mashada looked pained. "You believe I support the north's hate, their crimes against the people?"

"I'm not saying that. I just know you lived with your family outside of Khartoum. And that you've served the government for years."

Mashada looked down again, then across the room at Donovan. His round face was flushed and his curls were damp with perspiration, but he was still sleeping peacefully.

"When did I say this to you?" she whispered so softly that Mera barely heard her.

"I don't remember . . ."

"When did I tell you I was from north of Sudan?" she repeated, her voice even less perceptible.

"You . . . you never did say that. I . . . I just put together . . ."

Mashada reached beside the discarded brochure for the practice tablet of Arabic twists and curls. Silently, she wrote two words in English — *come outside*. When she looked up, Mera caught her gaze and held it. Pushing back her chair, she followed Mashada outside the tiny bungalow.

"Madam, you are anxious?" Mashada sank down next to her on the concrete steps of the red-dusted landing. The air was heavy from the rain and a silvery haze blanketed the moon.

"Why did you want to come out here?" Mera pulled at her damp, messy ponytail. She could already feel the sweat dripping down her back.

"It is not safe to talk of personal . . . private affairs. Not inside."

Mera knew why — and what — Mashada was talking about. But the fact that the woman might, too, was an unexpected twist. Could it be Mashada understood the link between Spectrum and the government?

"Do you not think so?" She made herself sound casual.

Mashada set her jaw like she was about to plunge into something big. In the filmy light, Mera noticed tiny perspiration beads glittering like diamonds on her forehead.

"Madam, I have worked for you two years almost."

"Almost." It would be two years in November and it was August now.

"We are like friends sometimes," Mashada suggested timidly.

Mera gave the woman's shoulder a light squeeze. "Like friends? We *are* friends. I don't know what I'd do without you here."

"I . . . there is . . ." Mashada stammered then fell silent, staring dully at the starless sky. Mera waited for her to continue, but when she looked closely past her *hijab*, she noticed tears streaming from the woman's eyes. A second later, Mashada drew her legs to her chest and curled herself into a human ball. Noiseless sobs racked her body.

"Mashada, what is it?" Mera exclaimed as she scooted close enough to put her arm around her friend's shoulders. "What hurts you like this?"

"Today, ten years ago on this day . . ."

"What? What happened ten years ago?"

"Oh madam, I am not from north," Mashada looked up and blurted out the words in staccato bursts of broken English. "I live in south village outside Babanusa in West Kordofan, me and my family. All my life." The sobs were subsiding but tears still coursed over her cheeks.

"But . . ."

"One night, the militia, they come . . . the night of my marriage . . ."

Like a sudden flash, Mera recalled the execrable image of nearly a year ago, the one of Mashada in the tattered gown beside the haunted soldier.

No, that couldn't be right . . . they couldn't have taken Mashada . . .

Mera dreaded what was coming, partly because it would require revisiting her own pain, partially because she knew Mashada's truth probably represented the sum of all hate and prejudice in this region.

"Our tribe . . . I am Dinka . . . we are celebrating my wedding," she continued between erratic breaths, "when they come on horses, the north army, with guns and knives." She fell quiet for a second, remembering. "It was . . . how do you say . . . so bad . . . so evil. They nearly kill my Francis . . . and many of them, so many I can not count . . . they tear my dress and . . . and . . ." Mashada burst into tears again. Like a small child, she hugged her legs even closer and rocked herself back and forth.

For a long time, neither of them said anything. Finally Mera broke the silence.

"Your husband, he's a soldier for the south, the SPLA?"

Mashada stiffened and sat up straight. "How do you know?" she said suspiciously.

Mera decided to skip telling her about the grisly vision.

"I didn't. Just a guess."

The woman relaxed a little.

"Francis is commanding officer. He moves often between villages to lead the soldiers."

That explained the fatigues and the other soldiers from Mera's apparition.

"I see." She returned to Mashada's story. "After the soldiers came and hurt you . . . and Francis . . . then what?"

"The northern guerillas, they kill many of our men that night . . . this I remember. And some of the women . . . they do to them what they do with me . . ." Mashada couldn't finish, like the recall, once verbalized, would be too much to subdue again.

"I'm so sorry, Mashada." Mera moved one of the woman's hands from her damp face then lifted her chin until their eyes met. "So very sorry." She said it softly, feeling both Mashada's violation and her own with a razor-sharp clarity. Hadn't she once heard rape was hell's imagination on earth? That had to be right because hell, like heaven, was supposedly eternal. And the images of force and flesh and fusion were vitriolic snapshots that lived on forever . . . and ever . . .

"I try to fight them away." The words clawed from Mashada's throat like they'd fought her and won. "This I swear . . ."

"Mashada . . . oh, Mashada, it wasn't your fault. You couldn't have resisted a platoon of soldiers." Mera shuddered at the thought. "It wasn't your fault."

"They took many of us to the north." The woman wasn't done telling her story. "We walk many days. Even now, I do not know how Francis got there. I think they do not kill him because he did not fight back. He listen to government soldiers." She took a deep breath. Blinked hard. "They know I am his wife . . . that we had not been together. So the soldiers . . . they make him watch while they use my body. This they do many times." Mashada was shaking and Mera felt her stomach twist and nearly heave inside out.

"We travel then to Khartoum. And there we are bought by Arab masters. Somehow Francis and I, we are were sold together."

Mera tried not to gape. "*Masters?* You and Francis were sold as slaves?"

Mashada steeled herself.

"Yes, madam. But our owner, he was not all bad. In fact, some say he is kind. He make me wear *hijab* and *jilbab*, recite his prayers. But he beat me only one time, the night I try to escape. And unless he is angry with all his wives, he did not use me."

"How nice of him," Mera quipped bitterly. "An irenic overlord."

Mashada ignored the commentary.

"One of his wives — I cook and clean for them all — she teach me to read and speak Arabic."

"What about English? Where did you learn that?"

Mashada's smile was wan. "Did you not know, madam? English is official language we teach in schools of south Sudan. When there are schools, we read and speak in English. In our tribe, we talk Dinka."

Mera let the information sink in.

"So how did you get from Khartoum to here?"

"It takes five years, but Francis, he make it when we plan our escape. He found embassy in Cairo that brings him to Iron Lung." Mera was startled to hear her call Onesphore by that name. So far, she'd only heard Seth say how he'd acquired it. Now the sound of it was surreal.

"Iron Lung, he tells me you know all about the north. And about Spectrum."

Mera figured Onesphore's trust in Mashada was either a crap-shoot or the woman was entirely safe. Considering the giant was about as confidential as a clam, she decided it had to be the latter.

"So Onesphore met Francis in Cairo." Regardless of Onesphore's estimation of Mashada, Mera still offered no confirmation of what she did and didn't know. "Then what?"

"You know how Onesphore works with SPLA," Mashada whispered. "Well, the embassy, they make contact with him, and he help Francis reunite with south soldiers. Francis told him about me, and one year later, Iron Lung brings me to him. By then, I have a small boy. A son by my master." Another spasm passed through her. "But he let me go when Iron Lung gives him news the government will pay for my release to Spectrum."

"You had a child?" Without trying, Mera saw the flash again. The dead toddler's vacant expression. Mashada holding him. And what had to be Francis hovering above them.

"A boy by my master," she repeated tonelessly.

"I see." What else could she say? The whole story was shaking out too much like her own. "And when you left, he let you take him?"

"Yes. I am *abeeda*, black slave. He can want no child with my blood, my color."

Thinking of children made Mera remember she hadn't checked on Donovan in nearly a half hour. Leaning forward, she peered through the barrack's cracked door. Sprawled on the couch in the little jean shorts and green alligator t-shirt he'd worn all day, the child's breathing was deep and rhythmic.

"Did you stay long with Francis before you came to Spectrum?" Mera wiped her forehead on her sleeve and settled back on the stoop.

"Iron Lung, he make it seem that the move from my master's home to here takes much time so I can spend two weeks with Francis before I come to here. The first week, it was very good. Francis is happy to see me, very kind to Saleem. He is not at all angry with me."

Mera frowned. "Angry? Why would he have been angry with you?"

"I had child and child was not his."

"But you didn't . . . you couldn't help what happened."

"Yes, madam. But in our culture, this is shameful. To the woman and to husband of the woman." A light came into Mashada's eyes. "But not my Francis; he does not have shame for me or Saleem. But second week, helicopters come to the village." She took a deep breath. "They drop bombs."

Without question, Mera knew what came next. Up to this point, the sequence of that night vision was flawless. She closed her eyes for just a second, not ready for Mashada's words.

"A big one, it came, very terrible. I will never forget because it looks like shiny black locust with dark wings that go *chop chop* at the air. Then it drop a bomb near our *tukul*. The pieces of metal . . . the . . ."

"Shrapnel." Mera opened her eyes and met Mashada's dead gaze.

"Yes, that is it. The shrapnel, it kills Saleem. It tears his body open."

There were no words to absorb her agony, no phrases to ease the torment of being caught in the crossfire of war. So they sat in silence again, listening as the tiny candle flame pulled and hissed in the lamp at the door.

"It's really warm tonight. We should go back inside," Mera finally said.

"Madam?"

"Yes?"

"You are very beautiful," Mashada made no move to return to their barrack, "and very good."

"That's debatable."

"When we make our return from Bentiu after the explosion last year, Iron Lung, he spoke of you."

Mera rested a hand on Mashada's bony shoulder. "You must've gone to check on Francis." A year later, the trip suddenly made sense.

"And my brother. They both are strong and survive. But my brother . . . he has no more arm now."

"I'm sorry." The words sounded trite, feeble in light of what was lost out here.

"When we travel back, Iron Lung says you have friend who recommend you come to here."

"This is true." The unexpected reminder of Seth took her off guard. Made something inside her tingle.

"He said your friend, he is very good man."

Hearing her talk about Seth was odd. Too personal, yet impersonal at the same time. Since she'd been in Sudan, their contact had been limited. Brief letters, intentionally vague in case they were censored. Occasional calls on sat phones or the company's land line had been no different since there were no guarantees her office or barracks might not be tapped. Obviously, the same thought had crossed Mashada's mind earlier.

"You know, I think he's the best person I've ever known." Without thinking, the words fell from her lips and the truth of them startled her.

"You love him, yes?" Mashada stared at her, eyes wide and serious.

"I haven't seen him, we haven't talked much in almost two years."

Mashada chewed on the evasive answer, thinking carefully before she spoke again.

"Madam . . . it is well to say this while you can."

Mera squinted. "Say what, Mashada?"

"Words of . . . how do you say . . . affection. Or love." She exhaled long and low like all breath was leaving her. "I think every chance you get, you should say these words. Because one day that you say it . . . or wish you would have say it . . . it will be final time." She dropped her voice. "Then if you did not say the words, you will wish always you can have the moment back."

Everything inside Mera was at attention. Fully alive.

"But it's been so long," she said thickly. "And . . . there were things that hurt . . . things that weren't easy." She had no idea why she was baring herself.

Mashada let a respectable silence pass.

"Time does not change love, madam," she finally said. "Neither does pain."

Mera thought about the way Seth's hair fell across his eyes before he pulled his fingers through it. She remembered his wide shoulders in flannel shirts, the clean smell of his skin when he stood close. Out of nowhere, she could feel his hands lacing through hers that night after the ballet. And suddenly, everything in her hurt, ached so deeply she could hardly breathe.

"Maybe you're right." Mera looked down at the concrete steps covered in African sands that seemed farther than ever from Chicago's bustling city streets. "Maybe I do." As she stood up to go inside, she said the last words so softly that she was almost sure Mashada hadn't heard her.

Chapter 36

The fact that sleep eluded her felt more like collusion than an irritation. It was as if her past had a contract with drowsiness and there could be no hope of rest until she surveyed long-forgotten vignettes that suddenly decided they would have lives of their own.

So here she was in an epic tug-o-war, part of her demanding to remember what the other part wanted so badly to forget. As if in sifting through these ashes — because that's all the past was — there might be some redemptive find that could move her somewhere new. Somewhere she hadn't been before . . .

Donovan slept sticky and hot, pressed close to her. Wiping his forehead with the edge of the sheet, Mera studied him in the moonlight. Just in the time they'd been here, he had changed so much. His legs, milk-white and baby-thick, had grown longer, gotten thinner and taken on a shape. His rosy lips were parted in sleep, revealing tiny even teeth that protruded where he sucked this thumb, but his chin and nose were still little fleshy dollops that had yet to take form. He was perfect, she thought contentedly, and for the millionth time, she thanked God that she'd taken him.

Scooping a hand under his head, she breathed in his smell, a pleasant miscellany of sweat, dried oatmeal and dust from playing outdoors. Smiling, she kissed his thatch of damp curls and a chubby cheek. Letting out a tiny whimper, he stirred and then turned on his side as she leaned back and crumpled a pillow into form. It was time to sleep now.

But instead of grogginess, all she got was an uninvited panorama.

They came quickly, these memories, and she wondered why now. Mulling over what couldn't be changed, what had happened epochs ago, was useless . . .

First, it was her positioned between Steve and Annalise on a sparkling white and emerald beach in Destin, Florida. She was little, around four, and clad in a pink bathing suit with violet polka dots. Next to her towered her twin brothers, Kyle and Derek, young teenagers with surfboards tucked under their arms. It was the only family vacation they'd ever taken and everyone looked happy as they squinted in the golden sunlight.

Then another flash. Her in a torn pink dress outside of Jack's house against a black sky that went on forever

It was the night Steve had first violated her.

There was Jack beside her on his creaking porch swing. Then Mark holding her while Emily stroked her hair.

More scenes followed, some dark, others benign, as they cooperated with an unseen muse, who was at least putting her life in chronological order.

Then came Jack again, strong and tall and handsome. This time, he was looking down at her. Asking her to marry him.

Without warning, a sharp image eclipsed his honest brown eyes. It was the shadowy outline of another Jack, this one wet and virulently consumed as he'd wrestled and pinned her down. The torrential rain — or was it the insufferable torment — of that night had blurred the sight and sounds of his betrayal. But the deluge hadn't shrouded his expression. She'd just blocked it out.

Now she saw it all again, a spectator watching someone else's demise.

His saturated hair was in ringlets. Tight little springs that dripped ice-cold rainwater onto her face. But everything else had been hot.

Sultry and torrid.

The sweltering air. Her flushed cheeks. The unreal clinging of skin to wet skin before his body overtook hers. Even the dizzying slowness of his first forceful motions were breathtakingly hot. And as it went on and on, deeper and sharper, the heat had felt more blistering than Saharan winds.

Oh God, there she was. That was her naked body, helpless beneath his. Her horrified features crumpling from disbelief to terror.

She was looking up at him, petrified at the fury that filled his eyes. His jaw was clenched and his eyes bored into hers, almost daring her as his breathing grew more and more shallow.

Then his body went rigid. A forceful shudder passed through him, and as it did, she felt it ripple through her. Gasping, he'd squeezed his eyes shut, and when he opened them again, she was crying. A second later a hand had slapped her face.

His hand.

The recall left her breathless for a second. Until now, she hadn't realized the numbing sting was Jack's hand.

Like the conquest of her body hadn't been enough . . .

He'd had to finish the deal with some reminder that he'd dominated her completely.

Lying in the dark, Mera waited for the usual wave of shame to follow. It always came, any time she even got close to revisiting that night. Ignominy that made her feel filthy and stupid and worthless for days after . . .

Instead something else happened. A realization, like an unexpected answer to a prayer.

Jack had stolen from her and it wasn't her fault. It never had been.

The truth hit her blindside.

Whether or not he wore a priest's collar was irrelevant.

Jack was a thief. A ravager who had plundered from her something that never belonged to him.

The understanding made her dizzy. Four years later, the crime made more sense than it ever had.

She'd just been in the wrong place at the wrong time under the false impression that her beloved Jack was anyone but the imposter who was playing priest, even playing God, to satisfy his own ambitions.

No wonder he couldn't face the truth she'd tried so hard to point out.

It wasn't her fault.

Heart pounding, Mera drank in the new revelation like cold spring water on a hundred-degree day.

She hadn't deserved the hell Jack had put her through.

Somehow it seemed like heaven might make the earth quake beneath the power of this truth, a truth that had her crying like a prisoner acquitted of a life sentence.

It all made sense now and she wasn't to blame. She never had been.

She tried to let it sink in.

She never had been . . .

Like an opened faucet, tears coursed over her cheeks, falling in little *plip plops* onto the crisply starched sheets. As they did, she felt a tight reel inside her loosen and start to unwind. She felt the secret shame and humiliation she'd carried for so long cut away like tether strings clipped to free a hot air balloon. And the release was so definite, so sharply final, that everything in her ached wildly and grasped for more at the same time.

Then she saw Jack again.

A little boy in the moonlight.

A young man beneath Martin Luther King, Jr.'s memorial statue.

A priest in an airport.

A rapist on top of her, naked and angry and stealing from her . . .

She felt her breath catch in her throat and start to stick. Consciously, she forced the air back out.

It was finished. Done now, she told herself. The agony could die and dim and start going away, because she could let it.

It was in her now, in this moment to let it all go. To release Jack once and for all until all that was left of him concerning her was whatever peace he'd need to make between himself and his God. And how and when or even if that happened wasn't up to her.

Seconds passed, then minutes, though she wasn't keeping track of time.

Lying in the silent room illumined in slabs of diaphanous moonlight, all that mattered was the curious stillness she felt inside. A wholeness she'd never known.

She had forgiven Jack Frasier.

It didn't matter he'd shown no remorse, sought no redemption. He was off her hook.

Studying the delicate art of Donovan's sleeping form, she felt her own eyes growing heavier. But the last thing she wanted to do was fall asleep.

Free. She was completely free for the first time in her life.

Still almost giddy with the largeness of it all, she started as another recollection edged its way from the periphery and crowded her thoughts.

It was she and Seth the night they'd gone to the ballet.

There he was, his wind-tousled head lightly touching hers, his etched features intense. But it was the look on his face she'd missed.

Until now.

He was completely caught up in the moment, in her, like he didn't ever want to be anywhere else. He looked so deliberately vulnerable . . .

They were near the door of her flat, laughing as he twisted his fingers through hers. She had said something, he traced the curve of her face with his thumb. Never taking his eyes off hers, he leaned down, his mouth closing softly over hers . . . and lingering.

She knew now. Love was the something else she couldn't, or maybe wouldn't, decipher. But it had been there, written all over his face.

Seth Langford loved her, really loved her.

Or at least, he had at one time.

She sat up then, something swelling inside of her, something greater than the infamy she'd outlived, powerful enough to shatter a lifetime of defenses. It swept through her, whatever it was, like pure light and fresh wind. And after it passed, the expanse cleared inside her was so wide open and real that she knew for the first time in her life she could choose to love — something she'd been paralyzed from all these years.

Chapter 37

The timing couldn't have been better, but it couldn't have been worse. The higher ups at Spectrum knew her now, knew just how easily she mingled among the locals. They knew, too, how she made things happen, whether it was navigating press calls or helping build schools in war-ravaged provinces. Bottom line, Meranda Kaine had long since trumped just about everyone's expectations. Despite ongoing turmoil in the oil fields, Spectrum still looked like a good citizen to the world. And for the past few years, she'd been behind much of that.

Which is why she got the call to head south with Onesphore after a series of landmine explosions and an aerial assault half-leveled a village near Torit.

Torit sat just north of the Ugandan border, south of newly government-occupied Juba, where from what Mera had been able to piece together, mercenaries had seeded the land with mines close to a new production bloc the consortium was exploring.

That done, the Khartoum government established a wider no-fly zone around the region and conveniently chose not to disclose the new boundary line, though it clearly infringed on southern property.

SPLA soldiers caught wind of the infraction and set out past the village where they fell into the first trap. Land mines were everywhere. Within hours more than a hundred soldiers had gone up in black smoke.

Trap number two fell a few days later when an Antonov bombed the village just after daybreak. Numbers of two hundred plus were reported dead and it was anybody's guess just how many were injured.

It looked bad for the company and the executive team knew it. Just two weeks ago, Spectrum had had to fight the press on charges of government planes refueling on their airstrips while NIF military opened-fire on a nearby village. It hadn't been an easy allegation to dismiss.

With that fiasco newly assuaged, there didn't need to be any more perceived collusion. That's why she and Onesphore were sent with orders to survey the damage, express condolences. The disaster had happened more than ten miles from the new bloc, distance enough to avoid too much suspicion, but close enough for the company to don its good citizen hat.

One of Spectrum's Cessnas flew them into Torit, and from takeoff, the six thousand-foot climb was turbulent. A late season storm made the skies gray and the headwinds strong while big raindrops spilled white weights over the windows. At about two thousand feet, the craft suddenly veered hard to the left, then back to the right while the winds piped from a loud hum to a howl. Occasionally, a thunderclap further rocked the cabin, and twice, sharp dips caused Onesphore to hit his head on the ceiling. Mera sat scrunched next to him, chewing her fingernails, clenching her teeth and reminding herself to breathe. To distract herself, she tried tracing the plane's pale blue wing between blinding sheets that had visibility at under three hundred feet.

Then the storm quieted as suddenly as it had started. Choppy air bursts still rocked the craft but the skies turned pale gray, the winds resumed a steady drone and the rain spattered in a soft shower. Onesphore, who had alternately set his jaw and mopped sweat from his forehead, dug a yellow tablet from his briefcase and began scribbling in Arabic. Relieved to the point of feeling limp, Mera stared outside and watched silver rain droplets chase each other like spilled beads across the window. The gentle *pit pat* amid the deafening *whirr* of the engine was music compared to the din of a mid-air tempest.

Now there was just the dread prospect of facing a war zone.

The Cessna dropped through snow-white clouds an hour later. As the little craft hovered just above the endless stretch of red dirt before touching down, Onesphore looked up from his tablet and stared at her.

"When we arrive, you will be surprised," he said quietly. She figured he was referring to the casualties.

But before the ancient Toyota they'd driven from Torit stopped at the ravaged village, she understood what he meant.

As the sometimes-wooded grasslands stretched into a holocaustal museum of debris and fire-scorched earth, two men stood out amid the huddled masses of hollow-eyed survivors. One was a young man, clean-shaven with a Latino appearance. He was in jeans, the stethoscope around his neck pressed against the bony chest of an old man on a makeshift stretcher.

The other one was Seth, his blonde hair cropped close. Cradling an emaciated child, he looked up as the Toyota's grinding engine sputtered, then clicked off.

The timing couldn't have been better, but it couldn't have been worse, either.

The moon rose high and full just before they left camp, a silver-clear orb that made the night glow eerie blue. The air was thick, too, and it only grew heavier and more suffocating with every passing step.

Both Seth and Mera were too tired to say much. The afternoon had been backbreaking and full, a non-stop mission of hauling rubble and clearing corpses so something resembling order might be restored. Then as if on cue, the locals ceased working at twilight to eat *acita*, a steaming cream-colored mush made from pounded, then boiled, sorghum and millet. A half hour later, nearly everyone slept. Since the *tukuls* had been razed in last week's siege, the locals had all settled in the open air on dusty hardpan pocked by rocket explosions and gunfire. But since the village chief must be protected, villagers, with the help of the relief team, had erected a temporary grass hut for him.

They walked on about a quarter mile past the village, navigating a mostly broken dirt path via bluish light cones shafting from headlamps strapped to their foreheads. In her hand, Mera carried a lantern knowing the trip back to camp would be far more black than this early darkness. The day's heat had baked the surrounding earth, and as if it were finally getting a chance to breathe, the air, the ground, even the tangled underbrush exhaled sweltering breaths that made inhalation almost paralyzing to the lungs.

Ten minutes later, they came to a clearing beside a *wadi*. The dried-up streambed cast dark imposing shadows onto the bank where they stood, compliments of towering black rocks that filled the deep gully. In the interest of light and repelling mosquitoes, Seth immediately started a fire with some scrappy sticks they'd collected along the way. As the dry branches hissed and crackled into iron-red flames, they tented a mosquito net over them and sat back against a thick tree stump.

"We're bending the rules, you know," Seth let out a long low sigh. "No one does this here."

She set down the lantern, adjusted the netting and moved a dirt clump from beneath her. "What? Sits against tree stumps?" She tried to sound casual but she was so nervous the words were sticking in her throat.

"No, no one lights fires after dark. Or not usually."

"True. In Kadugli, nature dictates lights out." She wanted to hit herself for sounding so dull.

The firewood snapped as a sudden wind fanned the blaze. Seth leaned in, ready to guard the flames, and as he did, their legs touched. The net draped over them was made for just one person.

"What a day." He pulled his leg back like an electrical surge had cut through him. Then raked his fingers through his hair before staring nonchalantly into the flames.

"When did you get here?" She picked up a long stick from the ground.

"Day before yesterday. Came in through Nairobi and flew on a charter to Lokichokio." Recently, the Kenyan border-city had been declared ground zero for all relief flights and humanitarian efforts heading into the otherwise restricted south. "Eeyore took us the rest of the way."

"Eeyore?" Mera smiled. "As in Milne's donkey?"

"As in the pitiful Jeep that barely chugged us here."

"Oh." Silence again, then, "Who's the doctor with you?"

"Juan Barrera."

"He's a nice guy," she said, referring to the steely sense of humor he'd shown all afternoon. Despite the bleak circumstances, Juan had managed to keep most of the native men laughing for hours. "Really good with the people here."

Seth nodded.

He was so blasé, she reflected anxiously. So much more guarded than she remembered. Maybe it was just being out here, so far from home. More likely, though, his feelings had changed. Nearly three years had come and gone and their contact had been so sparse . . .

"I came out here for a couple reasons," Seth broke her thoughts. "When Onesphore called me from the compound . . ."

"From the compound?" she interrupted. "About *this*?"

He shook his head. "If something's urgent, we use code. It's cryptic, mind you, something we've scared up over the years. But it works."

"Cool."

"Yeah," he continued as he stretched his arms in front of him and cracked his knuckles. "Any censoring would only report us talking about his parents. He's got me guardian for them when he's out of the States. So code language sounds like it's all about them even though they have nothing to do with it."

"Clever."

"It's definitely kept lines open between here and there." He said it like masterminding obscure language was an everyday affair. "Especially during red alerts like this."

She started to answer but he was talking again.

"Onesphore said it was bad," he sighed, ". . . really bad."

"I think it's the worst I've seen yet." She shuddered, recalling the corpses scattered over the earth like swollen seeds. Shrapnel had shredded some beyond recognition. Others lay bloated and maggot-embedded in pools of drying blood. Past the edges of the open graveyard had been lines of sick and infected natives waiting for Juan to stick them with penicillin needles.

Seth looked preoccupied and distraught at the same time.

"Well, UN relief's focused on getting into the Nuba mountains." The oil-rich Western Upper Nile region was an another battlefield between the NIF and the SPLA. Just the month before, Sudan's government had restricted all humanitarian access to the area, and with food and medical supplies cut off, thousands were dying. "They'll eventually try and help out here, but getting flight clearance in the banned space could take weeks. So we got what we could together. Moved it through Kenya."

She grimaced. "Wasn't it hard getting so much stuff across the border?"

"Onesphore had a guy waiting for us in Loki. Once we found him, he had connections the whole way here."

Mera shook her head, amazed. "That guy blows me away." Onesphore still appeared to have little use for her but that was neither here nor there.

"Know the other reason I came?"

"Your last letter said you finished the shelter. And you hadn't been here in four years . . ."

"Onesphore said you'd be along to do PR stuff while he checked out the bloc."

"He said *that* in code?" The how-to of the code thing was still fascinating.

"Sure did."

She inched closer, just enough for their legs to touch again. The effect was dizzying and she felt her heart pounding like a drum in her chest. "I'm glad you're here." She mustered up a little courage. "I've missed you."

"Have you?"

"I've never known anyone like you. It just took me a while to realize it."

He cleared his throat. Ignored the compliment.

"I bet it gets lonely here sometimes. This place is a world away from Chicago."

"Literally." She tried not to feel hurt at his brush-off.

"Do you like it?"

She thought for a minute, reaching outside their net to dangle her stick over the flames.

"It depends. I hate seeing the latest outbreak of meningitis or watching a five-year old pass out because someone's coaxing a six-foot guinea worm from beneath his skin. I hate it that I can't stop the machine guns or keep the next landmine from exploding." She poked at the glowing embers then fed the branch to the fire. "And I want to throw up when a government helicopter refuels on the company's airstrip before it goes and bombs only God knows who next while I crank out tomorrow morning's acquitting press . . ."

"God have mercy," Seth closed his eyes, digesting the horror. "That's gotta be the worst."

"Spectrum's as guilty of colluding with the north as I am of what happened with . . ." she hesitated for a second, like she wanted to elaborate, "with so many things."

Seth let a respectable silence pass before he turned to face her.

"Mera, no," his tone was firm beneath the gentle words, "Emily's dying wasn't your fault. None of it was."

She assumed the *it* he was talking about had to do with losing Emily Kate.

"You know, I know that. Or at least I think I do. But then I hit these every now and then moments when I just don't know."

"I *do* know. It wasn't your fault," Seth repeated adamantly. "Not any of it." He said it like he knew more than he possibly could, and for a second, she was almost sure he did.

"You can't know that."

"Maybe I do . . ."

"How? How would you know?"

He didn't answer. Instead, he changed the subject. "What do you like out here?" Her hair had grown past her shoulders and it gleamed golden chestnut in the firelight. She was still small, probably always would be, but she was healthy again. A far cry from the frail-thinness of three years ago.

"The anonymity. No one knows anything about me other than what I'm doing. I like that." She pulled her knees to her chest and wrapped her arms around them. "But mostly, it's the people."

He smiled.

"They're amazing aren't they?"

"Indescribable. One minute they're barely surviving, like it takes everything they have to just keep breathing." She paused, picturing highlights of the last few years. "Next thing you know, they're stacked shoulder to shoulder, ready to take out whoever's in their way." She studied Seth's face. "You know what I mean?"

He nodded as she continued.

"I guess when you've got a mission bigger than the hell you live with, you don't quit the fight until you either win or die." She looked up at the night sky awash in tiny glittering stars, took in the still-searing wind whispering lightly through the brush. "Before I came here, defending freedom was something that happened in history books. Here, it's in the air they breathe." She picked up two wispy sticks and tossed them into the flames. "I know I shouldn't feel this way, but every time I see a new drilling rig or get close enough to hear pressure moving through a line, I want to blow a hole in it. I want to wipe out these operations like the government and these companies massacre these villages."

Seth shook his head. Cracked his knuckles again. "I know. And any kind of help or aid, whether it's moving folks out or getting stuff in, seems like nothing more than snuffing out a campfire fifty yards ahead of a forest blaze."

They sat quiet for the better of a minute taking in the forlorn hum of the wind, the crackling of little branches in the fire.

"That's the hardest part," she agreed miserably, "watching it all happen and knowing your hands are tied. Realizing the only way it'll ever change is for the mask to fall off so the whole world can see this sham for what it is."

"Even then, the spade would have to be called a spade. And that's not likely considering what's been hedged and what's hanging in the balance." Seth thought some more. "But you're right, nothing's gonna change here. It can't until there's a clean reckoning of it all. The politics. The oil. The religious crusades. All of it needs to get tossed on a table and mediated until they can hammer out a fair peace everyone'll live with. And after that, the free world's gotta hold both sides accountable."

The fire flickered weakly now, puffing tiny ash clouds into the night air. Around it, a shimmering mound of orange and red and white kept whispering soft hisses. They needed more wood but neither of them got up to get it.

"You cut your hair," she said like she'd just noticed.

He touched his hand to his head. "Yeah. Getting too old to be a hippy."

She laughed at the retro word. "You couldn't be a hippy if you tried. But it looks good." It did, too. So did the ripped muscles of his arms and tight legs beneath his jeans, evidence he'd been working out.

"Quit smoking, too." The only time he was glad he'd kicked the habit was when he was telling someone he'd done it. Otherwise, he missed the things.

She smiled. "Now that's impressive. Was it hard?"

"Torture."

He looked right at her, the light of the dwindling fire catching at once the sharp blue of his eyes, the rough-perfect planes of his face.

"So what's been going on back home?" she inquired, trying not to concentrate on the fact that she would give just about anything to touch him right now. Instead, she made herself think about how this was the first time she'd ever referred to Chicago as home.

"Lower Whacker got shut down. The city passed proposals to get rid of low rent housing."

"You figured that would happen."

He nodded. "Handwriting was on the wall. Vagrants and drunks aren't good for the city's image. Anything remotely affordable for 'em now is out past the loop."

"Then your timing to expand the shelter was perfect."

"It was a God thing," he said with a smile. "The place is incredible. Twice as big as it was a few years ago."

"Awesome." She frowned a little. "But I bet that was expensive."

"Not bad. I got the property next door pretty cheap and we did the rest on a budget." He'd actually used some of the interest from his trust though he never made that public.

She had imagined this moment for almost a year, had longed for it. There was so much she'd never said. So much she wanted to tell him. But looking at the art of his chiseled profile, more defined now with small lines, made her tongue-tied. He seemed as much intangible now as he was desirable. And she wasn't sure how to deal with that.

"So, what are you doing in your spare time?" Maybe he was seeing someone else and hadn't said anything yet. It would be like him to wait and tell her in person even though there was no commitment between them.

"School."

"School?"

"I went back to law school. Just two nights a week, but it keeps me busy every spare minute."

She breathed a sigh of relief.

"What are you studying?"

"International law . . ."

She laughed, feeling almost giddy as she gave his shoulder a light squeeze. "You never got war crimes out of your system, did you?"

"I don't know what I'll do with it." Her touch had made his whole body tingle. "I just felt like I needed to go back."

"Maybe it has to do with this." She gestured backwards toward the sleeping village.

"I kind of think it might."

"You know," she mused, "no matter how I try, I still don't understand a government that sabotages its own people."

"Figure it out," he said, shaking his head, "it's crazy to us. But from where they stand, it's completely logical."

"For the life of me, I don't see how . . ."

"You've gotta remember, Mera, they're extremists. Radicals. And believe it or not, they're all over."

"The National Islamic Front?"

"No and yeah. Essentially the NIF's pretty much complicit in working with a bigger network that operates under different names though they're dealing with a lot of the same agenda."

She studied his face as he kept talking.

"You got these militant factions all over the Middle-East, spread throughout parts of Africa." He stopped to swat at a mosquito that had made its way inside the net. "You've read about fanatics who blow up embassies and buildings and scream 'in the name of Allah', right?"

She nodded as he continued. "Well, no one's paid much attention to them once the dust settles. But what we haven't put together until lately is their strategic link. It's not just a few random terrorists. Most of them are cells, trained and backed by governments that essentially operate like the Government of Sudan."

"Like?"

"The list goes on and on. Al Queda, Osama Bin Laden's network, had terrorist training camps in Sudan a few years back, right along with Palestine's Hamas and Lebanon's Hezbollah groups. The government here trades arms with Yemen officials, who harbor top dog Al Queda leaders, who support Afghanistan's ruling Taliban." He was reciting connections like a list of players in a line-up roster. "And I don't need to tell you about the right-wing factions in Somalia or Libya . . ."

"They're all Muslim nations . . ."

"True, but we're talking radical Islam. These groups are the poster kids for extremism. Fundamentalism. Not moderate Islam. So these insurgents may be marrying the crimes to their brand of *jihad*, but some of this holy war's just smoke and mirrors for something else."

"What do you mean?"

"For starters, they're using *shari'a law* like it's some broad-based license to carry out their treachery."

"*Shari'a law?*"

"From what I've gathered, it's this whole system of laws that control and regulate Islamic life. It's this how-to guide that hits everything from hygiene and raising kids to doling out instructions for prayer and social life. Which makes complete sense in their world since religion defines their culture."

"True," she conceded, "there's definitely no separation between church and state like we're used to."

"Exactly. For them it's one and the same." He yawned, then cleared his throat. "But things can get skewed real quick when there's no objective baseline in place. Meaning the explanations of *shari'a* can look totally different depending on who's doing the interpreting."

"Or depending on the motives of the interpreter . . ." The picture was getting clearer.

"My guess is a lot of the zeal here *is* religious, not that I get the twisted theology of slow motion genocide. But they're using this so called *jihad* to disguise their bigger passion . . ."

"The quest for power." She understood perfectly, though she hated the truth of it.

Seth smiled wryly. "Oil *is* power, isn't it, Mera?"

She loved the way he said her name, she always had. But the fact that he grasped the wider story of what she lived day to day — and they both anguished over it — was a whole other connection.

Staring into the ember-lit blackness, she pictured Mashada sobbing on the compound stoop, Deng's grave eyes locking with hers on a wide-open plain. She heard a landmine's furious blast, smelled the acrid smoke of a scorched village. Overarching it all, she saw drilling rigs. Tall proud raiders that methodically pierced the earth.

"You know, when you first told me about all this, I didn't believe it." She took a deep breath to keep the emotion at bay. "I mean who swaps human lives for something that oozes from the ground?"

She fell silent and he stared into the molten mound outside the netting.

"You know what I think?" she said softly.

"What?" His eyes met hers.

"That more stuff than what we think, things like oil and natural resources and all the geopolitical swashbuckling that goes with it are what's behind so much of the poverty and famine and civil wars that we arbitrarily write off as African strife."

"Right. But no one wants to talk about it. Never mind it's the freakin' elephant on the dining room table." He shook his head grimly. "We just act like it's not there. While corrupt investors keep coming in and aligning themselves with even more corrupt regimes, we turn a blind eye to the root problems and keep treating the symptoms." He sighed. "I guess humanitarian aid ops are easier than hauling out the dirty laundry that's sponsoring the need for them."

"Do you not think aid and relief's a good thing?"

His eyes sparked. "Sure I do, absolutely. Compassion and acts that demonstrate care for humanity are always good. But the real work of noble note, the work that could help move these folks toward a post-humanitarian aid society—which is what most people want anyway — would be stepping into the filthy river and setting up dams that stem the flow of the conflict resources—resources like oil and gas, diamonds and gold — these are what's sponsoring the tyrannical campaigns against innocent civilians."

She twisted a strand of hair around her finger. "I agree. The resources themselves, the oil, in this case, aren't what's causing these wars. The reasons for that are legion. But you're right. It's the revenues that the north is pilfering from this land that are fueling it."

Several yards away, two monkeys squawked loudly. Thumping ensued a second later along with a piercing screech as the duo tumbled over the bone-dry ground in a territory showdown.

Seth brushed the sides of his jeans like he was about to stand and call it a night. Tomorrow, she'd be back at the compound while he stayed here for however long before heading back to Chicago. She would go on with her life, he would move on with his. And that would be it.

Unless . . .

"Are you tired?" She let her fingers brush his elbow.

"Yeah." He stretched then rocked forward. "I really am. Why don't we head back?"

"Sure. But can I ask you something first?"

He sat back down and looked at her.

"Is it different now?" she stuttered, groping for words that would say what she meant.

"Is what different?"

"Do you remember what you said before I came here . . . that night at your shelter when . . .?"

"I remember," he interrupted, like he didn't want her to finish the thought.

"Did you . . . I mean do you . . . do you still . . .?"

"What? Do I still what?"

"Feel the same . . . about me?"

He tightened his jaw and looked away. For a minute she knew what he would say and she felt like she was drowning.

He waited to answer.

"Mera, what if I said I didn't?"

"I . . . I guess I would understand. Really. You were always so much better to me than I was to you." She bit her lip to keep it from trembling. "And it's been three years."

He looked surprised.

"Do you think that matters?"

"Yeah, maybe. I mean it could."

"It doesn't."

She was sick inside, scared to hear the truth, but more terrified of not knowing it.

"Then what caused . . . what made you stop caring about . . .?"

"You mean loving you?" he said bluntly, the words echoing into the starlit darkness. "What made me quit loving you?"

"Yes." She looked down so he couldn't see her face.

"How did you want me to feel?" His voice had an edge to it.

"I . . . I've had . . . a lot's happened since I've been here. I know it's probably too late. But I was hoping you might still feel the same." The pit in her stomach was swelling.

"I don't." He reached to tilt her chin up. "A lot's changed in three years."

She tried to move her head, but it was hard. He had no intention of letting her go. Numbly, she let her mind chase a hundred thoughts about what had changed and why. About how she hadn't deserved him in the first place but how safe and good her hand had once felt tucked into his. And how when she'd kissed him, it wasn't just his mouth on hers. It had been him, the wider, deeper part of what made Seth so whole and beautiful . . .

"I love you ten times more than the day I put you and Donovan on that plane." His words were gentle rain interrupting her thoughts. "And time's just made me more sure."

The fire was out and from inside their mosquito netting they watched the embers glow coral and white, a liquid sort of dance moving through them. Occasional sparks from the ashes flecked the black air, and for what seemed like an eternity, neither of them said a word, neither moved, as if the slightest sound or stirring might vaporize the magic of the moment.

"Answer something for me, now." He broke the silence.

She looked up and the expression on his face made her stomach hurt.

"I want to know how you feel about me."

"I . . . I told you."

"No. You asked if I felt the same as when you left," he said patiently. "And I gave you an answer. So, now I'm asking, what does that mean to you?"

She could barely make out his features in the shadowy glow but his voice was so raw with emotion that she knew her next words would find the same place with him as the rising sun found in the morning sky. Just as she was about to answer, though, he reached under the netting and pulled the lantern inside.

"Wait." He fiddled with the lamp until it burned softly between them.

"That's too bright."

"I want to see you answer me."

"Please . . . turn it off."

"I will, as soon as you look at me and . . ."

"I love you, Seth. I've loved you longer than I knew . . . and I think I'll love you my whole life . . ."

He didn't let her finish before he snuffed out the flame and pulled her so close she could feel the beat of his racing heart against her own. In the dark, his fingers twisted and wound through her hair, and reaching up, she found his face, half-feeling, half-memorizing the sharp-smooth angles of every inch of it with her fingertips. Like he couldn't take anymore, Seth stopped for a second. Waited. Then cradling her head, he leaned in slowly until she felt his mouth rest on hers, tentatively at first, then with a sweet wildness that matched the beauty and savagery of the Sudan.

Chapter 38

It would have been déjà vu but she could actually remember being here. It was seven years ago to the date, though she couldn't recall the particulars anymore. Back then, she'd been a starry-eyed *Tribune* reporter, an enamored neophyte commissioned to a fairy tale journey into the spheres of Chicago's rich and famous.

Like tonight, lacy snowflakes and crystal lights had decorated the air, framing an enchanting floor-to-ceiling picture from the Gold Coast Room's perfectly arched windows. And like this evening, The Drake's exquisite ballroom had been bustling with moving tuxedoes, swirling chiffons and floating organzas, all sported by society's most genteel and influential movers and shakers.

But tonight was different, definitely so. As Seth strode past the orchestra and bent to kiss the cheek of his regal, smiling hostess, Mera felt that despite the crowd of local dignitaries and philanthropists, she belonged here. Like she was somehow integral to the evening's purpose.

"Thank you, Astrid. Your introduction was entirely too kind." Seth smiled warmly as he gave the woman's sparrow-thin shoulder a light touch. "Only my mother's dearest friend would regard me so well, *despite* the fact that she knows me."

A polite laughter rippled across the room as the silver-haired woman nodded almost imperceptibly, an enigmatic smile playing at her lips. Then she sat down, queen-like, as the grand chamber silenced, a gathering of nearly six hundred elegant patrons.

Seth shifted easily then clasped his hands together like he was about to commune with friends rather than address an audience. For several seconds, he merely looked around the room.

"My friends, Albert Einstein once said that imagination is more important than knowledge," he finally began as adeptly as a politician. "For years, now, I've loved this thought. I've been compelled by this idea. But tonight, I want his words to move us." He leaned in toward the crowd like he was inviting them into something big. "So good friends, this is what I'm asking of you this evening — to imagine with me. As we ring in 2001 on this perfect evening, let's think and dream together of far away lands . . ."

He paused, as if he knew the timing of his words was as critical as their message.

"Lands now at war, battle-worn and weary, that come to meet peace and prosperity, safety and equity — because somewhere on the other side of the globe, there were men and women who decided to be the change they wished to see in the world."*

Mera glanced sideways at Astrid and Stan Levenkron, the benefactors hosting this evening's gala. Eyes rapt on Seth, they sat composed and expectant. They didn't appear at all surprised by his unimpeachable social graces, his flawless precision.

But she was, albeit she was doing her best not to let on. This Seth Langford was a radical departure from the socially irreverent renegade who usually marked territory with something less than conventional propriety.

To his credit, though, he'd told her this was something out of the ordinary when he had invited her.

Two months ago, just a week after that night by the campfire outside Torit, he'd ask her to join him for this. The timing must have been perfect, she figured, because Jake Wellington immediately agreed, pointing out that she hadn't been home in three years. And, he added, a fundraising gala for the war-torn regions of Sub-Saharan Africa was the perfect catalyst for a long and well-deserved break.

So with no further adieu, Spectrum juggled the profusion of drivers and flight arrangements that had landed her in Chicago late last night. The company had even arranged to put her up at

* Mahatma Gandhi

The Drake for the next two months, an extravagance she certainly hadn't expected.

She hadn't known, either, until early this evening that Seth was the Levenkron's distinguished guest and the evening's keynote. He'd conveniently left out that detail until he had shown up at her suite thirty minutes ago, hair damp and face flushed in a perfect-fitting tux. He was holding a small blue box.

"It's an advance peace offering," he said softly as he drew out the most beautiful pearl choker she'd ever seen.

She stared for the better of a minute.

"It's gorgeous, Seth. But I'm not sure what you're saying . . ."

Seth reached to take her hand.

"I should've told you something, Mera. And actually, this is just part one of my confessions." He swallowed hard. "Part two comes later tonight."

A little frown creased her features.

"What are you talking about?"

"This shindig we're headed to . . . remember I told you the Levenkrons were hosting it to raise money for remediation in Africa?"

"Right," she confirmed, "when you invited me."

Seth hesitated.

"What I didn't tell you was Astrid and my mom grew up together. They were like sisters until the day she died." He looked sheepish. "So I guess that makes her and Stan . . . like . . ."

"Like an aunt and uncle to you?" Mera finished his sentence.

He nodded.

"Actually, Seth, that's really cool."

And it surely doesn't merit a pearl choker.

"Yeah. She and Stan are great, really amazing. In fact, Stan's dad, Abraham, survived Auschwitz. Years later, he wound up being a rabbi."

"That's pretty incredible."

"It is. So as you might guess, Stan and Astrid are pretty serious about fighting hate and prejudice. They've known about — and really supported—my work for years," he continued somewhat self-consciously. They were actually on the board of his foundation, but he'd save that for later. "As of late, though, they've both felt compelled to really get the Sudan story out, along with giving a voice to other plights throughout Africa. So to raise awareness in their circles, they put together this gala tonight. And . . . well . . . a few weeks ago, they asked us to be their guests of honor . . . and I'm . . . I'm the keynote."

Hearty applause broke her thoughts and she noticed a few of the women were delicately dabbing at the corners of their eyes.

What had she missed?

"My longtime friends, the Levenkrons, and our generous gala committee, appropriately named this evening '*Star Light, Star Bright.*' When Astrid first called to tell me, I think a thousand thoughts must've crossed my mind."

A half-smile pulled at Seth's lips as he paused another few seconds for effect.

"I'm sure all of you here know it from memory. It's a saying I think most of us learned at our mother's knees." He dropped his head for a second, put his hands in his pockets then started in a very slow whisper. "Star light, star bright . . . first star I see tonight. I wish I may . . . I wish I might, have the wish I wish tonight."

The vastly adorned room fell completely hushed, all eyes on Seth.

"My friends, tonight as we celebrate the advent of 2001 beneath Chicago's starlit skies, I'm reminded of other nights, other evenings under the wide canvas of African skies . . ."

Suddenly he was gone. Mera watched in wonder as something in him left the pristine gathering to return to stifling African nights, evenings that might as easily have been aglow in orange gunfire as they were bright-lit by a million dazzling stars frolicking about a ghost-white moon.

"Skies that have become highways of destruction . . . places where arms do their worst after being illegally traded, where bombs are dropped on unassuming civilian targets. In southern

Sudan, much like other African regions, long-running civil war has brought famine. It's bred pandemic disease, slavery — yes, I did say slavery, sickness and death tolls in the millions, not to mention more than four million displaced. Like Angola and Eritrea and many other African countries, Sudan's south is studded with hidden landmines that kill hundreds every day."

Mera looked at the faces around her. Some were clearly affected while others appeared barely moved. She noticed Seth was sweating even before he skimmed his hand across his forehead.

Where had he learned this kind of composure, this consummate skill over a crowd?

"The list, I assure you, is endless, and our evening, short. But as our African brothers and sisters gaze up at the night stars, I can assure you their wish, their prayer, is for peace."

He was an unofficial ambassador, baring their deepest hopes with graceful temerity.

"It's for the safety of their children and a future that's brighter than navigating hidden mines and government assaults on their villages. It's a longing that someday there might be enough food for their families and the knowledge that they can develop and sustain their lands without fear."

It suddenly occurred to Mera that he had no notes with him. No paper at all. As he spoke, his eyes implored one patron after another.

"Socrates once said, 'the unexamined life is not worth living.' And over two and half millennia ago, Israel's King Solomon wrote, 'Do not withhold good from whom it's due, when it's in your power to give it.'"

He paused again, letting the words sink in before he continued.

"Tonight I invite you to join me in examining our conditions, our circumstances . . . our very existences. As most of us here will concede, we're a blessed people. We're a people who wake and work, live and sleep in a nation of unparalleled status, a nation that knows unprecedented wealth and security and prosperity.

And if all that weren't enough, this great land we call America promises us that every man, woman and child here has a voice." Seth took a deep breath. "Everyone matters."

He was looking right at her now, his eyes sincere, and she thought for the hundredth time tonight how incredibly beautiful he was. So much so, that for a minute, she lost track of his words, caught up, instead, in the art form of his expressions.

". . . freedom and prosperity, safety and peace . . . these things aren't birthrights. They're divinely given gifts."

He was winding down the address.

"But I believe as God has lavished them on us, we can, and should, pass them on by laboring for what's good and right in these places, these often forgotten corners of our world . . ."

Without meaning to, Mera caught Astrid's eye. The older woman nodded approvingly and let a smile turn her lips up in the corners.

"So as we celebrate this perfect evening," Seth concluded smoothly, not realizing the passion that edged his voice now had almost everyone in the room hanging onto his every word, "it's my hope that the light of our efforts will bring sunrise and strength into these dark regions still awaiting a future and a hope."

More clapping echoed, followed by a sequence of camera flashes before Mera noticed a few reporters moving through the crowd. One was flanked by a news crew with equipment that kept bouncing and floating above the perfectly coifed heads of Chicago's gilded society. Meanwhile, Seth wound through the masses, entirely self-possessed as he stopped to shake hands, kiss cheeks.

A second later, something else dawned on her. A handful of tonight's attendees were celebrities — and a few senators dotted the landscape, too, including one said to be hard at work on a Sudan peace document. He was a silver-haired man, she noticed, mid-fifties, with a cultivated anonymity that belied that he was up to anything important. When he stopped in front of Seth, the man smiled broadly and shook Seth's hand like an old friend.

Tanner, that's who he was, Robert Tanner. He looked different in person, much more affably handsome than he did bordered by the poker-faced throng of politicians he'd been featured with in last month's *Time* and *Newsweek*. And as a camera froze the Tanner-Langford encounter for the morning paper, Mera remembered, too, that Seth once said this work meant rubbing shoulders with names that could make things happen.

Her feet ached terribly as they walked beyond the west wall of The Drake's crimson-decked lobby, past the gleaming mahogany and polished brass of the front desk. Opposite, a uniformed bell-hop and concierge offered stately nods though it was obvious by their bleary eyes and wilted expressions that helping guests ring in the New Year had exhausted them. A second later, the concierge gestured lightly toward a secluded foyer housing old-fashioned elevators. Each elevator had a white-gloved attendant waiting.

Without a word, she and Seth stepped on and the attendant pressed a button that made two musical *dings* before it lifted them to the Executive floor.

Seth never asked if he could come in and Mera didn't invite him, but somehow it was clear the evening wasn't over. Inside, she excused herself for a minute, relieved and paid the woman attending Donovan, then slipped out of the fitted velvet formal she'd worn all night into jeans and a gray sweatshirt.

When she returned to the parlor, soft-lit by only white moon-beams and glowing colors that shifted with the city lights below, Seth was standing at the window looking out over Michigan Avenue. Even with his back to her, she noticed he, too, had made an attempt at getting comfortable, or at least as comfortable as someone wearing a tux could possibly get. His cummerbund was off, draped over the back of a nearby Queen Anne chair, and she saw his shirt was untucked and loosened at the collar even before she slid her arms around his waist.

"Have you noticed," he said softly as he turned and drew her close, "that this city never sleeps?" She smiled up at him, breathing in the clean of his skin, feeling the hard warmth of his body beneath his starched shirt. For what seemed like minutes, they watched the endless lights flashing below — passing cars, changing traffic signals, blinking marquises.

"You were amazing tonight." She whispered as if the moment was glass and speaking any louder might shatter it.

He smiled. "You think?"

"Definitely. It was like this whole other side of you showed up."

"Don't you hate it when that happens?"

"I'm serious. Your speech, the way you worked that crowd. I would've sworn you were campaigning. And you sure had my vote."

His cheeks flushed with the compliment. "Well, you know what they say . . . when in Rome . . ." He took her hand in his and led her to a prim sofa upholstered in cream-colored damask that shimmered silver in the moonlight. "But now, we're back in Chicago, and it's just you," he kissed her lips lightly, ". . . and me." He kissed her again, glad there was nothing to interrupt them.

He had no idea how long they sat like that, partially intertwined and completely engrossed, no clue a kiss could become some crazy masterpiece that made every part of him alive and aggravated with want. But when he felt his body cleave toward hers, first softly, then with an ardor that ignored caution, he forced himself to pull away.

"That's not gonna work." He took a deep breath, raked his fingers through his hair.

"What do you mean?" She looked up at him, perplexed. "What's not going to work?" Then taking in his expression, she got it. "It's okay, Seth. Nothing was going to happen."

He half-smiled, wondering if she'd remembered his long-ago decree about what lines he would and wouldn't cross. "Not yet."

"It wouldn't have," she assured him.

"I'm smart enough to know *that* wouldn't have worked much longer," he repeated. "And I want to do this right."

She leaned back and looked at him. In the dim light, his blue eyes were almost wild and a frown darkened his chiseled features.

"What's wrong . . . what is it?"

He breathed in deeply again and leaned forward until his elbows rested on his knees. "Remember earlier when I told you I had another confession?"

"Yeah."

"I need to tell you something. And then there's something I want to ask you."

"Okay."

"But how you feel about what I tell you might effect your answer."

"Are we playing *Clue* and you forgot to tell me the game started?"

"Are you always such a smart mouth?"

"Just in swanky hotels after midnight."

He didn't know how to say it, so he just plunged in.

"I'm not who you think I am. I . . . I haven't been totally honest with you."

"What are you talking about?" She seemed amused, not at all ruffled.

"My last name," he began.

"Langford . . . it's beautiful . . ."

He set his jaw. Squeezed his eyes shut for a second.

"But Langford's not my last name."

"Oh," she flashed him a good-humored grin like she was going along with a game, "so you have secret identities, different last names?"

He decided to hit it from a different angle.

"Do you remember when we first met?"

"Sure. At the shelter . . . when I went with . . . about Taize . . ."

It was like she couldn't quite get Jack's name out in Seth's presence.

"Right," he said gently. Now the conversation was headed just where it should. "Jack needed information that his bishop told him to get from me."

"So?" She sat up straighter as it occurred to her that Seth was serious about whatever he was getting to.

"You slipped in the interview, remember? And Jack covered it up real quick."

"Slipped . . . how?"

"Well, you mentioned the bishop's name and Jack interrupted you before you even finished saying it."

She shrugged.

"What, Thomas Kahlier? Why would it have mattered if I said his name?"

Seth felt every muscle in his body tense.

"My guess is that Jack was told to keep his name under wraps. Because Kahlier and I don't get along too well." His heart was beating like a drum and his mouth felt like he was chewing cotton.

"From what I know of him, that's understandable." Then something registered. "But how do *you* know him?"

For a minute, the world was still. Noise and sound and light and color were edited out. Transferred to another dimension. For several seconds, it was him and silence with nothing but the truth throbbing inside of him.

Then he just did it.

"Look, I need you to forgive me for not telling you before now," he scraped out. "I wanted to . . . I meant to before you left . . . but the time was never right." He took a deep breath and rubbed his pounding temples. "Thomas Kahlier was . . . is . . . my father."

She stared at him, speechless.

"Your *what*?" she said, after several seconds passed.

"My father," Seth repeated, knowing just how well acquainted she was with the bishop's effect on rookie priests. "Though he didn't do much more than sire me."

"Your father . . ." Mera echoed, still incredulous.

"In name only," Seth cut in, clarifying this point like it was supremely important. "But that's it. In name only."

Mera blinked, listening as he continued.

"We never got along, even when I was a kid. Early on, he was consumed with clawing his way up to bishop, way too busy for anything or anybody that didn't facilitate that pursuit. And later when I didn't buy into his whole climb-the-church-hierarchy thing, I turned into the proverbial black sheep. My trip to Taize, he swore, was about cheap thrills and I don't know how many times he said the shelter was nothing more than a den of losers under one roof." He shook his head and winced slightly. "So it was no surprise when he wrote me off for good after Mom's funeral. Far as he was concerned, I was dead anyway. Until he gave Jack a green light to call me about Taize."

Mera breathed in sharply. "He mentioned you," she whispered. "Jack mentioned Thomas Kahlier had a son and a wife who died." She was referring to the conversation in Chicago when they'd eaten at Scoozi's after she'd collected Jack from the airport.

"But Kahlier never let on that he was sending Jack to interview his son, I'm sure." A rueful smile twisted Seth's lips. "That, he wouldn't have done."

"True, Jack had no idea. But how . . . where did you get Langford?" she asked weakly, like she was hoping the answer wasn't too far-fetched.

He rubbed his forehead again. Cleared his throat.

"Mom. Her maiden name was Langford. Lucy Langford. I took it as mine after she died."

"Why *then*?"

He didn't hesitate. "Something my father did. Something big enough to make me want to eighty-six that name for good."

He had expected her to be angry or go cold. Either way, he wouldn't have blamed her. She'd deserved the truth from him long before now. But looking at her, he realized she was neither. Her eyes were soft and expectant and her index finger traced the scar over his top lip while she waited for him to keep explaining.

"He sued me after she died," he resumed.

"For what? Hadn't they been married for years by then?"

"More than thirty. But she . . . she had money from her side of the family. A lot of money. She kept her trust separate . . ."

Mera was shaking her head like she needed no further explanation.

"And when she died, she left it to you," she finished his sentence, everything suddenly making sense. Seth wasn't possessed by want. He was the type who could live around money and resist its lure. "Probably because she knew you didn't care about it."

"You're right, I didn't care," he confirmed. "I still don't. It's stayed in trust all these years. The only thing I use is a little of the annual interest to subsidize the shelter."

She giggled. "So that's the grant from the anonymous donor you talked about. You were so poker-faced when you mentioned that."

Seth nodded disconsolately. "Dad was furious when the probate judge ruled in favor of her will. It made him hate me worse. That's when I took on Langford."

"Langford fits you," she said gently, reaching for his hand. "Langford's perfect."

"Then you forgive me for not telling you until now?"

She laughed almost bitterly before letting her eyes fall to the floor. "Forgive you?"

"Yeah, I need you to do that for me . . ."

"Are you serious?" Studying his face for the jest in it, she found none. "There's nothing to forgive, Seth."

"I should've told you."

"Never mind," she said with feeling. "You won't find me casting stones. I have way too many secrets of my own."

Just as she started to look away, he took her face in his hands.

"Look at me. Please." He was dead serious. "About these secrets, these ghosts . . ."

"No. Don't, Seth." She tried to turn her head, though he wasn't making it easy. "Really . . ."

"Meranda, there's nothing, I mean absolutely nothing, you could say that would make me love you less. You need to know that."

He wanted so badly to tell her that he knew her story. But now wasn't the time.

Like she needed a diversion, Mera stood up and walked to the window, taking in the dwindling noise and color of the Magnificent Mile below. Seth waited a minute, then joined her as he pushed his hands in his pockets.

"Look, I've never done this before, so if I mess it up, be patient with me." He took one of her hands in his and laced his fingers through hers.

"When have you ever messed up?" Her voice quaked a little.

"I'm in love with you, I'm sure of it." He paused, choosing his words carefully. "I know we haven't talked about it and I know there's a million things we'll need to figure out. But I don't care. I want to spend the rest of my life with you."

She glanced down, her face catching at once the flickering lights of the city below, the pale moonlight that streamed from above. And for a second, she was a still-life portrait so sublimely beautiful he couldn't breathe.

"I . . . I'm not sure what you're saying, Seth. Are you . . . ?"

He reached deep into his pocket and pulled out a tiny silk bag. "I'm saying I want to marry you, Meranda. I'm asking you to marry me." He said it slowly, taking his time.

For a minute, all she could hear was a loud ringing in her ears, and through a tunnel, her heart beating wildly. He stood close, facing her, his hand light on her elbow. When he moved, she could smell his skin, clean and barely scented with cologne.

"I love you, Seth, everything about you . . ." She couldn't finish, like a lump in her throat had barricaded the words.

"But . . ." He sensed her hesitation.

"There's Donovan and . . ."

"I'll love Donovan like he was mine." He let her hand go and then fumbled with the bag until it opened. As it did, a ring fell into his palm, with its perfect little diamond that glittered every time the lights below caught its facets. "Please, Meranda, say yes."

Just as he reached for her hand, a long shrill buzz cut their hushed whispers. For a second, neither of them moved.

"You should get it. That was part of the deal." Seth's eyes met hers, then gestured toward the persistently bleating telephone. "Remember . . ." Spectrum's only condition in her leave was that she would be available in an emergency.

"It might be a wrong number," she objected.

"And . . . it might not be."

Like she knew he was right, she headed past the parlor into the foyer. A minute later, Seth heard her cry out.

"No! Oh, God . . . no. This can't be happening. It's wrong . . . it has to be. Are you positive . . . what about Mashada . . . is she okay? Where were they when it happened?"

As she pelted the voice on the other end with questions, Seth made his way to her side.

Then: "Of course . . . through Vancouver . . . for what? Okay . . . let me go so I can start making arrangements. Oh, and Onesphore, I want someone to find out if Deng is alive . . . please."

She hung up then sank limply onto the foyer's Italian marble.

"That was Onesphore . . . at the embassy in Cairo. My village outside Kadugli was . . . was bombed yesterday." She repeated the information like it wasn't real. "The school . . . the hospital . . . the locals were gathered for a UNICEF drop . . . They bombed a relief site, Seth . . . a *food* site."

Numbness gave way to tears spilling over her cheeks.

"He said more than five hundred were either killed or hurt."

Seth groaned. "Dear God . . ."

Her eyes flashed green fire before a look of helplessness filled them. "I want to know, oh, Seth, I need to know . . . why? Why does this keep happening? If God is so real . . . if He's so good, where is He?"

Seth drew her close, not even trying to come up with an answer to something so incalculable, when out of nowhere, a peculiar hush fell over them. It was a half-grace, half-power that was more a presence than just plain quiet.

"I think," he finally answered, "I've *gotta* think this is the last thing God wants for Sudan . . . or for any country."

"Then why?" She was tormented. "Why, this?"

Again he deferred to silence knowing her question was a riddle no man could solve.

She watched his face. The pulsing of his temples, the sharp cut of his jaw where he'd clenched his teeth together. She took in the clouds that had moved in behind his eyes. It was obvious that he cared with everything in him.

"Ten years . . . even five years ago, I could've rattled off something," Seth finally whispered. "Probably some platitude about how anthropology and ethnology works in all of this and how corruption feeds the ethnic rivalries and religious clashes, but never mind, don't worry, there's bound to be some higher purpose in it anyway . . ." his voice trailed off.

She wiped her nose against the sleeve of her sweatshirt. "But now?"

More quiet.

"Now?" A darker shadow dulled his eyes. "Now, the only thing I'm sure of is I'll never get the bigger why of this whole thing." He shook his head sadly. "All I know . . . all I know is we get to choose. All of us. And in the end, that kind of freedom's behind this hell."

Silence again, only the sound of their breathing and cars passing on the streets below.

"I've got to go," Mera said, after what seemed like an eternity. "They need me to come back since Kadugli's so close to the Halig bloc."

"I know." With the pad of his thumb, he wiped away a tear clinging to her eyelashes.

"I don't know what it'll be like when I get there. Donovan . . ."

"Leave him here with me."

"I don't know when I'll be back."

"It doesn't matter." He put a hand on her shoulder. "Leave him with me."

She took a deep breath. Then reached up and took his face in her hands. "The answer is yes."

"Yes . . .?" He looked baffled.

"My answer's yes," she repeated softly. "I want to marry you more than anything else in this world."

He'd forgotten until now that he was still holding the ring. Without a word, he slipped it over her finger, then lifted her hand to his cheek.

Chapter 39

She had no clue what was making her shiver, the fever that had set in this morning or the jet's cabin that refused to get warm. Already the plane was delayed an hour, a mammoth blue truck outside spraying round two of Glycol to de-ice for takeoff. Vancouver was under glacial clouds, beneath thick snow blankets, and over the aircraft speakers, an Indian-brogued AirCanada pilot announced the ice storm was the third in two days.

Trying to keep her teeth from chattering, Mera accepted two navy blankets and a small square pillow from a smiling flight attendant who had noticed almost immediately that she was feverish. The attendant offered her shoulder a sympathetic touch, and through a fog Mera thought how exquisite she was, how the cabin's yellow light made her smooth chocolate skin like velvet.

She nodded weakly, an attempt at gratitude, then braced herself for the effort it would take to wrap the covers around her. Fortunately, it wasn't as bad as she thought, and once settled, she groped with her feet for the long thick envelope she'd situated on the floor beneath her. Finding it, she planted one foot firmly against it and resettled as deeply as she could into the stiff economy seat. Then she waited for the thin blankets to do their magic.

Her head was excruciating and the perpetual chatter that filled the cabin seemed like screaming.

It had to be the fever.

She should take a few ibuprofen since they were just inside her purse. But her bags were on the floor and she was cold, freezing cold. The medicine would have to wait.

A long sleepy wave washed over her just as she felt the plane start to taxi. She had intended to do so much to fill the hours between here and London. But this flu, or whatever it was, was rendering her all but useless . . .

Smashing her foot against the package again, she drifted off into a delirious sleep and dreamed of flight attendants serving ibuprofen as big as cookies on trays that looked just like the package Nick Phelps had handed her as she left his office this afternoon. The attendants wore the same expression Phelps had, severe. Almost menacing. And even in the dream, Mera thought the deadened smirks terribly odd for their line of work.

All she wanted to do was sit down, but that wasn't likely anytime soon considering the Customs line was barely inching for what appeared the better of two hundred feet ahead. She rechecked her briefcase for Phelps' prized parcel then started ferreting through her purse for a second envelope he insisted she take. This one was small, the size of an index card, and amber brown.

Just in case, he'd said. A little insurance in the event of complications.

But so far, so good. The changeover at Heathrow had gone off without a hitch, just as Phelps predicted. Customs and Immigration worked like a well-oiled machine, travelers practically cascading through the lines. Only the occasional baggage search was performed. Otherwise it was quick glances at declarations, swift, though careful, examinations of visas and passports.

But Cairo International was a different story. Here, the serpentine lines inched just a couple of feet every fifteen minutes and threaded yards ahead to the shabby Terminal 1 counter. There, a handful of swarthy officials mopped their brows every few minutes and splayed open the belongings of every second or third person. The bags were yanked and tugged and all but turned inside out by foul-tempered agents in rumpled clothes who looked like they despised their jobs as much as they hated travelers.

The airport reeked of stale cigar smoke and body odor, no doubt a result of poor ventilation and endless lines that crammed people together like canned sardines. The din of multilingual chatter droned on and on, interrupted every few minutes by sharp apprisings over the airport intercom. In front of Mera, two men with chipped, yellow fingernails argued in Arabic over investments headed south on the Nikkei exchange, and a pudgy young couple behind her was trying to persuade their whiny toddlers in German. Mera understood the heated monetary debate, compliments of Mashada's teaching. But with the exception of catching the strained "pleases" and the infinite use of "no," the German was as good as Greek to her.

Another stiff heat wave passed through her, this one so virulent her knees started to buckle. It had to be the fever rising, she knew. The low-grade heat that had simmered in her all day now felt like fire roasting her from the inside out. She had no idea what her temperature was, but given the shivering and watery eyes, she figured it was well past the 100°F mark.

Trying to steady herself best she could, she tore her purse apart with one hand, balanced her briefcase in the other. She was freezing again, and with the combination of her chattering teeth and mounting anxiety, her nerves were growing rawer by the second.

Her efforts proved futile. The little caramel envelope Phelps had laid atop the tightly taped larger one just hours ago was nowhere to be found. She turned her coat pockets inside out. Inspected every compartment in her purse.

Nothing.

She thought about her briefcase then dismissed the possibility. Other than slipping in Phelps' premier package thirty miutes ago, she hadn't put anything else in it today. She checked her jean pockets again. Tried to take a deep breath.

No small envelope to be found.

Now she was so nauseous and lightheaded, she felt her body break out in cold sweat. She attempted a few deep breaths because the world was suddenly pressing in from every direction while tiny flecks of colored light decorated her peripheral vision.

Was she sicker now because she was scared half to death? Or was whatever flu she had just bringing on the worst it had to offer?

She didn't know and either way, she didn't really care. All she could think right now was how badly she wished that she'd listened to Seth yesterday. He'd predicted just this, that she was getting sick, after she'd downed nearly a pot of coffee at his shelter in an attempt to defrost. After her second dose of Motrin to stave off the aches, he'd pointed out the flu epidemic this year had shot past the higher than usual mark. All things considered, she might do well to postpone her trip back to Sudan for a few days.

She would have gladly agreed only she'd already made the arrangements between Chicago and Khartoum. On short notice, this hadn't been easy. Besides, Phelps said the stop in Vancouver was urgent. Spectrum had critical documents the government was expecting and since explosion damage was widespread, there wasn't time to waste.

So she'd kissed Donovan and Seth then boarded the plane to Vancouver. If all went according to plan — and there was no reason it shouldn't — she'd be back in Chicago in less than two weeks.

But sitting on the runway at O'Hare, she hadn't even fastened her seat belt before she knew Seth was right. She was too sick to make this trip. Looking at the perfect, still-unfamiliar diamond on her finger, she wondered if he was ever wrong about anything.

An hour later and no closer to finding the missing envelope, she faced the balding inspection agent with a cigarette dangled between his lips. As if his downward gaze was the result of his heavy purplish lids, he didn't glance at her passport, didn't even look up, before he waved her on. She breathed a grateful sigh of relief.

But just as she'd re-shifted her bags, another official flagged his attention. "Search the bags," he hissed in Arabic. The official took the agent with the smoke's place so he could forage through Mera's things.

She donned her best game face, but her chattering teeth gave her away. For the first time, the official glanced up, a glare that morphed into a lusty gaze. His eyes narrowed in his sweating face like he was working hard to undress her, and between puffs of his cigarette, he licked the corners of his lips like he was hungry for more than food.

Mera stood silently, hoping the path of least resistance would be her best bet. She couldn't help wishing that she had Phelps' missing mystery envelope. Whatever it contained, whatever magic it might conjure, would be a welcome alternative to this.

Then it hit her. As the agent opened one compartment after another, first in her purse, then her briefcase, she snapped.

She hadn't even thought to question the secrecy of the larger package's contents.

Why would Spectrum be so willing to pay off a Customs agent to keep her bags intact and an innocuous package secured?

There was no need to conceal a few damage assessments and reconstruction plans.

The agent pounced on the well-taped parcel like a cat on a mouse. He shredded a corner open. Then stopped, waiting for her reaction.

"Papers. They're reports my company is sending to Sudan," she explained in Arabic. "I'm on my way to Khartoum."

The official's jaw slackened a little, a gape indicating he was stunned that a near-perfect guttural accent had come from her very western mouth. Then he took a small knife from his pocket and offered a sly smile before he sliced the package open. Fanning through the thick stack and finding nothing, though, he crammed them back into her briefcase.

"May I go now, sir?" Again in Arabic, between lips shivering from the fever.

"You'll go when *I* say go," he growled under his breath. Then he motioned her on, giving her bag an angry final shove.

Thirty minutes later, she sat sipping sludgy black tea while waiting for the delayed Boeing to arrive. With another hour, minimum, to kill, she would reorganize her briefcase. It was a good distraction. Something to take her mind off her pounding head and sticky clothes. The last time her fever broke, her clothes had soaked through.

She couldn't move, though the loudspeaker decreed the final boarding call to Khartoum. Instead, she looked down at the disheveled paper stack in her shaking hands. And tried again to decide what should happen next.

The smoky gate seating area was spinning. Swirling. Closing in on her.

She would miss the flight. That's all there was to it. Something had to be done about these documents and she had to make choices here and now. Not in Khartoum.

Feeling the weight of the thick pile, she was torn. Half of her wanted to drop the sick evidence and run. The other half ached to kill the faceless players behind this whole travesty.

But she would do neither and she knew it.

Actually, she wouldn't do anything at all until the lies, the truth and what needed to happen because of both came at least quasi-clear. Until then, she'd just sit here.

These papers were what she'd hoped for when she'd left for Sudan in the first place. She had waited for this.

And yet she hadn't.

Not for *this*. This was past the scope of anything she'd imagined finding.

Sifting through the documents that Nick Phelps planned to safeguard with payoff at Customs, Mera understood completely the company's reasons for veiling the contents. It made sense to her, too, why she'd been dubbed the errand girl.

On two levels, she was the best choice. A cash-carrying Anglo-American, easy on the eyes, she would move unimpeded between borders. And if for some reason the documents might be opened, she was safe.

The papers were mostly in Arabic and no one at the company knew she read or spoke the language almost fluently now.

At first glance, the papers were exactly as Phelps promised. Endless numbers in itemized rows and columns that added up damages. Prepared statements to be delivered to the local press. Plans for remediation asterisked to denote attachments, appendices.

But these were the end of civility.

Because filed neatly behind rebuilding plans for the explosion site was a stack of other documents. Official papers calling for consecutive regional clearings. And Kadugli was the first of the packets in the file. In a letter written by the government three months before, the village was indexed to Spectrum's nearby Halig bloc, suggesting two more blocs just past Halig were drill-ready.

The problem according to the letter: the area was inhabited by a sizeable village outside Kadugli.

The village Spectrum had hired her to help rebuild. Deng's village.

The next attachment was dated two days ago. A document indicating Spectrum's regret of a major explosion in the region. The cause: rebel offensives at the drilling site. Artillery fire sparked flames, the report read, igniting a full-blown explosion. Two hundred civilians were verified dead, another three hundred engulfed in an ensuing blaze that traveled for miles before it was contained.

Mera stared in disbelief at the alien black and white words.

Lies.

This was nothing but deception. To the western world. To the African and Arab worlds. To any viewer watching this theatre of deceit.

There was no drilling site near enough Kadugli to cause an explosion.

The two areas cited in the memo were reserves. Not operational facilities like the second attachment implied.

Flipping the page, she found work permits, drilling contracts for the "cleared" blocs. Innocent enough, except until a few days ago a village was settled on top of them.

Mera stared at the heap in her lap. Numbly, she traced her fingers along the sharp edges so quickly the paper sliced her forefinger. Blood pooled then dripped on the top two pages before she stuck her finger in her mouth.

There was just one explanation, and as bad as it was, it was precisely what she'd thought — what she'd been waiting for. In black and white and Arabic, these papers confirmed Spectrum's connection with the NIF. They spelled out a mutual intent to eradicate anything and anyone subsisting atop oil-rich land.

Sifting through the stack revealed a sick sequence, an order first kicked off by a government letter specifying where reserves lay, who was in the way of the crude. Shortly after, an explosion would occur, usually a result of so-called insurgents opening-fire on drilling rigs and into company pipelines.

Of course, the company would express condolences, sometimes agree to help pay certain damage costs back to the government. Technically, though, they weren't to blame. The NIF wasn't either, though they would regret loss of lives. The cause would rest, invariably, with the opposition.

And the quest for oil could continue unabated.

That was the plan, she learned. A strategy that included four more regions in quick succession. Western Equatoria down to Torit were designated high priority, all of them attached with drilling contracts, land-clearing permits and estimated dates of clearing completions.

She had no idea how long she sat in the terminal, an odd figure bundled in her long coat as she rocked back and forth. But clutching the illicit proof in her hands as she watched her EgyptAir flight lift into the violet evening sky, she made two decisions.

The first was she would not be an accomplice to murder.

The second was after she'd handled the first, she would go back one last time. There was unfinished business in Kadugli, and she'd once made Deng a promise she intended to keep.

Chapter 40

At first, she moved with a rote ease, devoid of emotion. It crossed her mind that she might be in shock, though she dismissed this idea quickly. There was too much to do and no time to mull over a personal reaction to it all.

With the exception of the overstuffed briefcase and handbag at her side, her luggage was headed to Khartoum, a thought that would've been otherwise odious considering she had nothing to wear but the fetid sweat-soaked clothes she had on. At the moment, though, all she could think of was how long it would take to get where she needed to go. And how long it might be before the sweltering fever broke again.

Leaning her throbbing head back against the seat as the taxi cased through the winding, unfamiliar streets, she noticed her briefcase had inched its way open.

Again.

With an absentminded tug, she pulled the zipper closed for the third time in the past hour.

Then she saw it.

A little square of gold-brown paper peeking from an inside pocket.

She sat up straight and lifted it out. A very small envelope.

Nick Phelps' ancillary envelope, puffy with cash.

Somehow between the fever and her panic to find it, she'd managed to overlook it.

Careful to keep her find concealed, she forced the parcel deep into her bag before splitting it open.

Twenties. Fifties. Some hundreds.

The cash was in Egyptian pounds, or *guinehs* in Arabic.

Currency equal to about a thousand American dollars or five thousand Egyptian ones.

Plenty enough for a quick sleight of hand at the Customs gate.

If she'd just happened on it a few hours ago, it would have been her ticket past the surly official. Spectrum's package would have remained sealed, she'd have boarded her flight as planned, and if all things were on schedule, her EgyptAir flight would be touching down in Khartoum just thirty minutes from now.

But that's not what happened, she thought, looking at the engorged little envelope. Perhaps that wasn't what was supposed to happen.

She kept repeating the conviction to herself, though it did little to quell the adrenaline surges that kept her heart pounding like a jackhammer and stomach seem like it had no bottom. These papers at her side might have some catalytic value in aiding the south's ongoing saga. Something in her knew that. But it didn't change in the least how panicked she felt. Or how badly she wished this were all a dream.

Gripping her things and trembling through the latest fever spike, she took a deep breath. Then stepped from the taxi in front of 5 Latin America Street, American Citizens Services office of the United States Embassy in Garden City, Cairo.

The telephone's double *bleep* startled him from a sound sleep and even as he groped in the dark to answer it, he felt his whole body start tensing.

"Seth, Seth, are you there?" The phone lines snapped and crackled wildly, but still he could make out Mera's voice. It was low and strained.

He sat up and squinted at the numbers on the clock by his bed. 4:05 A.M.

"What's wrong, honey? Where are you?"

"Cairo." She sounded squeaky now, high-pitched like a frightened child. "I just booked another flight into Khartoum . . ."

"What? Why are you in Cairo? You should've been almost back to the compound by now." His sluggish mind was starting to wake up.

"Seth, you're not going to believe what I stumbled on." In less than sixty seconds, she hit the high points of the last several hours.

"What I want to know is where are you now?" he cut her off before she could finish. Her news made perfect sense, like the long-awaited missing piece to a jigsaw. If it had been anyone else on the other end of the phone, he would have been elated.

"The embassy, the U.S. Embassy in Cairo. I caught a taxi from the airport several hours ago."

"Who are you seeing?"

"American . . . Citizens . . . Services." Her words faded in then out. Then they cleared again. "And they're supposed to get word to the consulate general, who . . ."

"Who needs to see the documents . . ." he finished the sentence.

"Right. So I'm leaving the most implicating one here for them to . . ."

"Copies or the original?"

"The original."

"Forget going back then."

"They need the original for . . ."

"I understand that," he interposed bluntly. "Completely. But that means you're not going back."

"Yes, I am. First thing in the morning."

"No way, Meranda. You're getting on the next plane out of there and you're coming back home."

"No, I'm not." She was almost defiant. "The company's expecting these papers and I can't just cut out on them, Seth. And I need to see how Deng and the people in Kadugli are."

"You can find out from home," he lowered his voice in an effort to sound far more composed than he felt. He knew what could happen to her next. And the barbarous possibilities struck a lead fear into his heart. "Look, you don't know what you're up against now. You've already missed a plane . . ."

"They think I got held up at Customs and missed my flight."

"Yeah, and they're tracking you like a Fed-Ex package. If they think for a minute you've narched on 'em, you're history, sweetheart. They'll have you on grounds of tampering with government documents, and you won't be able to do a thing if they so much as suspect you. You know as well as I do, the rules are all different on foreign turf."

"The document I'm leaving with Services was the first in the stack." She wasn't backing down. "It's a logical confiscation if they ask me about it. Besides, almost all of it was all in Arabic and they have no idea I could make sense of it."

Seth exhaled into the receiver.

"Think Meranda, that's the most incriminating piece out of the stack. You just told me, all the others are future tense. Nebulous proposals. No detonation reports attached because they haven't happened yet."

She was quiet, and for a second Seth wondered if they'd been disconnected.

"I'll have to take my chances, then," she said slowly.

"You need to come home," he pressed. "You have a nephew . . . you have a life here . . ." He knew it was useless even as he said the words. He would have done the same thing in her shoes.

"I owe one more trip back to the village. I . . . I love them, Seth. I need to know what happened. And I promised Deng something a long time ago."

"Promised him, what?"

"Maybe the old chief's some kind of prophet, who knows? He said something like this would happen someday. And he asked me when it did to tell the truth."

"What do you mean, what truth?"

"I had no idea what he meant. But a long time ago, he asked me to tell the truth when this calamity struck. He asked me to tell their story." She steadied her voice so as to check a whole range of emotions descending at once. "Today I held the truth he was talking about in my hands, Seth. And as far as I was concerned, whether or not to tell it wasn't even an option." Her words faded to a whisper. "Now, I need to go back one more time . . ."

Seth looked out of his open window at a sharp crescent moon flanked by God only knew how many burning white lights. Then he blinked. "What's the moon like there, Mera?"

She hesitated. "Did you just ask me about the moon here?"

"Yeah. The moon. And what are the stars like?"

He heard her take in a deep breath like she was getting braced for a contest of wills.

"Seth, it's day here. You know that."

He waited to answer.

"It's night here. Or still dark anyway. And the moon is this clear crescent that looks like a sideways smile. The stars, I swear, the stars are sentries tonight. Like they're out just to make sure the moon gets to keep smiling and . . ."

"Come on, Seth, what are you saying?" She sounded drained. The last time her fever had broken, it zapped whatever lasting energy she'd had.

"Meranda, I'm saying that all that's separating us right now is time and sands. And that's enough. What if they figure you've taken that document? Do you have any idea what could happen then?"

"They won't. And as soon as I hand Wellington the papers and look things over, I'm out of there. Besides, the embassy said they'd make sure I was safe before anything leaked."

"Stuff happens, Meranda, mistakes get made."

"I know but . . ."

"I don't want to lose you over a stack of papers. I've waited a lifetime for what we have."

She looked at the glittering ring on her left hand. Drank in the gravelly-smooth of his voice.

"You won't, Seth, I promise."

"You can't make that kind of promise and you know it." He knew she'd just resisted some final lure to come back home, something bigger than herself pulling her deep into Africa. He understood completely. "But I get it. Really."

"I know you do. They're as much your friends, and in a way, your people, as they are mine."

"That's true. But I don't want to choose between them and you."

"You won't have to."

"Just be careful, Mera. Be careful." His words were soft.

"I will. And Seth?"

"Yeah?"

"Nothing. Never mind."

"What? What were you thinking?"

She hesitated.

"If I were a writer . . . you know, a Tennyson or Shakespeare instead of a journalist, I'd find . . . I'd even make up just the right words to say how much I love you."

He waited to answer, moved as much by the absence of her inhibition as he was by the tenderness of the declaration.

"You *are* a writer, Mera." He was glad he'd mastered his emotions, glad she had no idea he was blinking back tears. "And I think you just did," he whispered as they hung up.

Chapter 41

A scorpion loosened itself from a crevice in the stone barricade and scurried over the dirt floor. Her prison cell was black for all but an hour a day; at sunset, a shadowy beam from the west passageway illumined her cell through a crack in the door. Now, as an anemic ray showcased the insect's inch-long stinger, Mera tried to move, no easy feat considering the limitations of her shackled ankles and wrists. Luck was on her side, though. The thing switched courses and disappeared under the iron gate.

Heart beating faster, she scooted backwards to align herself with the brightest angle of gray light, and as she settled into place, she was surprised to find a pea-sized rock had pressed itself deep into the palm of her hand. Greedily, she picked it out then cradled it as if it were a gem of infinite worth. She knew exactly how to put it to good use . . .

Just two weeks ago, she'd started losing track of the days in these barracks. Alone in the foul-smelling blackness that knew no difference between day and night, time melted into endless nothingness until she happened upon the serendipity of occasional pebbles beneath her hands and feet.

The little rocks were turnkeys. Tiny watershed saviors that gave time form again and set one day apart from the next. Now approximate twenty-four time periods could be tracked by maneuvering sandy stones into a straight line under her left thigh, one pebble for each day.

Today was day nineteen according to the lineup that lauded her artistry at dusk, but missed the vigilant scrutiny of military guards who came and went. Nineteen days in the morbid dank of solitary confinement, twenty-one since two government officials and Jake Wellington had turned up at her bungalow.

~

It was a blur mostly. One that opened with a string of questions about the missing document. For an entire week, she'd been under the impression that the executive team completely bought her story about the papers' whereabouts. It was no problem, they'd assured her, just an unlucky twist of fate that didn't and wouldn't amount to anything.

Since she was functioning in a stupor of half-denial, half-grief, she'd been convinced. Her one expedition to the scorched and still-smoldering wasteland had happened via a Spectrum chopper since the cratered and blackened landscape was rumored to be seeded with mines. But even from the air, the macabre universe of charred huts, maimed corpses and bloodied livestock had left her so shaken that she hadn't thought to be wary of the company's seeming empathy.

So when three stony-gazed men turned up at her barrack, one being Jake Wellington, the other two entirely unfamiliar, she was petrified. Nonetheless, she steeled herself, summoned her best poker face and made what she thought was colorful small talk while Mashada sweetened freshly brewed tea and served *kisra* bread drizzled with honey. In the meantime, the restless trio grunted between themselves, telegraphed messages with serrated glances. Based on snippets of conversation, Mera was eventually able to piece together that they were high-ranking government security.

And they weren't happy.

Then the inquisition started. Sharp, accusing queries began flying with long pauses where Jake and the duo conferred, mostly in Arabic. Whether fortunate or not, she understood everything they said, though she never let on. Even when she gleaned things were heading in a terminal direction, she'd smiled and answered questions, sipped more tea and feigned innocence.

All the while, she held onto the fact that the documents, thank God, had largely been in Arabic, and no one other than Mashada and Onesphore knew she spoke or read the language. That, she kept telling herself, should surely be worth something.

It wasn't. An hour after the interrogation started, the two at Wellington's side suddenly pulled rusty steel-cuffed chains from a drawstring pouch they'd carried inside. Trying numbly to grasp the lurid turn of events, her feet hadn't had time to take flight before they'd shoved her to the floor and flipped her face down. Then one of the officials ground a heavy-booted heel into her left thigh while the other twisted her arms behind her back and manacled her hands together. She felt something wet hit her cheek before she realized Jake had spit on her.

The last thing she remembered was attempting to flail at one of the officials before a blindfold eclipsed her sight and someone shoved a sickeningly sweet cloth over her nose.

Everything went black.

Sometime later, she saw a slice of white-gold moon where the blindfold gaped open. She felt a continuous rush of sticky night air amid the excruciating sensation of tumbling helplessly around in what had to be the bed of a truck. For seconds or minutes or hours — she had no idea which — she faded in and out, back and forth over the whirring in her ears and pummeling knocks that never stopped.

When she finally came to, her body was an agonizing knot that nearly collapsed as a feculent prison warden with yellow-furred teeth and vile body odor shoved her into a stifling cell that resembled the inside of a cave. After slamming her hard against a stone side wall, he chained her to it, grabbed a handful of her hair and yanked. Then before everything went black and silent, she overheard him order a nearby guard to feed her once a day, at sundown.

That was it. Then came days indistinguishable from night, eternal heat and darkness interrupted by a brief sanctuary of refracted light beams an hour before sunset. In between were footsteps on the other side of the wall, creaking and clanging of prison gates. On interesting days, there might be a muffled exchange between what she assumed were jailers and wardens. But there was nothing else.

Nothing.

The air she breathed now was different. Heavy and rancid, it was the oxygen of the long forgotten. At first its reek had nauseated her to the point of gagging, but lately she'd almost grown fond of the stench. In this sweltering purgatory with its ceaseless penance, it was a touchstone that made this confinement real.

As shrouded insects and small rodents scurried over and around her, their chirping sounds and crawling sensations, even the sharp bites, were inverted megaphones echoing backwards that she was not mad. She was in prison, probably in southern Juba, since it was the military barrack nearest Spectrum's Bentiu headquarters.

Day forty-nine started identical to every other until light footsteps stopped outside her cell and the grind of a key wrangling in the door made her heart start pounding.

It was just after sunrise, she was certain, based on the slightly cooler temperature and inward slant of dusty streaks she'd discovered by leaning at just the right angle. The worst hour of all, she'd decided. The silver of morning light signaled the tyranny of yet another endless day.

But today, something different. Today there was the *clink clank* of keys in her cell door . . .

A minute later, the iron door moaned open and she felt air move inside the chamber.

Released. That had to be it. She was going to be released.

She figured it was just a matter of time before the red tape got untangled and she'd be out of here. No doubt, the embassy had set whatever it was that got her here straight. And at this point, she didn't even care if she got an explanation . . .

"Miss." Her eyes burned wildly as they adjusted to the light filtering in. She noted with satisfaction that the jailer was one of her favorites. Depending on his mood, this one sometimes talked to her, something she coveted more than whatever food scraps he might be bearing. Conversation between two people made the fact of existence real, a truth she'd never realized before.

Today, though, the jailer's dark features were tight and cold. It was obvious he was in no frame of mind for conversation.

"Am I leaving, *sahib*?" she asked in Arabic. Her heart sank as he thrust a handful of ripe tamarind pods at her and splashed murky water into her clay pot. Even with the chains, the long curved fruit wouldn't be hard to break open, but sometimes she could feel little worms tickling her mouth after she'd sucked the bittersweet pulp. Besides, food was the last thing on her mind.

"No."

"It's morning, why are you here?"

The nameless jailer narrowed his eyes, squared his sinewy shoulders. He studied her face, suspicious. "The miss can tell night from day?"

Watching his reaction, Mera thought quickly. If he figured out her secret crack in the door, he might move her to a cell where she'd find no light at all. Raising her leg over the makeshift pebble calendar, she offered a disinterested shrug.

"No. Not so much. I figure it must be day since I'm not so hungry yet."

The jailer nodded. "The miss thinks right. It is morning."

She'd derailed his suspicions so she decided to toss out what she knew was a useless question.

"*Sahib*, please tell me, when am I leaving?"

"When are you leaving?" he muttered, returning fully to his funk. "Stupid woman, how would I know? I just bring food, make sure you have straw." The straw was in a corner she could inch to, intended as a place of bedding. But it was infested with bugs and what had to be lice. Since the first day, she'd done her best to stay clear of it.

"However, I have news today," he continued. The door was barely open, but even in the cell's weak light, she could make out the sly smirk tugging at his lips.

"Tell me," she demanded greedily.

The jailer fished a pocketknife from his threadbare pants, flashed it open and began splitting a tamarind pod. He sucked on the squishy henna-colored pulp.

"A visitor comes to see you." He licked the juice off his lips. "Very soon now."

"You said we get no visitors here." She wasn't falling for the trick. Maybe instilling false hope was how they drove prisoners insane. Who knew? Already, there were days she barely held on. Days when thoughts of Seth and Donovan and Chicago were parts of someone else's life. Then like the mythological daughters of Danaus eternally sentenced to carrying water from the River Styx in jars that leaked like sieves, what was real slipped further and further away before she'd recount her pebbles and strain harder for another pathetic glimpse of light.

But now, dangling the hope of someone from the outside world . . .

"He knows the warden. Your visitor knows the warden. Now that is all." Like he was possessed, the jailer's beady eyes turned to black slits and he growled through clenched teeth. "If you ask more questions, I will send him away and tell warden you are ill-tempered this day."

He threw down the pod, crushed it with his heel and didn't even bother to rinse her waste pail before he left.

～

Nothing could have prepared her for the look in Onesphore's eyes, a disquieting mixture of shock and horror. Without question, he was the last person she expected to see, but when his huge ebony frame filled the doorway of her cell, a wave of relief washed over her.

She'd heard them coming. Light footsteps sauntered alongside heavier ones as they shuffled through the labyrinth of musty corridors, and the muted exchange of conversation grew louder and more distinguishable. Eventually, they stopped outside her barrack and something clanged against the iron door before a key crunched inside the lock.

Then nothing for a minute.

Finally, whispers ensued in a lyrical language before the impenetrable bastion swung open and lit up Onesphore's towering form. The jailer thrust a crude lantern at the giant then motioned him inside the cell. From outside, he shoved the door to a terrible rasping close, leaving Onesphore in stifling blackness tinged only by the hazy, amber glow of the light he held.

For what seemed like hours, Onesphore waited for his eyes to adjust. When they finally did, he surveyed her quarters in silence.

"What, in the name of . . ." He didn't finish before he turned away like he couldn't take anymore.

Mera was all but unrecognizable. Her sweaty face was streaked with dirt and mottled with bites and marks where she had tried to scratch. Like a maple helmet, her matted hair stuck together in clumps and her arms and legs were bones wrapped in pale flesh. She sat sprawled facing a stone wall embedded with rusted iron rings. From these rings, her hands and feet were shackled so that movement could be nothing more than synchronized scooting. Her only clothing was a thin gown of muslin. And it was stained with dried blood, urine and whatever other filth was indigenous to this world of dark captivity.

"Anyone ever told you, you stink in the encouragement department?" The words stuck in Mera's throat as she took in his bewildered expression. "You're finally here . . . it's been almost two months . . ." she stammered, words trailing off as she noticed Onesphore appeared anything but hopeful. "You . . . you did come to . . . to get me out?" Speaking in English sounded unfamiliar to her ears and strange coming out of her mouth.

He bent down next to her though the stench made him start to retch. In the flickering light, her eyes searched his, greedy for an answer.

"Meranda," he was groping for the right words, "God help me . . . I do not know how to say this . . ." He slumped over, trying hard to breathe in the scorching air.

"Say what, Onesphore?" An icy shot of terror cut through her. "What do you mean?"

"Meranda," he was struggling to get the words out, "this thing you have done . . . this . . . this courage . . . it has a price."

"Courage? Price? What are you talking about?" She wasn't getting any of it. The gist of what he was trying to say. The open emotion. None of it made sense.

"What you did back in Cairo has nearly every government in the free world cueing into the south's plight."

"What?" She stared at him in disbelief. "How? How would they know . . . how would anyone know what happened?"

It was Onesphore's turn to gape.

"Wellington did not tell you?"

"Tell me *what?*" she nearly shrieked.

"The embassy in Cairo, they did a routine employment check on you. Your report, the documents you left, they were classified . . . they were supposed to be handled by a special investigation team."

"I know that. They told me before I left."

Onesphore inhaled a shaky breath.

"But things did not happen as planned. The papers . . . the documents you found got picked up." He paused. "Some imbecile clerk called Spectrum to verify your position with the company. Making sure you were legitimate."

"What?" She couldn't believe it. That kind of blunder wasn't even possible. "There's no way. They were pending investigation until I got out of . . . Sudan . . ."

It hit her blindside why she'd ended up here. That night at the compound Spectrum and the government already knew she'd been the one to take the documents.

"A stupid clerk grabbed your classified stack, treated it routine."

Onesphore's words rung in her ears, but her mind wouldn't compute the implication of them. Hadn't Seth warned her, begged her, to go back home? "*Stuff happens, mistakes get made,*" his words echoed in her head, "*. . . don't want to lose you . . . I've waited a lifetime . . .*"

"No. This can't be happening," she echoed in disbelief. "I go to our embassy to report crimes against these people and I get . . ."

"Screwed," Onesphore finished the sentence, "you are getting screwed. The NIF has you on tampering with government documents, possibly espionage. That is why you are here. Spectrum is fuming because you have blown their cover. They have had to suspend operations until a full investigation report comes out."

"Investigation for *what?*" She still wasn't catching on. It was too much, too quickly.

"Conspiracy. Between Spectrum and the government, the consortium and the NIF." Onesphore shook his head wryly. "It is everywhere. CNN, BBC, Nightline, every major news entity in the free world . . ."

The still air was suffocating like it had nothing life-giving to offer. They sat in silence listening to the sound of the lantern's hissing flame and the invisible insects lightly rustling the straw. She dreaded asking the next question.

"So what happens now?"

"I am trying to . . ."

"Come on, Onesphore, the truth. That's why you're here, isn't it? To tell me something."

"They have scheduled your execution at sunset tomorrow," he said flatly, taking her manacled hands in his giant one. It was the first gesture of kindness he'd ever shown her. "But there is still a possibility of an out on grounds of . . ."

"Does Seth know?"

Onesphore's words weren't real and they couldn't be right. Any minute now, he would end the cruel joke, remand the barbaric sentence and they'd both head out of here.

"Does he know?" She was hysterical now.

Onesphore nodded. "He is back home driving D.C. crazy, doing what he can to get a stay on this. He has been working with the U.S. envoy to Sudan . . . been to the embassy in Cairo . . ."

Onesphore's voice faded to a thin whisper as Mera's cell door swung open.

At the threshold, the jailer's reed-like frame stood in full view though the glare rendered his face featureless. Like he had no time to waste, he emitted two short grunts then began speaking tersely in an unfamiliar rhythmic dialect, obviously African. After a few seconds, Onesphore stood abruptly and faced him, a heated stare down. He uttered something back, sharp, indecipherable sounds that made the jailer recoil before he slammed the gated door.

The tiny golden flame cleaved the blackness again, half-illumining the wretched cell in coppery light.

"What did he say?" Mera finally asked.

"Warden says my time is up."

Mera reached to pull the hem of Onesphore's pants. "Please don't leave me," she begged, starting to cry. "Please."

He bent down again to take her hand. And nearly gagged.

"Do not worry, this man owes me. I will not leave yet."

She searched the giant's dark face. "You know him?"

"Your jailer?"

"Yes."

"Once, long ago."

"He . . . that jailer is sometimes better than the others. We speak some, in Arabic, but that wasn't . . ."

"No," he shook his head, "it is Nuer. Another tribal language."

"Oh." Her voice was hollow, the sudden reality of her fate starting to sink in. All she could think about was Seth and Donovan and how she might not ever see them again. Not even to say goodbye. Slowly, she scooted to the stack of hay in her cell corner, dreading the deluge of tiny insects that would attach themselves to her flesh.

"What are you doing?" Two strides and Onesphore was standing on the stale straw.

"Getting this." She fished around with the hand that had the most play in the chain until she pulled out a square of tightly folded papers. Disturbed from her shuffling their nest, a spray of gnats and lice misted the air. Like tiny gray snowflakes.

"It's for Seth. In case I . . . in case I don't make it home." She handed it to Onesphore.

"When did you write this?" The parcel looked tiny in his huge, open hand.

"About a week ago, I found an old pencil by this wall. It was just a stub. But I knew I could keep sharpening it against the rocks. So when he was in a good mood, I asked that jailer, the one you know, for some paper. He hadn't a clue why I wanted it, but a few days later, he brought me a little stack."

"I see." Onesphore traced a finger over the dingy folded square.

"Promise me you'll get it to Seth. There are things he needs to know in here. Things I should've said long ago . . ." She bit her lip to keep from crying again.

Onesphore leaned over and laid an awkward hand on her shoulder. She was slimy with grit and sweat. "Never mind, Meranda. We all have these thoughts . . . these secrets and words we never find a voice for."

"Do we?" She looked away. "I don't really know anymore."

Onesphore knelt down in front of her and took a deep breath.

"I should say this before I go. In case I do not get another chance."

"Iron Lung . . ." She had no idea why she said it. The name just came out.

A look of raw shock flit across his tight features before he cut her off. "Do *not* honor me with that name," he said sharply. "Such esteem is blasphemy."

"Blasphemy, Onesphore?"

He dropped his hand off her shoulder.

"I can do little to help free you now."

In her head somewhere, she heard a faint aria that must have belonged to her childhood. She couldn't place its context, couldn't remember much about it at all. But the high clear voice sang of a long-ago friend of God in prison. An apostle visited by angels and earthquakes and deity who was yet able to do what no man could.

Then the airy tune stopped.

"*Look* Onesphore, I need you to look at me. I need you to see past these chains." As the words came out, she felt new life come into them. Into her. "Maybe I don't get to walk out of this place. Maybe this is where it all stops for me. But I know this. If exposing the truth here, whether it's some little thing or some watershed evidence that changes everything, is what God made me to do," she slapped best she could at an insect buzzing near her ear then motioned her shackled hands across the cubicle, "none of this is an accident. No matter how jinxed it all seems."

Her words hung in the motionless air, resolute and uncompromising. Onesphore stared at her like he'd been dumbfounded at the depth of them and confounded by the way this crucible had alchemized only deeper conviction in her, no trace of bitterness.

"I . . . I was wrong about you, Meranda Kaine," he began slowly. "Very wrong."

"It's okay, Onesphore . . ."

"No," he interrupted, looking at her with anguished eyes, "it is not okay. I am a fool, a blind fool . . ."

"Onesphore . . . stop . . ."

"I misjudged you, Meranda Kaine. I could not see . . . I would not see what you really were . . ."

"Onesphore, please. How you feel or felt about me has nothing to do with this."

"Does it not?" His lament was almost a shout. "What might I have done differently if I had believed you to be the most courageous person I know?" Onesphore exhaled, one long breath, before he let his shoulders slump like he'd utterly failed.

"This is not your fault," Mera repeated.

"Maybe not," the words scraped out of him. "But I was wrong about you. And this . . . before your God or any other one . . . this is the most inconvenient sacrifice anyone could offer." He stared dully into the corroded lantern.

"No. It's really not," she said after a minute had passed in the searing silence. "Not in the scheme of things."

"What the hell . . ." For a split second, he seemed to yield to an inner fury, like the world of prisons and guards and oil and gods that made the universe a spinning orb of injustice was too much to bear. "Understand me, Meranda, hear what I am saying. Unless some mythological god saves you, some miracle of fate . . ." Despite his intractable stoicism, Onesphore's voice broke.

She waited a minute to answer.

"I *do* understand. Clearly. It's just there have been bigger sacrifices than this. Bigger scandals than mine." She was getting strength from somewhere because her tranquility was surreal. "And right now, that's helping."

Onesphore just stared at her.

"Do not tell me about your God, your Christ." He spit the words out like acid, knowing what she was inferring.

Her nod was almost imperceptible.

"Did I say the name of either?"

His steely gaze met hers before he looked away.

"You mean to trust in this crazy deity. I know this. You mean to say that this God of yours, this moronic God, who let his son hang on some Roman cross is yet wholly good." Onesphore's eyes sparked dark fire. "And yet I know better. If gods exist, and if perchance, there is but one God, he would not let a good child dangle at the hands of bad men. This God, damn it, would not be crazy like the sons of men."

She sat quiet, taking in his heated words. Then worked to move her shackled hands until they rested on one of his.

"Tell me, Onesphore," she whispered, "why do you work for Spectrum?"

He tried studying her face though it was masked in shadows.

"You . . . you know why."

"You work for a company you can't trust, doing work that could get you killed because you care about people who don't even know how dependent they might become on whatever mercy you might be able to offer." She breathed in then hacked out a dry cough. "Is that not moronic? Is this not crazy?"

He didn't answer as he mopped his forehead against the sleeve of his shirt.

"Love, Onesphore, drives you to places you wouldn't imagine in your wildest dreams. It causes you to take measures that seem anything but sane."

"So your God is crazy . . ."

She shook her head.

"No," she answered, looking up at him. "I just think He took crazy measures to offer freedom. Sort of like you do, Onesphore."

Onesphore ran his hand over the dirt floor before he answered.

"And this . . ." he tugged in disgust at the heavy chains binding her wrists, "you call *this* freedom?"

She dropped her head, chin to her chest, like it was suddenly too heavy to keep holding up. In the feeble light, all Onesphore could make out was the continual rise and fall of her bony shoulders.

"I wonder, Onesphore," she whispered after what seemed like minutes, "I wonder if there's a whole new freedom that could come on the other side of these." She touched her shackled wrists before she looked up. "For all I know . . . these could be part one . . ."

"Part one of what . . .?"

"Freedom isn't free, Onesphore. You know that. I know that. It's something you have to know before you decide it's worth fighting for." She paused, as if getting the words out was requiring the sum of all that was in her. "What we don't know, though, what we can't know, is just how much it can cost."

Footsteps sounded outside her door, signaling the jailer's return.

"I must go, Meranda." Onesphore took a deep breath like he was hoping the air might reinforce him. "But I am still trying. I will keep trying."

"One more thing . . ."

"Anything."

"Deng . . . how is he? I never found out."

Onesphore grimaced. "He died, Meranda. In the explosion."

She tightened her jaw and closed her eyes, picturing the old chief's weathered face. His mostly toothless smile. Without trying, she heard his haunting oracle, words spoken years before their reality, "*One day something will happen in the south because of the north . . . when it does, the world will be ready to listen . . . tell the truth miss, that is what will free us . . .*"

"I see." Again, she was oddly composed like she already belonged to an unseen world that promised far more than infested hay and heavy chains.

"I am sorry, Meranda." The door opened again. This time Onesphore approached the guard, looking back at her. "Very, very sorry."

"Don't be, Onesphore." His eyes met hers and the fleeting connection made her heart skip a beat. "This one's worth whatever it takes."

The Eritrean giant offered a solemn nod before her cell was enveloped in complete darkness. Just outside her door, a heated dispute between Onesphore and the jailer began then went on and on.

Chapter 42

Seth held the loose papers between his fingers, still not believing the erratic scrawl. This was it, he told himself numbly. The last thing she'd written.

The last thing she'd ever write.

He shook his head, made a conscious effort to breathe in, then out, before allowing himself to look down again.

Right here in his hands were Mera's final thoughts penned from a dark prison barrack.

He couldn't take it in, couldn't bend his mind around it all. Not yet.

"Are you sure, Onesphore?" His eyes shifted to meet the giant's sober gaze. "Maybe there's a mistake."

For a second, Onesphore looked like he wanted to say something, like there was something to be added to Seth's deliberation. But he quickly took command of whatever thought it was.

"Langford," he was tenuous, "there is little margin for error. I got the call yesterday from Juba. They said she was moved in just after sunset night before last."

Seth knew the answer, but he asked anyway. "Moved where?"

"According to a preliminary report, the hanging barrack . . ."

"What do you mean, preliminary?" Seth went cold at the word 'hanging,' but picked up on what sounded like a possibility.

Onesphore sighed.

"My friend, do not have hope in this matter. The prelims are always consistent with the final report findings. You know this regime." Onesphore leaned over to shut the conference room door. As usual, quiet at Wings Like Eagles came at a premium. For the past thirty minutes, they'd sat side by side at the table saying very little, side by side taking in the hustling, bustling and echo of voices up and down the hallway. Outside, the irony of afternoon sunlight flickered through tree leaves and cast a lively mural on the west topaz wall. "The report said they dropped the floor at 7:32 P.M. The body . . ." Onesphore took a deep breath and continued, "the body was gone exactly ten minutes later."

"Who was there?"

"Apparently the warden and a jailer."

"What . . . happened . . . what did they do with Mera?" He felt the question fall from his lips though his mind refused to believe it.

"The jailer's report said it was bagged and sent to be incinerated."

Seth shuddered. This wasn't real. Especially since there was no empirical evidence.

He turned to accuse Onesphore. "I thought you said you knew the jailer."

"I do," the giant concurred. "The warden, too. Look, Seth, I tried," he said, swirling the water at the bottom of his styrofoam cup. "I even left Laos with the cash in case he could do something." Looking dejected, he downed the rest of it and crushed the cup. "And told him there was more where that came from."

"How much?"

Onesphore looked up. "How much what?"

"How much did you leave? How much did you promise? C'mon Onesphore, you know the drill."

Seth sounded so raw, the giant kept his cool.

"Ten grand in the hand for Laos," he said, referring to what he'd pressed into the jailer's palm, "another ten grand for Laos to get to the warden. And the promise of twenty more apiece. If she got across borders alive."

Seth looked hopeful.

"So how do we know she's not out there being escorted by some eleventh hour posse? Who knows, she could be anywhere right now."

Onesphore laid a firm hand on Seth's shoulder.

"Langford, stop. You cannot do this to yourself. The report said . . ."

"What about the warden?" Seth interrupted, like he hadn't heard a word his friend had said. "Didn't you see him?"

"No. With all the commotion, the militia was swarming like flies on a bloody carcass. So, I never got to him. But I left him the envelope," Onesphore repeated. "With Laos."

"Probably never even got it." Seth shook his head. Speculating on what might have happened was easier than dealing with the reality that Mera was dead.

Onesphore snickered. "He got it. Damn straight he got it. Laos owes me big. I bailed him years ago and he is not likely to forget that."

For a second Seth was interested, but the pain on hand swallowed his curiosity, and he returned his full attention to it.

"Give me specifics on the warden," he said, feeling dull enough to disappear.

"There are none to give. He knew I was there for Spectrum. He did his good deed by letting me see a prisoner in solitary confinement."

Seth closed his eyes and tried hard to fight back images of Mera alone and frightened in some verminous African prison cell.

"I should not have been able to get in, but when Mohammed heard it was me, I got clearance . . ."

"Mohammed is . . .?" Seth interrupted.

"The warden."

"Then what were you thinking? Why didn't you demand to see him?" Seth slammed his fist on the splintered table where he'd first sat across from Mera and Jack, years ago now.

"My friend, one does not order the military personnel, no matter what his alliance. I stayed with protocol, left one envelope for Laos, another for him to deliver to Mohammed. Neither of them knew

I was acquainted with the other. It was sheer coincidence that Laos was her jailer."

"Coincidence, Onesphore," Seth exploded, "is that what it was? Is that what all of this is?"

Onesphore waited to answer.

"After all that has happened, I am not certain anymore." he finally said.

Seth looked down at the letter and tried again to read it. There were things she had written here that he knew he'd ponder for years. Maybe forever.

The things she hadn't told him yet.

But right now, they wouldn't sink in and he was glad. Too much had to be done. He stood up to walk Onesphore out.

"Thanks for breaking your neck to get here." When his friend had shown up, Seth had immediately known that the news couldn't be good. But the fact that Onesphore had such recent contact with Mera brought him strange comfort, like she was somehow nearer.

"She made me promise to get that letter to you," Onesphore nodded at the rumpled stack of papers. "Her words were those she wished she had spoken. She said so."

Seth was quiet for so long it seemed no response was coming. Tentatively, Onesphore began making his way to the door.

"When it's all said and done, she said the most important things," Seth broke the silence. "This other stuff . . . these . . . these secrets . . ." The full impact of the last several weeks hit him, gale-force.

Without a sound, he faced the wall and gave into noiseless sobs that shook his whole body. Like he was unsure what to do with this new experience, Onesphore moved beside him. He placed a hesitant arm around his friend's shoulders.

"I love her, Onesphore . . . more than I ever thought I could . . ."

"I know." The giant helped Seth sink into a chair before he sat down again to continue. "I know you do. But you would have been proud of her, my friend."

"Like that's something new." Seth lifted a shoulder to his wet cheek, a makeshift handkerchief.

"I know I should wait until later to tell you this . . ."

"When's the final report out?" Seth demanded, thinking this is where Onepshore might be headed.

"I am not talking about the report, Seth. That should be out in the next month or two. For some reason, the paperwork in Juba always gets held up. Few, there, are in a rush." Onesphore took a deep breath. "Just trust me on this, though. The preliminaries and the finals are always the same. They are written on the same day. The final is just protocol summarizing the preliminary. The sign-off just comes later."

"Then what is there to tell me?" Seth's dead gaze met Onesphore's.

"I told her, Meranda, the . . . the execution was scheduled. I know her heart was grieved for you, for Donovan. She said so. But she did not cry. She was not even angry." Like he was agitated by the memory, Onesphore shoved his chair back and rose to his towering seven feet. He walked to the window facing the tired and dingy side streets.

"Was that . . . it?" Despite the pain, Seth wanted to hear what came next.

"No." Onesphore turned abruptly, his eyes haunted as they searched Seth's. "No it is not. She said if exposing this . . . this hell was the call of your God, what He made her to do, it was worth whatever it took." Onesphore dropped his head. "Even if the whatever was everything."

They fell silent again, the predictable din outside the door a welcome background noise. Without notice, Seth started reading.

"If you do away with the yoke of oppression, with the pointing finger and malicious talk and if you spend yourself on behalf of the hungry and satisfy the needs of the oppressed, then your light will rise in the darkness and your night will become like the noonday . . ."

"What is that?" Onesphore interrupted.

Seth gestured down at the thin pile of papers.

"She wrote *that*?" Onesphore frowned.

"Recited it."

"It is a quote?"

"Yeah."

"By who?"

"Isaiah. A prophet."

Onesphore rubbed his ebony head. "I do not know this name. Is he like Gandhi or Siddhartha Gautama?"

"He was a Hebrew prophet. She quoted him from a passage in the Bible."

"Sounds more like lofty code."

Despite himself, Seth smiled a little at Onesphore's crusty reaction.

"Once, long ago, a friend of hers pointed it out. Supposedly wanted his own life to answer it." After reading these letters, the thought of Jack made Seth's gorge rise. He swallowed hard.

"This friend, he had big plans."

"Yeah. Well, he got sidetracked. But after she read it twenty or so years ago, I think she sort of took it on as a life goal. Like a personal mission statement."

Seth pictured the endless expanse of lush green beneath infinite African skies. He saw hollow eyes in gaunt ebony faces, jutting bones wrapped in paper-thin flesh. Without trying, he could smell death. The rancid-sweet odor of decaying flesh only hours after the latest round of artillery drops. And the cries, the inconsolable, hopeless wails that went on and on . . .

And if you spend yourself on behalf of the hungry and satisfy the needs of the oppressed . . .

The words echoed in his head like a rifle shot splitting the air.

Spend yourself, the verse said. Give it everything you have. Relieve and tend the needs and pains of those so downcast they can't do it for themselves.

For God's sake, don't waste this life on selfish pursuits and vain interests.

Seth traced his fingers over the words on the crumpled paper.

"Right now . . . right now, just breathing in and out is about to kill me . . . and I have no idea how or when . . . or even if I'll ever make peace with it all." He sat up straighter, painful resolve distorting his features. "But she's right, Onesphore, and I know it. She's right. There *are* some things worth tackling. No matter what the end looks like."

Quiet again, this time even more noticeably so, since the clamor outside was at a standstill.

"It will get worse, now, before it gets better," Onesphore said slowly. He was talking about the sudden outbreak of interest, from NGO outrage and investigative efforts underway to the media's frenzy to spotlight what, if any, breaking news came next. Amazingly, one culpable document seemed to be opening international eyes to Sudan's concealed horrors.

"I know. Remember ten years ago when we used to hope for something like this?"

"I remember, my friend. But not this . . . we never hoped for this . . ." Onesphore sighed like he was bracing himself before his next question. "What will be done about the boy now?"

Seth let out a bitter laugh. "That poor kid's a tin soldier in this battle. A clueless little nomad." He shook his head. "Best part is, he doesn't even know it."

"So what will you do with him?"

Seth didn't hesitate. "That one's easy. I'll fight to keep him if it takes everything I have."

They lapsed into another silence as late March winds rattled the thin windows and dappled sunlight chased shadows over the stuccoed walls.

Watching the marigold yellow and black taxi swerve around the corner and pull to a smooth stop, Onesphore looked back over his shoulder at the painted looming eagle above the shelter doors.

The bird's black eyes seemed to know everything, and he was perched in such a way that he almost swore himself protector to all who entered this place.

Wings Like Eagles. He'd always thought it a peculiar name, even though Seth had long since explained its origin. Some whimsical notion about those trusting in God finding strength enough to soar about as if on wings like eagles.

Crazy thought. Faith in some unseen, abstract master of the universe. A master who, despite lack of intervention in the worst of human imaginings, had managed to commandeer the unalloyed allegiance of Seth Langford and Meranda Kaine.

It made no sense and he was a man who would have nothing to do with foolish speculations or misguided endeavors. Still, there had been something so gallant, even brilliant, in their separate, though concerted, responses to this hell of a scenario . . .

Climbing into the taxi and pulling the door shut, he shook his head in semi-satisfaction. At least something in this saga would be simple. Donovan's parents, any next of kin, were deceased.

The child and Seth could find mutual comfort in each other.

Chapter 43

Jack had decided that Helene either had hearing problems or she just liked everything loud. Nearly five years into married life, it was something he'd had to accept in the interest of domestic tranquility. But as soon as she left a room, leaving behind a blaring television, booming stereo or anything of the like, he couldn't wait to lower the volume.

This morning was no exception. Breathing in a whiff of something buttery as he came in, it was an easy guess that Helene was in the kitchen frying something. Probably pancakes, Jack decided, since she loved the things almost as much as he detested them. Meanwhile, the television in their empty den echoed the morning headlines loud enough to vibrate the dishes in their china cabinet.

Kicking off his running shoes and mopping his forehead, Jack hurried from the front door to crank down the journalist-in-stereo.

"Jack? You back already?" Helene was on the phone, but she poked her head out from the kitchen and waved. "That was quick."

He rubbed his muscular leg with one hand and reached over to turn down the volume with the other.

"Knee's acting up again. I really . . ."

"No! Don't touch it." Helene was somewhere in the kitchen again, but her shrill command was enough to make his hand recoil like he'd stuck it in a light socket. "They've got breaking news on that journalist in Africa. The one who was captured last month."

Helene was always up on current affairs, something Jack had admired before they married. Before he learned that she kept informed by watching television at least half of her waking hours.

"What journalist?"

"Shh, here it is." She was back in the den, clad in a fuzzy yellow bathrobe. Her auburn hair was twisted in hot rollers.

The WCVB anchor was on again, and to Jack's horror, so was a picture of Mera Kaine.

"The Boston native turned Chicago resident and a former syndicated columnist for the *Tribune*, Ms. Kaine was on assignment just north of Bentiu in southern Sudan. An employee of the Canadian-based Spectrum Energy, Ms. Kaine had been in Sudan for nearly four years as the public affairs representative for the company's regional operations . . ."

Jack gaped in disbelief as the blond woman prattled on, pleasantly detached. "Ms. Kaine's death has launched investigations into what is looking like one of the most horrendous campaigns of systematic destruction in modern history . . ." The anchor kept talking, but Jack couldn't hear anymore.

"Jack . . . Jack what's wrong with you?" With bony alabaster fingers, Helene gripped his biceps, an attempt to break his daze. But she was talking through a watery channel. "Answer me." She flipped off the television, a sacrifice for her.

"I . . . I knew her." It was all he could get out.

"How?" Helene's denim blue eyes searched his. "When? I've never heard you talk about her." Before he could answer, she smelled the pancakes starting to burn. ". . . story is so sad. She was beautiful, too. Gorgeous. Those eyes . . . did she look like that when you knew her?" Helene was firing off an inquisition from the kitchen while she dialed the phone again.

That was one of the great things about her, Jack had learned. She loved to ask questions, really probing ones. But she rarely wanted an answer. She just liked hearing herself talk.

"By the way, this man called while you were out running." With the phone pressed to her ear, she re-emerged to dangle a torn sheet of paper at him. "He said it was important." Her lips drooped into a slight frown. "We don't know an Evan Childress from the parish, do we? I mean maybe . . ."

Suddenly, she redirected her conversation to whoever answered on the other end. Without another thought of Mera or Evan Childress, she was on to plans for the day, lunch downtown and shopping up toward Maine.

The trip had been miserable. An unforeseen and expansive storm rocked the 727 for the first hour after takeoff, and by the time it touched down at O'Hare, it was all Jack could do to make it through baggage claim and land a taxi.

But five minutes into weaving through Chicago's streets, it occurred to him that air turbulence wasn't his problem at all.

The pounding headache and gnawing in his gut had actually started this time yesterday. After he'd hung up the phone with Evan Childress.

Pulling the cleric's collar at his throat, he tried hard not to think about Mera, about the possibilities that lay in the hours ahead. He tried not to worry about how hacked Helene was or what groveling he'd have to do once he got back to Boston. She had wanted to come with him, had been insatiably curious why Meranda's attorney would summon him in the first place. And he couldn't blame her.

"I told you, honey," he tried explaining, "I don't know why they've called me." According to Evan Childress' office, a summons had been mailed to him, certified. It had never reached him, though. Hence, the phone call. "He said it had to do with her estate."

"You never take me anywhere," Helene had whined. "Not to delegations or conferences. You could at least bring me along for this. It's not like we have any kids to take care of." Their infertility was a hot button she pushed when she wanted to hurt him. She wanted children. But Jack wanted them even more and she knew it.

"Besides, I love shopping in Chicago," she pouted seductively, "and we could stay at The Four Seasons." Helene was the only child of Wilson Stutgartt, a Dallas born and bred petrochemical magnate who had recently sold his business for untold millions. Now he split his time between travels, horse races and lavishing ridiculously expensive gifts on his daughter, who was without a doubt, the apple of his eye.

"This isn't a boondoggle." Jack held firm, though he knew telling her 'no' would come with a cost. "I'm just going up for the night and I'll call you from the hotel after I meet with Childress."

She sulked in earnest then, while he made last minute calls and tossed clothes into a suitcase. When he bent down to kiss her goodbye, she turned her cheek. It was a gesture he knew well.

It meant weeks might pass before she'd be civil again.

But Helene's scorn was something he could deal with and it certainly wasn't new. What had him now were two things: the fact that Mera was dead and the quandary of why he'd been summoned. After what he'd done to her, how could she have named him to anything in her estate?

As the taxi driver wound past the loop toward suburban Chicago, a dam of protracted memories broke wide open.

There was Mera in a little polyester short set with a messy ponytail. He was six, she was five and they were in his basement playing racetrack and nibbling on cookies.

Then she was nine, skinny in her pink dress. The dress that her father had torn and stained with her blood before she showed up at his house and huddled next to him on an old porch swing beneath the cold moonlight.

Next came the night of Louis' party. The night he'd found her naked on the floor with Creech — and nearly gotten himself killed trying to stop the deed.

A few more scenes flashed.

Outside the Marsh Chapel where Mera told him she couldn't marry him.

That first glimpse of her when she'd picked him up at the airport to meet the Taize guy.

Until then, he'd forgotten how beautiful she was and when he'd
held her, an unquenchable longing filled him.

A yearning that grew until it consumed him.

Looking at the blur of greening landscape outside the taxi
window, Jack did something he hadn't done since that fateful
rainy night in Boston.

He made himself remember it all.

The ride around the city. Their stroll through The Commons.
The melting ice cream eaten with wooden spoons in his Jeep.

Like it was yesterday, he recalled long-suppressed images of
crystal rain needles glistening in the halo of distant headlights. He
saw the wet outlines of two bodies cleaved together by force.

By his force.

He felt gritty mud between his fingers as he tried to brace
himself. Remembered the brackish metal of his blood as Mera's
teeth bit his lips. Somewhere in between, there was his voice, the
vibration of cruel, bitter words spilling from his lips before he'd
slapped his hand, hard, across Mera's cheek.

Then the worst part.

As he'd grabbed and wrestled and finally pinned her down,
the brilliant silver from a bolt of lightning captured her stricken
expression.

It was a look he knew he would never be able to put into words
if he lived a thousand more years.

The unadulterated agony on her face, the horror in her eyes stabbed
him like a knife now. How could he have hated her like that? How
could he have done what he did and then live with himself?

The taxi turned onto a side street, slowing. Abruptly, Jack
straightened, gulped in a ragged breath and glanced at the driver.
For a second, he was sure his thoughts must've been audible.

But the cabbie was unaffected, alternately smacking gum and
changing the radio stations. Relieved, Jack sank back against the
torn leather seat that had faded from a prep school khaki to a
listless shade of oatmeal.

"103 Riverview?" The driver had a bald head, no neck and a New York accent. He nodded at a line of low-slung tan brick buildings situated on a stretch of green grass.

"We there, already?"

"We been drivin' good part of an hour, pal." He said it over his shoulder just before he blew a bubble nearly half the size of his round, meaty face. "That'll be forty bucks."

As the car stopped, Jack adjusted his collar. He reached into his pocket while the driver tugged his bags from the trunk.

"Need help inside?"

Directly behind the nearest building was a pond, glass smooth, with the exception of graceful ripples tracing outward as three mallard ducks glided across. Near the sloping bank was a little boy with wavy dark hair. He was leaning toward the ducks, trying to entice them closer. Behind him was a petite older-looking woman with dainty features and a silver bob.

The scene struck Jack as peculiar, out of context. The office park was serene and outer-urban, but it hardly seemed a place for children.

"No. No, I'm fine." Jack turned his attention back to the taxi driver. "Thanks." He handed him a fifty. "Keep the change."

The cabbie grunted his appreciation before he climbed back into his yellow Impala and pulled out.

Chapter 44

Seth hadn't let Donovan out of his sight in days. The media had been relentless for the better part of a month now, an omnipresent flock of vultures that swooped down anywhere they thought he or the child might be. Ever since word got out he was Meranda Kaine's fiancé and the child's guardian, privacy had become a thing of the past.

But he figured it was safe to give the boy a little space out here. Evan Childress' office was somewhat obscure and Seth had taken particular care in making sure no reporters had trailed them. Besides, Sally had volunteered to come along. For moral support, she said, although he knew it was mostly to help him keep an eye on Donovan.

Standing at a window overlooking the pond, Seth couldn't help thinking that the boy looked as lethargic and pathetic as the weak little duck he was trying to coax from the water. He'd slept fitfully after Mera left for Sudan, but ever since Seth tried explaining her death to him, Donovan rested only after heaving sobs racked his small body into an exhausted slumber.

"That's him." Seth nodded as a yellow taxi pulled away, leaving behind a tall, dark-haired man making his way toward Childress' office.

A few minutes later, the attorney's secretary tapped on his door and Childress stepped forward to exchange formalities.

"Thanks, Dr. Frasier, for joining me on such short notice." Childress was smooth. Thirty years in estate law had done more than line his face and streak his hair silver. "With your schedule, I'm sure it was an inconvenience."

"More of a surprise, actually. This whole thing with Mera is still . . ." Jack stopped abruptly as Seth turned from the window to face him. "What is he . . . why is *he* here?"

Childress cleared his throat.

"Dr. Frasier, let me introduce . . ." he began.

"No introductions necessary," Seth cut him off. "Jack and I have met before, haven't we, buddy?" The blood drained from Jack's face as Seth continued. "When my dad suggested you look me up several years ago."

Jack eyes narrowed. "Your *Dad*? No, it was Dr. Kahlier . . ."

"One and the same . . ."

"*What*?"

"I won't underwhelm you with details today." Seth was curt. "For the record, though, I'm Seth Kahlier . . ."

"What . . . what are you talking about? Your last name isn't . . . wasn't Kahlier . . ." Jack stammered, studying Seth's face like he was searching for some hint of deception.

"How hard's a name change? Especially when there's no alliance with your kin?"

Jack looked like his head was reeling. "You're Thomas Kahlier's son?"

Seth acknowledged the question with only a disinterested look.

"What are you doing here? How do you know . . . ?"

"Gentlemen, let's continue this over here." Evan interrupted the tension and led them to an oval bocote table next to a window that framed the pond. When all three were seated and Jack poured himself some water from a carafe on the table, Childress nodded as Seth slipped worn sheets of paper from a thick binder.

"Mr. Langford will begin by reading a document that pretty much summarizes why we're here today, Dr. Frasier."

Seth filled a small glass of water and downed it, one gulp. He tried picking up Mera's letter, but his right hand shook so hard, the papers fell and scattered over the floor. Jack offered him a dirty look, though his grayish pallor attested to a mounting anxiety level.

"She wrote this late February . . ." Seth stammered as he reassembled the wrinkled sheets.

"I can't hear you." The priest rolled his eyes.

Jack's arrogance was just what Seth needed to snap out of the grief-fog that often commanded his full attention for days on end now.

"Then listen up, pal. Because in ten minutes, your life won't be looking the same."

Seth started reading:

"My Dear Seth,

I'm in a prison cell in Juba and it's dark for all but an hour a day, just before sunset. It's nearly dusk now, so I'll need to hurry.

Seth, there's so much I wanted to say to you. So much I meant to say. I just never had the courage. Forgive me please; now the absence of my confidences will be costly to you."

"What on earth is all of this?" Jack sneered like he'd been thoroughly inconvenienced. "Why are you . . . what does this have to do with *me?*" He shot Childress an exasperated look.

"Sit tight, Dr. Frasier, this is just background," Childress instructed, then gestured toward Seth. "Go ahead, Mr. Langford."

"What I never told you was who Jack Frasier was to me. I should have and I meant to. It just never happened.

I grew up the child of an alcoholic. My father was cruel when he drank and my mother was terrified of him. When I was nine, he started sexually abusing me . . ."

Jack closed his eyes like he was trying to restrain a flood of images that belonged to what Seth was recounting.

". . . probably wouldn't have made it if it weren't for Jack. He was the best friend anyone could've had, and for years, he loved me, protected me. No matter what I did, what kind of trouble I got into, he was the one person who refused to give up on me.

Then just before high school graduation, he was almost killed — defending an honor code I never had — or even wanted to have. And as I watched him unconscious in his hospital bed, I started thinking about his life, about how good he was. I thought about his family and his faith, about his love for people. It was then that I realized I needed what he had. I needed the forgiveness and grace of his God.

Quite simply, Jack showed me what faith looked like—what real friendship meant. So several years later, long after I declined his offer of marriage, I made the choice to cover something he did."

Seth stopped reading and looked at Jack. The priest sat like he was watching the four horsemen of the Apocalypse loosed and coming his way. Every few seconds, he wiped perspiration from his forehead.

"You remember the night I got the call from Jack after his mother died. By then, Jack had changed and not for the better—something that I somehow knew had a lot to do with Thomas Kahlier's influence. Still, he'd always been there for me . . .

It never even occurred to me not to make that trip to Boston.

But something happened while I was up there. I wanted to tell you when I came home, but I was afraid. At the time, I thought you might blame me like I blamed myself. So I lied to you and said I was with someone else.

I never told you that Jack raped me while I was in Boston.

I might have eventually come straight with the truth. But I found out I was pregnant, something I never told Jack. After what happened, I couldn't stand to see him again. Not to mention, a baby would've hurt his chances of getting that parish he wanted.

Seth, I guess the cords of friendship really are stronger than the whip of betrayal. Jack still doesn't know that our daughter was born or that she died the same day."

Like he was trapped in a bad dream, Jack shook his head in disbelief. "God . . . oh, God . . . please . . . no . . ." he moaned like he'd been socked in the gut.

"Sit back, Frasier. There's more," Seth ordered. Numbly, Jack complied and Seth continued:

"And what I never told you or him was something even greater.

Emily Kate was scheduled for adoption, a family on the East Coast. When she died, they never got her.

But they did get my son.

Let me explain. Since I'd never had a baby, I didn't think anything of the fact that my stomach had gotten huge, especially near the end of my pregnancy. But after the doctor delivered Emily, they found another heartbeat. Somehow I'd carried twins the whole time without them ever picking up on it."

The air in the office was so stifling that a wet crescent smiled from under the arms of Childress' blue starched shirt. Jack's collar was completely soaked as he reached to loosen it.

"After you left the recovery room that night, the doctor told me. He said to take a few days, decide what I wanted to do. But before I left the hospital, I had Emily Kate's adoptive family contacted. I wasn't sure what they would do, especially since they'd been expecting a girl. But to my surprise, they welcomed her twin. So before I went home, I kissed my little son what I thought was goodbye and handed him to the agency worker.

Then it all changed again. For whatever reason, you were back and loving you, even from a distance, made me live again. Next, came the plunge into your work, into what became our work, for these people here.

But before I left for Sudan, I got two calls. One was from my mother telling me Kyle and Leanne had been killed. The other was from the agency. The couple who adopted my child was divorcing. According to their state law, it takes a year before an adoption is final, and with all the confusion and grief, they decided to give him up. The agency had called to notify me.

Seth, I'm so ashamed. I lied to you again. When I came back to Chicago after Kyle's funeral, it wasn't with my nephew. Kyle never had a boy. He had a daughter who went to live with my mother.

Donovan is my son, Jack's son."

Seth stopped for a deep breath. He poured another glass of water and polished it off before he continued.

"Here's the hard part. If you'll have him, I want you to take Donovan. I know you don't know him well, but something in me is sure that there's no one, anywhere, who could love my little boy like you could.

Then there's this one other thing I need to ask, not because I want it, but because I can't leave here without knowing I did the right thing.

Seth, Jack needs to know. He needs to know that somewhere out there he has a son and a little daughter who died. I need for you to tell him for me . . ."

Evan Childress reclined in his chair and tapped a pencil against the table while taking stock of Jack.

The priest was a petrified rock. His angular body was frozen in place, his face a mask of mummified horror.

Feeling sore all over, Seth glanced out the window to check on Donovan. For some reason, the child had seemed extra small and vulnerable these last few days, a fact that served to bring out in him a fierce sort of protectiveness he'd never known before. Now, as he watched the skeptical brown and green ducks inching closer to the child's popcorn-filled fingers, Seth marveled at how easy it was to worry about him. But seeing all was well, he kept reading.

"Jack once said something I never forgot. It was about how we measure whether or not a person really answers God's calling. He said it was a debate that gets tossed around a lot in religious circles, but ultimately, Jack's point was we couldn't know. There's no way to tell without a person's full biography to look at.

I don't know what it was, but when he said that, I got to thinking for the first time that I really might be here on purpose, that God might have something intended for me to do.

A contortion twisted Jack's features as if Mera's words were stabbing his conscience with an anguish he should have suffered years ago.

I think I found what it was when I came here. I found this crazy meaning and purpose in pulling endless guinea worms out of toddlers, praying the things wouldn't break. I found it in helping my village turn their rubble into a community again, in seeing Deng smile for the first time. I swear, Seth, there were times I saw God's reflection in all of their faces. Split seconds when I heard His heart-beat while I pried out shrapnel or helped bury the latest malaria or landmine casualty.

But now, as I finish this, I'm wondering if there's something else. I'm wondering if my life isn't meant to make another kind of difference. If I'm here on account of that document, maybe it could set off a spark once the politics come out. God knows the south needs that. The world needs to know that it keeps sweeping aside a slow motion holocaust while the oil exported from that port might as well be human blood. What a strange thought . . . my being here, even if it means dying, might begin to help free these people . . . our people, Seth."

Seth stopped reading and tucked the letter back into his folder. Stiffening, he took a deep breath and rummaged through his top pocket until he produced a wrinkled strip of once-white cloth. It was frayed now, whatever it was, torn and stained about the edges.

"Recognize this, Father Frasier?"

As if he were in a trance, Jack stretched across the table toward the article. Just as he was about to touch it, though, he flinched and pulled his hand back sharply.

"Sure you do." Seth was incensed, but he'd waited for this. He had no intention of letting the moment turn into an emotional outburst. "It's yours. You had it on the night you raped *my* fiancé. The night you raped the best friend *you've* ever had."

Childress started to say something but decided against it. Instead, he leaned back in his chair.

"Your *what*? Mera was . . . ?" Jack cut in, shaking his head incredulously.

"My fiancé, you . . . you crossways . . . never mind." Seth recomposed himself. "Fact is, Mera's trusted priest betrayed her, *with his sacred collar on.* Tell me, Frasier, did the irony of that ever eat at you? Keep you awake at night?"

Seth leaned in until he was less than a foot from Jack's face. "I want to know why it didn't choke you when she tore it off," he snarled, barely restraining his fury. "Or maybe it did, but you were so busy gettin' off . . ."

"Stop it, shut up. Just shut up . . ." Jack bellowed, not able to take anymore. He looked across at Evan, as if hoping for some kind of intervention. But the attorney said nothing.

"She trusted you, Frasier. She believed in you. And you . . . you hurt her," Seth's voice broke for a second, ". . . left her with a weight she should've never carried."

Jack's cell phone rang and numbly, he reached to flip it off. Evan got up for coffee, lit a cigarette and, on the way back to the table, brushed his fingers over the rank and file of a chess set he'd bought years ago in India. He let his touch linger on a pawn, then the king.

"All my life, I've been around men of the cloth," Seth continued without much feeling. "Ones who loved God . . . ones who swore allegiance for reasons of their own." He let out a bitter laugh. "The riddle is always in figuring who's who." He stood and picked up the tattered vestment from the table. Then twirled it in his fingers.

"But I've never seen anything like this. *Ever*. Tell me something, Frasier. What does wearing this mean?" Seth looked evenly at Jack, pain clouding his eyes, and it occurred to the priest that this man loved Meranda. Really loved her. And death had done nothing to change that.

"When you put it on, is it a promise to your God, to the community that trusts you? Is it some unspoken oath that your private and public man are one and the same?" Seth threw the stained relic in front of the priest. "Is *that* what this thing means?"

Jack stared out the window, avoiding Seth's scorching glare. A gaggle of geese had landed, and just behind the glass tiptoed Donovan. He was dropping popcorn, hoping to have more luck with this fowl than the bored ducks. But looking closely at the small wiry frame, the dark head, it dawned on Jack who the child was.

"Is that child . . . that boy . . . ?" His mouth was so dry he couldn't finish.

"Your son," Evan offered.

Jack's eyes met Seth's, a look of stark agony. He reached onto the table and touched the torn collar.

"She grappled with the dark side, didn't she? While you docked yourself on high and preached from your sanitized pulpit, she risked her life for a people even more tortured than she was. But since she's dead now . . ."

"Don't say that, oh, God, please don't say that," Jack pleaded. He looked like a man who had just been sentenced to life in prison.

"Why?" Seth cried, emotion getting the best of him. "The loss is more mine than yours. She's dead, Frasier . . . Mera's gone." Saying the words never made it fact. It was like it was a mistake and somehow the final report that was due any day now would cite this whole thing was erroneous, that she'd been released and was making her way back home.

But deep down, he knew better. So he made himself say the truth sometimes so it would eventually register.

Jack dropped his head into his hands. Seth stood to pour himself a cup of coffee. Deliberately, he took a long drink, letting the hot liquid sear the inside of his mouth.

"But now that we've got the panoramic shot of her life to look at, help me out, Jack." Seth paused, more to steady himself than for dramatic effect. "Who is it that really answers God's calling? Is it the priest who covers his tracks, hides his sin, while he talks about God? Or is it the ordinary pilgrim . . . the one who decides this life should be lived on purpose . . . and last time I checked, most divine purposes have nothing to do with success and fame and power . . ."

Shaking his head mechanically, Jack looked up. Tears filled his eyes for the first time in years.

"Reverend Frasier," Seth said slowly, "you might wear that collar, you might even look like all it stands for . . . but right now . . . right now, I'm trying hard as hell to figure out what kind of calling you've answered."

Without a word, Jack stood and walked to the window framing the pond, his back to Seth and Childress. Mesmerized, he stared as the child twirled in circles, one after another, making himself so dizzy that he finally collapsed onto the grassy bank, the wind lightly feathering his hair.

THE END

Afterword

As our Cessna 210 lifted off the red dirt airstrip into clear azure skies, I wondered how this near two week odyssey into southern Sudan would further contour the way I'd live and work going forward. To be sure, I'd seen a whole other world during this March of 2007, a universe of devastation, starvation and extreme poverty that might easily have produced a despair and ensuing paralysis. After more than two decades of civil war, this country remains a wasteland that redefines the ends of the earth. With no health or education systems, no paved roads and only minimal access to clean drinking water, the bush of southern Sudan epitomizes the idea of no man's land.

But as the little aircraft carried me closer to the developing world of Uganda's Entebbe, I felt no dejection at all, just a sense of urgency and hope. Because after five years of writing this book, interviewing and befriending Sudanese refugees in America and entering into the ever-winding labyrinth of human rights advocacy, I'd finally been an eyewitness to the history I had read and written about. I had seen that which I knew was true, but just couldn't quite grasp without experiencing the context of it. And no, this trip hadn't etched deeper resolve in me or caused me to care more deeply about the tragedy of Sudan. That was somehow already a forgone conclusion.

Instead, it had shown me what and who it was that I'd been learning to champion this half-decade. Now when I lobbied or wrote or did whatever it was a moment required on behalf of this land and its suffering people, I had more than statistical data or the latest IRIN and Reuter's update to reference. Now I'd be able to feel the cratered rust hardpan beneath my feet. I would recall sweltering air that refused to buckle and an unforgiving sun that burned this African cosmos into an endless stretch of blackened trees and tan brush. Best, though, I would see the people, the gap-toothed grins in dust-shellacked ebony faces, the yellowed eyes of children, the blue-blind gaze of a young man crouched in the corner of a *tukul.* He, along with many others in some remote southern villages, had been struck with river blindness caused by the bite of a black fly. Now, without trying, I would remember how the smell of unwashed bodies hung in the stiff air and how the odor wasn't at all unpleasant or distasteful.

Sudan was further away from my Texas home than I'd ever gone, yet crazy as it sounds, it was home. I'd never been somewhere that I'd felt more shaped for than this place. And as I caught my connecting flight back to the States in Amsterdam, I reflected on the power of a witness, the nature of a purpose and the exigency of answering a call to justice.

For more than twenty years, southern Sudan lived with uninterrupted civil war, most of it at the hands of a militant government (based in Sudan's northern capital, Khartoum) that sponsored a systematic destruction policy responsible for the deaths of more than two million civilians. Another five million were displaced. This war ended in 2005 with the signing of a peace agreement that promised wealth and power sharing, among other commitments. Some two years later, this accord is fragile at best, rapidly unraveling as the international community fails to birddog its implementation. Instead, all eyes seem to be on the tragedy of Sudan's western Darfur, this century's first named genocide. What often remains beneath the radar, though, is the fact that the northern regime of Omar Al-Bashir that obliterated Sudan's south is the same one arming local Arab herdsmen in Darfur with weapons, horses and a mandate to burn villages, kill men, rape women and kidnap children. To date, some 200,000 to 400,000 have died in Darfur. Another two to three million have been displaced.

Let's talk straight here. Genocide, acts of genocide or crimes against humanity aren't accidental and they aren't acceptable.

We have the Holocaust to remind us of this. More recently, we have Cambodia and Bosnia and Rwanda as witnesses. And to our shame, as the world has watched, we have the tragedy of Sudan. I wonder if human suffering and oppression in any realm creates a problem in every dominion. Like it or not, our humanity inextricably intertwines us. We really are our brother's keepers, and if sacred texts and divine precepts don't inspire nobility — or even fundamental moral responsibility — we have international laws written to protect the rights and dignity of all.

So what is it that compels man to act so cruelly against his brother? I'm certainly no theologian, no psychologist or sentry of human motives, but I'd venture to say that the hate driving Al-Bashir's regime (and others like his) to such incomprehensible tyranny has its roots in greed. Espousing a plan to Islamize all of Sudan, this nefarious leader has used religion as part of his reasoning in scorching and securing southern (and now western) land. But what lies beneath the charred and evacuated earth, what's left once a village has been scorched, depopulated and strewn with rotting corpses, has eluded the media spotlight. Because what remains is untold amounts of oil — and oil is power.

Back in the mid-seventies, the black gold was discovered in southern Sudan, but it wasn't until the late nineties that a Chinese-constructed pipeline extending from the south to Port Sudan at the Red Sea was built and operational. Yet for much of the oil to be accessed, obstructions must be cleared. Even when those impediments were the black African villagers who had tended the land for millennia before.

So the combination of tribal infighting, deep-seated ethnic tensions and Islam versus animism and Christianity got tossed into the already simmering cauldron of "quest for oil." The lethal mixture, as you might guess, caused the pot to boil over, scalding and killing millions of innocent civilians in its wake.

Please hear me. Oil and other natural resources are good. Products of the earth like gold, gems, timber and more are, I believe, divinely of the earth like gold, gems, timber and more are, I believe, divinely given gifts. But using destructive and illicit measures to acquire the resources is unpardonable. Turning villages into killing fields to lay hold of diamonds or gold or oil is a preventable catastrophe that must be interrupted via aggressive international collaboration. Helping devise global initiatives that foster good governance via transparency is one of the best ways to help fledgling economies like southern Sudan escape the "resource curse" that often impedes the forging of a post-humanitarian aid society where community development becomes sustainable. Natural resources like the oil in Sudan's south may not be directly responsible for the wars and strife that seem to keep much of Africa aflame. But they're certainly fueling and funding the intractable corruption that keeps parts of this continent in a state of permanent crisis.

Friends, we have a moral imperative to help end tragedies like southern Sudan and now Darfur. We have a responsibility to help create a world where genocide or gross human rights abuses will not be tolerated. Human suffering and oppression anywhere is a stain on our humanity everywhere. Perpetrators of despotism must become convinced that their dark schemes will not be met with impunity and that the village of this world will stand strong against those oppressing our weaker brothers and sisters. When we make the world a safer and more productive place in one village, one locale, one nation, we make it more secure, more prosperous, everywhere.

In this book, you've hopefully seen the best and worst humanity has to offer (fyi: *The Calling* has a forthcoming sequel that picks up where this story stopped and goes through the end of southern Sudan's civil war and into the Darfurian tragedy). You've explored the horror that greed and religion, any religion, can inflict. Hopefully, though, you've been able to examine the good, the true and beautiful that authentic faith inspires. There are, I'm convinced, noble-hearted disciples in all faiths. And even when such believers cannot agree on doctrines, we can demonstrate mutual respect and remember that before we are Christians, Jews, Muslims, Buddhists, atheists, agnostics, or anything other, we are together human. Always, this gives us common ground from which to work and I pray we could remember and practice this.

I remember my last night in Sudan. I couldn't sleep. Instead, I lay in the cool dusty air beneath a canopy of a million plus stars that glittered like Lazare diamonds scattered on bolt upon bolt of black velvet. All night, to the cadence of babies crying and children coughing, these witnesses to darkness blinked and orbited about as if they had some secret delight. They played, these carefree heavens, and I'd never known until that moment, that heaven frolicked while we were sleeping.

Thinking back on that night, I'm reminded again of the power of a witness. Just as stars guard the night by piercing the darkness, those who work for justice on behalf of our world's voiceless cut the blackness of human suffering. They ease the yoke of oppression. True, the impact happens in degrees and not spades, but when one person says "no" to using religion for personal gain, the world becomes a little different. When a concerned nation adopts nascent initiatives like the Kimberly Process and Extractive Industries Transparency Initiative to help stem the flow of conflict resources, this planet becomes a little more secure. When a caring citizen e-mails a letter to a legislator or hosts a vigil or tells a friend the story of an afflicted nation or people, he bears witness that tyranny is real, anguish is the consequence and change can happen when we decide part of our work in the world is helping end the suffering of others.

May each of us do the good work of a witness. May we join with voices across time and space and embrace the brilliant mission of lighting dark places.

Acknowledgements

The journey of writing this book has been anything but solitary. I owe a deep debt of gratitude to Bonnie Abaunza, Lizi and Matthew Bailey, Annetta Box, Melanie and Duane Brooks, Cindy and Tommy Brown, Rebecca Buckner, Amy Burns, Kevin Cristadoro, Diyo Deng, Chelsea and Kim Deutsch, Beth and Chris Ducker, Achel Gak and David Mou Giir, Buttrus Jok, Stephen Jones, Carol Kleckner, the awesome folks at Living Water International, Amy MacDougall, Kim and Chuck Martin, Leigh McLeroy, Abraham Nhial, Sandra and Rob Perkins, Shauna and Peter Swann, Meredith Van Meter, Joel Vestal, Toby Whitby and Laura Winchell.

Without these, this story wouldn't have been possible: Richard Denham, my college English professor who insisted I think past the edges; Kathy and Jim Kidd for the once upon a time that's landed us here; John Morrison, who taught me the value of plowing a field while never forgetting about a kite in the sky, Shelly and John Berryhill, for believing this story existed years before it was even an idea; Bill Hinson, who now belongs to heaven and time, but first demonstrated with his life that the collar and a divine calling could be stunning, one and the same; Betsy Smith, for always being fully present in a moment; Lynn Fredriksson and Faith McDonnell, who helped (and continue to help) demystify the daunting matrix and language of human rights advocacy by generously coming alongside; Lee and Lish Ashels, who stayed with this story—even when it spanned five years; my beloved parents, Joni and Cris for their unfailing support; and Jana Whitby, who read and offered insights on this manuscript maybe a million times and never once acted like she was tired of it. Words don't capture how much I appreciate all of you.

Special thanks, too, to Wes Yoder, venerable sage and agent extraordinaire and the exceptional, talented team at Key Publishing. Your contagious enthusiasm and support have made this an unparalleled experience.

Finally, thank you, David, for everything. Your grace, your goodness, astounds me. I still can't believe you chose me . . .

Working for Change:
What You Do Matters

A Conversation with Amnesty International USA's Advocacy Director for Africa

Shortly after I'd completed *The Calling*, I had the good fortune of catching up with Amnesty International's Africa advocacy director in Washington DC, Lynn Fredriksson. Lynn is a veteran human rights advocate and scholar who has championed human rights in both Southern Sudan and Darfur. Amnesty International envisions a world in which every person enjoys all of the rights enshrined in the Universal Declaration of Human Rights and other international human rights documents. There are more than 2.2 million Amnesty members, supporters and subscribers in over 150 countries and territories in every region of the world.

So readers of this book can learn how to get involved to help end the suffering in Sudan, I asked Lynn, "How can the average citizen make a difference? What is it we can *do* to help combat injustice and bring peace to Sudan?"

Here's what she had to say:

If you were inspired by *The Calling*, and Elizabeth's moving call to action, please consider your own personal witness by utilizing a few talking points and websites to take one or more suggested actions listed below.

TALKING POINTS:

• While progress is being made toward critical deployment of the UN Security Council-authorized UN-AU Mission in Darfur (UNAMID), conditions in Southern Sudan are deteriorating.

- The Comprehensive Peace Agreement (CPA) signed by the Government of Sudan and the Sudanese People's Liberation Movement (SPLM) in January 2005 is now in real danger of unraveling.
- A number of critical provisions in the CPA (regarding allocation of oil revenues, border demarcation and essential development) have made little or no progress, while the deadline for a referendum on self-determination in Southern Sudan approaches in 2011.
- The U.S. government, which played a crucial role in securing the CPA, must now re-invest itself in its full implementation.
- Contact your Members of Congress, the Secretary of State and President Bush to tell them: "Follow through on Darfur but do not forget Southern Sudan. Save the CPA."
- Our work requires a long-term re-commitment to support reconstruction and development even after conflicts end in Southern Sudan and Darfur. The President and Congress must fund essential relief and peacekeeping now, and essential development programs post-conflict.

TAKE ACTION:

1. Call, fax or email your Congressional Representative and Senators. Find your Members of Congress at www.congress.org.

2. Call the White House comment line at 202-456-1414.

3. Write Secretary of State Condoleezza Rice at the Department of State at 2201 C Street NW/ WDC 20520.

4. Organize a book discussion of *The Calling* at your high school, university, place of worship, local bookstore or library. Brainstorm creative ways to take action to educate the public about Sudan.

5. Consider hosting a Sudanese speaker or human rights advocate at your school.

6. Give to your favorite international organizations carrying out relief and development and/or carrying out essential advocacy and activism in Darfur and Southern Sudan.

7. Visit www.aiusa.org for up-to-date actions to help bring peace and human rights to Sudan.

8. Visit the International Crisis Group at www.crisisgroup.org for more information.

9. Visit the International Rescue Committee at www.theirc.org.

10. Visit the UN High Commissioner at www.unhcr.org for Refugees.

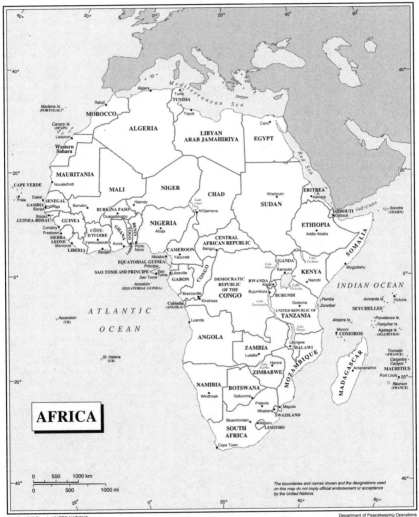

AFRICA

| 0 | 500 | 1000 km |
| 0 | 500 | 1000 mi |

The boundaries and names shown and the designations used on this map do not imply official endorsement or acceptance by the United Nations.

SAUDI ARABIA

EGYPT

Lake
Nasser

Administrative
boundary

Halaib

RED SEA

Selima Oasis   Semna West   Wadi Halfa   Salala
                Lake   Kumma
                Nubia   Nubian   Muhammad
         Laqiya Arba'in   Qol
N O R T H E R N   D e s e r t

Nukheila   Dongola   Kerma   Abu Hamed   RED SEA   Port Sudan
                                                            Suakin
El'Atrun   Old Dongola Karima   Merowe   Tokar
                                                            Karora
                           Ed Damer Atbara   Haiya
                                               Gadamai
CHAD   Abu Dulu   Meroe

                           Shendi

Abu 'Uruq   Omdurman   KHARTOUM   KASSALA   ERITREA
NORTHERN   Khartoum   Halfa al
DARFUR   Gadida   Kassala   Asmara
Miski   NORTHERN
             KORDOFAN   EL GEZIRA
Umm Badr   Sodiri   Wad Medani
El Geneina   Dar Hamid Gedaref   GADAREF   Tekezé
WESTERN   Al Fasher   El Obeid
DARFUR   Kosti   SINNAR   Gonder
             En Nahud   WHITE   Sinnar   T'ana
Nyala   Abu Zabad NILE   SENNAR   Häyk'   Abay (Blue Nile)
Tullus   Ed Da'ein Al Fula   Renk   BLUE   Ed Damazin
Buram   Muglad   Nuba Mts.   NILE   Famaka   Abay
SOUTHERN DARFUR   Kadugli   Kologi   NILE   ETHIOPIA
Radom   Talodi   Paloich   Ãdis Ãbeba
Kafia Kingi   Abyei   UPPER   Kigille (Addis Ababa)
CENTRAL   Lol NORTHERN UNITY Malakal NILE
AFRICAN   Aweil BAHR Bentiu   Omo
REPUBLIC   Raga EL GHAZAL   WARRAB Fathai
WESTERN   Akobo
BAHR   Wau   JONGLEI   Ukwaa   Administrative
EL GHAZAL   boundary
             Rumbek LAKES   Bor Kenamuke Towot
SUDAN   Li Yubu WESTERN   Swamp   Ch'ew Bahir
             EQUATORIA   Amadi EASTERN Kapoeta
             Yambio Maridi   EQUATORIA
DEMOCRATIC   CENTRAL Juba Torit   L. Turkana
REPUBLIC OF EQUATORIA Yei   Nagishot (L. Rudolf)
THE CONGO   UGANDA
             L. Albert   Victoria Nile   KENYA
             Kyoga

SUDAN

- ◎ National capital
- ◉ State (wilayah) capital
- ○ Town
- ✈ Major airport
- --- International boundary
- State (wilayah) boundary
- Main road
- --- Track
- ┼┼┼ Railroad

0   100   200   300 km
0   100   200 mi